The Summer House

A TRILOGY

The Summer House

A TRILOGY

ALICE THOMAS ELLIS

PAUL DRY BOOKS
Philadelphia 2013

First Paul Dry Books Edition, 2013
Paul Dry Books, Inc.
Philadelphia, Pennsylvania
www.pauldrybooks.com

Cover design by Karen Horton

Printed in the United States of America

Library of Congress Cataloging-in-Publication Data

Ellis, Alice Thomas.
[Summerhouse trilogy]
The summer house : a trilogy / Alice Thomas Ellis.
— First Paul Dry Books edition.
pages cm
First published under the title: The summerhouse trilogy.
ISBN 978-1-58988-086-3 (alk. paper)
1. Man-woman relationships—Fiction. 2. Friendship—Fiction.
3. England—Fiction. I. Title.
PR6055.L4856S86 2013
823'.914—dc23
2013003226

For Colin

CONTENTS

The Clothes in the Wardrobe   1

The Skeleton in the Cupboard   127

The Fly in the Ointment   245

THE CLOTHES IN THE WARDROBE

I remembered her all my life. For years the image of her had hung in my mind like a portrait in a high room, seldom observed but unchanging. Sometimes, unawares, I would see her again suddenly revealed in the vaulting halls of my head. She was sitting on a grassy bank, leaning forward a little, a cigarette between her fingers, and she was speaking. I could not remember what she was saying, nor even if I had understood her, but I knew that what she was saying must be, in some sense, significant. She wore a cream-coloured cotton frock with large puffed sleeves, sprigged with tiny brown flowers; her stockings were cream-coloured too and on her feet were white, barred shoes. Her hair grew in dry red curls, dark red like rust or winter bracken. She was not at all beautiful, but even with her likeness before me I had always assumed that she must be, since she carried such conviction in her forgotten words and her enduring appearance. Her name was Lili.

'Margaret,' called my mother, and 'Margaret' again, her voice taking on the faint exasperation that had flavoured her tone as she used my name for many years now. I sometimes wondered whether she had been angry with the infant Margaret and whether I had feared her always.

'The guest list,' she said, standing in the hall before the looking-glass, removing her hat and jabbing stiff-fingered at her hair. 'Have you thought about the guest list?'

I stood in the doorway of the sitting-room and said that I had.

'Invitations,' said my mother. 'I must send out the invitations.'

She came into the sitting-room and sniffed. 'I wish you'd eat in the kitchen or the dining-room,' she complained.

I had eaten an orange and thrown the peel on the fire just as I lit it, and the smell of orange zest and smoke embittered the air while the peel lay, mock flame, amid the cold coals.

'If you'd chosen to be married in June,' remarked my mother, doubtless moved by the aroma to an association of ideas, 'the mock orange blossom would have been out.'

I thought that I hadn't chosen to get married at all but that Syl had chosen to marry me, since it was time for him to marry and I offered no threat to the way and integrity of his life and character, and that my mother had chosen to see me wed because I was good for little else.

'On the other hand,' added my mother hastily, as though she feared that I might take the chance to postpone the ceremony in order to accommodate the philadelphus, 'chrysanthemums are more reliable. They don't wilt so quickly, and those dark red ones are really very attractive against the grey stone.'

I told my mother with timid spite, hidden terror and a certain mad braggadocio that in some countries chrysanthemums were considered appropriate only for funerals.

'This is not some countries,' retorted my mother, perhaps wondering again whether the money she had spent so that I might learn French and a little grace had been utterly wasted, for I had learned only superstition and discontent.

'For goodness sake go and put some lipstick on,' she said. 'If Syl comes he'll think you're dying.'

I was too meek to tell her that I wished I was. Nor would it have been true, for I greatly feared death, suspecting myself to be damned.

My mother glanced at the clock before looking at the window to ascertain that the garden was already retreating into night, and drew the curtains.

'I don't suppose you've written down the guests you want to ask?' she remarked.

'I've got a list somewhere,' I said.

My mother, quite properly, did not believe me, but as I was now clearly an adult, even if an unsatisfactory one, she could not directly accuse me of lying. Frustrated, she went towards the kitchen and I pulled the curtains apart to watch night fall.

'It doesn't fit,' I said with satisfaction.

My mother couldn't deny it. The wedding dress hung loosely on me and I appeared to myself, reflected in the cheval mirror, gratifyingly ridiculous.

'It looks silly,' I said more positively.

My mother irritatedly seized two handfuls of the old brocade and dragged them behind my back.

'You've lost weight,' she observed in a tone which indicated that she could have expected nothing else of me. 'It'll have to be taken in at the seams.'

Already the tiny triumph had withered in me. I thought the dead whiteness of the dress made me more of a corpse than a bride but hadn't enough energy to infuriate my mother by telling her so.

'For goodness sake liven up,' she said. 'Syl will think he's going to a funeral not a wedding.'

This was not percipience in my mother, but a belated riposte to my revelation, the day before, of the role of the chrysanthemum in foreign culture.

'I've never known such a miserable bride,' she went on, standing back and looking at me with some affection, but more disapproval. 'What's the matter with you?'

This was the first time she had admitted openly that all was not well; and I was forced to reassure her, for otherwise she might find herself in sympathy with me, she might come to my side, and this was unthinkable, for to be understood by her was a prospect beyond endurance.

5

'I am only cold,' I said. 'It is cold after Egypt.' And dark, I thought. Dark, dark.

My mother wasn't one for silences. As she pulled the dress over my head she said that she thought it would still fit *her*, that she could see the hole at the neckline where my grandmother had pinned a pearl brooch as something old, that the classic line never dated. Moved by an ancient sentiment as she cradled the dress, so that it lolled in her arms like someone drowned, she said that she was glad she had a daughter to wear it; and I said, politely, that I could see it must be a pleasing economy.

My mother couldn't refute this without venturing further into sentiment, and this she would not do.

'I had a letter from Lili this morning,' she said. 'They're back in England.'

I was silent, for the news meant nothing to me.

'She saw the announcement in *The Times*,' continued my mother.

As I was still silent she went on, 'You must remember Lili. She was my bridesmaid.'

'I don't remember her,' I said, but I lied. I remembered her now. It was a small shock to know that the neglected image in my mind was real, that she lived and breathed, read *The Times* and wrote letters to her old friends.

'I shall ask her to stay for the wedding,' said my mother. 'Her and Robert.'

Suddenly I remembered Robert too. A man behind Lili. A bearded, shapeless man in brown and purple woollens. A painter.

'He's an artist,' said my mother. 'It's years since I've seen them. They stayed in Egypt. Lili's father was tremendously rich until the government sequestered all his property. If I'd thought, you could have stayed with them, but I don't suppose you'd have learned much French.'

I hadn't. I had learned very little, but my mother had no means of testing me. I had learned other things.

*

6

In those days I slept a great deal, and sometimes I dreamed: not of what had happened but of emptiness and occasionally of chaos when the tenuous mosaic that was life shattered into its constituent parts and whirled away into unknown infinities. I would wake sleep-logged and weary, and every new day was dull. After a while it seemed to me amusing that such preparations as a wedding involve should surround the plain, pale husk that was me and that no one had commented on this incongruity. Even my mother had closed her eyes and ceased to speak of bridal nerves, and my groom, who meant as little to me as his mother's dog, was just as he had always been.

I was trapped, not only by the ordering of the caterers, the priest and my mother's new hat, but by an impotence of spirit. Sometimes in the evenings I would hear myself laughing, and the sound was like wind passing over an empty vessel. One day I overheard my mother speaking to a friend, or rather to an acquaintance, since she was clearly deemed worthy only of instant or cliché speech. My mother said casually, 'Oh, the honeymoon will soon put the roses back in her cheeks.' And for a moment despair was overwhelmed by something more lively: by a sensation of such disgust that for just that one moment I was almost galvanized into rebellion. My mother had intended no lewdness, but the connotations of her remark had made me feel a greater, more immediate sense of defilement than that which I already experienced. Then I shut my mind to the picture that her words had conjured, for after all – what did it matter? My mother had lived my life until half a year ago when I had so briefly lived my own and in the process destroyed it. Now I was to be given to Syl. I had nothing to lose. For Syl I felt no sympathy, since if he was fool enough to want me he deserved none. In the course of time I would die and then it would all be over.

We went to the theatre and to dinner and I believe I must have talked and, as I have said, I know I sometimes laughed and I think no one ever knew that I was empty of everything except perhaps madness.

I spent as little time with Syl as I possibly could. He didn't seem to mind. He had few friends but many acquaintances. He played tennis and golf and sometimes went swimming, determined to give no appearance of succumbing to time, to age. I saw that he could not marry a woman of his own generation, for that would double his chances of seeming old. It was sad for me, I thought, that I was the only girl in the world sufficiently stupid to permit herself to be sacrificed to his vanity. I had few friends, just one or two left over from school, but on the infrequent occasions when we met I could see from their faces that they pitied me, finding me foolish and Syl a bore. He somehow seemed familiar with the jokes that the young were making and used their slang. He embarrassed my friends, and I saw them less and less. He even behaved to my mother, his exact contemporary, as though she were much older than he, deferring to her opinions with an air of youthful *naïveté*. She colluded with him. I had seen her ruffle his hair as though he were a little boy. I knew myself to be stupid, but I sometimes felt that I wasn't alone, and that stupidity was a condition which age did not ease. This was against all that was implicit in the way I had been taught – people increased in wisdom as they grew older, so that they were able to guide the young in the paths they should follow. But my mother had no learning, no wide experience: merely the prejudices, the powerfully surviving clichés, of her own upbringing. Knowing this, I was still impotent, for I had nothing to put in its stead, no one to turn to for advice or support, and I had learned for myself nothing of life except that I was bad at living, and that where I loved I met only rejection and disaster. My father feared my mother as much as I did and wished me to please and agree with her always, for when I did not she would complain to him of my behaviour and I suspected that when this happened his new wife would complain in her

8

turn that he paid too much attention to us and too little to her and her own children. I didn't like to cause trouble. Troublemakers were visible by reason of their demeanour and I wished to be observed as little as possible. I wished to get through life along the lanes and side roads, unseen.

One weekend I went with Syl to stay with some people in the country. I don't remember much about it, only dim rooms and firelight, a dinner of steak-and-kidney pudding and broccoli, which I recall because I disliked it – the smell of urine in the meat, laughter at conversation I did not understand.

There was a boy there of my own age and we got drunk together at the far end of a room with a bottle of Martini. He put his head on my shoulder and undid the buttons of my blouse. As fast as he undid them I did them up again, so that when he got to my waist and sighed he recoiled with indignation and astonishment to find that his labour had been in vain. I was too drunk to wonder whether we had been observed and too remote to care. I had no fear of him and was pleased with my own ingenuity.

My head spun that night, and all next day I felt weak and disordered. The boy in the daylight reminded me of a bird, a bold curious bird. He asked me questions about Syl and about myself without any pretence at politeness. I felt even more fearful than usual faced with this clever inquisitive boy who showed no further desire to undo my blouse and who was only interested in the incongruity of my relationship with Syl. I wanted to tell him calmly that I knew perfectly well that it was absurd and quite understood the point of his questions. Clever as he was, he wasn't sufficiently clever to see this, and his assumption that I was halfwitted made me stubbornly worse.

Syl was away all day with our host, shooting something, and I was too shy to say I was tired and would like to go and sleep in my room. I spent hours with that wretched boy evading his

9

questions and seeming more stupid by the minute. I never did discover who he was, the son of the house or just another guest, and my own obtuseness and incuriosity now appear to me more revealing than anything else of my state at the time. Healthy creatures do not behave so in strange surroundings.

Our hostess scarcely showed herself at all. I suppose she was in the kitchen, perhaps avoiding me, and perhaps the boy had been instructed to entertain me. I didn't wonder about it then. I was no more alert to my environment than a sick animal and I must have somehow been aware of that, because it was then that I remembered the starveling cat.

When we got home my mother asked if we had had a good time and Syl said with great enthusiasm that we had.

Perhaps he had. I never knew him.

When Lili came to stay the emphasis shifted slightly, away from me and on to the strange woman.

She hadn't altered. Her clothes were different – foreign, and smart – but her hair was red, and although I could see she wasn't beautiful I thought she was. She had such colour, such brightness, that sometimes she reminded me of the whirling mosaics, except that she wasn't fragmented but unusually complete. She seemed, if anything, younger than I remembered her. Only one thing surprised me – I didn't recognize her voice and I had thought I would.

She said as she entered, 'My dears ...' in a very English fashion, and she said all the usual phrases, and then to me, 'I hope you're doing the right thing.'

'Now then, Lili,' said my mother.

'You must just forget I'm here,' said Lili. 'You must go on with the preparations as though you were alone. I promise I won't even offer to help. I shan't get in the way for a moment.'

'Where's Robert?' inquired my mother accusingly. 'I thought Robert was coming with you.'

'Oh, he *is*,' said Lili. 'Robert always comes with me. He had to see a man about a gallery.'

'Will he be here for dinner?' asked my mother, the cook briefly taking precedence over the hostess.

'I shouldn't think so,' said Lili. 'I shouldn't think so for a moment.' She moved to the foot of the stairs. 'Am I in the same room?' she asked.

'Yes, Lili,' said my mother.

I thought she sounded rather as though she too had forgotten the essence of Lili, was now reminded and was regretting her invitation.

'Margaret will help you up with your bags.'

Lili glanced at me. 'You look quite strong,' she said, picking up the largest of the suitcases and dragging it up the stairs. 'I remember the smell of this house. I remember you when you were little.'

In the bedroom she turned to me, 'You look tired,' she observed. 'Aren't you sleeping?'

'I sleep too much,' I said, startled into the truth.

'It sometimes takes one that way,' she said obscurely, hunting through her handbag for her cigarettes and lighter.

My stomach tightened. My mother took a firm line on smoking in bedrooms.

Lili lit her cigarette and looked in the mirror.

'Hag,' she addressed herself.

'I'd forgotten how loud and exhausting she could be,' remarked my mother later as I peeled the potatoes.

I looked nervously at her face, but it wore a smile, a reminiscent smile that I hadn't seen before.

'She was expelled from school,' said my mother. 'But I never thought she was really bad – just mischievous and high-spirited.'

It came to me that my mother was *proud* of her friendship

with this high-spirited outcast, and I felt resentment as I thought of my own upbringing, of the fuss when my school reports weren't all that my mother would have wished, of the scene when once I had sworn. My mother is a hypocrite, I thought incredulously. Then I forgot about it as the carrots boiled over. But already Lili had added a new dimension to my view.

'And how is Syl?' asked Lili over dinner.

This, too, astounded me. Syl was more of my mother's genera-tion than my own but it had never occurred to me before that he and she and Lili must all have been young at the same time. I realized that until recently I had thought very little, had taken life at face value, as though, until I was born, nothing on the earth had moved.

My mother, it seemed to me, looked shifty. She said, 'Syl's fine.' She added, 'He's very good to Margaret,' and I felt that simultaneously she had nodded towards the past while affirming the present and that I had fallen somewhere between the two: nothing but the body of a ghost, nebulous and deserted.

'Is he still as good-looking?' asked Lili.

Again I was astonished, for Syl was hard and red and, as I had just realized, old.

'It seems like for ever since we were last here. Hasn't he changed at all?'

Lili looked sideways at me and then away. I thought it the gesture of someone who has noticed a fellow human being about to step in something horrible but who is too polite to draw attention to the fact by seeming sorry for her. I didn't yet know Lili.

'He plays games,' said my mother. 'Keeps himself in trim.'

'Hmm,' said Lili, mashing a carrot.

'Prime of life,' said my mother, sounding to my ears de-fensive.

'But of course,' said Lili. 'Aren't we all?'

Not I, I thought. And not you, Mother.

Then Lili laughed and seemed to gleam with deathlessness and, I thought, the pride of life. Then I remembered, the lust of the eyes and the lust of the flesh, and thought of the quiet convent and cool water.

'Egypt,' my mother was saying; 'tell Lili what you thought of Egypt.'

I said, 'It was very nice.'

Lili laughed again. 'She has the right instincts,' she said. 'She is too polite to bore us with a travelogue.'

She lit a cigarette and asked what I had thought of Marie Claire.

I said I had found her very kind.

'She was always kind at school,' said Lili. 'She used to share her sweets, but I never thought she had the sense of a hen.'

'She was cleverer than all of us,' protested my mother. 'Top of the class.'

'I'm not talking about cleverness,' said Lili, 'I said *sense*.'

My mother said she thought the two qualities went together and Lili said they didn't: not necessarily, and in many cases they were mutually exclusive. My mother couldn't understand this and accused Lili of talking drivel.

Unwisely, I spoke. I felt relief that someone who had known Marie Claire for so long should share my opinion of her. 'She was *daft*,' I said.

'You are in no position, Margaret,' said my mother, 'to judge Marie Claire.'

I knew she was angry because this appraisal reflected badly on her judgement. She could hardly bear to be contradicted, and no good mother, in my mother's view, would send her child to stay with a daft person.

I think it was now that Lili decided I stood in need of care. As she went on talking, making occasional references to the length of my fingers or the breadth of my brow, I thought it ironical that this odd woman should be defending me, not from outright attack but from my mother's protectiveness. I felt like the babes in the wood concealed by leaves lovingly given. I consoled myself; for if it is not possible to be free, perhaps to be hidden is the next best thing, and Lili's presence gave me, as the hours went by, the feeling that I was growing less visible. I was scarcely called upon to say a word as she talked, pale smoke drifting from her mouth and her nose and hanging in the light.

Just before bedtime Lili reverted again to the topic of my marriage.

'And will Derek be coming?' she asked. Derek was my father.

'Yes,' said my mother looking consciously civilized. She had been outraged when her husband left for another woman, had addressed him with religious vehemence and spoken of hell, but as time passed she had realized that life was very much more pleasant without him, that he was generous with money, and so she had, not forgiven, but ceased to revile him; and I know she found grim amusement in my stepmother's harassed countenance and the irritating ways of her two small children. They would come sometimes for my birthday, or at Christmas, and my mother, whose material circumstances were very much more comfortable than those of my father and his new family, would patronize them and condole with my stepmother on my father's drinking habits and the undisciplined weeping of her little boy. The girl bade fair to be pretty but fortunately was extremely dim.

'He'll be here with his family,' said my mother. 'The children are going to be page and bridesmaid.' She wore a momentary look of almost angelic forbearance. 'I was doubtful when I first had the idea, but Margaret has no cousins or ...' Here she bit a potato, because she had been going to say 'close friends' but had thought better of it. She had lost her temper with me on the subject of bridesmaids. Of course there were friends whom I

14

could have asked, but I had seen an opportunity to be stubborn, and had dismissed each of her suggested candidates with tiresome and irrelevant objections – too fat, too blonde, too tall, too many teeth. 'Then we'll have Jennifer and Christopher,' my mother had said in a barely controlled fury. 'All right,' I had said listlessly, disconcerting my mother considerably, since I was perfectly aware that she had expected me to turn down this preposterous proposal with as much intractability as I had turned down the others. She was now determined at least to win admiration for her enforced magnanimity.

'What's his wife like?' asked Lili.

'She's a nice little thing,' said my mother damningly.

Lili, who I could tell understood her very well, laughed and lit another cigarette.

'She's called Cynthia,' said my mother as one who says, 'She's called cat-sick.'

'Ugh,' said Lili obligingly.

There was a small summerhouse at the bottom of my mother's garden, half wood, half glass. I used to, as my mother put it 'curl up with a book' on a broad shelf which ran the length of one wall under shaky moorish windows which looked out over the golf course. On the opposite shelf stood my mother's collection of cactuses. She refused to have any pets in the house, but even the hardest of hearts need some discharge of sentiment. This usually presents as sentimentality and my mother talked to her cactuses with affection and called them sweet names. I very much resented them, because they drew my mother to what would have been a private retreat for me. Most days she would, sooner or later, walk down the lawn to examine her plants and I learned to wait until she had done this before myself settling in the summerhouse. Once I waited so long and stayed so late that I gave myself away to Syl, who had called in the usual way at the front door, to be told by my mother that I was in the summerhouse and he should go and bring me out and back to the drawing-room where, like normal people, we should converse. After that Syl took to walking from his garden along the edge of the golf course to my mother's garden. He would look in the summerhouse before coming in by the back door but he seldom found me there now.

'If you want to do something useful,' my mother said to me one day, 'you can help me propagate the cactuses.'

When bits of them broke off you had only to plunge them into the earth and they grew into new cactuses. I didn't want to do anything useful. There were very few human beings I cared for and I cared nothing for cactuses.

'You're very selfish,' my mother said. 'If you took more of an interest in things you'd be happier.'

I knew I was selfish. I knew that people who loved God were supposed to love their neighbour too. But Syl was our neighbour.

I said I'd go shopping for her instead, and she said that that was unnecessary since Mrs Raffald had already done it. I said I'd tear out the dead Michaelmas daisies, but the gardener had done that. There was really very little I could do actively to refute the charge of selfishness. Even the local cats were, without exception, well-fed and cared for, and there wasn't a needy creature for miles round. In order to express charity and compassion I would have to travel far, since nobody near would have thanked me for it.

'When you're married you'll have to be less selfish,' said my mother, who was particularly displeased with me on this grey, wintry morning. 'You'll have to brighten up.'

I was disposed to argue. 'Why?' I asked.

'Syl won't put up with all this nonsense,' said my mother unwarily.

'I'd better break the engagement now,' I said, thinking my mother very foolish for not realizing that what appealed to Syl

16

was my very paleness, my silence, my hostility, which he mostly construed as shyness, until I was unpleasant, and when I was unpleasant he took it as evidence of some depth in my feeling for him and found it sexually alluring. I had once or twice been goaded by his obtuseness into cruelty and he had wanted me more. I had been brought close to another sort of despair by my inability to draw blood: a cat with no claws and ineffectual teeth. Such a cat can seem only like a toy.

'You can't break the engagement now,' said my mother.

'Why?' I asked.

'You know perfectly well,' said my mother, not going into details.

In a sane world, I thought, we would have discussed the state of my feelings, debated whether I loved Syl sufficiently to commit the rest of my life to him, questioned my views on the institution of marriage, examined my mother's motives in striving to introduce me into this state, have said *something* of some interest. But the cake had been ordered and that was that. There was no more to be said.

I was ill at ease in the mornings in those days. I would wake sour-mouthed, unwilling to get out of bed. My mother would bring me China tea and toast, succulent with butter, and I would eat it, knowing that afterwards I should feel sick and heavy. I would remember, against my will, the fragrance of coffee and hot bread, the energy that had possessed me so short a time ago, when I had felt supple as an eel, as powerful as a salmon, as sure and quiet and graceful as an owl. I would remember the sunlight that I had thought was like wealth, redeemed and transformed beyond the reach of cupidity, and the shadows that were not black but the colour of great half-forgotten riches. My own country now seemed mean and meretricious, and my feet clashed awkwardly with the ground, jarring my body and jangling my bones so that the sound of my clumsy movements echoed hollowly against thin walls, and I was never at peace. So short a time ago? It seemed like aeons of time ago in an unimaginably distant world. My childhood felt nearer. The useless girl that I was might have grown without diversion, etiolated and bland like a stalk of grass under a stone, from those early days, represented still by the dolls and bears that lay on the cupboard shelves. The living creature that I had briefly been might never have existed. My mother would not have recognized her, and now I scarcely recognized her myself.

I was so cold.

'I'm only spoiling you like this,' lied my mother, 'because when you've got a home of your own you won't have time for breakfast in bed.'

I sat up so that she could put the tray on my knees. She brought me breakfast in bed to ensure that I was awake and wouldn't spend the morning half sleeping in frowsty, tumbled sheets.

I said, like the child who had played with the dolls and bears, 'Syl would bring me breakfast in bed, only his mother wouldn't let him.'

'I certainly hope you wouldn't expect him to,' said my mother. 'Syl is a busy man. No time to make breakfast for a lazy wife.'

She picked up my underclothes from the floor and laid them on a chair. 'I just wish you'd pull yourself together,' she said half-despairingly.

But I knew what was really worrying her at that moment. It was the mention of Syl's mother who lived in his house and showed no intention, although she was nearly eighty, of ever dying. My mother frequently inquired after her health and was constantly disappointed. 'She's wonderful,' Syl would say, 'got the heart of a sixty-year-old.' He seemed not to dislike her, which was odd since apart from him all who knew her were united in this emotion.

'You'll hardly have to see her at all,' said my mother, voicing her worry tangentially, 'in a house that size.'

'We'll have to eat together,' I said in a doleful tone which I knew would upset my mother as much as the vision which my remark would conjure up. These petty revenges were my only source of pleasure, pallid though it was.

'Of course you won't,' said my mother, almost squeaking with exasperation. 'Why on earth do you think Syl went to all the trouble of making her a separate kitchen?'

Syl had indeed done this. He had taken the pleasantest, south-facing rooms of the house and turned them into what he described as a 'suite' for his parent.

'I could hardly expect her to eat alone,' I said. 'Poor old lady ...?'

But I had gone too far. My mother glared at me suspiciously and told me not to be so ridiculous.

Already the satisfaction of teasing her had faded. While I spoke like that I could pretend that Syl and his house were unreal and my projected presence in it merely an extension of that fantasy, but the wedding loomed ever closer like a rock and I, poor ship, was about to founder on it. I had had a sudden image of Syl bringing me breakfast in a bed which we had shared, and I heard myself saying aloud, 'No!'

My mother who had reached the door turned to look at me.

'What?' she said.

'Nothing,' I said. 'I just thought of something. It wasn't anything.'

My mother was the sort of person who regards talking to yourself as the first sign of madness.

'What you need is a couple of babies,' she observed. 'That'll give you something to think about.'

I did so wish that my mother hadn't said that.

'How's the bride?' asked Lili when I came downstairs.

For some reason I didn't mind Lili talking about my wedding. I think I knew already that she didn't take it seriously.

'I'm dying to see Syl again. When is he coming?' She looked at her watch. 'Robert should be here soon.'

'Syl will come this evening,' I told her.

'Goody, we can have a party. It might cheer you up. On the other hand,' she added, 'it might not. I often find parties depressing. All that yelling and drinking and getting too hot. Parties have been known to make my make-up run. That's annoying.'

I found her calm assumption that I needed cheering up restful after my mother's blind denials.

'It isn't any fun being young,' said Lili. 'But people forget. I don't. I clearly remember it being detestable – one's hormones haven't yet learned their place and one is full of uncertainties.'

My mother came in, flustered.

'I'm short of a chop,' she said. 'I just looked in the larder and I've only got four. Now if Syl stays to dinner we'll be five . . . '

'I'll go and buy you one,' said Lili. 'I'll buy you half a dozen if you like. It isn't like you to fuss about a missing chop.'

'I've got so much on my mind,' said my mother irritably, letting us know that she was bearing the full burden of the forthcoming taxing ceremony.

'Me and Margaret will go,' said Lili. 'It'll be a nice little outing for us.'

My mother looked less harassed.

'Margaret could do with some exercise,' she said. 'She hardly leaves the house. No wonder she's so pale.'

'Exercise is good for you,' said Lili as we walked, 'but I hate it. I can't see the point in going for a walk unless a chop lies at the end of it.'

'I used to walk in Egypt,' I said. Egypt.

I could sense Lili turning her head to look at me, but the urge to talk, to confess, had left me as suddenly as it had come.

'How did Syl propose?' asked Lili. 'Did he go down on one knee, hand on heart?'

I considered. What had happened was that Syl had, one evening, flushed with wine, remarked that he thought it would be a good idea if we got married. I had said nothing and he had assumed that we were engaged, telling his mother that night and mine the following morning. He had moved to kiss my mouth, but I had turned my head and he had kissed my cheek. Incomprehensible as it may seem he and I had never shared an embrace. He had made many attempts to put his arms around me, but I had always evaded him. As I thought about it it seemed extraordinary that any man should endure such behaviour and still wish to marry the object of his desire. Sometimes he would whisper that I was an innocent little thing, a primrose, a little white pony and other endearments: strange, understated fantasies that I could not comprehend.

'He asked me to marry him,' I said at last, 'so I said I would.'

'Why?' asked Lili.

'I don't know,' I said, because of course I hadn't agreed at all. Simply I had known that I couldn't go on living with my mother. I had nowhere else to go and now I was being carried along – that ship bound for wrecking.

'I wonder if he's queer,' mused Lili aloud. 'I always used to wonder if he might be. And now he's forty, unmarried and still living with that old termagant he calls Mother.'

'He's had girlfriends,' I protested, just to be fair.

'I know that,' said Lili, 'but he was always a bit strange with them. Too *helpful*, if you see what I mean.'

I did. Syl would have liked to take my shoes off for me, brush my hair, and once he had muttered that he would gladly wash my clothes.

'Tell you what I think,' said Lili cheerfully. 'He's either a masochist or, in view of your age, a paedophile.'

I thought that this was a most extraordinary conversation to be having about one's intended groom, but I was feeling lighter. Lili, I thought, would be ruthless with cobwebs, dauntless in darkened rooms, relentless with dust accumulated in hidden corners. I wanted her to go on talking, but she lost interest, turned into the butcher's and struck up a conversation about meat.

This was the first time I had seen her exercise her charm. After two minutes I believe the butcher would have followed her out of the shop had she beckoned him. With talk of sweetbreads and liver and fillet she captivated him – I couldn't quite see how she did it. She would look at him sideways, smile at unexpected moments, and while she was never coarse there was the vaguest suggestion of the gentlest possible obscenity as she spoke of the bodies of animals. However, she did it well, and I shouldn't think the butcher ever quite forgot the lady with the red hair.

I felt inclined to congratulate her on her performance as we left with our solitary chop, but her interest had turned again and she was speaking of Egypt. I tensed myself, but Lili's Egypt wasn't mine. She spoke of painting and antiquities while I thought of rivers, dark faces and the shadowed cloisters of the convent.

We stopped again to buy olive oil and garlic, for Lili said that although she had vowed not to interfere she was going to cook dinner and, while my mother would complain, she would be grateful in the end.

'I shall cook an Egyptian meal,' said Lili.

She put her arm around me briefly.

'Make you feel at home,' she added.

I wondered if she could see into my mind, and I didn't care, for during that one short walk I had come to believe that Lili would not harm me.

Robert, unlike Lili, had changed considerably. He wasn't the bulky, bearded man of my memory but thin, clean-shaven, dark and angry.

'Do stop worrying,' Lili ordered him, after he had spent some time fulminating against the iniquities of the gallery owner. 'It'll be all right on the night.'

'You haven't seen the lighting,' he said.

'We'll make the man change it,' promised Lili. 'You mustn't bore the bride's mother with art-world horror stories. She has enough to think about.'

Robert then spoke to my mother about the time when they were young. He only mentioned the gallery once more when Syl arrived, clapped him on the shoulder and asked him what he was up to now.

'Syl,' said Lili coolly, as he turned to her, 'how nice to see you. You've hardly changed at all.'

I said without thinking, 'I wonder what you were all like when you were young?', realizing as I spoke how young I was myself as four people in early middle age turned to regard me with varying degrees of indignation and amusement.

'I do wish you'd make some effort to grow up,' said my mother before she could stop herself, for she didn't want her future son-in-law to know how much I could irritate her.

'I keep myself in trim,' said Syl.

'I expect you do press-ups,' said Lili, playfully pinching his upper arm. He did. I had seen him.

'You look well, Lili,' he remarked, also without warmth, and I wondered why they had ever been friends since they didn't like each other.

I drank too much at dinner and missed whole stretches of conversation, noting at one point with tipsy clarity that people who could converse were a great boon to the inarticulate who yet, when in the company of their tongue-tied fellows, felt it essential to say something. As it was, Lili chatted easily and Robert timed his eating to synchronize with her fluency; when Lili stopped talking to eat he carried on, not in the same vein but sufficiently in harmony with her style not to upset the balance of conviviality.

I found it curious that when everyone had finished Robert still had a plateful of food before him and we had to wait as he ate it and Lili talked and smoked her endless cigarettes. None the less I had found the evening reassuring and felt no difficulty in saying that I was sorry but I was suddenly most awfully tired and if no one minded I thought I would go to bed.

Lili said that of course I must, but I made the error of looking at my mother for approval, found none and saw only displeasure at my childish crudity.

It was this that made me unable to sleep, so that coming downstairs, parched with alcohol, for a glass of lemonade, I heard my mother and Lili talking. Syl had left and Robert gone to bed and the old school friends were talking as they must have talked in their manless dormitory: my mother careful, Lili dashing.

My mother said, 'I've never discussed anything with her, I'm afraid. *You* know ...'

Lili said, 'You don't imagine she's a virgin, do you?'

My mother said, 'Lili, you can't be suggesting that Syl ...'

And Lili said, 'Darling, you can be so stupid sometimes.'

I went back upstairs, drank water in my hands from the bath tap and slept without dreaming.

At breakfast Lili for some reason spoke of fidelity, and I noted my mother as she went in and out with bread and boiling water, looking at her, not with the disapproval she reserved for me but with half-amused incredulity.

'You see,' said Lili, 'there's no real experience to be gained by promiscuity. We're all called to understand ourselves, and to do this it's necessary that we should understand one another, and this is only possible after a long while of living together. Leaping from bed to bed one learns nothing of any depth.'

'What have you learned, Lili?' asked my mother, at last sitting down with a cup of tea before her.

'You challenge me,' said Lili. 'What have I learned? What have I learned of myself from learning through Robert . . .?'

Her husband lowered his paper and regarded her over the top of it.

'I don't know,' she admitted. 'But I've learned something. Isn't it obvious that too many relationships will teach one nothing except that men are much alike?'

My mother sniffed. She had no very high opinion of men.

'So are women,' said Robert, turning back to the paper.

Lili looked affronted. 'I am quite unlike other women,' she observed.

'Yes, you are,' agreed her husband, and Lili smiled.

I thought that Robert loved her and wouldn't mind her having lovers if she always came back to him. I wondered how it was possible to love many men when you had once loved one more than your immortal soul, and whether Lili had ever loved like that, or whether this was a torment saved for ridiculous people like myself.

'What are you thinking about, Margaret?' asked Lili.

'I was thinking about what you were saying,' I told her, while memories of Nour flooded my being so that I felt I couldn't bear it but must instantly take that gleaming knife and open my body to let him out.

'I sometimes talk nonsense,' said Lili, 'and sometimes I don't. Mostly I don't, but you must be careful when you listen to me.'

'*Don't* fill her head with a lot of nonsense,' said my mother, rather oddly since, on the face of it, Lili had been recommending the path of virtue. I understood that my mother was ambivalent about marriage, bitter about her own experience of it while seeing no possible alternative for me, and that this must make things difficult for her.

She said that sensible people weren't led astray by infatuation. She implied that only a fool could allow what was known as 'love' to enter into consideration in the matter. She stated that a wise woman would choose her mate on the basis of his qualities of character.

Lili's cigarette smoke went down the wrong way. 'Nobody ever married anyone because he was virtuous,' she protested. Then she recanted. 'Yes they did. What nobody ever did was go to bed with someone because he was virtuous.'

My mother looked annoyed and inclined to dispute this but, naturally, she couldn't. What could she say?

There was still so much I didn't understand. The revelations of evil that I had experienced had brought me only to confusion and powerlessness. I remembered a night by the river when daylight faded, darkness fell and the moon rose at once with a new light and I thought I understood everything and that everything was good. Now I knew myself to be bad in a bad world, a vessel of poison afloat in a sea of poison, and I thought that this was all there was to know.

'We have to go into town,' said Lili. 'I'm going to take Margaret with us.'

I protested. I wanted only to go down to the summerhouse and watch the leaves falling until night fell with them.

'You go,' said my mother decisively. 'It'll do you good.'

That was that, for if I now refused my mother would see to it that I regretted my foolishness.

'What are you going to wear?' asked Lili.

'Wear your grey tweed,' advised my mother. 'You look nice in that.'

'Let me look,' said Lili. 'I adore other people's wardrobes.'

She looked through my chest-of-drawers after she had decided that the grey tweed would do.

'Haven't you got a grey jumper?' she inquired. 'How elegant you would look all in grey – like a little nun.'

Elegance was not a concept I associated with myself, nor with nuns, but as I thought about it I realized that Lili was right. The sisters had indeed looked most neat and lovely in their colourless habits, stark against the brightness of the country.

'She should wear a red jumper,' objected my mother. 'A nice colourful contrast.'

'No, no,' said Lili. 'That is a very English notion and quite misplaced. I shall lend her a jumper. She shall go all in grey and you shall lend her your seed pearls. Now a pale lipstick and some powder and she can slip into Bond Street without looking as though she came from Croydon.'

'She does come from Croydon,' said my mother.

'There is no need for her to *look* as though she does,' said Lili.

My mother in her mustard-coloured coat and skirt, with a green jumper for her nice colourful contrast, looked minutely offended but wasn't sufficiently interested in clothes to argue the matter further. 'She'll look very drab,' was all she said.

Lili brushed my hair with a brush wrapped in a silk scarf and pinched my upper lip to refine the line of lipstick.

'You must never underestimate the power of clothes,' she said. 'Clothes *are* the person. Take away the clothes and you take away the personality. Naked people are nothing. You wouldn't recognize me if you met me in the bath.'

I thought of the river and Nour.

My mother said, 'Since you're so mad about clothes, Lili, you can help me alter the wedding dress.'

'OK,' said Lili nonchalantly.

Someone had lent Robert a car. He had the expatriate knack of being lent things and getting himself looked after on his return to the native land, and as they talked it became apparent that we were to be entertained to lunch by the gallery owner.

'Won't he mind if I come too?' I asked.

'I don't care if he does,' said Robert rather ungallantly.

'No one cares about *him*,' said Lili.

My heart misgave me. Together with the other pains of youth, I was shy.

'We were going to stay with him,' said Lili, 'but it's much nicer staying with you. The least he can do is buy us a decent lunch.'

I wondered if Lili and Robert were short of money since his government had impoverished Lili's father. I had the impression that unless you were famous there was little money to be made from art.

I asked, 'Is it difficult to sell paintings?', thinking this a quite decorous way of framing my question.

'Yes,' said Robert.

'Not if you know how,' said Lili. 'I shall sell a lot at the opening. I shall spike the wine and tell people how beautiful they are.' She sounded excited at the prospect, alert, like any animal at the beginning of something – a race, a hunt, a battle.

'How beautiful who are?' asked Robert.

'The people and the paintings of course,' said Lili. 'I must flatter people and arouse their acquisitive instincts at one and the same time.'

'You're good at that,' said Robert, but he didn't sound, as I thought he might have done, condemnatory.

'I enjoy it,' said Lili. 'It's good for *me*. It gives me a role in life. A positive helpmeet to my husband. Now if you were rich I should have nothing to do. I should be a silent shell, wealthy and withered and bored. As it is, I have been forced into positive action, into vitality and life.'

She spoke to her husband, but I thought she was addressing me, for he must have heard this before, or at least known what was in her mind.

He said mildly, 'I always told you you shouldn't have given up dancing.'

Lili said, 'I was tired of dancing. I wanted to stay with you, not go all round the world, dancing.'

'You wouldn't have gone round the world,' said Robert. 'Summer seasons in Fayyum perhaps.'

Lili laughed.

I thought – if it had been my parents who had been talking, they would have been doing it at the tops of their voices, for surely on the content alone that conversation had been a row. I wondered whether Robert and Lili had spoken so often like this that neither had any longer the energy to shout, or whether there never had been anger between them. They were quite outside my experience. It was as though they were creatures of the same species, possessed of a venom which might kill an outsider, but were powerless to injure each other.

'If I had been married to a successful man,' said Lili, 'I should never have discovered myself, or my potential.'

'You've always been the same, Lili,' said Robert. He was right, for I remembered her and she hadn't changed.

The gallery owner sighed when he saw us. Only I saw him sigh, for Lili and Robert were looking not at him but at the walls, and he found me too negligible to bother to disguise his ennui.

'Robert, Lili,' he said and didn't inquire as to my identity.

'This is Margaret,' said Lili abstractedly. 'I don't know why you were worried about the lighting, Robert.'

'It glares off the surface,' said Robert.

'No it doesn't,' said Lili. 'Not if you stand here.'

'Everyone won't be able to stand there,' said Robert. 'Not if you're standing there.'

'I have booked a table for midday,' said the gallery owner, 'and I have an appointment at two.'

As we walked to the restaurant I felt miserable, foreseeing argument and dissent and wishing that I possessed the charm and the experienced polish to ease the tension between these people.

Lili said suddenly, 'What I like best in the world is to see *men* dancing.'

Robert said, 'I was telling Lili in the car that she shouldn't have stopped being a dancer.'

'I don't mean ballet,' said Lili. 'I gave up ballet because I found the artifice irksome. It isn't natural to dance on one's toes. People can't fly, they can only jump, and once you've realized that you must either laugh or cry. I like to see men stamping all of their foot on the ground – Morris dancers and Russians and Greeks – and jumping, like people who are resigned to mere jumping, without any pretence at flight. I don't think I like to see women dancing at all – when they're not hopping they're undulating.'

'Don't you enjoy the ballet?' asked the gallery owner, who, I think, had not been listening.

'*No*,' said Lili with emphatic patience. 'I dislike the artifice, you see.'

'You must suspend disbelief,' advised the gallery owner, bored.

'I don't see why I should,' said Lili, argumentative.

She stopped walking suddenly, so that the two people behind nearly collided with her. We also stopped after a few paces and turned to look back at her. She seemed poised to make a speech, then and there, in the middle of Tottenham Court Road, but all she said, before she came forward to join us, was: 'Art can be a snare and a delusion.'

'If it wasn't for art,' said Robert, 'we wouldn't be about to eat.'

We had reached the restaurant, and the gallery owner held the door open for us as we went in. It was called El Misr and Lili exclaimed, 'Egypt again. Egypt is surely the motif of the year.'

'I thought it would make you feel at home,' said the gallery owner – untruthfully, I felt. I suspected that the restaurant was cheap and that this was the reason we had been guided here. Also I could hear irony in his tone and I thought that for some reason he was very annoyed indeed.

I could hear foreign voices raised in the kitchen and stopped listening to my companions. When I again became conscious of what they were saying I heard Lili arguing. '... Not soft and soggy,' she was saying.

I must have looked inquiring, for Robert explained, 'We are debating whether beans should retain some bite.'

'It doesn't really matter,' said Lili, losing interest. 'They'll bring it the way it is anyway. They think we're stupid about food.'

I said, 'I think they're right.'

Everyone looked faintly surprised, for I hadn't previously volunteered a remark.

'Hashed mutton,' I said by way of explanation, 'and tinned spaghetti on toast.'

'Oh yes,' agreed Lili gloomily. 'No wonder the English look so awful.'

'Margaret doesn't look awful,' said Robert, as though it was expected of him.

'We,' said Lili, 'have *just* managed to force down sufficient amounts of fresh veg and protein to retain some shapeliness and complexion.'

I found it odd that Robert had chosen to distinguish me alone as English and wondered how he saw himself and Lili and I found it odd that Lili had chosen to lay claim to Englishness. I hadn't yet learned that she was able to change her nationality as she changed her accessories, to suit the occasion. She was skilled at being English, but she was more interesting when she was half-Arab.

They talked about art, and I drank too much because I had nothing to say. I felt that my life fitted me as ill as a garment designed for somebody else.

I don't know how I got the following impression from Lili. I don't believe I was listening to her very closely. Not listening was always one of my faults and one of the reasons I so frequently found myself isolated in misunderstanding: like a careless rider, cut off from the company, alone and benighted for failing to pay attention to the prevailing agreements as to intention and direction. After a while the other riders don't even bother to come and look for you. They leave you to amble into the desert on your own, and when you come to think of it you can't really blame them.

One day she was talking about love again. She said – or I heard – that we should only fall in love once, that it was an experience of such profound significance that to repeat it would be to devalue it. This seemed to me so true that I couldn't imagine why it was not universally acknowledged. Even in my limited experience I had seen people falling in and out of love, as though, soiled by sorrow and loss, they had to go in search of comfort from one used and lukewarm bath to another. The marriage service, I conceded, did insist on exclusivity, but clearly people other than myself were prone to not listening. It was sad for me that I had fallen in love with someone who did not love me, but it was not an experience I cared to repeat – for more and better reasons than the fear of pain. If it had been an illusion, then other illusions lay ahead, a hall of mirrors, a series of mirages. I had lost faith, not in God but in the carnal love which so preoccupied almost everyone I had ever known. How they talked and sang and wrote and thought about it, as though union with another were the entire purpose of existence. And how could they believe it when disillusion, of one sort or another, sooner or later was the almost invariable result? Perhaps it was not I but the other riders who were hell-bent on the wrong route. I was too unsure of myself to believe that this could be possible. Mother Joseph seemed utterly remote, her voice lost in the clamour of my mother's voice, my mother's certainty that marriage represented sanity, security, good behaviour in a dangerous world of hostile winds and people who were 'not one of us', talking to themselves. It couldn't be that I was right, and while I yearned to return to a certainty I already knew, I heard only my mother's voice, insisting, on one dead note, that she knew of what life should consist. All the other voices around me were saying the same and the distant peal of the convent bell mingling, not incongruously, with the cry from the minaret went unheeded.

When Lili stopped speaking I wished I could ask her to repeat what she had said, but already she was lighting a cigarette and talking about linen.

'I've never seen the point of keeping piles of the stuff,' she said. 'It goes yellow if you keep it for too long and I don't see how anyone can be expected to use fifty tablecloths even in a lifetime – not mucky-looking yellow ones. And where are you supposed to keep them all?'

'I don't know,' I said. I already had a great many tablecloths in boxes with bows on. Presents from relations.

'There'd be no room for one's clothes,' said Lili, 'not with all those tablecloths and napkins.'

'The nuns have three habits,' I said. 'One to wear, one in the wash and one in the wardrobe.'

'I wouldn't mind that,' said Lili. 'It is possible to look very beautiful in a habit.'

'The habits are blessed when they make their final vows,' I said. 'They have a robing ceremony.'

'I know,' said Lili.

I knew it was probable that she knew. I just wanted to talk about it. 'Inside the main door there's a holy water stoup of blue-and-white porcelain,' I said. 'They brought it from France. The walls of the visitors' parlour are blue, and the rest are white.'

'And a statue of Our Lady in a blue-and-white dress with a golden crown,' said Lili.

I realized that I had been talking about the convent without explanation or location. 'Did you know Mother Joseph?' I asked, 'and Sister Bridget?'

'A long time ago,' said Lili, 'when we used to stay with Marie Claire.'

My mother had come in. 'Wasted lives,' she said. She was a

very English Catholic and opposed to religious excess in all its forms.

I wanted to ask whether she thought her own life unwasted and whether the fact that she had given birth to me was sufficient justification for it.

'I don't think so,' said Lili. 'I should have liked to be a nun, except they wouldn't let me smoke and I couldn't live without cigarettes. I wouldn't want to.'

'*You*?' said my mother. 'A fine nun you'd have made.' She moved to empty the ashtray. I thought, Be still and know that I am God. 'Some of them are very good and quite useful, but it's a selfish existence.'

'I don't want to appear awkward,' said Lili that evening, 'but she looks like something the cat dragged in.' She was sitting on her heels with a pin in her mouth, eyeing me with pity as I stood yet again in my mother's wedding dress.

'That's why I want to alter it,' explained my mother wearily, too tired to argue.

'I'm not certain that it's salvageable,' said Lili.

'That's rubbish,' said my mother. 'It's in perfect condition. All it needs is to be made to fit. It looked lovely on me.'

'Hmm,' said Lili abstractedly, leaning forward and tweaking at the hem. The fact that she was doing this and not looking at her old friend made her doubts about this statement less evident, but all the same my mother protested. 'It *did*, Lili,' she said. 'Everyone said so.'

'Oh yes, it did,' said Lili, 'though, mind you, I think it highly unlikely that anyone would tell you on your wedding day that you looked the most frightful frump – not,' she added hastily, 'that you did. All I mean is that brides are always described as beautiful.'

She sat back on her heels again. 'They so seldom are,' she reflected. 'Tulle is terrible, and lace is worse, and white is woeful.

34

Nothing white should ever be taken in at the waist. White should either flow in an unbroken line from the shoulder to the ground or be superbly cut and tailored. Veils don't help. They make the poor girls look as though they hadn't been properly unpacked, as though they'd been taken out of the box and someone had left half their wrappings on.'

'I don't know why you have to be so contrary,' snapped my mother. 'Brides always wear white veils. They always have.'

'Murder is fairly common too,' said Lili. 'It always has been.'

'Don't be silly, Lili,' said my mother. 'The white is meant to represent purity and innocence.'

'That's pretty stupid,' said Lili, 'considering that marriage means an end to all that. I can see why nuns wear white when they take the veil, but when you think of the way everyone goes on at the prospect of the wedding night innocence is the last thing on anyone's mind.' She now had a cigarette between her teeth and squinted against the smoke.

'Don't be disgusting,' said my mother.

'There you are,' said Lili. '*You* said disgusting.'

'Oh, anyway,' said my mother, 'I don't know why we're talking about it. She's got to wear that dress come what may.'

'Why?' asked Lili.

'Because I wore it,' explained my mother. 'I've saved it for years for my daughter to wear.'

I thought she might add, 'And she's bloody well going to wear it,' but my mother had said her piece for the moment. Her insistence seemed absurd in view of her own failed marriage, but I had always been too nervous to point this out, to ask what she made of the break in connection between the symbolism of the dress and the unassailability of the marriage vow.

'I wore crimson at my wedding,' said Lili. 'Heavy wild silk, calf-length.'

'I know,' said my mother acidly. 'I was there.'

'I looked *wonderful*,' remarked Lili dreamily. 'I should have been marrying a prince.'

My mother said nothing, and Lili stubbed out her cigarette in a pin tray. She said, 'Well, if there's nothing else for it,' and began to fold and manipulate the wedding dress while I stood like a doll, cold and alien and powerless.

That night my mother went to bed early and Robert walked through the wood, past the golf course to the pub. He would pass Syl's house on the way, since it stood close to ours on the same side of the private road, behind hedges of cypress and box, flanked by lawns garnished with birch and all manner of ornamental trees.

'Why don't you pop in and see Syl and say hallo to his mother?' suggested Lili, malice flickering in her bright face.

'He'll be busy,' said Robert, 'studying briefs, or whatever it is he does.'

'Oh, go on,' said Lili. 'He'll be delighted to have a break and go off for a pint. Perhaps he'll play you a tune on his oboe.' Syl's oboe was another of the things about him that I couldn't bear. He must have been playing the beastly thing for years.

'I'll see,' said Robert – I think in deference to me, for he gave his wife a nasty look as she beamed up at him.

I thought – it isn't just me. Nobody likes Syl. I'm marrying a man whom nobody likes. I could see the room beginning to spin as though I had had a dreadful shock or a moment of unbearable fear. That I myself did not like Syl was almost immaterial, since I deserved nothing better, but even with my penitential self-disgust it seemed unfair to me, and otiose, that my future husband should be so generally unpopular. With a glimmer of self-preservation I began to reason that to be a martyr to an unwanted marriage was one thing, whereas to look like a fool in the eyes of all the world was another. Then I suddenly saw that Syl, too, must look a very great fool, for he was twice my age and

I wasn't beautiful, nor talented, nor in the least degree interesting. We were, I suddenly perceived, an entirely incongruous and idiotic couple. I thought that he was already a man when I was born, that he had seen me growing up, and I thought of the strange, sad, frightening creatures who haunted the borders of the woods watching the children play.

'Oh Lili,' I said, and I grasped the table's edge.

Her expression, to my fearful eyes, was enigmatic. It might have been compassionate, or amused, or even hostile.

She lit a cigarette, and when she spoke her tone was cool. 'Sometimes there are things you have to do,' she said, 'and sometimes there aren't. Sometimes other people can make up your mind for you and sometimes they can't. Sometimes you have to grow up – not just once but all through your life. Even very old people sometimes have to suddenly grow up a bit.'

I didn't really understand what she was saying, but I could see that she despised me.

'You think I'm stupid,' I said.

'No I don't,' said Lili. 'I think you've lost hope, and the only thing I can tell you is that if you hang on hope will come back, and you mustn't do anything until it does.'

My wedding was close. Would hope return in time?

'I've got to go through with it now,' I said.

'Oh well,' said Lili.

She seemed again to have lost interest, in that swift way she had, and I felt useless and bereft.

'Tired,' said Lili. 'Bed.'

The next day was Saturday, and Syl called in the middle of the morning. He had been playing golf and was wearing cavalry-twill trousers and a plaid tie round an unbuttoned shirt-neck.

'How boyish and negligent you look,' cried Lili.

She reminded me of a wasp as she flitted round him, a wasp suddenly aware, in the way wasps have, that there is rotting matter in the vicinity, for she had been upstairs when he arrived by way of the garden and couldn't have seen him.

'I've been noticing how very much roof you have,' she said to my mother. 'I've never known a house with so much roof. In places it almost comes down to the ground.'

'It was designed like that,' said my mother, 'on purpose.'

'But why?' asked Lili.

'I don't know why,' said my mother. 'It must have been some idea the architect had. Does it matter?'

'No, it doesn't *matter*,' said Lili. 'It just seems so peculiar.'

'It's no more peculiar than the other houses on the drive,' argued my mother, and she was right. Ours was glancingly Tudorbethan and called 'The Oaks'; others had clearly been inspired by visits to Spain and were called '*Casa*-something-or-other'; one or two bore hints of castellation and crenellation and were appropriately named after some of the statelier English homes; while Syl's house had been conceived in a dour Regency style by a less fertile imagination and its grey dressed stones were covered by a great pelt of ivy. It was the only house on the drive that I could imagine Syl's mother living in. The haciendas, the castles and the oast-houses would not have suited her at all.

'I wonder what it's worth now?' mused Lili, scandalizing my mother. 'It's much too big for you. Why don't you sell it?'

'It's my home,' said my mother stiffly.

'Oh silly,' said Lili. 'You sound as though your family had lived here since Sir Eggleswyke slew the great eel.'

'I came here as a bride,' said my mother, and Lili giggled.

My mother insisted when my father left that she should keep the house, and all its contents, and continue to receive a major part of his income. I felt guilty about sharing in this bounty, for my stepmother and her children could clearly have benefited from some of it.

'And I couldn't now adapt,' said my mother, sounding grand, 'to a smaller house.'

Nor could she then justify employing a cleaner and the odd-job man who kept all the local gardens more or less under control. Nothing would persuade my mother to lower her standards, for that might ease my father's lot.

'Well, the place certainly suits you,' said Lili – I thought ambiguously, but my mother looked gratified.

'It would be foolish to sell now,' said Syl judiciously, and I thought that apart from wanting young girls he wanted to inherit another big house, and I wondered how on earth I could be going to marry someone whom I detested so much.

'Why did you disappear like that?' he asked.

I had left the room without speaking and gone into the garden. Now he stood behind me, so that I could feel the warmth of his body, but I was facing the box hedge, so close to it that I couldn't turn.

'I won't marry you,' I said. My voice was high and it shook and I didn't convince even myself.

'Yes, you will,' said Syl.

He sounded like my mother at that moment and I was surprised, for I had thought him weak. I saw that I was intended to be subject to people like these two, was doomed to marry Syl as surely as I had been born of my mother.

'You and your little nerves,' he said and he put his fingers in the back of the collar of my dress and pulled it slightly as though I was a recalcitrant dog.

I didn't like to be touched by almost anyone. I said, 'Let me go, Syl', because I felt ridiculous, crushed between this man and the garden hedge. I spoke calmly since now revulsion had given way to hopelessness. I had remembered the last time I had stood in a garden with a man.

'I don't love you, Syl,' I said. He stood back and let me turn. I looked at his face, which was something I did seldom, for I didn't like it, and saw that he didn't believe me; that he found it inconceivable that I shouldn't love him; that, ageing and unmarried though he was, he believed himself to be irresistible.

I stepped round him and went back to the house.

Lili was alone in the sitting-room. I wanted to tell her that I had told Syl I wouldn't marry him, but I didn't, for I felt that once I had told Lili she would somehow prevent me from recanting and that, freed from Syl, I should be bound even tighter to my mother.

There was a hangnail at the side of my thumb and now I took it between my teeth and tore it off so that the blood ran, leaving a scarlet spotting on my dress where it bloused out above my waist.

'That's attractive,' remarked Lili, regarding it distastefully. 'Spilt blood is quite the untidiest thing I can think of – much worse than milk.'

I sucked my thumb and mumbled that I hadn't meant to do it.

'You've probably ruined that dress,' said Lili, and I said it didn't matter.

'Come to the kitchen quickly,' she said, getting to her feet.

She took one of my mother's gingham breakfast napkins from a drawer and wrung it out in cold water.

'You keep your thumb in your mouth,' she advised, 'and I'll try and get these stains out.'

'What have you done?' asked my mother from the doorway, her arms full of branches of copper beech.

'It's all right,' said Lili. 'Not a road accident. She just bit her nail.'

'Well, don't soak her,' said my mother. 'She'll get pneumonia. How did she bite her nail?'

Lili regarded her, her head tilted thoughtfully.

'Like this,' she said after a moment, gripping her own thumbnail between her back teeth and worrying at it.

'It was a hangnail,' I explained. 'I pulled it off and it bled.'

'You'll get blood poisoning if you're not careful,' said my mother, putting her leaves on the draining-board.

I wondered, since my mother was principally concerned for my health, and Lili only for my dress, why it was that I had felt secure until my mother arrived.

'There,' said Lili after a final rub. 'There may be a mark, but it won't show too badly. You'd better find a plaster for that thumb or it might start bleeding again.'

It was a very small wound to have caused such concern. That night by the river there had been so much blood . . .

'It's nothing to cry about,' said my mother contemptuously, and I said that I wasn't crying. Lili agreed with me, saying that a reddened nose didn't count as crying, not in her book.

'I have a good cry sometimes,' she said, 'in the same way that I sometimes have a spring-clean. I close the house and take the phone off the hook and I cry.'

'Why?' asked my mother.

'It's good for me,' explained Lili. 'You should try it yourself. It would do you a world of good.'

'I can't think what you've got to cry about,' said my mother, managing to imply that she herself had far more to cry about than Lili and far too much strength of character to do so.

'All living beings,' said Lili, 'have something to cry about.'

I could tell by her voice that she had just said something which she believed, and I was surprised, because I had somehow thought her too clever really to believe anything.

'Sometimes,' she said, 'I sink into a grand black horror of depression, but I don't cry so much then. I stay in bed and pluck at the counterpane and listen to the winds of solitude roaring at the edge of infinity and the wolves of evil baying down the void, and I look into the darkness.'

My mother obviously considered this to be both morbid and affected. 'For goodness sake, Lili,' she said, 'do try and say something cheerful.'

'I can't think of anything just at present,' said Lili. 'Can you?'

'The wedding of course,' said my mother ill-advisedly.

Lili frowned, and I wondered what would happen if I should say that the wedding was cancelled.

'It's going to be so jolly,' said my mother.

Lili and I were silent and I wondered for a moment how I would be feeling if I was going to marry the man I loved – *had* loved, I amended in my mind, for surely even I couldn't be so idiotic as to love still where I had met with such treachery. But I could. I was sufficiently idiotic to love with a longing that weakened me as though I was bleeding.

'We're having canapés,' said my mother doggedly, 'and asparagus rolls and vols-au-vent.'

'Of course,' said Lili, 'and champagne and speeches and confetti.' Her tone was flat and glum and my mother looked at her suspiciously.

'What's wrong with that?' she asked.

'Nothing, nothing,' said Lili, 'only I do hate weddings. I wish I'd had a gypsy wedding, jumping over the fire and fleeing into the night.'

'You'd have burned your red frock,' said my mother acidly.

'Then Robert would have stamped out the flames and carried me still smouldering into the thicket.'

'Robert would have turned the fire extinguisher on you,' said my mother with what I thought was unusual perception.

'Well, then I should have married some gypsy who would have trodden all over the fire with his bare feet,' said Lili. 'One with earrings and a spotted scarf.'

'I thought Robert was the only man in the world for you,' observed my mother.

'He is,' said Lili. 'I was toying with fantasy.'

'You do too much of that,' said my mother, putting the kettle on. If she had seen the man I loved she would have thought him a figure of fantasy too. Foreign, unsuitable. And, I admitted to myself, she would have been absolutely right.

'When is Derek coming?' asked Lili, perhaps because we were on the subject of husbands.

'The night before the wedding,' said my mother without much enthusiasm. 'We're having drinks here in the evening.'

'No stag night for Syl?' asked Lili.

'Of course not,' said my mother.

'I suppose he's a bit old for that sort of thing,' said Lili, 'although with that ridiculous car he drives he does seem to be trying to give an impression of boyish insouciance.'

My mother ignored this, while I felt myself flush with vicarious embarrassment. Syl went out of his way to preserve a semblance of youthfulness, wearing his clothes untidily and even eating in a haphazard fashion as though he wasn't quite old enough to have learned proper manners. He liked to be the centre of attention and would sulk in any gathering where people talked and laughed without him.

'And you must go to confession,' my mother told me.

I knew that.

Our Irish priest was not a person I felt I could unburden myself to. He was quite aware of my childish misdemeanours, but I hadn't been to confession since I returned from Egypt, and I thought he would be profoundly shocked by what I should have to tell him. He came several times a year to have a glass of sherry with my mother and I always felt awkward in his presence, fearing that instead of 'Would you care for an olive?' I might remark 'Bless me, Father, for I have sinned'. At the sight of him I would smell the dust of the confessional and remember the mixture of boredom, shame and relief as I said my penances. I was familiar with the view that the priesthood is beyond shock, being entirely cognisant of the whole sum of human folly and evil from the outpourings of the penitent, but I wasn't convinced. I also had a feeling that my mother would never forgive me if she thought I had admitted to fornication and worse to a person who came to her house and drank her sherry. I sometimes thought that the social considerations of people like my mother militated more against religion than atheism or simple sin. I had discovered in Egypt what seemed like a different religion: a thing of unimaginable heights and depths, of light and shadow with none of the vertiginous darkness of which Lili had spoken. Now that I was home, my religion seemed compounded of polite appearances and the prospect of eternal hell. It was unfortunate, I thought, that at the same time as I had realized the grandeur of God I had fallen in love with a mortal, and that the two experiences should have proved to be mutually exclusive, leaving me with the sensation that I was being sundered by equal forces. Destroyed.

I went to confession. I took the bus to the neighbouring parish and told an unseen, unknown priest all that had happened. A sad little tale it sounded, a trivial matter to consign a soul to perpetual separation. I felt apologetic for boring the poor man and was as brief as possible in order to spare, not myself, but him. Afterwards I had no sense that I had been forgiven, but I had done what I was called upon to do and there it must rest.

I told my mother where I had been without explanation as to why I had chosen not to go to our own church, and she said nothing. I wondered whether she believed in God. I knew that she didn't believe in him as I did because in that case I would have recognized her as I had recognized Mother Joseph, who inhabited a territory which I had visited. My mother, I felt sure, had never been there. She had no travellers' tales, no air of a person who had been on a journey, and I knew she would be both disbelieving and resentful if I should try to describe the eternal vistas I had glimpsed. To her, religion was morality and appearance, and she kept it in the same compartment of her mind as her dinner napkins. Suspicious of excess and what she thought of as theatricality, she lived – quite adequately and blamelessly – on the lowest level of religious experience. If I should cry, trying to express the inexpressible, that I had walked the wind with archangels, she would have been worried and annoyed; and if I had gone on to say that I had forfeited those heights and lived now in an unremitting shadowless glare of exposure in a runnel of Hell, she would have feared for my mental health. I did myself.

'I like to go to confession straight after I've been to the hairdresser,' said Lili. 'It makes me feel so complete, body and soul.'

'I don't think you've got quite the right idea, Lili,' said my mother.

'Yes, I have. It's all about ease, you see,' said Lili.

My mother looked irritable. She subscribed on the face of it to the proposition that we are not put here to be happy, although she was the first to complain if she, or the few people she loved, were not. Lili, the hedonist, on the other hand, was clearly familiar with some of the regions of hell. She had described them earlier and I had known what she meant.

That night I was again subjected to the ordeal by wedding dress. I imagined what would happen if I should tear the sleeves out, or cut it up, or run to the kitchen for tomato ketchup and pour it all over the bodice; if I should rip out the collar with my teeth. I could hear the sound of rent cloth in my head, but I stood on a wooden chair while Lili pinned the seams closer, standing quietly like a broken horse to be saddled and bridled. Bridalled and saddled. I said: 'I feel sick.'

'Don't be silly,' said my mother.

I wished I did feel sick. I wished I could be sick on my mother's wedding dress.

'It's beginning to fit much better,' said my mother.

When I tried to take it off I found that Lili had pinned it to my petticoat and I was trapped in it.

'Well, *what* a performance,' remarked my mother rather breathlessly after a short urgent scene.

Lili watched me thoughtfully as I put on my skirt and blouse. I was shaking and my eyes were blurred.

The dress lay on the floor and my mother picked it up tenderly, as though it was a child. I think she may even have said a few words to it.

'Robert will be getting lonely,' said Lili. 'Downstairs all on his own.'

'You can join him now,' said my mother. 'I think it fits as well as it ever will. We'll all go down and have a Martini.'

I could smell a sour smell of old cloth, of old weddings, old sorrows.

'I could do with a whisky,' I said.

'I hope you're not becoming an alcoholic,' said my mother with the unfairness of the recently offended.

'She's got some way to go,' said Lili. 'Unlike me. I often fear I drink too much.'

'Nonsense,' said my mother tartly, as though she thought Lili was showing off.

'You are not of that opinion?' inquired Lili, her head tilted in a way that I was beginning to be familiar with. 'You have no fears for *mon foie*?'

'I've got better things to worry about,' said my mother, not letting us forget for a moment her onerous wedding duties. 'Margaret has to have tea with Syl's mother tomorrow.'

She spoke as one implying, 'And serve her damn well right.'

'I do think she might have offered to do something to help, but then it's always up to the bride's mother to make the arrangements, even when she's on her own.'

The implication here was that Syl's mother was very much richer than mine and a mean old beast.

'It's the convention, my poor duck,' said Lili. 'You like convention.'

My mother looked as though she wasn't too keen on this one. 'Syl is very good,' she said, consoling herself. 'Where's your ring?'

I said I thought it too valuable to wear constantly and had put it in my dressing-table drawer. My poor mother, I am sure, couldn't determine whether to commend my prudence or berate me for my lack of romance. I hated the hoop of diamonds which, although I had washed it, looked somehow dirty. It reposed in a box of plum velvet on a bed of harsh white satin, reminding me, whenever I saw it, of the inherent vulgarity of marriage, that combination of contract and concupiscence.

'What are you doing about your going-away clothes?' demanded my mother.

I had promised to go round the shops looking for something suitable, since my mother had shown that she wished to accompany me. I had said that I would find it easier on my own and she had been hurt, for normal mothers and daughters went together on this expedition, lunching in a department store and discussing the newly acquired contents of the carrier bags that lay at their feet. My trousseau had been taken care of already – underwear, nightgowns and some light dresses for my honeymoon. I had said that we should go to Egypt for this, not believing that the occasion would ever really arise; that I should be married to Syl and taken to the country in which I had come to life and lost it. My perversity had seemed to me amusing. I didn't even realize how unhappy I was, as the wounded suffer merciful shock.

'You are such a lump,' said my mother ill-temperedly. 'You don't enjoy anything.'

'Pity she couldn't get her clothes in Cairo,' said Lili.

'She didn't think of that,' said my mother.

'She didn't know then she was going to get married,' said Lili – on the face of it reasonably.

But I had thought I was, though not to Syl. Not to Syl. By now I was past weeping.

'Why aren't you seeing Syl this evening?' asked my mother, who knew.

'He has to see a man,' I reminded her tonelessly.

Now my mother did something rather risky. She said, at the end of her patience, 'Don't you love Syl?'

And I said smoothly that of course I did, for I wasn't going to be inveigled into an emotional uproar.

'Love?' said Lili sardonically. 'What's love?'

'I thought you knew,' said my mother. 'I thought you were the expert.'

Lili must also have realized that here was thin ice: thin ice over deep waters.

'I know absolutely nothing about it,' she said airily, dismissing the subject.

My mother looked dissatisfied, but I switched off my bedroom light and we were moving downstairs towards Robert and the tray of Martinis.

Tea with Syl's mother was a taxing experience. She had a little pug-like dog who wore an expression of perpetual outrage, its eyes bulging as though someone had just said something unforgivable to it. She and this animal treated each other with mutual contempt, like an old unhappily married couple, and I always thought that the only reason he didn't bite her or she have him put down was that they disliked the rest of the world even more than each other and would have been even more miserable and lonely than they were in their trap of hostility.

'Cootchy, cootchy, coo,' said Lili to the dog. She had insisted on coming with me to refresh, so she said, her memory of that ghastly old trout. Syl's mother was highly displeased to see her and made a great to-do of fetching an extra cup, saucer and plate, worrying aloud that there wouldn't be enough for three of us to eat.

Anchovy-paste sandwiches, scones and Dundee cake seemed to me an ample repast, particularly as I had a nervous, irrational distaste for eating the food of Syl's mother in her house. I crumbled a scone and left the raisins and crumbs all over my plate.

Syl's mother disapproved of this most bitterly and rebuked me for waste.

'You should empty the teapot over the old horror's head,' suggested Lili when our hostess had gone to replenish the jug of milk.

I said 'Ssshh,' cravenly, for I was scared of her, although not as scared as I was of my own parent.

Lili had already smoked three cigarettes and stubbed them out in her saucer, devil-may-care, and Mrs Monro had said nothing. Now she jabbed the toe of her smart Italian shoe in the dog, who was snuffling about under the table. We were sitting in the window embrasure looking out over the laurustines, cupressus and other seemingly indestructible plants.

'Bugger off,' said Lili to the dog, incurring the insincere wrath of his mistress, who chose that moment to reappear.

'He was making love to my foot,' explained Lili.

'He's not capable of that,' said Syl's mother with a Yorkshire accent.

She seldom sounded Yorkshire and I had never known her to make a joke. For an instant I saw a different woman: not the sour, bored old creature I had grown to expect, but someone strong and humorous. She was gone again in a flash, leaving me faintly confused and in doubt about my capacity to judge people. No one liked her, so why should I suddenly? Was it possible that people were even more complicated than I had imagined, and had Mrs Monro once been young and funny? I couldn't remember her ever having been any different, and even Lili couldn't have known her as a young woman, for Syl's mother was old enough to have been his grandmother.

'Well, he was thinking about it,' said Lili.

I would never have dared to speak so, but she was quite unselfconscious, although I suspected her of an intention to shock – to shock me as much as anyone.

'You can read the minds of animals then?' said Mrs Monro, more like herself.

'Some of them – yes,' said Lili judiciously. 'Some of them are remarkably transparent. I've known horses I could read like a book. Cats aren't so easy – more opaque, you could say. Camels are unexpected, but dogs on the whole make their intentions quite plain.'

'And their likes and dislikes,' said Mrs Monro.

I envied Lili and her social skills. I felt she would be at home in an arena with starving lions. It was hard to imagine anything eating Lili, even being rude to her. Rudeness and aggression, I felt, would merely amuse her.

'I don't think he likes me,' she said of the dog. 'He is simply overwhelmed by purposeless lust.'

I hadn't noticed anything untoward in the animal's behaviour, but I believed what Lili said. She was too secure to lie, it seemed to me. Only the doubtful, those who were bad at living, needed to dissemble.

'He's old,' said Mrs Monro, and I wondered whether she was thinking of herself: that old age bred inanition, that the longer one lived the less one cared for one's fellows. With perverted hope I wondered if with time love might fail, and all the pain ease. I almost envied Mrs Monro, who couldn't now be far from blameless death, beyond desire, perhaps beyond regret. I had lost all joy in youth. Mrs Monro was old, but she wasn't debilitated as I was. She had energy and opinions, and I had none. I was tired, and she was not. I was such a weary girl that I bored myself.

'Do you ever bore yourself?' I inquired of Lili on the way home.

'I just did,' said Lili.

'You weren't boring,' I protested, surprised.

'Yes, I was,' she said. 'I was doing a solo. I kept hearing myself uttering a light laugh.'

'I'm sorry,' I said humbly. 'I just find her so difficult to talk to. I can never think of anything to say.'

'There isn't really anything to say,' said Lili, 'not to the old. One can only talk with conviction to one's peers. Shared experience, shared uncertainties – that's the stuff of talk. General conversation is a nightmare. Gossip, that's what makes the world go round.'

My mother claimed to disapprove of gossip. I wondered what I would have been like if Lili had been my mother, but it was impossible to imagine Lili in the depths of maternity. Mothers, no matter how disparate, had something in common, some elusive quality which Lili conspicuously lacked. I pondered what this quality might be – not unselfishness, which it might have been, for I knew selfish mothers; not *gravitas*, not responsibility. I wondered if it might be an admission of mortality, an agreement that as birth precedes so death must follow. I couldn't imagine Lili dying. She was ageless and even in age would, I knew, be careless.

'I wish I was like you,' I said suddenly, still childish enough to speak like this, to say what I meant without recourse to subtlety.

'You are a bit,' said Lili.

I wasn't altogether surprised. There was about her something inhuman, and while I saw her as fey rather than remote, I was aware of my own inhumanity: something in me which was arid and incapable of desire. I wished for nothing but the absence of pain, and Lili seemed beyond harm: as secure and unassailable as the morning star.

'But you're happy,' I said foolishly.

'I make it my business to be happy,' said Lili. 'Life is bloody awful enough without being unhappy.'

I wanted to ask her how she did it, how she attained the condition of happiness, but this question cannot be asked outright for there is no one answer. There must be a myriad ruses and devices in the pursuit of happiness, and I could think of none in order to conjure up a complementary question. I knew she liked smoking, but I did not. She took pleasure in clothes, and I did not. She liked the company of men, and I did not. Yet I knew that none of these, nor all of them, made her life complete. It seemed I could learn nothing of happiness from Lili unless I could first discover her secret. Then I could frame my question, but then, of course, I wouldn't need to. I thought that after all we weren't alike; that I was a fish, perhaps, and she a bird, and all our requirements were different. Sometimes when my mother told me how fortunate I was, how lucky to live in a nice house and be engaged to a good man, I felt like a fish in a gilded cage. It was no use her demonstrating the comfortable appointments of my environment. I was out of my element, and the air itself could have been made of gold for all the use it was to me. If I was a fish then I needed water and I had given up my right to it.

I wondered as I thought of secrets if I might find some release in telling Lili the thing that festered in my soul, and I asked her if she would listen.

She said something I found so odd that my vision of the world faintly changed and my despair lessened. If the world was not as I perceived it then it was possible that I was not damned. I felt no great assurance of comfort, but my conviction of evil grew a little less.

She said, 'If you have a secret you don't want the world to know you must never tell it except to an enemy. And if you must tell your dearest friend your secret then you must tell others too, for inevitably the world will get to know and you will blame your dearest friend and lose him. So tell him, if you must, but also tell his brother and the butcher and the baker and the candlestick-maker and then you will never know who has betrayed you and you can, to some degree at least, go on loving your friend. If you tell your enemy, your hatred will be even more satisfactorily justified, but the best thing to do is tell the priest. No one else. He won't tell. The trouble is, sometimes people *want* to be betrayed. It makes them feel more at home and less lonely.'

For once I listened carefully, and I understood. I would never again speak of sin, certainly not to Lili, for one of the messages I had gathered from her speech was that it would bore her. I was happy that Lili would be bored by my sin. It made it less significant. I had learned something else that I am sure she wasn't conscious of teaching me. I had learned that it was possible, if tedious, to speak of evil, but that it wasn't possible to speak clearly of God. I had no intention just then of attempting such a thing, but as I lay awake that night I realized that if it hadn't been for Lili I might have felt it necessary to attempt to describe to someone, anyone, what I knew of God and what he had asked of me. I might have felt it as a duty. Now I knew that it wasn't to be said. For one thing it was impossible to say, and for another it would be a deplorable waste of time. Finally, the matter lay solely between God and me and had nothing in time or eternity to do with anyone else. So I haven't spoken of it, here or anywhere.

'A good time?' asked my mother when we returned.

'Oh, wonderful,' said Lili. 'What do you think?'

'I expect she gave you a good tea,' said my mother.

'I hate tea,' said Lili pettishly. 'What I want now is a good Scotch and soda to take the taste away. I think she puts moth-balls in her cake.'

'She buys her cake,' said my mother. 'Do you really imagine she makes it?'

'Then she shoots them in afterwards,' said Lili, 'with a special little pistol she keeps for the purpose.'

Her mood had changed again. She told my mother she had been bored silly by Mrs Monro and was tired out with making conversation. She even looked pale.

My mother was once more in a difficult position. She cared no more for Mrs Monro than did anyone else, but the mother of my groom should, by rights, be beyond criticism, a positive bonus to my marriage, and even my mother, inclined as she was to the bright side, couldn't overtly claim this. 'She's marvellous for her age,' she said.

'Oh, marvellous,' agreed Lili sarcastically. 'Can you imagine how she ever conceived Syl?'

I couldn't. I wondered what would happen if I should say that I wished she hadn't.

'Don't be coarse,' said my mother, adding, 'She's actually a very good cook. We had dinner there only a couple of weeks ago. Stew.'

'Stew,' said Lili gloomily.

'It was all right,' protested my mother, regretting her remark about the cake.

'Was it all right, Margaret?' asked Lili, and I said I couldn't remember.

'Not that it matters,' said my mother. 'Margaret will have her own kitchen, so she'll have to learn to cook herself.'

'On a plate with parsley round,' said Lili.

'What?' asked my mother, staring.

'Cook *herself*,' said Lili. 'Oh, never mind. I shouldn't make jokes. It isn't funny.'

'Of course it isn't funny,' said my mother. 'Marriage is a serious matter.' She had again unwittingly revealed her misgivings, for on the face of it we hadn't been speaking of marriage. Hastily and irrelevantly she asserted that Mrs Monro was very fond of me.

Lili looked at her squarely, and for a moment I entertained a mad hope that she would deny this, would announce that my engagement was a travesty and a cruelty, would say that she was going to take me away and teach me how to dress or dance. She might have done. I felt Lili might have done anything, but she didn't. She got up and poured herself a glass of whisky without asking, and my mother didn't seem to mind. She must have briefly feared what I had hoped for.

Robert arrived then and my mother let him in and offered him a drink.

'Hallo,' said Lili as though he were only an acquaintance. 'How did it go?'

Robert had been back to the gallery, to the annoyance, I felt sure, of the owner.

'It's coming together,' he said. 'Slowly.'

'Perhaps we should ask him to dinner,' said Lili.

'Who?' asked my mother, and I replied for Lili, 'Robert's gallery owner.'

As it was I who had spoken, my mother responded sharply. 'We have no time to entertain strangers at the moment.'

'I wouldn't give him a ham sandwich,' said Robert. 'He's a mean sod.'

Relieved, my mother showed some compunction. 'If it would help, we could have a simple dinner – Syl, and maybe a couple of the neighbours.'

'No point,' said Robert. 'He can hardly back out of the exhibition now.'

'Did you think he might?' asked Lili with a momentary show of anxiety.

I was surprised at this and wondered again if they were short of money.

'He always might,' said Robert, draining his glass. 'He's un-predictable, as well as mean.'

'I wouldn't let him,' said Lili. 'Just let him try.'

'Even you,' said Robert, 'could do very little to deflect him if that was his intention.'

'Watch me,' said Lili with that determined faith in herself that I found so enviable.

When we stopped talking about art, she began to talk about love. No one else had ever spoken of love in my mother's drawing-room and I imagined that Lili's conversation would cling to the curtains and the cushion covers like tobacco smoke so that the room would never be the same again.

Robert went away. I don't know where. I supposed that he must have heard it all before, although I didn't think he was ever bored by Lili. I knew that men didn't enjoy talk about emotion. My father had been embarrassed when my mother or I had wept at the time of his leaving. My mother had wept very little, her tears dried by her wrath, but I had cried for her.

'What are you thinking about?' asked Lili. 'I was just explaining something very important and you've got a glazed look.'

I said I was sorry.

'Lovers,' said Lili, 'lovers are even more valuable after they've stopped being lovers. One's own lover, that is. Their function is this. When you fall in love with someone new and it goes wrong you go and fetch an old lover and remember how much you loved him once and how you don't any more and can't imagine what you saw in him, and then you feel better. It's like tying an old sock round your neck when you've got a sore throat.'

'Why?' asked my mother.

'I don't know quite,' said Lili, 'but that's what it feels like.'

I said, 'You can't do that when it's your first lover', and my mother frowned.

'I know,' said Lili, 'That's why it's vital to find a new one quickly.'

'They don't grow on trees,' said my mother, and I agreed with her silently.

'People always imagine they'll never love anyone else,' said

Lili, 'like when you're freezing cold you can't imagine ever being warm again. We are silly creatures.'

I wanted to tell her that I was just a silly creature and couldn't believe that I would ever be warm again.

Only once had I feared the heat of Egypt and that had been in a waking dream. I had thought that I might ride in a *caretta* to the edge of the desert, and then walk away over the sand into the sun. Sand was cleaner than water, the desert dead cleaner than the drowned dishevelled things which I had seen thrown up on shores. I had told myself that the heat was cleansing, because I had grown fearful of water. Water, which I had loved, had become an agent of corruption. Perhaps only the sun could purify – burn me, burn the world into characterless dust. But dust lay all around me, a matter of constant irritation to Marie Claire, and the servants' principal task was fighting and dispersing it. I remembered that I too hated the dust, and as I imagined the walk into the desert I felt the sky come low and very close. There would be no room for the birds to fly, and dead birds would fall on me as I walked.

I had opened the louvred shutters and let in the real sun. The sun I had been dreaming of was dark, and the real sun was nothing: nothing but what it was.

Below, on the terrace, Marie Claire had heard me open the windows. 'Close them,' she had cried, 'you'll let in the dust,' and I had gone down to drink *citron pressé* with her in the shade. That had not been long ago.

It was a lifetime ago.

My mother hadn't mentioned the matter of invitations for some days. She was waiting, hopelessly, for me to present her with a completed list and I wasn't going to. I saw my marriage as a kind of pointless secular martyrdom, but I baulked at putting brushwood around my own pyre.

'Right,' said my mother, holding a pen and a sheet of paper and looking nonchalant. 'Let's start on this list, shall we?'

Lili and Robert were out, and anyway there would have been no escape. I recited the names of some relations and friends, and my mother wrote them down in a businesslike fashion until I ran out of ideas.

'Marie Claire,' said my mother suddenly, beginning to write again.

After a while she looked up at me. 'Do think,' she said. 'We must have forgotten dozens of people.'

'Not Marie Claire,' I said.

'Don't be ridiculous,' protested my mother. 'You stayed with her for all that time. She's one of my oldest friends. Of course she must come. She may not be able to, but she must be asked.'

My mother and Marie Claire and Lili had all been at school together in Egypt. They had married in Egypt and been young matrons together. Marie Claire had married an Egyptian but since he was rich and cultured my mother hadn't minded and had continued with the friendship. They had sent each other Christmas cards. The fact that they had scarcely met for twenty years was immaterial and the bond between school fellows and fellow expatriates seemed stronger than ties of blood.

I dared not say any more, but my mother didn't mention Nour. She had never expressed much interest in Marie Claire's child. I suppose she had sent bootees or a matinée jacket on the occasion of his birth, and sent him her love on the Christmas cards, but she didn't want to know what he was doing now. Marie Claire in her turn hadn't been interested in me. I thought that people were always disappointed in their old friends' children, seeing them as diluted, distorted versions of their parents, not nearly as much fun and full of peculiar new ideas. The fact that Lili seemed to take an interest in me led me to think that she had never been very close to my mother.

'Who was your best friend at school?' I asked.

My mother was surprised and undoubtedly gratified by this question.

'Well, Lili was first, then Marie Claire, then a German girl called Ilse ...'

She went on talking and I half listened – just enough to be able to make a response when she stopped. If it didn't upset me too much I liked to make her happy. I wondered whether Lili would agree that they had been best friends. So I asked her.

'Oh yes, I think so,' said Lili, 'for a while. One's best friends kept changing.'

Everything kept changing. I hadn't known that this would happen. None of the people I knew had changed very much in my lifetime. My father had left, but everything apart from his absence was as it had been. To accept change took more courage than I possessed. All change was a forerunner of the last change. Death would come as a bridegroom and nothing then would ever be the same again. Yet I would prefer that contract. I would rather lose my self than share it with Syl. How inconvenient, I thought, that I should know that death was a suitor I could not seduce, that the choice of date lay only with him. No one could take death by force. It was my lot to live on the desert fringes where the rubbish lay.

My mother, wild with exasperation, one day again described me as a lump. I thought it an apt and correct description, with its connotations of inertia and lifelessness. She could just as well have been arranging my funeral for all the co-operation I offered her. I remembered what Lili had said about brides being gift-wrapped, and thought of them in their boxes. Dead people, like presents, were put into boxes. Brides were given away.

It didn't matter.

I began to think too often of the starveling cat. It had appeared in the garden of the villa one morning soon after Nour had returned for the holidays. I knew Nour was beautiful with the same sort of tutored, obedient awareness that led one to comprehend the merits of, say, the head of Nefertiti, but I didn't care. He meant no more to me than a painting or a sculpture. He wore nothing except shorts, and was unlike the head of Nefertiti in that he was self-conscious. I could see that he was pleased with himself, and yet I couldn't dislike him any more than I liked him. He was just there, with his long legs and his smooth shoulders and his golden hair and his pride.

I saw the little cat first. It crept towards the table where breakfast was laid, and it had the demeanour of a creature that wasn't loved and yet must survive. It was half-blind and its fur was staring and it expected nothing and desired nothing save the crust by the table leg on which its half-gaze was fixed.

There were mangoes on the table and flat bread and a dish of scrambled eggs, so I took a spoonful of egg and put it slowly down on the terrace, as I thought any human being would do. Then Nour turned and saw us, and he leapt from his chair and took a cup of coffee ready-poured and threw it at the cat, who was near my foot, so that my foot was covered in coffee and the cat fled. I said, 'No English boy would have done that.'

I sounded to myself absurd and thought he would laugh, but he said nothing except 'It's diseased', and he sat down again.

He was furious with me. It was an odd situation, since we didn't know each other well enough to be suddenly on such bad terms. Intimacy, I had learned, can begin in a strange variety of ways, and we now had a relationship where previously there had been nothing. And now again there was nothing. I was not loved yet must survive.

'What are you thinking about?' asked my mother.

'Nothing,' I said.

I was thinking about Nour and Marie Claire, and I was thinking about Syl and Mrs Monro. Each couple was like a parody of the other, their attitudes much the same. In some ways Syl and Nour were identical. It was like the sudden revelation of a pattern where none had been suspected, and I didn't at all care for it. I appeared twice like an inkblot on a folded sheet of paper: a passive, meaningless blur. I vowed to question Lili about predestination. It was, I felt sure, something about which she would have something to say.

She said she hadn't, but I don't think she was listening to me. She wanted to talk about Robert's exhibition. They were both out for most of the time, and my mother was torn between relief that they weren't under her feet all the time and resentment that they were treating her house like an hotel. Lili placated her with the occasional presents marked with the stamp of central London – things from Soho, cheeses and pâtés, jam from Fortnum's, chocolates from Charbonnel et Walker. They made me think of beads and mirrors for the benighted natives.

'What do you find to do, out all day?' asked my mother, who only ventured out with a specific purpose in mind and always got back at the time she had decided she would. Lili's excursions, I felt, seemed to her gypsy-like in their apparent aimlessness, and vaguely immoral.

'Shows, exhibitions,' said Lili. 'Shops.'

My mother who did virtually nothing except cooking and the housework Mrs Raffald didn't do, and who went hardly anywhere, clearly considered this a terrible waste of time. She couldn't help disapproving of people. It seemed to be essential to her sense of identity, but I was finding it wearisome. So was Lili, who now proceeded to give us an account of the contents of the British Museum.

'Yes, I remember,' said my mother after a few minutes.

'Do you remember Old Ginger in the Egyptian room?' asked Lili.

'Yes,' said my mother. That was probably true since I, also, remembered Old Ginger. He had been curled up there, dead in his basket, since I had been a child in a velvet-collared coat.

'Morbid,' said my mother.

'And the winged beasts of the Babylonians,' said Lili. '*So wonderful.*'

My mother, who could have held nothing personal against these creatures, remarked that she had never liked them. She had got to the point where, if Lili had announced a passion for sun-kissed babies, she would have said she found them overrated.

Lili relented, or perhaps she could think of no more artefacts to describe. I was almost certain that she had been to the British Museum no more recently than I had myself. I was almost certain that she spent the afternoons in a drinking club in Soho. She had never come home drunk. Nor had she ever come home footsore, as she surely must had she been quartering the city in the fashion she claimed. She smelt of the exhalations of other people's cigarettes and spilt wine, and she was expansive, with the air of someone who has spent time in the company of her like-minded fellows, not distracted and irritable as people are when they have tired themselves on the trail of trivial knowledge. She now set out to please my mother, not by pretence that she had been spending her time worthily, but in shared reminiscence.

This, as almost always, proved efficacious. My mother softened at once at the words 'Do you remember . . .?' when they referred to her youth and not to her knowledge. There was no competition here, no assumed superiority on the part of another to make her uneasy or defensive, only what she saw as shared experience, delightful in retrospect. She seemed not to notice what I realized almost at once – that Lili's memory differed, not in essentials, but in flavour, from her own.

The Egypt of which they spoke was not the Egypt I had visited. It seemed to have been a place of school and tennis, of clubs and tennis. Of the people they spoke not at all. I wasn't surprised that my mother was silent on this subject – she acknowledged the existence of rather few people. Mrs Raffald was to her somehow unreal, a creature from another world; and foreigners, even in their own country, must have seemed infinitely remote. But Lili, I thought, should have known them, *must* have known them, for if she could see in me something to address then she could see something in any human being.

'The people were funny,' I said, as Lili stopped speaking, cigarette between her teeth, searching her pockets for her lighter.

'We have a sense of humour,' she agreed, unexpectedly becoming half-Egyptian as I watched.

The veiled women had reminded me of the nuns. They were much more like the nuns than were my fellow-countrywomen and co-religionists. Marie Claire was nothing like a nun and made a noise as she walked in her high-heeled shoes. The women, away from the men, used to laugh, and the nuns too were much more often merry than any European lay woman I could remember. I thought that the presence of men disinclined women from laughter and saw how Lili made my mother laugh as no man had ever done. My mother would often smile when speaking to men but dignity forbade hilarity in their presence. Or perhaps she simply didn't find them all that amusing. Once Nour had made me laugh, but then I had laughed – like the nuns – more from happiness than mirth. I had laughed like the veiled women. Syl frequently made jokes, but I seldom smiled.

Mother Joseph, speaking her confident but imperfect Arabic, often had the beggars in stitches when they came to the convent gate for food. I had thought it a measure of their love and generosity that the nuns would make the suppliants laugh.

Marie Claire had been like my mother. She could speak to no one who would not have been admitted through the front door of her school.

Mother Joseph and the Mother of God, I thought, were quite unlike the mothers I knew. I wondered whether it was because neither of them had stirred herself to go through the contortions attendant upon attracting men, but it wasn't that. Nothing so simple. I decided that it was perhaps because they weren't possessive and had given no other human being the feeling that having been once disgorged he wasn't safe and at any moment might find himself gobbled up again and back in the confines of a body not his own. I thought, with revulsion, of my body in my mother's wedding dress.

I had drunk too much again. God was at the other end of the room. I thought perhaps he was smoking and reading. I knew he was there, but I couldn't see him and I thought he was unaware of me. Then I thought that he wasn't really there at all, and he wasn't God but my father, who also wasn't there. I had been abandoned. Now I can understand that isolation, but then I felt like the stray cat of Egypt, not only unloved but undeserving of all regard. And when my father came he wouldn't be the father whom I missed. The father I missed had never existed.

My mother had said to Lili one day that she thought I was marrying Syl because he was so much older than me and would take the place of my father. Lili had said inconsequentially that Syl had been chasing young girls for years, and my mother had asked her crossly how she knew.

I was in the scullery washing mud off my shoes, still as I listened.

My mother hadn't denied Lili's assertion. She couldn't, for it was true. When I was a little girl and scarcely aware of Syl except as one of our neighbours, I had known that he was old to be unmarried and that the girls he brought home in his sports car were too young. It was a fact of life, like the tic in our milkman's left eye, and had meant no more to me. Lili had said, 'His mother told me.'

I wondered when Lili had seen Mrs Monro.

'Why should she do that?' my mother had asked scornfully, slapping something down on the kitchen table – a fish, I think.

I remember picturing the wet grease-proof paper it would be

wrapped in and how my mother would cut off its head and scrape out its insides. There was nothing symbolic in my reflections – I didn't see my mother as a butcher of fish or of me. I just preferred to think of dead fish rather than Syl.

But Lili went on. 'Women are proud of their sons' prowess,' she said. 'She couldn't stand any of the girls, but she liked to think of Syl hauling them in. She said she used to get annoyed at the way he tired himself out running round after them, but she obviously thought it was jolly clever of him.'

'I can't imagine her telling you all that,' observed my mother. 'Why should she?'

'I asked her,' said Lili. 'I asked her why he wasn't married, and she didn't want me thinking there was anything wrong with him, so she told me. She says he likes looking after young people.'

'There you are then,' said my mother. 'That's what I said.'

'The truth about chaps who want to be father figures,' remarked Lili, 'is that they actually want a mummy figure themselves. A little-known perversion.'

'Oh, fiddlesticks,' said my mother. 'He's got a mother already.'

'That makes no difference,' said Lili.

I had gone out into the garden, closing the scullery door as quietly as I could. Although I found it impossible to imagine such a conversation with Mrs Monro, I had no doubt that Lili was telling the truth, and whatever the psychological convolutions the facts were there. My mother had discovered that Syl sometimes disappeared in the night, was not at home when a respectable bachelor should be. She had sometimes called to find him absent and his mother's explanation, when she deigned to give one, unconvincing.

It had happened several times. The first time my mother had been indignant and remarked that Syl had no right to disappear for the evening without telling us where he was going. That had been when he had just engaged himself to me. I had said that her view was unreasonable and Syl was free to go out in the evening as he wished. 'Nonsense,' she had retorted. She had telephoned at nearly midnight to tell him I wasn't very well and he should call before office hours in the morning to cheer me up, but he wasn't back. I suspect that she may have telephoned yet again in the small hours. She said no more about it, but I knew she worried when these unexplained absences occurred. The trouble was that Syl was usually expansive about his movements. He liked to tell anyone who would listen where he was going and what he was doing, and so my mother found his silences ominously strange. I thought he had probably made an arrangement with a brothel-keeper, and sometimes I pictured him clinging to the branch of a tree peering in the darkness through the window of some schoolgirls' dormitory. Naturally he wouldn't wish to tell anyone where he was.

I had stood in the garden, and the wind, like a dressmaker, fitted my clothes to me, cold and indifferent. Stupid, I said to myself, stupid, stupid . . . I spoke to myself and I didn't listen: meaningless words on deaf ears, although they were true, and whoever I was meant them, and whoever I was speaking to knew them for the truth. I wished I could turn to stone, or put down roots like the spotted laurel and forever let the adjusting wind tweak and fiddle with my clothes to no purpose.

Syl's previous engagement had ended only a few months before. I think it was his fourth, but as I had been a child during this proliferation of fiancées I wasn't certain. My mother undoubtedly had been counting, but she would have put the numbers out of her mind since they were evidence, at the very least, of instability on the part of her future son-in-law.

Syl didn't see it this way. He seemed to think it evidence of a malignant fate that he had had the misfortune to link himself to a succession of mad women. 'She was crazy,' he said of the last reneging fiancée when he first turned his attention to me. 'She used to burst into tears when we were having our happiest times.' She had tried to get out of the car when he was driving and he considered it lucky that they hadn't been killed, but as he and I were together more I came to admire her resolution and good sense. She had been as insignificant in appearance as all the other girls I had seen him with: as insignificant as I was myself. I wondered whether he eschewed beautiful women because he feared competition from them, or from other men.

'She was always arguing,' said Syl, sounding bewildered. I felt then that I understood her. If I hadn't been weak and without hope I should have quarrelled with almost everything Syl said. If I had been brave I would have hit him. He was, I think, even more solipsistic than I was: self-centred as only a man constrained within his own view of what constituted his masculinity could be. I wasn't trapped within a vision of my femaleness. I had no consciousness of it. I saw that despite his good looks Syl was a little too short and a little too fat, that when he went about his garden stripped to bathing trunks he aroused not desire but embarrassment. I was too miserable to giggle, but I wondered if the fiancées had when he postured on his lawn. Even his kindness was repellent. One day he put his hand on mine and said he wanted me to be happy, and distaste, or perhaps anger, made me cruel. I knew he was convinced that if he made love to me I should be happy. He had frequently said as much.

'You're like my mother,' I said. 'You're exactly like my mother. You sound like her and you even look like her.'

But he only listened interestedly because whatever I was saying I was talking about him.

'You're womanly,' I said. 'You behave like a woman, running round looking after people. That's why your girls ran away from you. Because you ran after them, flapping like a woman.'

I had no wish to marry anyone now that I couldn't marry Nour, but I was particularly averse to the idea of marrying my mother. I didn't say so, because the idea was too unpleasant to be clothed in words and made visible.

I said again I didn't love him, but he didn't believe me.

He went on listening, not saying a word.

'You're babyish too,' I said. 'You're a baby with your car and your games.'

He still listened, but now I don't think he was hearing me, not believing that I meant what I said. There was something so wrong between us that he grew instantly fonder of me, and oddly enough I didn't mind the rest of the evening we spent together. He seemed less absurd, more mature, and I don't know why. I know he paid no attention to my words. Perhaps, because I had really addressed myself to him for the first time, he thought we were in accord. I wondered then whether when two people speak together they ever really hear anything but what they say themselves, and what they wish to hear from the other.

I seldom speak now. There is no need for speech. Perhaps there never was.

Events that seemed to me to lie in a past as remote as the Second Kingdom were as vivid now to my mother and Lili as the day they happened. They both remembered a party at the Yacht Club in Alexandria that had taken place fifteen years before: the food, the people, the clothes. My mother remembered the food and some of the people, and Lili remembered different people and the clothes.

'There was style then,' she said. 'How old that makes me sound.'

She got up and looked in the alcove mirror.

'I, of course, still have it,' she remarked, 'and I always will, only everyone else has lost it. How unfortunate for them.'

I saw perfect truth in this, and even my mother didn't trouble to deny it.

'The King was there,' Lili said.

'He wasn't,' said my mother, perhaps because she had concurred for too long and now it was time for contradiction.

'I danced with him,' said Lili. 'I was wearing lime-green chiffon and my mother's emeralds. He was a nice king. My father loved him. The people loved him.'

I had taken no interest in Egyptian politics, but this struck me as a novel view. My mother was, I think, almost as ignorant on the subject as I was myself, having lived only in the nutshell of the English enclave, and she was silent.

'He didn't stay long,' said Lili in a comforting tone. 'He was a very busy king. Do you remember? We walked home, along the Corniche and all the way back to Camp Caesar.'

'I didn't,' said my mother. 'You wouldn't have caught me walking the streets in my dancing shoes.'

'I remember you,' said Lili. 'You had a little cream velvet coat with feather trimmings round the sleeves.'

'I remember *that*,' said my mother, 'but I went home in the Embassy car.'

'We went past a house where there'd been a wedding,' said Lili, 'the night before. We walked past in the dawn and there, hanging from the window, was the bride's nightdress, all bloodstained.'

'Why on earth ...?' said my mother, who knew less of the native customs than she did of their politics. 'Had he killed her?'

She looked alarmed, and even though I knew the significance of this rite, because Nour had told me, for a moment I shared her confusion, her small anxiety at the thought of the violence of that long-past nuptial night.

'No, of course he hadn't killed her,' said Lili impatiently. 'He'd have killed her if there hadn't been any blood. They'd all have killed her. Her own family first. They'd have lapidated her. Put her in a hole and stoned her and covered her up with earth before she was dead. And then forgotten all about her – even her name.'

My mother thought about this for a moment until

comprehension came to her, whereupon she changed the subject out of deference to my youth and inexperience.

'What was the name of that chef?' she asked. 'The French one. The one who would go round to all the different clubs and people's houses and do the cooking there. Pierre? Jacques? Jean ...? He was wonderful with fish.'

'I don't remember him,' said Lili. 'I preferred Egyptian food in those days – *baba ganouche* and ...'

'Oh, I know,' said my mother laughing crossly. '*Foul medames*, I suppose.'

'You pronounce it "fool",' said Lili placidly, 'as you very well know.'

'I know you used to drag me to native cafés,' said my mother. 'I used to think I'd die of cholera on the spot.'

'You never ate the salad,' said Lili. 'You don't know what you were missing.'

I couldn't visualize my mother in one of the Arab cafés. I just couldn't. 'Where was I?' I asked, with dim disjointed childish memories of dark, blinded rooms and sudden blinding sunlight overlaid by newer memories of similar rooms and the same sunlight.

'You were usually with me,' said my mother virtuously. 'Or with Nanny in the villa garden.'

Now that Lili was here my lifelong image of her had become confused. She had leaned forward on the grassy bank and she was speaking and I couldn't remember what she was saying. I wished I could, for I couldn't forget that what she had said had seemed significant, and of greater, stronger import than anything she had said since she had come back. I wondered where the grassy bank had been. In the villa garden? Or had we travelled out to one of the villages? It seemed unlikely.

'Another drink,' said Lili. '*Emfadlek*.'

I forgot their talk of parties and food and clothes and felt the unknown bride's nightdress around me, wet with blood, marked by change. Again I saw change as the enemy. I had heard my mother's friends sometimes whispering ruefully of The Change, but I saw the loss of innocence as the greatest and the worst change. Once accomplished it left one spoiled for ever and forever incomplete, all integrity gone. It was nothing to do with morality, I was thinking. It was more to do with the jars of jam on the pantry shelves. Once opened they were as good as finished. I knew what Syl would say if I tried to explain my thoughts to him, because Nour had said it already. He would say that it was the purpose and blissful destiny of a pot of jam to be opened and eaten up. To give pleasure and be obediently laid on bread was its *raison d'être*. Jam left in the jar, he would say, would turn bitter and go off and be of no use to anyone. Nour had said it all, although of course he hadn't spoken in terms of jam, but more directly. His words hadn't affected me at all. I had been lost because I loved him. There was, I thought, something shoddy, pathetic and defeated about an opened jar of jam. How much more pleasing to the eye and the higher senses were the gleaming unbroached jars in the pantry, and how I suddenly hated the men who had assured me that in their attentions lay my fulfilment. I wished for the first time that I had taken that knife and turned it on Nour and let *his* blood.

Then Lili said, 'I must go up and change.' And I laughed.

I soon stopped, since as far as my mother knew there was nothing to laugh at and she was looking at me. Inexplicable laughter would, I was sure, seem to my mother yet another of the first signs of madness.

Lili came down again in a black jersey frock and fresh lipstick and carrying the scent of some strange perfume.

'That takes me back,' exclaimed my mother. 'Now that really does take me back. It's that dreadful stuff you got in the bazaars.'

'I like it,' said Lili, 'though I wouldn't wear it every day. Just for a change.'

'It's overpowering,' said my mother, fanning her nose with her hand.

'It is *verree erotique*,' said Lili, affecting a foreign accent. 'It *is*, actually,' she went on in a normal voice. 'It drives men wild. Even camel drivers, and you wouldn't think they'd notice.'

'Nobody could fail to notice it,' said my mother.

'Derek used to like it,' said Lili. She stood lighting a cigarette and looking at my mother out of the corners of her eyes.

My mother was again plunged into a version of that dilemma common to all divorced wives. Either she could say that Derek was the biggest fool the world had ever seen – in which case she would stand, self-confessed, as an even bigger fool for having married him in the first place. Or she could say that Derek had always had charming manners and was in the habit of commending ladies on their scent, even if it smelled of Alexandrian sewers, and sound as though she had lost something worth keeping – and inevitably regretful. Or she could, if she thought of it in time, say that Derek had always been the most frightful liar.

We watched her, Lili interestedly and I apprehensively.

'Derek had very little sense of smell,' said my mother.

Lili was kind. 'You're quite right,' she said. 'He never complained like the rest of you when it was really hot.'

She had said 'the rest of you' and I had never heard her so distance herself before, but what astonished me was the realization that my father must have been at that party, must have returned with my mother to the villa in the small hours, must have been aware of me in my little white pyjamas and Panama hat. My mother had several photographs of me in this attire. She said, with satisfaction, that she had never made the mistake of the other English wives and forced me into liberty bodices and starched frocks. Yet I remembered a pale-green crêpe dress with rosebuds on it that was too tight under the arms and prickly round the neck, and a navy-blue sailor suit with a white collar that chafed. I remembered wearing English sandals and white socks, and a white lambswool cardigan for the cool of the evening and lawn nightdresses and winceyette knickers, aertex shirts and grey flannel shorts. I remembered all sorts of things and my young father hardly at all. There had been an office somewhere near the Corniche: tall rooms with charts on the walls, Arab coffee in tiny cups, secretaries smiling, silent . . . But the glimpse of memory had gone and I was furnishing the room from later experience. Marie Claire had friends with similar offices.

My mother said with patient scorn, 'Speaking of Derek, we'd better ring him and make sure he hasn't forgotten about the wedding.'

I said, 'Cynthia wouldn't let him,' which was silly of me because it aroused several emotions in my mother.

I think what had happened to my father was this. He had been married to my mother for fifteen years and had been called a bad husband, whereas she had been what is known as a good wife. That is, she had been faithful, and domineering, and had demanded proper behaviour of him. Under her crumpled linen skirts had been concealed the pants. Since she had begun by taking charge he had let her continue doing so, and had responded by being more feckless, lazier and more contrary than he was by nature. A marriage only needs, can only support, one strong partner, and my mother had claimed that role for herself. When my father tired of the pretence involved in this relationship (for he wasn't as weak as they had tacitly agreed) he had hastened to the other extreme and married a woman who, as my mother was fond of remarking, you could pour into a jug.

Cynthia was given to what used to be known as the 'vapours'. She would call my father home from his place of work because there was a spider in the sink. She wept if the milkman seemed disrespectful. She had refused to breast-feed her two children because she thought it disgusting, and my father in middle age had spent many wakeful nights, not cavorting in the pleasure grounds of a foreign city, but walking the floor feeding his children from a bottle while his new wife lay in a sedative-induced slumber. My mother couldn't understand it, but her rage and jealousy had long since given way to contempt and the occasional satisfaction of genuine sympathy. I wouldn't have changed places with my father's new children who, although they were five and seven, still seemed to smell of damp nappies and regurgitated milk, but I used sometimes to wonder what I would have been like if he had devoted similar time to me and not left me entirely to the women.

'Cynthia wouldn't let him, indeed,' my mother repeated after me, italicizing her words. 'Huh,' she said.

But I knew that Cynthia liked weddings and parties and dances. At least she said she did. I didn't see her often, but whenever we met she would complain gently that they never went anywhere because Derek was always so busy or the babbas were teething or undergoing the whooping cough. And when, by good fortune, they had contrived to attend some glittering function Cynthia would delight in describing it, with especial reference to the people she had met, the important positions they occupied, and the deep respect in which they held her husband. She was a desperately tiresome female, but I always felt constrained to be pleasant to her merely because she was so uninspiring. I had wondered once whether that was the reason my father had married her, but that was before I had learned that men are not much given to acts of altruism, and certainly not in sexual matters. Improbable as it was, he must have been in love with her. She had been nineteen like me, and youth, as I knew, even when its possessor is unattractive, has an appeal of its own. She was still young, but her teeth stuck out. Perhaps one day my father would leave her too. He gave little appearance of being unusually happy. On the other hand he wasn't particularly sad. Not as I knew sadness. Perhaps, after all, anguish died with time, and life became a simple matter of bills and procreation and sometimes going to parties. The prospect didn't give me new heart, offering as it did yet another barren dimension to the future with Syl. It wasn't that I thought myself deserving of more delight than was offered the mass of mankind (I told myself) but that the common lot seemed so dire. I wouldn't let myself think how I had hoped to marry Nour and the happiness I had anticipated. Incredulity at my own stupidity almost made me laugh, for Nour would, without a shadow of a doubt, have many, many wives and not one of them would ever be happy.

Lily and my mother were still remembering. They were talking of Mr Monro, who had died, it seems, of whisky and soda many years before: before I was born. They spoke of him as 'Syl's father' and I thought that death, like marriage, depersonalized people. Now he was dead he was no longer Jack Monro but only Syl's father, the dead husband of Mrs Monro, and soon I would be Margaret Monro. Everything was a reflection of death, not only birth but marriage.

'I brought you a bottle of gin,' said Lili.

I got up quickly and fetched three glasses. Too quickly, for my mother looked at me as I put them on the table. She would have liked to deny me the gin and vermouth I was craving, but I would soon be a married woman and she couldn't. The vermouth was dark red, and I wondered what my mother would do if I poured it on the mushroom-coloured carpet – very slowly. That would not be the action of a responsible woman on the eve of her wedding. Perhaps she would cancel the wedding, would say to Syl, 'You cannot marry my daughter. She has poured vermouth on my carpet and is not a fit person to wed.' But Syl would be angry. I had seen him angry. He hated to be thwarted and went white with rage when his car wouldn't start. Once he had taken me to Brighton for the day. I had said I didn't want to go, that I was tired and that I didn't like the sea.

I meant the people who gather by the sea and the noise and the colours and the smell of frying, but Syl had gone pale and sworn at me, using a word I had never been called before, and saying only a moron would say she didn't like the sea. I had to agree with him. But how could I explain to a man shaking with fury that it was candy-floss I didn't like, and crowds, and being with him?

One of Syl's ways of expressing displeasure was by tightening the purse strings. He was naturally mean but aware that this was an unattractive characteristic; therefore he was always swift to take an opportunity of indulging his parsimony with a clear conscience. When I annoyed him he would punish me by economizing on whatever it was we were doing at the time. Should I express a taste for wine he would order half a bottle, or sometimes say outright that it was bad for me and I should drink lemonade. He would drink lemonade himself if he was sufficiently offended, and then add to my other transgressions the blame for spoiling his outing by denying him wine. Today he walked past the expensive fish restaurant where he had planned to lunch and into a steam-clouded fish-and-chip shop.

We had driven in silence and walked in silence and eaten fish in silence. I had wondered how a man in his right mind could want to be with me and decided that no girl in her right mind would want to be with him. I was the only one he could control. I was afraid of him.

'Syl's late,' remarked my mother. 'He said he'd call in on the way home.' She spoke to Syl more than I did. They seldom had a conversation but they arranged things together: things like my life. I poured myself more of the sweet red vermouth.

'Don't drink too much of that,' said my mother, unable to stop herself; but it made me feel better, more like the early girl of Egypt and less like the starveling cat.

Syl and Robert arrived at the same time and my mother poured them drinks. They talked about Robert's exhibition, and to an outsider the scene would have appeared normal: a group of friends in an English house on an English evening. I don't remember much of it. The last I remember thinking was that Syl should marry my mother, his contemporary, and that then perhaps I would have to call him Daddy. I must have smiled, because Syl smiled back at me and leaned across and took my hand. My mother had looked cheerful and I had gone to bed seeing her cheerful face.

I had drunk too much and woke in the night knowing I was damned. There is nothing to do about being damned. I lay in the darkness but my soul lay, the insect's child, washed in endless light. Light made me powerless. In the dark I could manoeuvre, hide in the alleys of incomprehension, crouch behind the walls of indifference, know that I existed, and hope because I couldn't be seen. Only perfection can flower in the light. It is eternal and it illuminates despair. Hell is the absence of God, the absence even of his shadow. Much grief, much pain is experienced in the shadow of God, but despair comes where he is not. You can pray, you can say the words, but there is no communion, and you cannot close your eyes.

I sat up and turned on the bedside light to see the shadows in the room. There was really nothing else I could do. I had been party to a murder, and I didn't care.

Robert's exhibition was the next highlight in our lives. We went in Syl's car, his mother and mine in the back and me in the place of honour beside Syl. I felt childish and rebellious and irrelevant to all that was happening.

The gallery was full and the gallery owner looked happier than when I had last seen him. Already there were red stars on some of the pictures. I saw Robert and I saw Lili. They looked odd to me. It was as though Robert had given birth and Lili was handing out cigars. He wore as pleased but modest look and Lili looked as though she knew she was expected to appear proud. I thought she was proud but aware that she should be prouder. This made me uneasy, and I was glad when someone gave me a glass of white wine.

I was caught in a group near the door and it took me some time to realize that I ought to be looking at the pictures, since that was why we were there. They seemed to be mostly line-and-wash with an occasional burst of colour, and even when I got close to them I found I had to concentrate to see what they were about.

Not for too long, though. I immediately recognized the subject of the third picture I looked at. It was of the gate to Marie Claire's villa: a clear bold drawing of the tall wrought iron gate I had watched the girl go through on the first night I saw her. One of the scrolls was broken. I had always put my hand on that attenuated strip of iron to push the gate open.

She had appeared one evening at the kitchen door with her hands outstretched, though not very far. She wasn't like the other beggars, not quite a supplicant; fairer than the maids and with her head uncovered. I was sitting under a tree in the evening coolness and I watched her. Both maids came out, and although there were only two of them they seemed to surround and overwhelm her, not threateningly, but eagerly as though she brought gifts. They spoke in Arabic, but I thought they didn't understand each other very well. Her voice was harsh and she gestured with her outstretched hands. The maids laughed as they did when they were alone and they brought her bread and half a roasted pigeon. She sat on the ground and ate them while the maids watched in the fading light. I could smell the citronella that I put on my skin to ward off the mosquitoes and feel the breeze beginning to rise from the river. Fatima brought out an oil lamp and sat beside her. She stopped eating and threw the bones of the pigeon away. Secretly the maids used to leave food in hidden corners for the dogs, but not when

Marie Claire was around. Marie Claire held that this practice encouraged rats and snakes, but the maids thought Allah smiled upon their benevolence. At least I think that's what they thought. Like the nuns they never refused a beggar and, no matter what Marie Claire's opinions of that were, there was nothing she could do to prevent them.

The girl stretched out a hand and took a fold of Fatima's dress between her fingers. She sat still, and I believe her eyes were closed. Nobody could sit so still with her eyes open. After a while she began to speak again and Fatima listened, her elbows on her knees and her chin on her hands. There was something enthralling about this scene, the three girls in the circle of insect-laden light, so that I hadn't wondered what she was doing and only now did I realize that the girl was a fortune-teller. She spoke – more slowly than she had spoken before – and Fatima listened with a concentrated intensity that she never lent to Marie Claire's requests and detailed instructions. It was evident in all their dealings that no matter how Marie Claire bestirred herself the maids would do things as they had always done them. Now, watching her, I thought that Fatima might, at this girl's behest, change her life, her ways, and I wondered what she would do if she was hearing that she would find no husband, have no children, lose her life to Leviathan. What if the fortune-teller was destroying her hope and joy with that strange, harsh voice. But Fatima was laughing and loving herself with crossed arms. The husband, I thought, was assured, and the many fine sons. The fortune-teller would hardly relay bad tidings, for who would be generous, learning of coming sorrows? Hala took Fatima's place and the girl reached out and plucked a pin from the scarf which concealed her hair. Hala giggled and rocked back and forth and Fatima moved closer to watch. They were full of movement, the maids, but the strange girl was as still as a hunting cat, her fingers closed over the cheap pin and her eyes open now. I saw them gleam in the lamp-light. Hala was little and round and fat like a quail, and the girl, like a cat, stared at her in unblinking silence. I thought I should clap my hands and shatter the scene, send the cat leaping into the bushes where the snakes lay coiled, send the quail flapping into the house and safety. I no longer thought the fortune-teller would foretell only good things, for the girl had a cruel face.

Marie Claire called from the balcony. Supper was late. Nour came into the garden. The maids skipped into the kitchen. The girl slipped away, not to the bushes but out through the curled iron gates to the earth lane that bordered the river.

Somebody said, 'Can I give you more wine?'
I said, 'No.' There might be crocodiles in it.

I heard Ahmed, the porter, boasting to Marie Claire in the heat of the following morning. He had come as he did each day with bread from the baker's iron oven that stood open to the lane in the souk. I felt hotter than I need have done as I thought of the man who fed the dough on long, long shovels into that blazing hole. Once Nour had said to me, 'Margaret, would you like to be that man, burning all your life, or would you rather marry me?'

His mother had made him take me out to see the sights and he was bored and resentful. He would lead me through small flocks of goats, or to where the traffic was worst, and then briefly hide from me in the narrow alley-ways or the open shops. 'I would sooner swim in the pool with the crocodiles than marry you,' I had said. I wasn't brave then; I was never brave, but I was not yet broken.

Ahmed had come from that dizzy town to boast that he had seen a bad strange girl leaving Marie Claire's house and had shouted and thrown stones at her. He boasted in French, but I understood him. He should have seemed ridiculous, the big man, demonstrating how he had put a girl to flight, but I felt sorry for him. I believed that a murrain would fall on the hens that he kept on his housetop, a wasting illness on the sheep that he kept by his door. I feared for the health of his mother and the aunts who lived with him. I wondered about the future of his wife and his little children. I thought that perhaps I would sooner have swum in the pool with the crocodiles than draw to myself the hostile attention of that girl.

I called, '*Ahmed, elle est mauvaise, cette fille.*'

He turned to me, smiling with his few teeth.

'*Mais oui,*' he said, and I shrugged in the sunlight, trying to disregard the foreign mists of foreboding. It was nothing to do with me if the porter wished to bring himself to the notice of Shaitan. I said to myself, Don't be stupid, Margaret, for my religion forbade superstition, and I sipped bitter black coffee.

'Which girl is bad?' asked Nour, his hair dark gold from the wetting of the shower, and I felt I would rather swim in the pool with the crocodiles than tell him about the girl like a cat. Perhaps I had always been in love with him.

'The peasant,' said Ahmed in English, 'who troubled the house last night. She is a bad girl.'

'I saw her,' said Nour, and I looked away.

'Pretty,' said Nour, and the cup I was holding shook.

'Nour,' said Marie Claire, giving him the warning glance that only a mother can command.

'*Ooh là là,*' said Nour, looked up to smile directly at me with the triumph of the creature who knows himself to be irresistible.

When he saw my face he stopped smiling and his eyelids lowered. I had given myself away. I had bestowed myself on Nour, and from now on he could do with me as he would. I knew what he was thinking, as I watched him realizing this. For a while it made him like me.

He reached over to touch my wrist, and his look was tender. I was more surprised than gratified, for without having really considered it I would have expected unsolicited adoration to annoy Nour, to lead to stone-throwing ...

*

It was as though I had slept and had dreamed. I awoke to find myself still standing before the water-colour painting of the curled iron gate. I could almost feel the river running behind me, beyond the earthen path.

'Like it?' asked Lili. 'Have some more wine.'

'It's Marie Claire's gate,' I said.

'Do you think so?' asked Lili, her head tilted. 'I don't think so. It's just a typical villa gate.' She wandered away, bottle in one hand, cigarette in the other.

I stared at the opposite wall. Robert had used pastels to draw a group of earthenware pots and jugs.

'That's nice,' I said to a stranger, speaking only to reassure myself that I could.

He didn't answer. It was a pleasing picture. I looked at it for a long time until Marie Claire's kitchen began to form itself around the pots.

Syl was trying with kindling glances and *doubles entendres* to enthral the girl who worked in the gallery. I couldn't hear what he was saying, but I didn't need to. I had heard it all before and could only think how differently she would be responding if Syl had been Nour. She looked puzzled and rather angry, and Syl looked old and silly. He saw me watching him and leaned forward to touch the girl on the shoulder, and then came towards me.

I turned and pushed my way through a group of people to the end of the room. It was unbearable that the gallery girl should imagine that I belonged to Syl, that his glances and suggestive remarks had ensnared me. I forgot that sometimes he could be quiet and kind, and I hated him. I stared at a picture of a cedar tree in curious perspective. The paintings seemed to bear the same relation to reality as prayers to the vision of God. In a word I found them inadequate, not to say hopeless. Perhaps vision can never be recaptured or reconstituted. Perhaps there are no words or pigment capable of carrying meaning, and all our flourishes are a waste of time.

Lili was talking to someone behind me. 'Being the object of many men's desire,' she was saying authoritatively, 'makes one feel like a bus.'

I thought she must at least be a little drunk, for it seemed an odd remark for even Lili to make to a stranger, but the stranger said, 'What can you mean, Lili?' So she wasn't a stranger but a friend: one of the friends of Lili's London afternoons; a woman dressed in black wool with silver hoop earrings.

'Your average whore,' explained Lili clearly, 'goes round like a taxi cab touting for trade, but the innocent irresistible woman is like a municipal bus. It isn't her fault that people keep running after her, and it's unpleasant for her, people jumping on and off . . . '

Somebody pushed between us and I could no longer hear what she was saying.

Few people were talking about Robert's paintings. The ones who were looking at them were looking silently and glancing at their catalogues, and the rest were talking about other matters – mostly about where they had last met. I moved along past the drawings to look at a blurred water-colour with a wild smudge of cobalt in the centre. The blue, after a while, revealed itself as the dress of a woman walking behind an ox. This painting was larger than the others and more like everybody else's Egypt, the Egypt the traveller expected. There were date palms in the middle ground and I shouldn't have been surprised to see a pyramid in the distance.

This was a little reassuring. To find a country unlike your imaginings of it, and then to find a series of representations by somebody else of your own experience, gives a sense of intrusion. I felt as though Robert had used my eyes.

'The assumption is that women like to be desired by many men.' I could hear Lili again as the crowd shifted. 'A wrong assumption,' she said, 'as any woman in that situation will tell you – if, that is, she has the wit to recognize her reactions. Many people don't . . . '

I heard Syl's voice saying, 'Oh, come on, Lili', and I moved further away, not wishing to hear his opinion. I thought it likely that an unruly argument would develop between them, with Syl insisting that no woman could get enough admiration and Lili denying it. Lili could be difficult, and Syl was irredeemably convinced that men were the principal object of every woman's thoughts.

The next picture I looked at was of Marie Claire's bedroom. Marie Claire was in it, her back to the viewer, her hair down, naked. The gilded chair by the dressing-table was strewn with clothing, just as I had seen it when I had sometimes taken in her morning tisane. I told myself it could be any bedroom, and the woman any woman, but even in Robert's blurred, shadowy style it was unmistakable, and Marie Claire's back recognizable. I thought that this was a painting I shouldn't discuss with Lili, but only when I had walked to the end of the gallery to look at an innocuous picture of a group of long-haired sheep did I ask myself what Robert had been doing in Marie Claire's bedroom.

I should have stopped looking at the pictures then, when past and present had clashed in my mind and made no meaning, but I went on. Some of the scenes were unfamiliar, though not many. Again and again I recognized vistas, buildings, details of tree and ditch. He had even painted the convent where I had sought consolation in my early homesickness and had agreed with Mother Joseph that I should apply to the Mother House to be accepted as a postulant and return in the course of time, if God so willed, as a professed nun to help her teach the children and grow the herbs and milk the goats and say the prayers in the cool chapel. I looked at Robert's painting, reflecting how I had spoiled my life: a life that I had muddied and bloodied and ruined.

I looked for respite at the catalogue. None of the places was named. The paintings had silly names like 'Gateway' and 'Woman in Blue' and 'Vespers'. I thought that Robert had covered his tracks well and then that it was inconceivable that Lili, who knew everything, shouldn't have known all that her husband did.

I came to a picture called 'Crocodile Pool'. I don't know how long I stood in front of it.

'Like that one, do you?' Syl was behind me, his hands on my shoulders.

'Lovely,' I said, as lifeless as the painted image. It was a good picture, if, I told myself, you liked that sort of thing. There were no figures in it. None of the villagers would go near the pool, which was what made it such a suitable place for a rendezvous. There was an old broken mud house near by with a fallen tower where the pigeons had lived, and trees like willows hanging over the still water.

'None of the villagers would go near it,' said Lili beside me. 'They said it was full of crocodiles, but that was nonsense. There hasn't been a crocodile there for donkeys' ages. It's haunted by some awful phantom, or a devil or something. Robert had a terrible time painting it. People kept waving warnings at him from a distance.'

'How do *you* know?' asked Robert. 'You weren't there.'

'You told me,' said Lili.

I turned to look at her face and saw her smiling.

'You said they were always yelling at you from the fields, and brandishing sticks.'

Her smile seemed to me to be defiant and triumphant and accepting all at once, which was ridiculous since a smile is only a smile: sometimes honest, sometimes forced – no more. I was reading into it what I thought she must be feeling, certain that she wasn't threatened by Robert's infidelity, yet challenging him with her smile. Robert seemed unnaturally unperturbed.

I wondered what he would say if I should remark that just outside the right-hand frame there lay a disused water wheel, and that the low wall of the ruined house had a hollow place where it was comfortable to sit, shaded by what remained of the pigeon tower. I knew that he too would tell me I was wrong and that it was in another part of the country. Perhaps he would be speaking the truth and this small scene was repeated the length of the Nile.

'They kept finding bodies in it,' he said.

It was agreed the next day that I was run down. It was also agreed that the gallery had been overheated and airless and that I had drunk too much. I had held on to Lili, and Syl had brought me home insisting that our mothers should stay and go on to dinner with Lili and Robert and the gallery owner as planned. I remember looking into Mrs Monro's face and seeing that she looked concerned, and being surprised.

My own mother looked cross. Syl, too, was angry with me. It seemed that he wouldn't be kind when I was ill, but only when I was badly behaved and unpleasant to him. That night I felt too sick to be any such thing. He took me to my room but didn't offer to help me further. This was fortunate, for if he had touched me I think I would have gone mad.

Later in the day it was agreed that the honeymoon trip to Egypt should be cancelled. I wondered whether I had said something that I couldn't remember, perhaps had shrieked or whispered that I wouldn't go back, but Lili said she had heard it was unusually hot for the time of year and unsuitable for a run-down person. My mother argued for a while that the dry heat was known to be bracing, but Lili went on to speak of rumours of a cholera epidemic in the rural districts and disaffection among the fellahin and I said I would rather go to Bournemouth, which was a black lie but efficacious since we had gone there for our holidays and my mother seemed gratified that I should wish to return. Syl however was angry again. It appeared that he would lose money by this cancellation and despite his liking for the seaside he didn't want to go to Bournemouth.

Scotland, suggested my mother, and Syl said at least he would be able to get in some shooting, but I don't think he ever did anything about it. Already it seemed that the wedding was to be an ending and nothing lay beyond it but a prospect as vague and as shadowy as one of Robert's landscapes. It contrasted unfavourably with the structured clarity of the convent.

A little fat nun had once cried in the heat of Egypt's afternoon, in the accents of County Cork, that she wished she could take off her flesh and sit by the well in her bones. I day-dreamed that I could do the same and we would sit together unashamed in the afternoon sun. I could hear the click of rosary beads on bone and an Irish voice saying, '*Ave Maria, gratia plena* ...' And behind it another voice, '*Ora pro nobis* ...' that was mine. My soul breathed between my bones, and my flesh was an encumbrance.

'Margaret.'

I looked up. There was no ease among the people in the room. I had for too long been conscious only of my own concerns, but now I became aware that those around me were troubled and at odds. With the egocentricity of all human creatures, exacerbated by my youth and misery I assumed that I was the cause and source of this lack of comfort and stirred myself to attempt to dispel it.

I said humbly, 'I hope I didn't spoil the evening.'

'Oh no,' said my mother sarcastically.

'Not *you*,' said Robert.

I stared at him because he sounded so cold, but he was sitting looking down at the glass which he held on his knees and I couldn't see his face.

I glanced at Lili thinking that she must know and would somehow reveal what was disturbing him. I still thought of them as indissoluble despite the picture of Marie Claire's bedroom. On one level I knew that Robert had been unfaithful to Lili and on another I knew that he couldn't possibly have been.

I found no difficulty at all in believing both these things, having been forced to extend my capacity for credibility to accommodate stranger and more terrible inconsistencies. Lili looked calm and showed no sign of the guilt she must surely have felt had Robert meant his words as an accusation against her. But whom else could he be blaming? And for what?

I asked doubtfully, 'Was the exhibition a success?'

'Oh yes,' said Lili.

My mother spoke suddenly. It seemed to me that the question she asked had been simmering in her for some time. 'How do you know,' she said, 'when you left so early?'

She sounded ill-tempered and I realized that in the absence of me, Syl *and* Lili she must have dined alone with Mrs Monro and Robert and the gallery owner. It was, I thought, a measure of her self-control that she had waited until now to express her annoyance.

'It was a success from the very beginning,' said Lili.

I thought I heard her say that she'd packed the gallery, but she was lighting a cigarette and no one took any notice of this remark.

'I was tired,' she added without apology. 'I just came home, let myself in by the back door and went straight to bed.'

She had done no such thing. I had lain awake the better part of the night. My room was over the back door and it squeaked like a murdered rat. I had heard my mother and Robert come in and had gone to sleep much later. If Lili had come in by the back door it had been very late indeed.

Robert yawned and said nothing.

'We couldn't think where you were,' said my mother, 'we hunted for you for hours.'

'Oh sorry,' said Lili. 'Sorry, sorry.'

Syl left soon after that. It was Sunday the next day and he would be playing golf.

'You mustn't lose any more beauty sleep,' said Lili, and I

thought she spoke to me. I felt foolish for having mentioned the exhibition and caused the display of ill-temper. I should have kept quiet and remained as the focus of disapproval.

When I went to bed it was as though the night was last night and no day had come to separate them.

I had tried not to remember, but Robert's paintings made forgetfulness impossible. Even if I had no longer been able to see the real images in my mind I could see their representations as clearly as if they hung before me, and the two were beginning to run together. I could almost hear voices. '... see where the water moves ...' '... the wind ...' '... no wind from the Nile, there is never a wind from the Nile ...' '... there is, there must be ...' '... Herodotus ....' '... who? ...' '... Herodotus said there is never a wind from the Nile, never, never ...' Nour had laughed because I had not heard of Herodotus. We were in competition: competition of sex, of race. Nour drew me as an English Miss: Ingleesy, prim, uneducated, unsophisticated. I set him as a foreigner: untrustworthy, slyly clever, un-English. We were both entirely correct in our estimations of each other, only there was, as there always is, more to it than that.

'Once upon a time,' I said, 'people believed that horse-hair grew into eels.'

'Stupid girl,' said Nour, bored with me. He was sitting on the wall by the broken tower where the pigeons had lived.

'And they thought barnacles turned into geese,' I said, racking my brains for ancient nonsense.

Nour laughed again. 'Dirty girl,' he said.

I stared at him.

'Geese is Arabic for fart,' he told me.

I had never heard the word and unwisely said that I didn't know what it meant. Nour told me that too. I was more shocked than embarrassed and didn't blush. Where I came from no one spoke of such things. He was disappointed at my failure to react and puzzled. I had been at great pains to appear distant towards him and been more successful than I had thought I could be. Nour was beginning to doubt the evidence of his senses.

'How vulgar,' I said, not turning my face from him.

It was Nour who looked away.

'And what, pray, is the Arabic for those long-necked water birds?' I asked. I had never teased anyone before, but I felt a sense of power, for I had put Nour out of countenance.

'*Weza*,' he said sullenly.

But Nour, as I should have known, was not one to submit to defeat. He shouted suddenly and my fingers pricked with fright.

'There, see the crocodile,' he yelled. 'See it move the water. See it smile.'

'There isn't a crocodile,' I said. 'They've all gone miles and miles upriver. The consul told me. There haven't been any here for years and years.'

'What does your consul know?' asked Nour, coming close to me. 'Your English consul with his English rivers and his little fish.'

I wanted to say, as I believed, that the consul was an English person of good sense with a proper grasp of facts, but I was too well brought up to state unequivocally that all foreigners, including Nour, were superstitious and given to exaggeration and unnecessary alarms.

'Do you want to see?' said Nour. 'See for yourself? Shall I show you?'

'Stop it,' I said.

Nour had taken me by the shoulders and was pushing me towards the pool. I slithered from his hands and sat down on the ground and he dragged me up. There was nothing for me to hold on to to prevent myself from getting closer and closer to the pool.

'There's bilharzia in that water,' I cried.

'Crocodiles,' said Nour, 'no bilharzia.' He pushed me as far as the trees and I seized a trailing branch.

'I'll tell your mother,' I said, and he let me go. I had been afraid.

I stumbled from the edge and backed away straight into Nour. His arms went round me and I shook.

'I'll tell your mother,' I said.

But this time he knew I didn't mean it.

Lili and Robert went away that week. They went to stay with friends in Scotland. Alone with my mother I had a sense of impropriety. It was no less incongruous for me to live with my mother than it was for Syl to live with his, or Nour with Marie Claire. Mothers should be left behind. I seemed fated to spend my time with them and it made me feel incomplete as though I were yet unborn. Such intimacy as life with my mother entailed should cease with parturition, and since Syl so resembled her in his attitude to me I could see no end to my continued childhood. Lili and Robert didn't oppress me. Childless, they were free, not constrained – constraining – links between birth and death. I wanted no children of my own, not because I disliked them, although I did – my stepsister and brother were the only small children I had experience of and they aroused no feelings in me but exasperation and distaste – but because I didn't want to be a mother with the weight of life and death on me. Perhaps the only creature to rouse what could be construed as a maternal sense in my heart had been the Egyptian cat, and Nour had killed it.

I was once sitting in Syl's car when I heard Nour's voice.

I said aloud, 'No.'

'What?' said Mrs Monro from the back seat. We were going to a country pub for lunch. Just the three of us.

'Nothing,' I said. 'Sorry. I was thinking aloud.' I knew that Syl's mother, like my own, would consider talking to yourself the first sign of madness.

Nour hadn't killed the cat. He said he had and I believed him. After the first morning when it appeared in the garden I had gone on giving it food. It would eat anything – bread, even fruit – but I saved bits of meat for it when I could. We had a trysting place, the cat and I, a strip of tiled pavement behind the villa surrounded by bushes for it to take refuge in should Marie Claire or Nour approach. Ahmed was dangerous too. He liked to please the family and if it wished ill to the starveling cat then so did he. He was a funny man and good at making people laugh. I laughed sometimes when he chased intruders from the garden, but I wished he hadn't been aware of the little cat, although I think he only wanted to frighten it away, not kill it.

Nour said (he really did say it) that I was disobedient to him to persist in feeding the cat. I had laughed at him more than I had laughed at Ahmed. I had been happy and thought he wouldn't mind. I had been wrong. Ahmed liked to be laughed at, but he was a peasant and Nour was, in his own estimation, a prince and I was of an English generation which would have felt free to laugh at the Grand Turk if it had been so inclined. It made Nour very angry. I had put on a show of contrition all day, and behind it had been incomprehension and fright. My pride of race didn't go as deep as my fear of disapproval. I wouldn't have made a good martyr, for the frown of the tyrant alarmed me more than the threat of wild beasts or the rack. While knowing that being ingratiating was as unproductive as it was craven, I couldn't endure the wrath of those around me.

Marie Claire had some novels about English girls lost in the desert at the mercy of proud sheikhs, but those girls were as proud as the sheikhs themselves and defiant too – at least until near the end of the story – and the sheikhs were prepared to make some concessions themselves by that time. Nour would make none. He wore his mood wrapped tightly round him like a *galabeah* until he was prepared to throw it off, and there was nothing I could do to change him.

'I choked the dirty thing,' said Nour, 'and threw it in the street for the dogs.'

But I was sure I had seen it after that, slinking, a shadow cat in the tree shadows, black as Egypt's night. No Englishman would have boasted mendaciously of killing a cat. Even Syl seemed fond of his mother's awful dog. It snuffled near the gear lever and he occasionally patted its head.

'It's nice here in the summer,' said Mrs Monro when we were sitting in the pub by a window overlooking the river and the distant fields.

An artificial log glowed in the manorial fireplace and I wondered whether she was admitting that it wasn't really very nice now, and how often Syl felt it as an obligation to take his mother for drives around the countryside. I saw the future with the three of us lunching regularly in this horrid pub at all the seasons of the year. Mrs Monro would say, 'It's nice here in the spring ... or the autumn, or the winter ...' And after the course of years perhaps I should respond, 'It was nice when the primroses were out ...' or 'the leaves had turned golden ...' or 'the snow was on the ground ...' But by then I might have children and all I would be saying was 'Sit still', or 'Don't eat with your fingers', or 'Eat up all your peas'.

Mrs Monro had just admonished Syl, 'Don't eat with your fingers', because he had picked a roast potato straight from the vegetable dish and put it in his mouth. I waited for her to speak of peas, but she had no need. Syl was eating them all up without requiring any encouragement. She would be with us always, and I wouldn't have to say a word to her grandchildren because she would say them all. I thought of these imaginary children without hope and quite without fondness. Thinking of Jennifer and Christopher, I said 'No' aloud. It seemed to be becoming a habit.

'Yes,' said Syl, leaning towards me and smiling his smile. 'What do you think of her, Mum, talking to herself?'

'It's the first sign of madness,' said Mrs Monro.

I wished that I was less inhibited by my upbringing and could have done some extraordinary thing to confirm her diagnosis – danced on the table or stated that I wouldn't ally myself with a man with a face like a toothpaste advertisement. Or simply told the truth – told them there and now that it wasn't Syl's smile that repelled me but that I had an intuitive conviction that there was something unsound in him, something unwholesome by virtue of being undeveloped, something that would, sooner or later, cause me to turn on him with bitter cruelty as Nour had turned on me. It was probable, I thought, that what I disliked in him was what Nour had disliked in me, and that the whole world was mad. Why else should I still be yearning after a man whom I knew to be a murderer while shrinking from the innocent Syl whose only crime was that I found him unattractive? But I knew that reason was powerless to undo these matters and ate some Yorkshire pudding in silence.

'Look at those cows,' said Mrs Monro when the trifle had been put before us.

It was a boring remark, but at least she had thought of something to say. I could think of nothing, and Syl was busy with trifle, so I glanced, as bidden, out of the window. There was nothing unusual about the cows. They were only eating what remained of the summer's grass, but they had struck some chord in Mrs Monro.

'I was once chased by a herd of heifers,' she confided.

'Intrepid beasts,' said Syl through the jam and cream. He often teased his mother and I couldn't think why he bothered, for she seldom responded. Perhaps it was different when they were alone, and they laughed together.

'I had to jump over a hedge,' she said, 'and I tore my bloomers.'

I found this indelicate. I couldn't imagine her jumping over anything and I didn't think old ladies should mention their undergarments.

'Where was I?' asked Syl.

'It was long before you were born,' said his mother.

I knew I should show some interest in Mrs Monro's hedge-leaping girlhood. I even knew that if we talked about her past and all her life I might begin to like her, but I was thinking of a different countryside and different cattle and worrying about the oxen who ploughed the fields and turned the water wheels. The cows I could see grazed on and on, and I was trying to remember if I had ever seen an ox grazing instead of working. From the example of the cows before me it seemed that they were designed only and eternally to eat grass and, left to themselves, would never do anything else. I remembered the palms with clustered dates hanging like udders high in the air, and wished she had never mentioned the subject of cows.

'It was on the moors,' said Mrs Monro, laying down her spoon with a decisive air. She hadn't quite finished her trifle, so Syl leaned over and scooped up what was left.

'There were three of us,' she continued, ignoring her son, 'but all the cows were chasing me. I wasn't wearing red and I could never think why they were chasing me and not the others.'

She looked puzzled for a moment, and I wondered if she really still worried about this ancient happening. Did the elderly have minds like old wardrobes stuffed to overflowing with useless memories and take them out sometimes and look at them and ask themselves why they were there? My own mind seemed full of memories already and I couldn't imagine storing away the new ones as years and years went by. Some surely must be discarded as outworn, but some wouldn't let themselves be forgotten. Some would take up for ever more space than they were entitled to – like my mother's wedding dress, shrouded in sheet linen, suspended in time, uncrushed by the other more workaday but less significant garments that crowded together as though they were cold, waiting in a queue, inmates of a zenana to be taken up or not at the Pasha's pleasure, promiscuously gathered, at the mercy of their owner. The nuns wore always the same habit. Even when they changed, the habit remained the same, blessed, sure and unobtrusive.

It was ironic that while most of the men I knew seemed inclined to some form of polygamy, Syl, now that he was getting older and had less energy, should have decided on a monogamous relationship with me. He had once assured me, earnestly unsmiling, that he would be faithful. I had said, in revulsion at the intimacy his words implied, that he could do what he liked, I didn't care; and he had taken this as evidence of a previously unsuspected sophistication in me. He had smiled then and said that despite my generosity he would give me no cause for jealousy. Oh Syl.

How hopeless and ludicrous everything was: the seas of incomprehension, the misunderstandings that could never be cleared up because we seemed not only to speak different languages but to inhabit different countries. If I had told him I wished he was dead he would have seen this as a palimpsest of desire, but I only wished that he wasn't there.

I had wished Nour dead because he would not stay with me, and that had been a palimpsest of desire.

'I've been frightened of cows ever since,' said Mrs Monro, and I thought – her memories don't even have the moth.

When Lili came back from Scotland with a bottle of whisky and a biscuit box emblazoned with the tartan of the clan Campbell I told her that I was frightened of growing old.

'Well, it's that or die,' said Lili. 'You might as well hang around for as long as you can.'

I was disproportionately pleased to see her. She had the effect of an open window on a frowsty room, ice in a lukewarm drink, wind on a sullen sea. She was free of the shaming curbs of expedient morality. She would never smell of milk, or the urine of infants, or laundry-steam rising from linen indiscriminately washed. She wasn't a mother, and if she was a wife, she was, by conventional standards, a gloriously bad one.

'Did you have a good time?' my mother asked Robert as I whispered to Lili that I found old age unclean and a disgrace. When I was as old as Lili Syl would be an old, old man, but I didn't say that. I didn't want to think about it.

'You don't have to go along with it,' said Lili sitting down. I realized that I could have her full attention as long as I caught her interest, and I could only do this by telling the truth, for she could no more be bothered with the niceties of drawing-room small-talk than could a fox.

'You must wear false eyelashes,' she said, 'and very, very expensive scent, and you must never, never sit on a park bench with a person of your own age.'

'Is that all?' I asked. I liked this foolish image, which was so different from Mrs Monro.

'And you must try not to grow worse,' said Lili. 'Morality lapses as you get older and nothing seems to matter any longer.' She sounded serious and I knew that, this being so, she was talking about herself.

'I always wanted to die young and now it's too late,' she said. 'My mother died at the age I am myself and I never thought I'd be older than her. I was quite prepared to die – without giving it too much thought, you understand – and suddenly I find I've got up steam and I've puff-puffed past the station labelled "Death" and the track lies all before me, unsignposted.'

I saw myself chugging along a short track: a little side-shunting labelled 'Marriage' with unyielding buffers at the beginning and the end – cutting off the track and all the future. So I didn't say anything.

'The young are as good as gold. They fuss about fidelity. Even when they're not being it they're fussing about it. And they espouse causes and strike attitudes, and then after a while when they get old they think what-the-hell, and they start doing what they like and nothing matters at all. They still feel free to criticize the young though,' she added.

I always believed what she told me, but now as I considered her words I objected. 'I don't know any old people like that,' I said: 'not who are doing exactly what they like.' I was thinking of the mothers. But, so I found, was Lili.

'You have fallen into the common error,' she said. 'You are taking it for granted that when I say "what they like" I mean sexual experience. Hmm?'

She looked at me unsmiling and I opened my mouth to protest that I was the last person in the world to take such a thing for granted, that I was the only person in the world who held a low opinion of sexual experience.

'You do not know,' said Lili, 'how many women would gladly put away for ever their suspender belt and stockings – put them away with the relief of the weary warrior hanging up his shield after battle.'

I *had* assumed that everyone else was constantly in search of erotic adventure, of physical fulfilment, and I was affronted to discover that I was not, after all, unique. Realizing that I was piqued by the recognition that I was not singular even in what I had considered an inadequacy, I convicted myself of lack of humility. Pride is the subtlest of sins, affording the most morally destitute some comfort, like a rat in the barren cell of the prisoner. I was pleased with this reflection, and so convoluted is the human mind that I ceased to take pride in my lack of pride and was proud that I had found myself capable of it. I was not perhaps as gutless as I had assumed.

'You are so young,' said Lili, as though youth were a shame and a disgrace. 'You have listened too much to men, to what the men say . . . '

She went on, but now I could hear another voice. Mother

Joseph was saying ' ... and you see how the painter has painted her mouth so small. This is because Our Lady seldom spoke. She had no need for speech for she gave birth to – she uttered – The Word ... ' and, standing before the icon, so perfect in its gilded stillness, I had thought of the bodies of men, land-locked and mute, and I had felt sorry for them.

'... and we all know what the weary warrior wants after battle ... ' Lili was saying. 'The trouble is it is unimaginable to him that his women don't want it in the same way.'

She was talking quite loudly now and Robert and my mother were both listening to her.

'Read a book by a man,' she said, adding severely, 'and I don't except *Madame Bovary* or *Anna Karenina* – and you will find that he has put breasts and a silken skirt and long-lashed eyes and lustrous hair on himself and filled his *poupée* with his own desires.'

I was sure that my mother neither understood nor agreed with what Lili was saying, but the mention of these classic works of literature compelled her to reveal at least her knowledge of their existence. She wasn't going to let her old classmate get away with showing off.

'I never really cared for *Madame Bovary*,' she said, 'but Tolstoy is another matter.'

Lili ignored her. 'No man,' she said, 'has ever portrayed a woman as she truly is.'

Robert spoke mildly. 'And no woman,' he said, 'has ever been able properly to portray a man.'

'I know that,' said Lili impatiently. 'Why should she bother?'

'There's never been a great woman composer,' said my mother with an air of triumph, not because she delighted in this deficiency of her sex, but because she thought it percipient to have noticed.

I wanted to say that women, since they uttered human beings, had no need to make a noise, that all the bluster of music was a sad cry because the world was unevenly divided, but I couldn't think of how to put it. I had always felt embarrassed and had to look at my feet in the presence of anyone playing any musical instrument, and had realized once when watching Syl spitting and squinting at his oboe that this was because it was irresistibly evocative of masturbation.

'People look silly playing a musical instrument,' I said.

'*You're* silly,' said my mother, getting angry because she wasn't used to converse of culture. She had had precisely the same expensive education as her friend and would never concede that she was not as clever.

'You talk tripe sometimes,' said Robert to his wife.

I wished that I could talk well, and could continue this conversation until animosity was dissipated and we could all stand on some common ground, but I knew enough to admit that this wouldn't happen, and that the longer the talk went on the further apart we should all grow.

Lili and I should talk alone. She showed no inclination to argue further, but lay back in her chair, smiling at Robert, and I saw that it was not, as I had believed, understanding and acceptance that her smile revealed, not that their marriage was so secure it could sustain itself in the face of any disagreement, but that Lili could afford to be pleasant because she had no scruples. I knew that tonight she would make love to another man. If Robert knew it too, as I thought he must, he seemed not to care. Perhaps it made for a safer relationship if, instead of arguing to a standstill, the party who felt herself misunderstood took her grievance elsewhere and satiated it in transgression. I was thinking, in contravention of everything I had been taught, that this casual immorality would be more wholesome than the hidden hatreds of marital strife. Everyone was amazed when my father left, but when I came to consider it I had been relieved. He had taken with him more badness than goodness, leaving not a vacuum, but a breathing space.

My mother seized the dangling reins of conversation. After all it was her house and the choice of topic should lie with her.

'I have my doubts about Cynthia,' she said. 'I don't trust her or her dressmaker to get the children's clothes right.'

She had posted off a length of pale blue silk for Jennifer's dress, and another of velvet in the same shade for Christopher's pageboy suit. She had enclosed patterns and detailed instructions, and while she hoped, for the sake of appearance at the wedding, that the children's clothes would be properly cut and fitted, she also hoped that between them Cynthia and her dressmaker would have made a pig's ear of the business.

'Let's go and see,' said Lili. 'We can drive down and have lunch in Winchester and be back by dinner time.'

My mother was startled at this suggestion. I had been there once or twice but she had never set foot in my father's new home.

'I don't know . . . ' she said.

'I'm dying to see what Derek's landed himself with,' said Lili.

'You'll see them at the wedding,' said my mother.

'It's not the same,' said Lili. 'I want to see their little nest.'

'Well, I can suggest it to Cynthia,' said my mother. 'But I don't know what she'll say.'

We all knew it didn't matter what Cynthia said. If my mother decided to go, she would. And if she didn't, she wouldn't.

'Ring her now,' said Lili.

We listened to my mother talking to her successor, and I have never heard such an example of civilization and restraint. Her resentment was buried deep. Lili was taken by a fit of mirth and lay with a cushion pressed to her nose. Above it her eyes glittered.

'I don't know why you're laughing,' said my mother coldly as she put down the phone.

'I'm not,' said Lili, sitting up and straightening her skirt.

'Yes, you are,' said my mother, and briefly she smiled too because in some ways she was no fool.

'We'll go on Thursday,' she added. 'And Cynthia says she'll give us a snack lunch.'

'Did she sound surprised?' asked Lili, and my mother said that, yes, she did rather. She smiled again.

'I don't have to come, do I?' I said.

'No, of course not,' said my mother, and now she sounded surprised. I understood that this was my mother's wedding, and although I was necessary to it I was expected to do nothing but be there and appear contented.

I, in my turn, was surprised to find how much I was looking forward to a day on my own, and mildly surprised at my mother's willingness to leave me to it.

'You can go and see Mrs M,' said my mother and I wondered whether her sense of grievance towards me was inclining her to spite.

When Thursday came and they had gone I found myself alone with Robert. I thought neither of us was thrilled, and Robert looked at his watch. Mrs Raffald looked at both of us, for she wanted to tidy the drawing-room and suspected that when all the coffee was drunk we would go in there. It was strange how difficult it was to be alone, especially as no one was anxious to be with me.

'All right?' said Robert from the door. 'I'll be back soon.'

'All right,' I said. Then I heard the door open again, and turned, thinking Mrs Raffald would be there with her things for tidying up, but it was Robert.

He said, 'Are you sure you don't want to come with me?'

I said blankly, 'No – I mean, yes – I mean, no thank you.'

'Sure?' he said.

'I've got a lot to do,' I said. 'I'll be all right.'

He looked worried – or perhaps he looked thwarted. It did occur to me that since everyone seemed to be playing a game with rules unknown to me, Robert might not be concerned only that I would be bored by myself, but he might want me to go with him for reasons of his own. He was the same age as Syl, after all, and Syl wanted me to go with him for reasons of his own. There was a madness about and I couldn't tell whether it was within or without me, or either or neither. All the boundaries were blurred.

'What have you been doing?' asked my mother. She looked cheerful.

I had been to church, but I didn't tell her. I could imagine her discomfiture as a natural approval of this evidence of my religious feeling vied with her conviction that normal people did not go to church unless compelled by the Sabbath. I told her what she expected to hear – that I had not done anything much.

'Don't you want to know about the children's clothes?' she asked, adding that they had looked rather sweet.

'Except for the Peter Pan collars,' amended Lili. 'She'd put Peter Pan collars on them, so I took them off again, and fortunately there was enough stuff left to finish the neck lines.'

'If she'd stuck to the patterns,' said my mother, 'there'd have been no need, but Cynthia had to fiddle with them.' She still looked cheerful. 'Pork pies,' she said.

I could think of no response to this remark, so she went on to explain. 'Cynthia gave us pork pies and pickled cabbage.'

'How nasty,' I said tactfully. I loathed my father's new house, which seemed always to smell of damp washing, but her visit had clearly enlivened my mother. She would, I knew, have liked to categorize the shortcomings of her supplanter's domestic arrangements but was aware that it would seem too much like jealous triumph.

Happily for her, Lili had no such reservations and described the mess in the garden. I could visualize it. Mud and children's toys and a lopsided swing. Even the memory was depressing.

The children of Egypt played in the dust-laden sunlight, and as far as I could tell they were happy.

Happiness was not the first quality to come to my mind when I thought of Jennifer and Christopher. They looked as though they knew already that life was no laughing matter. I should have felt sorry for them, but I didn't because I was really only sorry for myself and their problems weren't mine. They might have belonged to a different species. I wondered briefly whether my father had a tendency to marry women who would make their children unhappy, but it seemed an unfair reflection. I couldn't imagine myself making my children happy, having no conception of how to go about it. Oppression lay on me like a dead beast, not gaunt and stiff-legged like the animals which lay where they had dropped along the desert road, but soft and smothering like something from which the breath had only just gone. Once when I had thought Nour loved me I had delighted in a garden full of roses surrounding a villa where his aunts lived. The aunts had sat half-veiled in the evening, talking in Arabic and French and sometimes in English for me, but I hadn't listened. I had been remembering another rose garden lit by shafts of lightning and somebody telling me not to be afraid and to go to sleep. I hadn't been afraid. I had wanted to watch the roses lit by sudden light, but they wouldn't let me. The roses in the garden of the aunts were covered by a thin, barely perceptible layer of dust. Spoiled gardens, dusty flowers, small animals cowering under wilting leaves. The convent garden harboured herbs and a yellow flowering vine flourishing over a falling wooden structure. I hadn't been aware of the dust in the convent garden. The nuns got rid of it. They were endlessly busy when they weren't praying and I remembered their surroundings as always faintly shining. They grew white lilies around a well and under the chapel wall for Our Lady who had sojourned once in Egypt. I wondered why I hadn't had the wit to take the starveling cat to Mother Joseph as soon as I knew that Nour might kill it. It would have been safe there.

'You're very quiet,' said my mother.

I thought with sudden exasperation that of course I was quiet. I always had been. Marie Claire had once commended me on this negative virtue. 'You are no trouble,' she had said, lying back against the satin cushions, smelling of rosewater and musk. I don't know why it had occurred to her to make this observation. Perhaps Nour had burdened her with noisy, tearing girls who had shattered the afternoon calm with screams of merriment and wild gestures, or frenzied weeping. I moved so quietly I barely stirred the dust, yet now in the English winter I could hear a spectral echo of angry laughter and I thought it was my own.

Marie Claire had written to say she couldn't come to the wedding and had sent a present of yet more tablecloths and napkins. 'How useful,' my mother had remarked. I hadn't read the letter. I imagined Marie Claire coming to England in the cold to be present at my marriage. She would have worn her furs and her jewellery and she would have struck an even odder note than Lili. She might have made Nour come with her, because she refused to travel alone. They both looked exotic even standing by the Nile and would have seemed remarkably out of place among us. It was perfectly possible that they could have come, and yet unthinkable. My imagination failed.

'I feel a bit deranged,' said Lili. 'I think it must be something to do with the pickled cabbage. Or perhaps it's just the effect of the Peter Pan collars. Cynthia is a remarkably inefficient woman.'

My mother looked pleased. 'I know what you mean,' she said.

'There's no need for such messiness,' said Lili. 'Messiness makes me feel like hitting someone. I get this inclination to take a broom and a pail and tidy up. I would start by throwing Cynthia away and I would sit the little children on a shelf while I swept the crumbs off the floor.'

'The place wasn't actually dirty,' said my mother with conspicuous justice, 'but it is dreadfully untidy. She doesn't seem to put anything away. There are clothes everywhere.'

'And such clothes,' cried Lili, who seemed intent on gratifying my mother. 'She dresses like the offspring of the vicar and his cleaning lady. When she goes to parties she will wear not a party frock but a summer frock with a bow at the neck and a tie round the waist. She will undoubtedly wear a summer frock for the wedding.'

'She's quite kind,' I said.

Lili went towards the drinks table. 'Where stands the sun in relation to the yard-arm?' she inquired rhetorically, pouring a Gin and It. 'As if it mattered. I drank brandy for breakfast in Tanta.'

'I'll have a Martini,' said my mother. She was sitting back relaxedly and looking more contented than she had for some time. 'Margaret?'

'Yes please,' I said, all at once looking forward to the mild dulling of the senses, the ease which the evening drinks induced.

'It is better not to drink in the daytime,' said Lili. 'Not so much because of the liver but because it spoils the effect of the first drink of the evening.' She was wearing a burgundy-coloured dress of fine corduroy and reminded me herself of foreign wine.

'I know,' I said.

'You shouldn't need it,' said my mother remembering her responsibilities, 'not at your age.'

'I have had this dress for ten years,' remarked Lili. 'I was ten years younger when I had it made. You see this tiny patch where the material is paler. That is where I spilled vodka on it the day I wore it for the first time.'

My mother gazed at her inquiringly with a so-what expression on her face.

'I have been drinking all my life,' explained Lili. 'And I am growing older. But my clothes are not. My clothes remain the same. They never wear out because I look after them so well and they stay young while I ... I ...'

'Portrait of Dorian Gray,' interrupted my mother triumphantly.

'Quite,' said Lili.

'Don't they date?' asked my mother. 'I find I have to change my wardrobe every other year or so.'

'Not really,' said Lili.

'What about hem-length?' inquired my mother.

It would be impossible to accuse Lili of being ill-dressed, but if she wore the same clothes for decade after decade while my mother did not, then there was something wrong somewhere and my mother was suspecting that, implicit in the situation, lay criticism of her taste and judgement.

'I always keep the same hem-length,' said Lili. 'Mid-calf.' She spoke casually without looking at my mother, and changed the subject. 'Did Marie Claire say why she couldn't come?'

'Oh, some family business,' said my mother. 'They have those dozens of cousins and aunts and there's always some sort of crisis going on.'

As far as I could gather, Nour's father had taken on responsibility for all his sisters, married or not, and for their offspring, and since his death Marie Claire had assumed the burden. Eventually it doubtless would fall to Nour. I wondered what sort of job he would make of it. I had once imagined that I too might one day be involved in that large, confusing family with its extended degrees of affinity. I wondered how it could be that I was going to marry Syl.

'I don't want to marry Syl,' I said, surprised to hear that I had spoken aloud.

'Don't be silly,' said my mother.

'Have another Martini,' said Lili.

'I *don't*,' I said.

'Now look here . . .' began my mother.

'I want to be a nun,' I said. I had wanted to be a nun before

107

Nour had made me love him with his golden hair and his golden face and his golden eyes. I wondered how long it would be before I stopped loving him. I had loved God before Nour. I had been a vessel of pure water and I had been spilled. I had loved God more than I had loved Nour and I had betrayed him. I had rendered myself purposeless.

'You can't change your mind at this point,' said my mother, carefully reasonable, and ignoring this imbecile talk of nuns.

Lili looked thoughtful, but I didn't know what she was thinking about. I was angry with her for not saying anything, not doing anything. I still had a formless feeling that she understood me where my mother did not. Perhaps it was despair that made me believe there was one person in the world who might know that I was in despair.

'Do have another Martini,' said my mother. 'Lili, you have one too.'

'Shall we all get very drunk?' suggested Lili.

'There's no need for that,' said my mother. 'Margaret is merely suffering from pre-wedding nerves. She should have an early night.'

'Why don't we take her out to dinner?' said Lili. 'I'll drive us to Soho.'

'We've just got back from Southampton,' said my mother, as though this circumstance presented a total barrier to further movement. 'What about Robert?'

'Robert will be all right,' said Lili. 'I think we should definitely go out.'

'Why?' asked my mother.

'It would be enjoyable,' said Lili. 'It would be interesting to try a new restaurant. It would remind us of the days of our youth mixing with Greeks and Arabs and Armenians in strange corners of the world.'

I still couldn't imagine my mother mixing with foreigners anywhere.

'We could go to Rules,' she said doubtfully, 'but we haven't booked.'

'Let's go somewhere more *farouche*,' said Lili coaxingly. 'Somewhere we won't see anyone we know.'

Maybe my mother thought it would take my mind off the convent, for she agreed.

Lili could be charmingly manipulative, but I would have thought my mother proof against her. I had no desire to go out, but it would be one way of getting through the evening.

Sitting in the back of the car I watched the suburbs going by under the street lights. They hadn't the appeal of the stinking lanes fitfully lit by naphtha flares in the souks when a fair went on long into the night.

Lili sang as she drove.

The restaurant was in a back street and was small and half-empty. My mother looked round with an expression of misgiving. 'Why here?' she inquired, too loudly.

'I was told about it,' said Lili. 'They do delicious *moules marinières* and they're not mean with the garlic.'

'Well, I don't know,' said my mother, extremely dubiously, but she permitted herself to be led to a table and sat down.

'I hope it's clean,' she said. 'It doesn't look terribly clean. I hope there aren't any cockroaches. Cynthia's house this morning – and now this.'

'Not your day is it, darling,' said Lili consolingly. 'Just wait till you try the *moules*.'

'I'm not sure I want *moules*,' said my mother. 'I'm never sure about shellfish.'

'They get them fresh every day,' said Lili.

'How do you know?' asked my mother.

'I was told,' said Lili, 'by the person who told me about this place.' She looked round. 'It has a certain character, you must admit.'

'When people say that about restaurants,' said my mother grimly, 'it usually means cockroaches.'

I thought this rather witty of my mother. Lili seemed able to make both her and Syl's mother passingly amusing.

I was sitting with my back to the door. I felt a draught as it opened, and half turned. Nobody came in, but as I looked round I saw my mother staring past me, her mouth open.

'Wasn't that ...?' she said. 'Did I see ...?'

'Who?' asked Lili casually, lighting a cigarette and shading the lighter flame with her hand.

'I could have sworn that was Syl,' said my mother. 'He looked straight at me and went straight out again.'

'He works somewhere round here,' said Lili. 'Perhaps it *was* him.'

'At this time?' said my mother. 'And why did he go like that?'

'Perhaps he had a secret assignation,' said Lili. She looked up, into my eyes, and grinned.

My mother recovered herself. 'Don't be ridiculous,' she said, 'I must have been mistaken. The light's none too good in here.'

The *moules marinières*, by the way, were unexceptional.

'And this is my present to the bride,' said Syl. He had been very noticeably kind over the past few days: thoughtful, and seeming more mature and sensible, as though the imminence of marriage had indeed begun to bring about that change of which my elders spoke – the settling down, as it was called. There had been no unexplained nights away and no displays of petulance, and when he set off through the gates of his house he drove slowly and with care. Nobody had spoken of this new responsible attitude, because to do so would be to admit that his behaviour had previously left something to be desired, and my mother had spent too much time in implicit denial of this to waste it all now. I wasn't deceived, for Nour had been kind when I had been what he called 'good', and I had thought that a new Nour had been born who was made for me, designed for all my needs and desires, and we would be unchangingly happy together until the end of time. I had thought that for about five days.

'Oh Syl,' my mother said effusively as he laid the oblong package on the drawing-room table. 'What is it?'

Clearly it was I who should have spoken these words, but already I had a feeling that I knew what the brown paper and the ribbed cardboard concealed, and I wasn't going to say a word until time or circumstance compelled me.

'Open it, Margaret,' cried my mother, and as I made no move she herself ripped off its coverings.

'Oh, how lovely,' she said less effusively, for after all it was only one of Robert's paintings.

I knew as I was doing it that I shouldn't be following them, through the snake-laced paths to the river in the moonlight, to the broken house with the pigeon tower: that shame would be the result – my shame, for I cared nothing what their feelings might be. I was used to shame. I had felt it for my mother before my father left when she would intercept his post, putting certain violet-scented envelopes into the pocket of her dress and steaming them open in the kitchen after he had left for work. The indignity of peering into other people's intimacies had appalled me, quite overpowering the acquired, accepted knowledge that reading other people's letters was one of the things that wasn't done. I had felt all my life that lavatory and bedroom doors should be kept firmly shut, for fear of what they might reveal. My mother had taught me that, just as she had taught me to change my underclothes daily and not blow my nose in public. Walking silently and in stealth over the harsh grass I remembered all the things an English gentlewoman shouldn't do, and the thing my mother had done.

Then when I came near the broken house and stood in the moon shadow I could hear and see nothing. I don't know how long I stood there while the world turned. After a while I saw Nour standing on the low wall gleaming naked in the dark light, looking defenceless and young. He knew I was there, for he called softly, 'Margaret, Margaret', and I went towards him.

The fortune-teller lay on her back behind the low wall and she was dying, or perhaps she was dead, for her eyes were open and she looked up at the stars. Her clothes were wet with blood.

Nour said, 'You must help me now, Margaret.' He added, 'The jackals will come tonight and lick up the blood.'

He sounded hopeful. I wondered why the girl was clothed and Nour naked, but I asked no questions.

'I have here part of an old plough,' said Nour.

He now sounded as though he were beginning a lecture and I thought he must have learned that intonation from his tutors. I expected him to continue, but he knelt and pushed the rusty metal through the brightly coloured rope that bound the fortune-teller's waist. Then between us we carried her to the river and rolled her in and Nour washed himself at the edge of the crocodile pool. I don't think I had any blood on my hands, for I had held her ankles just below the silver bracelets.

'Where did you get the knife?' I asked. Nour was holding it now above his head.

'It was hers,' he said and hurled it into the pool.

I watched it go regretfully because it was a beautiful Berber knife. I wondered why Nour had killed her and decided she had probably laughed at him.

He put on his shirt and shorts and took my hand. We went back to the villa hand in hand and no one ever knew we had been out, or if they did they didn't say.

Alone in bed I wondered for the first time whether the girl had been truly dead when we threw her into the river. Sometimes I still wonder.

'Well?' said my mother impatiently.

'I know this one was your favourite,' said Syl. 'We'll hang it in the bedroom where you can see it when you wake up.'

I gazed at the picture of the crocodile pool and all I could think of to say was, did the gallery owner give you a discount because you're a friend of Robert's? But I didn't, of course. Syl's mad little meannesses were not to be mentioned.

In the end my mother had invited fewer than fifty people. The wedding was not going to be the one she had dreamed of. She must have realized some years before that I wasn't headed in the direction of St Margaret's, Westminster, but she had still intended the occasion to glitter, a bright milestone in our uneventful lives. I knew how she envisaged it – all sparkle: the glass, the cutlery, the champagne, the eyes of the bride; gleaming white napery, carnations and maidenhair fern swaddled at the stem in silver paper; fallen flakes of expensive pastry, and the smart aroma of smoked salmon and asparagus blending subtly with the scent of flowers and wine; loud voices and muted laughter; sometimes a discreet tinkle of broken glass, because at a good wedding some breakage was unavoidable, indeed desirable and evidence of an expansive generosity. The weddings I had been to had been like that, quite different from the wedding parties in the villages along the Nile: a deafening noise of drums and flutes, bright hot colours and people saying words I couldn't understand. My mother's hat, I thought, would have looked very out of place at one of those Nilotic feasts. Despite the time of year she intended to dress herself in mauve silk, a coat and skirt faced with regal purple and embellished with a cream lace jabot. Her hat was mauve plush with a veil. Lili had given the outfit her qualified approval. 'Cut the jabot,' she had advised. 'Wear a string of pearls if you must, but cut the jabot.'

'I need the jabot,' my mother said, 'to hide the crêpiness of the throat.'

'Once you start thinking like that,' said Lili, 'you might as well go round dressed up like Whistler's mother.'

Lili was going to wear a crimson redingote of stiff taffeta with dull pewter buttons all down the front, a skull cap of crimson velvet atop her rusty curls, grey gun-metal stockings and gloves, and Egyptian crimson slippers. She looked a little peculiar, but she would make everyone else look pitifully ordinary.

'Don't you think your grey ...' my mother would say to her, 'or perhaps that nice beige facecloth coat-dress ...' But Lili said there were few enough times when she got the chance really to dress up and she was going to now.

The caterers had been in and out with boxes and covered trays. They were polite, professional and subservient, and reminded me irresistibly of undertakers.

My father arrived with his wife and children two days before the wedding. They had come only from Southampton where his shipping firm had now placed him, but Cynthia and the children couldn't be expected to face the rigours of the festivities on the same day that they had driven seventy-odd miles. Cynthia preferred to endure a night under the roof of the woman she had superseded. I thought this unexpectedly brave of her until I realized that she had no sense of incongruity whatsoever and wasn't aware that her presence might be unwelcome. She treated my mother as an older woman, not so much by deferring to her as by assuming that they had nothing at all in common, and never could have had. In one way this eased the situation, since it occluded any sense of unseemly rivalry, but it annoyed my mother.

Everything about Cynthia annoyed my mother, including the confusion attending her arrival. We stood in the doorway watching as she backed out of the car, immediately reaching into the back seat to extract her children. With them came carrier bags, dolls, bears, sandwiches, apple cores, orange peel and biscuit packets. A roll of lavatory paper fell on the drive and unravelled. My mother sighed. Then my father opened the boot. He had not so far looked at us waiting, a welcome party, in the doorway. Cynthia dropped a bag, out of which fell a beach ball and a clockwork mouse. My mother rolled her eyes but we stepped forward to help.

'Well, here we all are,' observed my father, forced into recognition of our presence.

Lili kissed him first, elaborately on both cheeks. Then she kissed Cynthia in the same fashion. Cynthia was surprised by this and dropped another bag. Then Lili kissed the children, who appeared less startled than alarmed. One of them stumbled over the beach ball and set it moving, and some of us ran after it. My father kissed my cheek in passing and asked how his little girl was.

'Fine,' I said.

'I've put you in the Blue room,' my mother told Cynthia, 'and the children in the dressing-room next door to it.'

None of the rooms was usually referred to in this stately manner, but my mother was determined to wring some enjoyment out of the situation. It was a little too early however to start frightening Cynthia, for she was engrossed with getting what seemed to be all her household effects upstairs.

'Bring Christopher's you-know-what,' she instructed my father, and my mother gave the object in question a meaningful glance. I gathered that in her opinion Christopher was now far too old to need a portable pot. Unfortunately Cynthia intercepted the look and explained. 'He won't do jobbies without it,' she said worriedly, going upstairs empty-handed while my father followed with the luggage.

'Aaugh,' observed Lili, lighting a cigarette, 'what a *revolting* thing to say.'

My mother looked gratified.

'I suspected she was unbalanced,' said Lili, 'when I saw that she had ashtrays fixed to leather straps on the arms of her chairs.'

'And no linen hand-towels in the bathroom,' said my mother with satisfaction.

Poor Cynthia, I thought, but my sympathy was wasted. Cynthia was oblivious of everything but herself and the children. This being the case I foresaw that she would inevitably go on putting her foot in it. The preoccupied frequently do, since their minds are not on the manners and mores of polite society and they express their anxieties without thought of the likely consequences. I was different, having no preoccupations apart from self-consciousness. This did not prevent me from making gaffes, but mine were in a different category – errors not merely of taste but of spirit – and in the main mine were sins of omission. I knew that it was inadvisable to attempt to paddle in deep waters. I tried always to stand quite still in the illusory shallows.

It hadn't occurred to me to scream at the sight of the dead fortune-teller or even to step back aghast, my hand to my heart, as the girls in the books would have done. Murder was a solecism and it would have been ill-bred to draw attention to it. A gentlewoman shouldn't make scenes, any more than she should read other people's letters. It was incorrect to appear to mind too much about anything. I adhered to this code more rigorously than my mother did, for often the pupil takes the teachings more seriously than does the tutor.

Besides I didn't care that Nour was a murderer. I didn't care that the girl was dead, except that it seemed unnatural that she should be. I had a long time ago, somewhere, seen a dead kingfisher, and that had been incongruous too and disquieting.

Once Nour said that he had found her dead, once that she had killed herself. And once he wondered aloud whether Ahmed had killed her because she had trespassed in the garden. He was trying to regain his innocence. I could have told him it was impossible. I found his state no more regrettable than my own.

Perhaps I was a moral idiot, or perhaps I was right and sin once committed has fewer degrees than we believe.

All I really cared about was that he didn't love me. If ever he might have done – and I knew in those moments when I could bear to be honest that he never would have – he couldn't now. No one can love a person who knows a secret about him that he would prefer not to know himself. Narcissus does not sit by his pool to see ruined and rusted detritus and the floating, bloated bodies of dead toads. And Nour could never be sure that I saw him as guiltless as he saw himself. The prince had blundered, to put it no higher. I had betrayed God for a blundering prince.

It was some days since I had been to the summerhouse.

'Darling,' said my mother, relaxed now that the wedding was so close and I hadn't yet disgraced her completely, 'go and see if the cactus is flowering. It will be so lovely if it comes out for the wedding.'

It was quite early in the morning or I should have suspected my mother of drinking. I stared at her.

'Well?' she said, turning from where she was making breadcrumbs at the kitchen table.

'Why?' I asked, and I sounded half-witted. I couldn't see that it would make the slightest difference to the occasion whether the cactus flowered or not. My mother seldom called me 'darling', and while I thought her fondness for her cactuses slightly silly I hadn't imagined her to be as sentimental as she was suddenly proving. Perhaps because I was so soon to be out of her care she was already growing careless, feeling free to express emotions that might previously have seemed like indulgence, might have spoiled me. She had a great detestation of a spoiled child.

She flushed when she saw my face, but it was with annoyance.

'It means good luck,' she said. 'There should always be something flowering, even for a winter wedding.'

I thought Lili was amazing. She had sown seeds of superstition in my mother and made them grow. It was a feat far more remarkable than my mother's cultivation of her cactus. I was sure that it had been Lili who had given my mother this idea. My mother's only previous obeisances to fortune had been touching wood and throwing spilled salt over her left shoulder to blind the devil. There was something crafted about this flowering myth, something touchingly, repellently obvious – like the gift which the honey-curled innocent is deputed to hand to the rich and evil-tempered old relation. What, I asked myself, was Lili up to? I felt that now I had been betrayed. It seemed as though she had been trying to help my mother sweeten the occasion – garland it with pretty conceits, as people pile wreaths on corruption.

'Who said so?' I asked without subtlety.

'Nobody said so,' squawked my mother. 'I don't *believe* it, but it's a pretty thought. *Isn't* it?' she added angrily as I still stood gazing at her.

'Yes,' I said.

'I'll go down myself later,' said my mother, 'but I'm busy with the stuffing for the duck. Go and get some fresh air.'

The air was more than fresh. It was freezing in the garden. It was nearly as cold in the summerhouse. There was a bud on the cactus but it looked unpromising. There was a small bottled gas-heater in the corner and I wondered if my mother had instructed the jobbing gardener to warm the place up further to encourage the thing to flower. There was a pile of my books where I had left them half-read. And there were some torn scraps of red crêpe paper on the floor. The moorish arches of the summerhouse windows framed a vista of dead grass and deciduous trees beyond the broken hedge of evergreens through which Syl entered my mother's garden when he came to call. Some black birds flew by with a stunned weariness like the survivors of a disaster. Winter must seem like a disaster to birds, and rain was on its way. I didn't care. I picked up a bit of red paper and twisted it in my fingers. It was the colour of the doubtless poisonous berries which gleamed here and there in the hedge and it stained my hands. The summerhouse was always untidy because my mother stored things in it besides using it as a haven for her cactus. Garden chairs and umbrellas were stacked in a corner with some flower pots. The cushions along the ledge smelled damp, and when I sat on them they felt chilly even through my tweed skirt. The paraffin heater which was left on constantly may have been sufficient to support life in the cactus, but it wasn't enough to comfort me. I sat under a travelling rug and looked at my fingernails.

Lili tapped on the window before she came in, wearing a scarlet wool coat with a huge collar. I hadn't seen it before. The collar stood up round her head and her rusty curls rested on it.

'You look warm,' I said from under my rug.

'I'm not really,' said Lili. 'I'm beginning to pine for the banks of the Nile.'

'Do you think that thing is going to flower?' I asked.

'Mmm,' said Lili.

I sat holding myself still against the cold. I wished Lili had stayed with me, hung about with cigarette smoke and laughing. I could still smell cigarettes. There were butts lying on the wooden floor. I missed Lili in her scarlet coat and her stench of scent and cigarettes. Nour had smoked incessantly and so had some of his aunts. My mother and Syl disapproved of the habit. My father didn't smoke. Nor did Cynthia. The house was smoke-free when Lili went out. At the moment it smelled of food and wedding preparations and children. Cynthia had said they couldn't go out because they might catch cold. My mother was trapped in her own house with her ex-husband and his new family. Nobody was laughing and the children were grizzling. I wondered if they would be happier on the banks of the Nile playing in the dust with the brown babies and the children or leaning against the knees of the covered, cigarette-smoking aunts. I pictured Syl's cold house invaded by crying children and wondered if I could alter the atmosphere sufficiently to make it bearable by taking to cigarettes. It seemed like a counsel of despair. I imagined myself creeping about in the night dropping smouldering stubs in conveniently inflammable corners till all the house burned down. Perhaps if I smoked in bed Syl would sleep in the spare room. Perhaps I could drop ash on the things I cooked and he would refuse to eat them and starve to death. I wondered if it was fair to wish somebody dead because he was going to marry me. I wondered if I was truly eternally wicked and how many people had turned to destruction because they had no strength in them. I wondered if the venom of weakness was more dangerous than the rage of power, more insidious with its content of despair, and if when the world failed it would be because it was heavy with inertia and the tears of deceit, not the fires of wrath. I wondered what would happen if I laughed at Syl. He might kill me.

I stayed in the summerhouse while it rained. The rain of winter was like the tears of the old: not sorrowful and not kind, bitter. Self-pity was a wearisome emotion. I wished I was dead, but I had been too well brought up to snatch at death without being invited. It was not there for the asking but had to be deserved or – sometimes – offered as a gift. I thought it remarkable how few people appreciated this offer. Did they like the rain and the pain and the boredom which constituted life? Perhaps the death-fearers perceived life differently from me. For me it was being a vessel of evil afloat in a sea of evil. If I broke, it would take the power of God to separate my elements from the elements of the sea – and why, I asked myself, should he bother, since if I took my own life it would be in full knowledge of what the act entailed? I drifted on a sluggish tide of badness unable to see help or hope, and silent: blind as a worm, as a bottle, faceless and limbless, incapable of any cry or gesture or expression that might call the rescuer to me. I reminded myself that she who has scuttled the ship cannot in all conscience summon the lifeboat, even were she able. I waited.

Lili had gone to the gallery, for Robert's exhibition was over and there were things she had to discuss with the owner. My mother had said earlier that Lili must remind him not to forget the wedding. 'What?' I had asked, thinking it impossible that she would have invited a virtual stranger – of whom she had been determined to disapprove – to my wedding. She had ignored me and I hadn't repeated my question.

'I think you should see Syl,' said my mother. 'He'll cheer you up. Perhaps he'll take you out to dinner or for a drive.'

Oh God. I said, 'Mother, I am truly all right. I don't want to go out to dinner or for a drive. I don't want to see Syl.' *I don't want to see Syl.*

'Rubbish,' said my mother, going to the telephone.

'Hallo?' she said. 'Ah, Mrs Monro.'

Serve you right, I thought. Now you'll have to talk about the weather and she may go on to complain about the government.

But the conversation was very brief.

'Oh,' said my mother. 'Oh, all right. Thanks.'

She put the telephone down slowly and I could see her wondering what to tell me.

'Has he gone out?' I asked.

'Er, yes,' said my mother. She paused. 'He had to see a client.'

'I didn't know solicitors saw clients in the evening,' I said. I was beginning to cultivate an air of *fausse naïveté* to disguise my real ignorance of the world and I wouldn't have blamed my mother if she'd thrown the decanter at me.

'Well, they do,' she said shortly. She said no more but left the room by gradual degrees, humming a little, straightening a cushion, pushing a silver snuff-box nearer to the centre of the table, until she reached the door and went out to the kitchen.

I wondered what I would have done if I had discovered Syl, redhanded, standing over a dying girl behind the summerhouse. It occurred to me that trysting places – summerhouses and ruined pigeon towers, hidden strips of tiled pavement – are by their very nature secret, and therefore perilous. Love and death happen in the unfrequented ways. A laugh at the wrong moment and a poor body, hoped-for vehicle of pleasure, would lie, wide-eyed, transfixed by steel with no one to know. My confessor had said I should have told the authorities, but he didn't know Egypt. I knew that the authorities would not have pursued the son of the Pasha, and anyway the girl was gone without trace to the bottom of the crocodile pool. I hoped that Allah had washed away the fingerprints of the murderer, not for his sake, but for hers. It was hard to be born formed and distorted by the mother body, intolerable to enter eternity fumbled and bruised by the hands of a stranger.

I would have screamed if I had apprehended Syl the murderer because I cared nothing for his good opinion. I would have run, screaming, to the real house where the lights were on. I would have screamed 'Mother' and 'Police'. I would have been glad. I would have been free.

I remember little about the night before the wedding. The house was full of people. Syl and his mother came for Martinis and she brought her little dog to show to Jennifer and Christopher. The dog didn't like the children, nor the children the dog. That part was a failure. The gallery owner was there and, it seemed, was staying overnight. I found this most strange and asked Lili why it was so. She looked at me oddly.

'Weren't you listening?' she asked.

'No,' I said.

'Your mother invited him after the opening night,' she explained. 'They got on so well and had so much in common.'

'Oh,' I said. After a while it became clearer to me. My

mother was unwontedly attentive to the gallery owner, especially when Cynthia was in the vicinity. My mother didn't care to appear as a woman without a man on this occasion, loaded as it was with hints of lubricity. Lili had a man, Cynthia had my mother's erstwhile man, I was about to have a man, and my mother had refused to be allied with Mrs Monro as a spare and unwanted female. This realization made me think less of her.

My father, when he could be, was unwontedly attentive to me. Cynthia dogged him but he did his best to talk to me. Unfortunately he could think of little to say and silences kept falling between us. In the end I was quite relieved that Cynthia was there. Her conversation was unmemorable but it made the awkwardness less obvious.

Syl and his mother left early. My father, still trying to make things go with a swing, said, 'Yes, you'd better have an early night tonight, old man. Ho, ho.'

I knew this was the sort of remark that was made at weddings, but my awareness made me feel no less ill.

Lili handed me a drink. She plied me with whisky until the horrible evening became as blurred as the boundaries of madness, and I remember nothing more.

I also remember little of the following morning until the moment we set off for the summerhouse. My mother went to early Mass because it was *comme il faut* but didn't even ask me to accompany her. She had looked at my face, haggard with hangover, and left.

She brought the parish priest back for breakfast and we crowded into the morning-room because the dining-room was being readied for the more important wedding breakfast which loomed in the afternoon. I hadn't bothered to dress, since there seemed no point when I should soon have to don the garment which hung over a chair in my bedroom. I sat in my nightdress and dressing-gown and drank tea.

Lili was already in her redingote and refused to sit down for fear of creasing it. She had her hat on too and looked alert and excited. I was drearily disappointed in her. She left the room and I supposed she had gone to charm the caterers who were adorning the table with maidenhair fern.

After a while she came back smelling of cold air and cigarette smoke.

'It's out,' she said.

'What's out?' asked my mother, who had a great deal on her mind.

'The cactus, darling,' said Lili.

'It *can't* be,' said my mother, now also looking elaborately excited. 'It showed no signs yesterday.'

'Well, it's out now,' said Lili.

'I must go and see,' cried my mother, vivacious for the sake of the gallery owner.

'No,' said Lili. 'Wait until everyone's finished their breakfast and you can all go and see.'

This idea appealed to my mother. 'We can go and toast it,' she said, 'with champagne.'

'What?' asked Cynthia. She had somehow managed to cram both her children on her lap. They were crying a little.

My mother took on a more staid expression and adjusted her voice to instruct. 'My winter-flowering cactus,' she said. 'It's a sign of great good fortune if it flowers on the wedding day.' This slight exaggeration of the myth I felt sure Lili had constructed gave her pleasure and she smiled at the gallery owner.

'You *must* come too,' said Lili to me. 'Go and put on something warm.'

An hour later we all set off down the lawn carrying glasses and a couple of bottles.

'Where's Lili?' asked Robert as we reached the summerhouse.

Lili was already there, and so was Syl.

She still wore her hat and her redingote although it was utterly unbuttoned and she had clearly ceased to care whether it was creased or not, but Syl was naked except for his socks and shirt. I thought, with the first touch of pity I had ever felt for him, that he must be rather cold.

This is my last memory of Lili and another one I shall keep until the day I die. We had all witnessed the scene; those who hadn't crowded to the door peered through the moorish windows to see the winter-flowering cactus and I noticed that it was made of crêpe paper. She was always clever with her hands. The gallery owner shouted, in an outraged roar, 'Lili.' And I thought – Lili has slept with every man present with the possible exception of Father O'Flynn. And then I thought that what would have upset my mother most was that Mrs Raffald who was helping with the preparations had also come to see the cactus flower.

I went back to bed, and I never knew how the caterers were dismissed and the wedding guests turned away, the cake and the maidenhair fern disposed of and the parish priest returned to his church.

The day came when I was aware that I had been forgiven, that I was free of hell. I think perhaps that such things happen in eternity and not in time and that we, mortal and profane, can only gradually realize the movements of God: that he is generous and unassuming in these matters, not demanding scenes of reconciliation, merely our souls' health. I was filled with a sense of flowering, of abundance and gratitude, which related me for a while to infinity. The feeling lessened, of course, for only the saints can bear to live close to God, but sometimes now when I listen to the convent bells ringing with the cry from the minaret, and I look at the lilies under the convent wall where we plant them in memory of Our Lady who sojourned for a while in Egypt, I feel another sense of gratitude. To Lili. For surely to make a great fool and spectacle of yourself for the sake of another is a form of martyrdom.

The fact that she also enjoyed it seems immaterial. I had caught a glimpse of her face and remembered that she had been a dancer and had capered on the stage to the gaze of strangers. She had hated it too. She had given up a lot for my sake – dignity, and the goodwill of my mother, although I don't suppose that bothered her too greatly. Robert would forgive her. He always had. It was a strange martydom. She had offered not so much a sacrifice as a gift. What she had given was of value only to me, and she had not in reality harmed or impoverished herself beyond redemption. I have long since ceased attempting to follow the processes by which God works out his purpose, but I know he sent me Lili. For who but he – or she – would have conceived of a wedding present so original as the scene in the summerhouse?'

I remembered one day what she had been saying all those years ago, seated on the hummock of harsh grass. She had been speaking of love and I hadn't understood her, and she had waved her cigarette, and Robert had asked her if she would rather live for the rest of her life without smoking or without love, and she had replied, 'What do you think?'

My only regret is that no one answered her, and now I shall never know.

THE SKELETON IN THE CUPBOARD

I hadn't given her a thought for years. I had had no reason to think about her – not really. I was old Mrs Monro and my life was over.

Monica called one morning to ask if I wanted anyone else put on the guest list and said, as though it didn't matter, that *she* was coming to stay for the wedding. She said '*Lili's* coming', and I put my cup down very carefully in its saucer. It was winter and I was cold. I could see my fingers trembling and put my hands in the pockets of my cardigan. Winter gets worse as you get older.

'Have some more coffee, Monica,' I said. 'Are they back then?' I remembered the relief when they had left. It was years before, but I still remembered the relief.

She said, 'Robert has an exhibition arranged. They'll be staying for a few weeks.'

'A few weeks,' I said. 'How nice.' I poured her another cup of coffee and put my hands back in my pockets.

At some point my flesh had ceased to be of much significance to me, and it was my bones of which I was always conscious. My bones were cold and they ached, perhaps to remind me that before too long they would be all that remained of me: the neglected skeleton's revenge, as the pampered flesh decayed away. I was reflecting thus gloomily because I was unfairly enraged with Monica, and spite and unhappiness frequently go together. I could not reach over and slap her for bringing Lili back into my life, but I could break a less stringent social taboo and embarrass her with talk of my age and impending death. I could remark reflectively, 'I suppose, after all, we are all only skeletons in our own cupboards, waiting to be revealed.' That'd serve her right, I thought, but I kept silent. Such subtle aggression would be wasted on Monica. She would respond with some bromide and make me even crosser. Years had gone by since I'd been able to say things as they came into my head, knowing that I should be understood. The people who would have understood had all gone away. Sometimes I made Syl laugh but he was my son and it was different. I had missed those who had been my friends for so long now that deprivation had become my element. I had adapted like some Darwinian prototype to loneliness and now could never revert to what I had been. I was sorry for myself, but I would have died rather than let anybody know. Dislike was preferable to pity since people mostly dislike from a distance. They seldom bother to come to you in order to dislike you, whereas pity brings them thronging, eager to express this gratifying emotion and gain whatever is to be gained of credit – in time and eternity. I had not, of course, always been so cynical.

When Monica left I went into the sitting-room and sat down. The dog was looking at me, lying with paws outstretched, his eyes filmed and bulging. Syl had brought him for me when Jack died, so he was an old dog now. I hadn't wanted a dog, especially not a small, peculiar pug, but Syl's fiancée's bitch had just had a litter and Syl had thought a puppy would be company for me. He had fully intended marrying the girl, although no date had been set, and his father's death had come at an inconvenient time. How could he marry when his mother had just been widowed? He and the girl came with the puppy and a mushroom basket for it to sleep in until we made more permanent arrangements. That particular girl was, in my view, too sweet to be wholesome. She would look at me with brimming eyes, rather like the dog, and bring me exasperating posies from her mother's garden – little bits of flowers and leaf and twig tied up with shiny ribbon. She would catch my eye with her brimming one and glare into it with deep compassion. I used to long to say how pleasant a change it was to be widowed, and watch her expression alter, but I had learned over many years to be guarded and to control my inclinations. Besides, Syl seemed fond of her. He fussed around her, as though she were made of porcelain, and it was already high time he was married, being well into his thirties.

Time: it seemed I could think of nothing else. So much had passed, and still it flew. It must be running out for me, but I went on, seemingly indestructible: a little bored but not unbearably so. I began thinking more and more about the past, and had to make an effort to return to the present. I would come back from the moors of my youth still feeling the wind in my hair and catch a glimpse of an old woman in the darkened windows. Looking in the mirror I could see no trace of the girl whose life I had been reliving. Old age seemed to me not so much a natural progression as a disguise: a suit of unsuitable clothes, ill-fitting and inappropriate. I fell into the habit of sadness and gave up the practice of hope. It made existence easier.

'I have a lamb's kidney for you, dog,' I said, and he got to his feet, shaking slightly. When he was a pup I had kept treading on him; whether it was his fault or mine I could never determine. He had squealed 'Pen and ink, pen and ink', and Syl's fiancée would leap to console him – 'Who's a poor little baby then?' All in all I was more glad than regretful when that engagement ended. Syl grew very white and quiet, and I know he telephoned her in the night to ask her to come back to him. She never did, not once, and I used to wonder why. Then after a few weeks he fell in love again. He never had any trouble finding girls.

I went to the kitchen and got the kidney from the larder. 'Soon, dog,' I said, 'soon, soon', as I sliced it up into small bits for his old teeth and his old gums.

He found it difficult to chew and his breath smelled, but I felt

I was in no position to criticize. I was, as they say, no oil-painting myself. I had never liked him as much as a dog should be liked, and now it was too late. I had never quite been able to dissociate him from his origins and the fleeing fiancée. Even now he reminded me of loss. That he had arrived at the time of Jack's death did not worry me. I had never liked Jack as much as a husband should be liked.

Considering this, I bent down and patted the dog as he snuffled the bits of kidney. My back ached as I straightened up, and he snarled briefly at me.

'You're an ungrateful little swine, dog,' I told him, 'and the world is too cold a place for you to bite the hand that feeds you.'

I had had a sheep-dog once who had leapt across the moors, his hair sleeked by the facing wind. I had gone home with him to golden fires, and sometimes I thought that all I retained of warmth and joy – and it was now little enough – had been stored up in those days and seldom since replenished. My memories of youth were of movement and life, of cold wind, bracken-and-gorse-scented, fire and a warmth of summer more significant in the North, more notable than it could be in a gentler climate. The clear air had seemed to clarify everything – sentiments and sensation.

I went back to the sitting-room and the dog followed. Syl had had the end part of the house converted for me, so that when he married I should be out of the way of the bride. I had suggested that there was nothing to prevent him from buying his own house but he had not seemed to listen. I was not blind to Syl's faults. He could be spontaneously and ridiculously generous, but he was also mean. I could hardly blame him for this trait, since it was from me that he got his Yorkshire blood and York-shiremen are known the world over as careful.

I was not delighted to be consigned to only a part of my own house but I didn't care enough to argue about it. One of my anxieties was that I knew Syl would spend a good deal of his time with me in my new quarters and Margaret would be left rattling round on her own in the rest of the house. I had ceased to wonder why Syl not only stayed with me but sought out my company. It had become very noticeable when his father died and I had tried once or twice then to tell him that he need not trouble himself about me – I was quite self-sufficient. Again he had not seemed to listen, and in the end I was forced to accept that, for some reason, he would stay with me. I knew it would appear to everyone that I was a possessive and demanding mother, but I didn't care. There was very little I could do about it. Some of the girls had complained that he spent more time with me than he did with them, but Syl could be stubborn. I also think that he believed he could have everything. He had always wanted everything – both sorts of cake at teatime, jelly *and* blancmange at parties – when he was a child. It didn't seem like greed – more like curiosity. I used to wonder if that was why he had so many girls. He was not truly an amorist since he always meant the latest girl to be the last, believing her to be finally the love of his life. Then she would run away – and I never did understand that – or Syl would tire of her, and look around for another source of sweetness. Or perhaps I mean a sort of sweetmeat.

I had not yet used the converted part of the house, despite all the trouble Syl had taken to make it pleasant. I was waiting until Margaret moved in. Margaret.

When she left school she stayed at home all day. I used to walk the dog along the path bordering the golf course and I would see her, most mornings, sitting in the summerhouse – sometimes reading, sometimes just staring into space. It seemed unnatural. When I was your age, I would say to her in my mind, I was preparing to go to college. I did not say in my mind what I really remembered: when I was your age I was in love, I was alive. That is not the kind of thing the old say to the young.

I had not seen her very often as she grew up because she was sent away to school. I remember that she always seemed to be at home during the holidays, for I found it strange. She never brought a friend home with her and whenever I came across her she was on her own. Most girls of her age spent at least part of their holidays in each other's houses, went around in packs or in pairs and lounged a lot – like wild cats – before marriage and responsibility domesticated them and dulled their shining fur, silenced their wails. Adolescence is usually typified by an un-answerable combination of innocence and insolence. As their elders require that they should conform to society's demands, to the hypocrisy – if we are to be honest – that makes life possible, the young often respond with a curious superiority. It is unlikely that they have yet done anything truly dreadful and they suspect that their elders probably have. To be told how to behave by a person steeped in moral turpitude is annoying to everyone, but more particularly to the young. And then the old grow exasper-ated by the stupidity of the young: by their failure to realize that moral decline is a matter only of time, and that as circum-stances alter they too will be forced to cut corners and com-promise their early – and unfortunately vague – ideals. Of course only the good die young. With a few rare exceptions only the young *are* good. Margaret sometimes struck me as too good to be true. She had not that quality of fresh and honest surprise and indignation that I have been speaking of. Rather she had a copybook conformity which only a fool could have taken for the real thing. The real virtue of youth lies in that impulsive gener-osity and Margaret was as contained and closed and mute as her mother's meat safe. On the face of it she was the perfect girl: obedient, disciplined, quiet, sober and undemanding, and yet she was wholly unnatural. Perhaps Syl was deceived by her appearance, by the way she behaved like a much older person, into imagining that she was unusually mature for her age. No, he wasn't. He found her similar to me, and also might have thought that behind her reserve lay those much-vaunted banked fires beloved of novelists. I'd never believed in them myself. Ice and fire do not coexist and all the romantic longing in the world will not make it so.

Monica was caught in the common trap between parental fondness and exasperation. When people inquired over the tea table what Margaret was going to do now I could see her torn between snapping 'Nothing', and explaining that Margaret was resting after the rigours of school before deciding between a career in the diplomatic corps or a suitable marriage. I recognized her dilemma, for Syl, while his problems were different from Margaret's, caused me similar feelings of irritation. One of the reasons I was seeing fewer and fewer people was that I was sick and tired of being called on to explain why Syl was yet unmarried. 'Mind your own damned business' is the response of those who are aggrieved because they have something to hide. I had evolved an air designed to give the impression that I could not understand their question, that to me there was nothing untoward in Syl's condition. In truth, of course, no one wondered more searchingly about it than I. My sisters-in-law, all of whom had grandchildren, had become particularly unwelcome to me as time passed. From resentment of Syl's undoubted beauty as a child to envy of his achievement in passing his law exams with honours, they had progressed to a shared *schadenfreude* at his failure to wed and breed. I frequently had an image, which visited me unbidden, of the backs of girls flouncing down the drive, never to return. Not the least worrying was the speed with which he recovered from these rejections.

Each sister-in-law, like a bad fairy, had a different form of words with which to attack me, from 'Syl not married *yet?*' to 'How good of Syl to look after you so well', an implication that I was a monstrous mother, destroying her son's chance of a future, of fulfilment and happiness. I could not explain that there was nothing I wanted more than that Syl should leave me:

go away and leave me alone. In a way I was protecting him by letting the world believe that his state was all my fault. It seemed preferable to the view that he was a hopelessly inadequate human being. My annoyance at being cast into this role was vitiated by my awareness that, like it or not, there was some truth in it. I did not like it at all. I did not care to remember that my own marriage had left much to be desired, that I had not married the man I loved and that when Syl had started to grow up I had indeed preferred his company to that of his father. Now I no longer needed company. I had had enough and I wanted to be left to think about things I had not had time to think about. Increasingly I remembered my childhood, the beginning: the dark spaces of the farmhouse, the endless moors and the perfection of smallness in the hawthorn, white with birth, bright with death. I thought more of winter than I did of summer. It seemed to me that those Northern moors were designed to receive snow; intended for the winds to pass untrammelled. Summer was a dull season. In spring things were growing; in autumn they were harvested; in winter they were waiting. Summer was pointless, designed for idleness. An inbred Yorkshire puritanism led me to despise it. I wondered why I was thinking of summer with winter all around me.

It was the egg sandwiches that reminded me. Shaking white pepper into the mashed egg, I was back in a more recent past than the one I habitually roamed: only about fifteen years ago, which is nothing. It was cold in the pantry. I had chosen this house because it was just a little like the stone-built houses of the North, of my childhood. Jack had favoured a more exotic residence which had also been on sale just up the road, but I put my foot down. There were some things I could be stubborn about, and I refused to live in a house designed, as far as I could tell, on the lines of a Dutch dairy. Jack had decided that we should retire to this neighbourhood, indeed to this particular road. One of the firm's bosses had lived and died here. Something about this ill-expressed, incoherent estate represented worldly success to Jack and I didn't really care enough to question the assumption.

Derek and Monica had shared his view and followed us here. Certainly you had to be well-off to be able to afford the absurd buildings that rose like apparitions on either side of the private road. Manifestations of architectural fantasy appeal to those who know no better. I never said this to Jack. There would have been no point. I was undoubtedly a snob in some matters but I kept silence. Jack had been dismayed by my uncle's farmhouse. I had (only to give him the benefit of the doubt) taken him there once when we were first married and its charm had escaped him. He was town-bred, the son of a cotton broker, and his aspirations were formed by the views of his father and his father's contemporaries. 'I don't know much about art but I know what I like and I've got t'brass to pay for it' was their attitude. I was never an aesthete, but I did not care for pastiche. The house in which I would end my days stood amongst a medley of wildly assorted historical and geographical styles, and I missed the assurance of roots, of houses built of local stone, of people speaking in the accents of the district. I had been homesick for most of my life. Inevitably I would have little in common with the others who had chosen to live here. I was a fish out of water. When Derek came back from Egypt bringing Monica and the baby I was not enthralled. He was some sort of distant cousin of Jack's, although much younger, and worked for the same shipping firm. There was a tendency in the North for relations to work in the same firm. They liked each other no more than relations anywhere but they stuck together. I used to think it was a kind of tribal imperative in face of threat from the South. Jack, who, to be fair, was not entirely stupid, said once that they would be company for me, friends from our days in Liverpool, but he didn't repeat it. Derek was cast in much the same mould as Jack, so he was the wrong sort of Northerner for me. I wondered whether North and South married more easily than Town and Country, yet that was absurd, for I had left the country when I went to the college and I had never been a rustic. Perhaps it was really very simple: I didn't love my husband, so I didn't like his house.

I sneezed, startling the dog who was hoping something might drop from the pantry shelf into his waiting mouth. The sneeze jarred me and I said 'Ouch'.

The dog sat looking at me and I felt foolish for speaking aloud to myself.

'How are *your* bones?' I asked him. 'You're as old as me. How do *you* feel?' Talking to the dog was in a more acceptable category than talking to oneself. 'Does your back ache when you sneeze?'

I stirred the pepper into the egg and started to butter the loaf. The dog, who had got up, sat down again, prepared to continue waiting. He wasn't interested in conversation at the moment. It was in the evening that he liked to be addressed occasionally, lying in front of the coal fire, dozing. Sometimes he had bad dreams.

'You eat too much,' I said to him as he watched me. 'On the other hand,' I said, 'I seem to be making too much tea for two.'

I put the sandwiches and cake on a tray, and the scones to warm in the oven. I think I hoped that Margaret, who was too thin, would be tempted to eat at least one of these offerings.

'You're too fat,' I said to the dog, who whined in response. 'I'm too old,' I said, like a character out of one of those serial fairy stories. 'And this pantry is cold.'

'Fee Fi Fo Fum,' I said under my breath and I knew how I would appear to an observer: an old woman muttering to herself. The old seemed always to look down and inwards, and speak, most of all, to themselves.

The smell of newly made egg sandwiches is not to be denied. It was again summer that I was reluctantly remembering now.

I was already old fifteen years ago but my bones were holding up better. I was remarkable for my age, as they say: quite frisky in fact. Jack had not yet died. Syl was engaged to what is known as a 'nice girl', which meant, when analysed to its smallest components, that she was as boring as hell but at least she wasn't a whore. I recalled now with wry regret that I had thought her not good enough for Syl.

There had still seemed some point then in the round of dinners, ladies' lunches, teas, picnics, bridge parties which constituted what was known in my youth as social intercourse. Not a great deal of point – never that – but rather more than now. Now I was moving towards the grave and would give another dinner party only over my own dead body. Even the small suppers and teas to which I occasionally entertained Monica and one or two other acquaintances were taxing and boring in equal proportion. If Syl would only leave home, I thought, I would never have to cook again. The dog and I could live on scraps and the contents of tins. But then I thought of the time a year or so before when I had fallen downstairs. Monica had come in through the back door calling my name. I had retained the custom of my childhood of not locking doors, and now I was rewarded. I heard her telling the ambulance men that she had found me lying there unconscious and icy cold and had telephoned them immediately. I'd come round by then, and on the whole I was rather annoyed. As I was saying, I was relieved to know that Syl was always around in case I should have an accident and lie helpless with broken bones but, having toppled downstairs and knocked myself out, it seemed quite pointless that at my age I should recover. I could have quietly faded into whatever comes next for the children of man, but as it was I had no more than a lump on the head and a black eye. I was doomed to go on going through the motions of life. Quite uselessly, it seemed to me, I was to live until I'd eaten more egg sandwiches.

How difficult it is to keep to the point when you grow old. Not only because the brain cells are failing but because there is so much to explain. So much unharnessed, uncategorized experience leads up to each new episode – no matter how trivial. Each new happening is not new, but an echo, a reminder, or a repetition of something that has happened before – and quite possibly before that, and before that again. Certainly I had eaten many egg sandwiches in my life.

As I carried the tray from the kitchen I thought of the last time Margaret and I had eaten egg sandwiches together. She must have been very small, since it was shortly after they had returned from Egypt and I had felt the odd wish which no other child (except Syl, of course, for whom as a baby I would have offered myself as a feast) had ever aroused in me, to cosset her. She seemed even then to be lacking something which was the birth-right of every child. I had no idea what it could be. She was well-dressed and, although tiny, clearly not undernourished, and her mother kept a constant eye on her. She was too quiet. Syl felt it as well. He kept offering her little bits of 'eggy samblidge. It'll make you grow up into a big girl.' 'No thank you,' Margaret would say. 'Anchovy samblidge,' Syl would offer. 'Little tiny fishes in it.' 'No thank you. 'You'll never grow up to be a big girl. Don't you want to be a big girl?' 'No thank you.' Lili and Robert were staying with Monica and I had asked them all to tea in the garden. There were rugs on the lawn, and garden chairs, but Lili chose to perch on an overgrown, neglected rockery built over the old air raid shelter because, she explained, she didn't want to ruin the lawn with her cigarette ends, and the rockery was conveniently full of little cracks and holes hidden by the wild grass which had seeded itself there. I could see her now. She was wearing white and her red hair stuck out all round her head.

Syl's fiancée was also making a fuss of Margaret. She had the air of a girl who believes that there is no prettier sight in the world than that of a young woman being kind to an innocent child. I never could be fair to that girl.

It was Lili who fascinated Margaret. She sat high on the rockery talking her nonsense and all the men hung round like flies. I had a feeling that she smoked so much in order to keep them at a certain distance. Then Margaret crawled up the slope to sit by her and I wondered at Lili's quality.

I lived too much in the past. I don't know why this should be considered reprehensible but I often resolved to cure myself of the habit and face the present. There was nothing too terrible about my life, no need to turn away from it or pretend it was other than it was. The truth is I was bored. I had not been bred to suburbia. I had not intended or imagined that I should end my days in a London suburb behind a screen of spotted laurels. I had never really expected to grow old. The wisdom that is supposed to come with age seemed to me only an accumulation of repeated experience, a realization that people and their emotions are much alike. I found it irritating that, this being the case, no one was able or prepared to learn from the experience of others. I had watched many people go through the motions of birth, marriage and death convinced of the uniqueness of their experience and I could think of nothing to say to them. Congratulations always seemed to me premature, and when disaster struck commiserations were otiose. I went through the forms with less and less conviction and came to be perceived as begrudging, negative and, I suppose, sour, although I retained enough *amour propre* to feel somewhat reduced by that description. The world has always feared old women, witches. I had known some cheerful old people, but their lives had worked on them differently and I found them tiresome. The optimism of others is always irritating and appears peculiarly misplaced in the elderly. In view of the way the world is constituted it appears misplaced (although more forgivable) in the young as well. I remembered being hopeful. I remembered sliding on a frozen tarn as a tawny sun retired obliquely behind a darkening hill, and the exhilaration of cold and shadow contrasting with my own warmth. I had sometimes felt what perhaps we should all feel always – that I was an integral part of everything, of everything that was huge and all that was small. Now I was part of hardly anything. I worried that Syl was aware of this. I worried more that he was using the evidence of my emptiness to excuse his own refusal to take any chances.

Margaret reminded me of myself. Not as I had been, but as I was. Syl fell in love with her. No one could understand why. She was very quiet and seemed to take no interest in anything, but I knew why. She was like me. Syl would need to learn no new lessons. She was not disruptive. She was not even remotely self-assertive. Also she was beautiful and unaware of it, and there is perhaps nothing so seductive as unselfconscious beauty. Yet I was always puzzled by Syl's attitude to her. I have to admit that, if I'm to be honest with myself. I had watched Jack when he was Syl's age making sheep's eyes at girls young enough to be his daughter and showing no signs of awareness of his own foolishness. I had thought that odd; had thought that even if he couldn't help himself and was compelled to behave like an ass, he should, at least, have shown some acknowledgement of his own ludicrous plight, a sheepish smile to go with the sheep's eyes perhaps, but he had been quite unaware of the effect he made.

Syl had never struck me as being as foolish as his father. I was prejudiced in his favour, and anyway his proclivities, even if they reflected badly on me as a mother, did not make me seem vicariously ridiculous as my husband's carryings on had done. With Syl I had never felt that common female compulsion to invert the soup tureen on a man's head as he goes into the old routine. Syl had begun by flirting with Margaret as he automatically flirted with any woman and I had been surprised – no, shocked – when he announced that he was yet again engaged to be married.

Of all the girls Margaret seemed to me the least likely as Syl's wife, or indeed as anybody's wife. Nubile, for some reason, was not a word one associated with Margaret. She had a cool clear quality and it was impossible to imagine her in a transport of passion. For one thing, she never giggled. Most of Syl's girls had giggled a good deal, and wriggled as well. Wriggling and giggling, regrettable as it seems, are the human female's means of indicating willingness to be courted, and Margaret had a curious dignity which was incompatible with sexuality.

I was never certain, to put it at its simplest, that Syl was really in love with her, because I couldn't see why he should be. I feared that perhaps vanity had led him to wish it to be known that he could still procure for himself young and beautiful women. He did care about her. He fussed around her and tried to give her treats, and sometimes I thought that what he really wanted was not a wife but a child.

He took her to Brighton one day, getting up early and spending some time with his head under the bonnet of his car, ensuring it would carry her safely. She was late, and Syl came into the house looking at his watch and wondering aloud what she was doing. After a while he went to fetch her, and when they came back I was standing in the doorway holding his sweater, since he had left it on the hall table and I didn't want him to forget it. It could turn cold by the sea. Something had made him very angry. He was white and his movements were hurried and careless and he threw shut the open door of the car. Margaret was unperturbed. The last girl had grown supplicatory when Syl was angry: penitent and fearful. But Margaret looked at him as though she thought he was mad.

'She says she doesn't want to go,' Syl had told me – and to Margaret: 'Why didn't you tell me before?' 'I didn't think it was important,' said Margaret. 'I'll come with you,' I offered, trying to lighten the situation, and Margaret said in her clear voice with no hint of a remorseful tremor: 'I've agreed to go if you really want me to.' 'Too kind of you to *agree*,' Syl snarled and I thought that if her small pedantries irritated him so much it boded ill for the future.

He was still in a rage when he got home. Or perhaps it was a fresh rage and they had had a pleasant day together. I never found out, since it would have been injudicious to ask. A few years earlier he could have taken her for donkey rides and bought her candy floss, and as I reflected on this I thought that the proposed marriage was the stupidest thing I'd ever heard of. She was too young for Syl and, to my own mortification, I found I was again thinking, too *good*. I examined this odd thought but could find no reason to reject it. Syl, much as I loved him, was an ordinary mortal and there was something strange about Margaret. Perhaps 'good' was not the word, but whatever the quality I had discerned in her it unsuited her for everyday human things and I could think of no appropriate uses to which she might put herself. I found it impossible to picture her pushing a pram.

The doorbell rang and the dog barked. I wished as usual that my visitor might have forgotten to come, but it was too late now. I opened the door, and although I was aware that Margaret was there all I could see was Lili. Of course I knew that they had arrived from Egypt, knew I would have to see her sooner or later, but not now. I was not over-zealous about the social niceties but I could have strangled Margaret for bringing her without warning. I was, for a moment, speechless.

Lili seemed not to have changed at all. I would describe her as garish, but that wouldn't be fair. She was vividly *alive*. A cartload of monkeys, I thought confusedly, and had a sudden hallucinatory impression of the Blackpool Illuminations as I submitted to her kiss. Considering the circumstances under which we had last parted, I found her attitude remarkable, even admirable. Or perhaps she led such a varied life that she had thought the event of no significance. Perhaps she had no recollection of it. I found myself quite unable to behave naturally and fell back on convention, wondering as I offered egg sandwiches whether she would remember the garden picnic. Her behaviour then had been impeccable, and if, as seemed possible, she couldn't remember the outrageous things she had done later it seemed improbable that she would remember a small party of no interest or importance at all where she had done nothing untoward.

Margaret seemed paler and quieter than usual. She refused sandwiches and fiddled with a scone. I could still think of nothing to say to Lili and grew exasperated with Margaret for being so hopelessly little help. I think Lili too began to feel the constraint, for she accused the poor old dog of assaulting her foot. I would not myself have chosen quite this method of easing a social situation but it was better than nothing. I had been on the point of screaming as Margaret made crumbs and looked as though she were waiting only for the tumbril to come and carry her off, while Lili gazed at me brightly as though wondering what had happened to my powers of conversation. I had always found her amusing – what Monica would have called 'stimulating company'. If she had not come unexpectedly I might have been able to cope, but as it was I could only gape.

I went to fetch more hot water for the teapot – unnecessarily since it was nearly full, but I had to do something. I stood in the kitchen and swore under my breath, determining to ask Lili what Egypt was like these days. It would surely make a more fruitful topic than the state of the crops, which was the only other thing I could think of. It didn't interest me at all, but then nothing did. As I realized this, I wondered why I wasn't bored when I was alone, and concluded with some surprise that, although by no stretch of the imagination could I call myself happy, I was content with myself and my own thoughts. I had not wondered about it before and no one had told me that this was one of the consolations of age. There weren't many.

I was extremely careful as I poured the boiling water into a jug, and careful as I walked back to the table. I had to be very cautious now of heat and height and distance. Ordinary things, all part of the world as it was made for humans, had become dangerous and threatening. Fires and steps and floors waited for me to pitch myself against them: not with malice, but with an unpleasant, alien patience. The world, it seemed, grew passively hostile as death loomed closer. I no longer felt at home in it. I had an impression that my frailty was somehow despicable, and that the forces of nature found me expendable. Looked at another way, this was undoubtedly true. The aged of other cultures have voluntarily lost themselves in forests or flung themselves off ice-floes when they have judged themselves to be of no further use. This purely utilitarian view has never struck me as totally unreasonable, even if a little harsh. Other people have paid great respect to their ancients and, considering myself, I thought it had probably been misplaced. I did not feel wise, just old. I have said before that the wisdom of age is merely an accumulation of experience. Repetitiveness is wearisome. Even Syl became impatient when I repeated myself, and I sometimes thought I could not bear to brush my hair once more. Now I hear myself saying again what I have said before, and find myself tiresome. Perhaps that is why the old mumble to themselves – out of consideration, not only for others, but for their own pride's sake. I must say, as I speak of pride, that I was never unintelligent. Intelligence is perhaps my favourite quality. There is something almost evil in real stupidity, and perhaps 'wisdom' is only a softer, larger, furrier word for the lithe, naked 'intelligence'.

I went reluctantly back to the tea table. Lili was intelligent and so, I believed, was Margaret, although she seldom gave evidence of it. Sometimes she would reveal an unsuspected wit, but then she would hastily cover it as though somebody might chide or punish her. I wished I knew what was wrong with her, what had so silenced her.

If only Lili would for God's sake say something which would keep my attention. I remembered her talking the hind leg off a donkey and how I had sometimes wished she'd shut up. That had been when I had something to say: before I'd said all I have to say again and again. She did give a brief description of the journey through Italy but she was not on her old form. Once, in these circumstances, I would have fetched a bottle of whisky to loosen her tongue, but I could myself no longer drink as I used to and I had come to realize that the only purpose of alcohol in an awkward social situation is to make the listeners less critical. The person holding the floor should ideally be stone cold sober since drink has never made anyone more amusing. It does greatly help though if the audience is half-seas over. Now in the evenings with my small glass of sherry I found the company unsurpassedly tedious as they waxed merry on their huge Martinis, as their own jokes appeared to them to be rib-splittingly funny and their insights profound.

'And how is Egypt?' I asked heavily as I sat down, remembering that it was hot, dusty, smelly and full of interesting antiquities.

Lili spoke for a while and confirmed this. I also knew it could not possibly now be as boring as she was making it sound and I was annoyed with her. She seemed guarded, careful, as though she feared committing some solecism. This was most unlike her and beyond my understanding.

'You liked it didn't you, Margaret?' I asked, growing very tired now. 'Syl said you liked the people.'

He had found this surprising, which was why he had mentioned it to me. The British soldiers had returned from the desert wars with tales of feelthy postcards and baksheesh and peculiar goings on in Port Said, but I don't think it was that which had influenced Syl and caused his perturbation. I think it was because it was unusual for the English to express a fondness for any foreigners at all, and he saw it as a sign of unexpected originality in Margaret: something he had not bargained for. I had tried to tell him once or twice that I thought her clever beneath her pet-mouse exterior, but he didn't want to hear me.

'It was very nice,' said Margaret at her most bland.

'I miss it,' said Lili. 'I miss the heat and the colour.'

'And the noise?' I inquired. 'I remember it being very noisy in the cities. Monica always complained about the traffic.'

'The cities can be noisy,' agreed Lili.

I fervently wished they'd go home.

They did go eventually, just as dusk was falling. There were plenty of sandwiches left, so I gave one to the dog and he was grateful. I seldom gave him bread or things that might make him fatter, for I had a fearful fantasy that his taut shiny skin might not be sufficiently flexible to contain him and that he would go off *bang* like a sausage in the pan. I had a similar meaningless fear that if I should fall again I would break into a million shards like a saucer. I used to wonder what Syl's reaction would be if he returned home from work to find dog spattered all over the sitting-room. I would have tried to get down on my hands and knees to sweep him up with the dustpan and brush and I would have fallen and shattered into pieces, dry, friable pieces compared with the viscous remains of pug. I was quite aware that there was an element of aggression in this distressing image. In a remote part of my mind I believed that Syl demanded too much of me, expected too much. I drew perverse satisfaction from the imagined expression on my son's face as he came upon the scene and realized that he had asked too much of me; that his well-meant gift of a dog had brought about his mother's demise, and that anyway he had forced me to live too long by his unnatural dependence; that I had survived past the time when I should make a normal corpse and had drily exploded as burned bones turn to splinters and ash. I hasten to repeat that this thought did lie in a *remote* part of my mind. I was not going insane.

I put away the tea things in their accustomed places and went to clear the crumbs from the tea table. Mrs Raffald, the charwoman I shared with Monica, would be in in the morning but I couldn't leave the crumbs and the cigarette ash until then. Some crumbs fell on the floor and I called the dog to snuffle them up. A few crumbs could do him no harm. I went back to the kitchen. The smell of Lili's cigarettes had drifted through the house reminding me, not that she had just been there, but of the last time I had seen her.

My mind had an increasing tendency to make these slightly wrong connections, as though reaching for one drawer I had pulled open another. The smell of stale tea in the sink took me back to the farmhouse where the kitchen had been like a cathedral with hanging hams and bundled herbs for icons and the smell of apples, porridge cooked overnight on the range and roasting meat for incense. My present kitchen was not small by contemporary standards but it would have fitted six times into my uncles' kitchen. We had not formed the usual picture of a farming family despite this kitchen. My aunts always took tea in the afternoon in a little sitting-room in the back of the houseplace. The kitchen quarters were known as the down-house and were more the province of the farmhands and the servants. The aunts had all smoked cigarettes when it was considered unladylike to do so, and the woman who worked in the dairy smoked a clay pipe. The shallow stone sink always smelled of tea leaves in spite of all the other uses to which it was put and – I was homesick after sixty years of absence.

I began to prepare dinner for Syl, concentrating closely on what I was doing, not because I thought it wrong to live in the past – I've already said I didn't think it wrong – but because of the dangers of the heavy pans and the hot water and the floor which could become splashed and slippery and because dog and I could trip over each other. Monica had once alarmed Syl by telling him that old people frequently suffered from food poisoning, and indeed inflicted it on others, because they had lost their sense of smell. My sense of smell was in fine fettle. I could smell Lili's scent behind the smoke, and the chrysanthemums in the sitting-room. I could smell blood on the meat as I brought it from the pantry. So could the dog. *Go away dog.*

I cut up the meat carefully, for cold steel can be dangerous in trembling hands, and looked back a few weeks to the time Monica and Margaret had come to supper. I sliced carrots and chopped onions and tried, for safety's sake, to live in the present. Syl had bought a rack to keep the vegetables in. Before I knew it I was feeling the chill of a stone-flagged floor under my feet and peering into huge stone crocks for root vegetables of a similar size to bake together over the range coals. I could no more forget the farmhouse than ignore my own outworn body.

Monica and Margaret, I reminded myself, had come to supper on the day that we normally had stew, because the butcher called the day before and I always used up the stewing meat first. Joints for roasting could hang longer but I mistrusted the keeping properties of stewing steak. How boring it was to live in the present, I thought; how banal the minutiae of everyday existence. How much more delightful to revisit the scenes where such details had ceased to matter, where I could see firelight reflected in the windows and not fear the flames, smell wood smoke and cigarette smoke, hear the laughter of someone I loved because someone else I loved had just said something funny and not remember the joke, smell onions frying and not have to worry about the washing-up. There was no danger and no inconvenience in the past. I supposed that not all of it could be held blameless since it had brought me to what I was now, but it would be as futile to repine as to regret the ocean's flow.

If I had been a more religious woman I would probably have been considering life after death, but I could only think of what had gone before. If I had any hopes for the future they were that the past should be restored to me.

I had floured the meat and put it on the stove to brown. It was beginning to catch. I stirred it with a wooden spoon I had had all my life. One of the aunts had given it to me for Christmas long ago with a pudding bowl and a checked apron. The following Christmas my needs, my tastes and desires had changed and she had given me a beaded evening bag. That I had long since lost, but I still had the bowl and spoon of the last Christmas of my childhood. I had to go to the dining-room to see if there was a half-empty bottle of claret. There were plenty of full ones but I couldn't open them; nor was I sure which were sufficiently undrinkable to be used in cooking. Syl had a friend who was a wine merchant and sold him crates at a time. Some of it was at least not poisonous, but some of it, I was convinced, was so awful that it could only be palmed off on a friend whose concern for the relationship would prevent him from pouring it over the merchant's head.

Monica and Margaret had been subjected to a bottle of this because Syl – quite sincerely – took his father's view that women had no palate and good wine was wasted on them. I had argued with him about it, pointing out that I was a woman and I would prefer to drink the gardener's bath water, but Syl wouldn't listen. It was one of the things he had made up his mind about.

It had been an unenjoyable evening. The only person who had had a good time was Syl. He had his father's taste for company, and while he did not drink as Jack had done – indeed a very little alcohol went a long way with Syl – he liked the whole business of opening bottles and pouring liquid into glasses. We had gathered in the drawing-room and he had been the only creature present who showed any animation. The dog and

I were tired as we always were in the evening; Margaret was as usual, and Monica was preoccupied. I had served supper with the minimum of fuss and formality and made no attempt to talk to Monica.

Monica had only once ever surprised me – some years ago now. One evening there had been a knock at the door. There was a summer storm going on, no rain yet but distant thunder, and lightning tearing up the night as though it were paper. It was so bright it shone through closed curtains, closed eyelids. It was late for visitors so, as Syl was in, I asked him to go and see who it was – not because I was nervous but I liked to remain on good terms with the neighbours and it was preferable for Syl to tell them that I was not in, rather than for me to appear unwelcoming.

I was in the kitchen mixing cocoa, quite a distance from the hall, but I could hear a woman talking. Oh God, it's some girl making trouble for Syl, I thought, and my skin felt odd with the apprehension you only feel for the people you love, a worse sensation than physical fear.

I went as silently as I could to the open kitchen door and listened. I could hear the woman weeping and then Syl said, 'Come and sit down, I'll get Mum.'

I was puzzled but reassured, for had it been one of his girls he would have tried to take her out of the house and soothe her down in the garden among the bushes so as not to upset me. It had happened before.

I went back to the stove to turn off the gas before the milk boiled over and waited for Syl to come and get me.

He said, 'It's Monica, Mum. I don't know what's wrong with her. Come and see, will you?'

I poured the milk into two mugs so that I could put the pan into cold water before it congealed, and I went to the sitting-room. She was sitting down but she got up as soon as she saw me.

I said, 'What on earth is it, Monica?' for she looked terrible.

She didn't even look like Monica. She was in her night-dress and resembled an elemental female creature from one of the more dispiriting myths – a harpy, a fury, a witch, somebody given to consuming the flesh of men. Her hair stood up all over the place, her face was wet with tears, scarlet and twisted with what I recognized as rage, and she was flexing her hands as though she was rending a living creature apart.

I said very sharply, 'Stop it, Monica. You look as though you're plucking a chicken.'

She laughed and I saw I had struck a wrong note, for these were days when women knew how to have hysterics. They had watched an older generation doing it and still found it a useful means of expression. The frustration of being forced into a role and told to keep quiet had caused many eruptions of shrieking hysteria in women when I was a girl. I had never needed recourse to it myself since I had refused the roles I was expected to assume and had always spoken my mind. Monica was normally so perfect an example of the English lady that this frenzy now seemed almost inevitable to me. I hoped I would not have to slap her face or dash cold water into it – two more clichés of the hysterical matrix.

I said again, 'What is it, Monica? Tell me at once and please sit down.'

When I had left college several people had suggested I should take up teaching, merely I think because I could so easily appear formidable. Even when I was a girl and not at all leading the sort of private life considered suitable to teachers I could put the fear of God into those around me by using a certain tone of voice. It was just another personal characteristic, of no more real significance than the shape of my nose, but it had often stood me in good stead

Monica seemed to grow quieter and sat further into the chair instead of perching on the edge of it, poised to fly and sink her teeth into someone.

She said, 'Derek's leaving me.'

Her face contorted again as she made this announcement and I said, 'Syl, go and get the cocoa and give Monica a glass of brandy.'

He went gladly, never having enjoyed scenes.

I now noticed that some of the redness of her face was due to a slap. I could see fingermarks. Clearly somebody else had been forced to apply the remedy for hysteria.

I said, startled, 'Did he hit you?'

Monica laughed again. 'I tried to kill him,' she said simply. 'He had to defend himself.'

This was by far the most interesting thing I had ever heard Monica say. I had never before seen so much as a crease in her conformity and this remarkable revelation put her in a different light.

'Where's Margaret?' I asked. I imagined that anxiety for her child would be uppermost in her mind after this scene of family violence, but it didn't seem to be.

'She's in bed,' she said.

'And where's Derek?' I inquired.

Monica was growing weary. 'He went out,' she said. 'I don't know where he went.'

I got up and called to Syl. 'Come and stay with Monica. I won't be a minute.'

He came reluctantly, bearing the cocoa, and poured out two glasses of brandy. As I went out I heard him beginning to talk about a committee meeting of the tennis club. It was probably the best way.

I went along the footpath that bordered the golf course and pushed through the gap in the hedge in Monica's garden. There was a light in the kitchen window and the back door was unlocked.

I called softly, 'Derek', in case he had come back, but there was no answer.

The house felt empty. The hall light was on too, illumining the way up the stairs.

I went very quietly to the nursery and opened the door. A night light glimmered on the chest of drawers and the child stood by the window looking out at the lightning over the rose-garden.

I was not what is known as 'good with children'. I had been well over forty when Syl was born. I couldn't remember how I had behaved towards him when he was very young and I couldn't remember ever dealing with other children. I had left all that to a succession of nannies.

I couldn't now remember how nannies behaved towards their charges; certainly no form of words came to me. Formality had been invented to ease those situations in which human beings find they have little in common and less to say to each other, so I said 'How are you, Margaret?' in a tone of great politeness.

She answered in her clear little voice, 'I'm very well, thank you.'

She showed no surprise at seeing me in her room, and no sign of fear. I wondered if she might be in shock and tentatively touched her hand. It was cold, but then so was the room; the window open top and bottom, the curtains drifting at their moorings in the night wind. I was silent and so was she. How could I ask whether she had overheard her mother trying to kill her father and whether she had minded very greatly?

She turned her head slightly to look at me but, it seemed, not in appeal – more as a well-bred adult might gaze at a stranger who had stayed too long and seemed to have no further purpose in remaining.

I said, 'Why don't you jump back into bed, Margaret?'

She obeyed at once and lay on her back, quite still. She was very small, her body scarcely perceptible under the bedclothes and I thought that in the circumstances I should take her in my arms and reassure her, but it would have appeared presumptuous. She was so self-possessed and undemanding.

I said, 'I'm going downstairs to wait for Mummy. I won't go away.' I wanted to tell her some comforting lie – 'Mummy came round to borrow a cup of sugar but we couldn't find any so she's still looking', or 'Mummy and I got bored with our own houses so we decided to change places for the evening'. There was no suitable lie, no explanation, and the truth seemed wholly inappropriate for that quiet child.

There was a book lying on the table beside her bed and I picked it up. It was full of brightly coloured pictures of birds and I turned over the pages. 'Oh, look at the robin, Margaret,' I said, feeling an awful fool. 'And here's a duck with its babies.'

To my surprise she sat up a little and leaned over to look at this tiresome duck.

Encouraged, I flicked through the illustrations of tits, starlings, wagtails until I came to a picture of a kingfisher, and suddenly faced with that vivid, unearthly green-blue I was back in the country by a deep tree-shaded river pool and there was a kingfisher lying, startling in death, on the shoaly brink; one small, flat space just large enough to contain it. I spoke without thinking, or spoke my thoughts aloud: 'I found a dead kingfisher once.'

She stared at me unblinkingly and said, 'It couldn't fly.'

'No,' I agreed, feeling more than foolish now.

She had leaned further over to look more closely at the picture and then settled back on her pillows.

As I went downstairs feeling remarkably useless, I realized that she must have heard something or she wouldn't be lying awake. It was too late now to do anything about it. Whatever damage there was had already been done to her.

After a while, as neither Monica nor Derek returned, I telephoned Syl to ask what was going on. He spoke softly but without whispering, so I gathered that Monica had not left the house but Syl had closed the sitting-room door before answering the phone.

'She's sunk half the decanter of brandy,' he said.

'Has she told you what happened?' I asked.

Syl hesitated. 'She's told me some of it but I think there's more. She keeps opening her mouth and staring at me in a maddish kind of way, then closing it again ...'

I interrupted him. 'Did she tell you she tried to murder Derek?'

'Well, she didn't quite put it like that ...' said Syl.

I interrupted him again. 'Do you think she did?' I asked, suddenly wondering if a corpse was lying somewhere in this silent house.

'Oh come on, Mum,' said Syl. 'Monica's just upset ...'

'How do you know?' I demanded, thinking of Monica's usual ladylike demeanour and the stories I had read of mild-mannered little men who the neighbours insisted wouldn't have hurt a fly and under whose cellar floors were found grisly things.

'I think what's really annoying her,' said Syl, now lowering his voice further, 'is that Derek's taken up with some teenaged typist.'

'Did he tell her?' I asked, reflecting that it was often this type of admission that led to murder.

'I think it was his parting shot,' said Syl. 'They were arguing about something or other and then he mentioned this girl – hang on ... Monica, I'm just talking to Mum ...'

'Hallo,' said Monica's voice still sounding high and strange as she took the phone. 'Has he come back?'

'No ...' I said, intending to tell her that Margaret was all right.

But she wasn't listening. She said, 'Can I stay here? I don't want to see him.'

'Well, of course ...' I said, but she'd hung up.

I sat all night wrapped in a rug I found in the cloakroom. I'd locked the doors and I must admit I took a cursory survey of the ground floor to ascertain that Derek's lifeless body was not indeed littering up some corner. Then I stayed awake reading one of Monica's novels in case Margaret should cry out. I thought it strange that Monica had not mentioned the child. She was usually an oppressively careful mother.

That one display of emotion had been as shocking and strange as if she'd suddenly taken all her clothes off. She had kept out of my way for months afterwards and I hadn't sought her out. Derek had returned, for I saw him several times and found it difficult to think of much to say to him. Eventually he left for good. I had no idea how the divorce went through, but Monica and the child stayed in the house and gradually we began to see her again – at the tennis club and in neighbours' houses. She never mentioned that naked night, and I certainly did not. There is fortunately a mechanism in us which works like the gate of a lock, interrupting and blocking the flow of memory, of immediate awareness. Once the gates are closed, although we know the water is there and it is still the same, we can disregard it, think of it as past and, often, forget it. This, I suppose, is what Monica did: put out of her mind the bad things drifting and floating behind the gates, and drove resolutely onwards, refusing even to acknowledge their existence.

Syl was late getting home. I heard him whistling in the hall and called out to him.

'Not in bed yet?' he said.

'No,' I said. When you have lived with someone for a long time, no matter who he is, this seems to be the sort of conversation you make. I asked if he had had a pleasant day and he said he had. Then, since it was his turn, he asked if I had had a pleasant tea with Margaret and Lili.

'Very nice,' I said. 'There's some cake in the pantry. Or do you want some soup?'

'I've eaten,' said Syl. 'Went to the pub in the city.'

'Who with?' I asked.

'Just a bloke,' said Syl. He looked at me sideways and grinned.

'Bloke?' I said. 'What was he like?' Syl seldom whistled when he came home from dining with a bloke.

'He was a nice little blonde from the office,' said Syl.

'You're nearly a married man,' I said. 'It's time you settled down.'

'I'm going to, Mum,' said Syl. 'Honestly.'

I believed him: perhaps not because I trusted his intentions but because he sometimes looked so tired. I could see that settling down would come as a relief. Married men did not have to prove themselves capable of attracting women – not, that is, until they grew rather older than Syl and in need of a further dose of reassurance. That had been Jack's trouble. When he was really quite old he had begun to strut in the presence of women. He had always fancied himself as a bit of a lad, as they say, but he grew silly, especially when there were younger men present. He could not resist the temptation of cutting out younger men, even if it was only by hogging the conversation. He was entirely predictable, and after a while I didn't go out with him if I could help it. It was boring. Besides I had enough residual fondness for him not to enjoy watching him make an idiot of himself. I could not, naturally, remonstrate with him because that would have been construed as jealousy and have led to long passages of misunderstanding. I don't suppose there's a man in the world who would believe you had only his interests at heart if you asked him not to flirt with other women. I had sometimes wished he would take a mistress, particularly after he retired and was at home more. Luckily the golf course was just behind the house and he spent a lot of time there, but it wasn't the same as when he had to spend weeks away and I knew I had the place to myself – and Syl of course.

I have often noticed that when a man takes a mistress it greatly improves his demeanour in the marital home. Whether this is because of guilt or satisfied desire I do not know, but I have always remarked it. It is important for the wife that the mistress should be a serious, responsible sort of person, and luckily they frequently are. Men tire quite soon of the dizzy gold-digger of legend, and a surprising number of 'other women' are more homely and steady than many wives. These excellent creatures help to ease the pressure put on a couple by the exigencies of married life; they uphold the man's self-esteem so that he does not need to wear himself out demonstrating his virility, and they enable the wife – if she is capable and prepared to do so – to uncover an identity of her own, to escape, to some degree at least, the stifling confines of wifehood. Jack unfortunately had not enough self-confidence to take a permanent mistress but contented himself with ogling girls. I was painfully ashamed of (and for) him, but I could think of no formula by which I could make him understand his error. I think he believed that if his liaisons were brief, shallow and impersonal no harm could come of them. He was unaware that his loss of dignity which should have, and did not, trouble him caused me sleepless nights. I could have borne the compassion (not infrequently mixed with respect) which is accorded to the wife whose husband has another ménage, but not the pity, the mirth, to which a husband's ceaseless, pointless, trivial dalliance exposes a wife. How does one explain such things to a man?

Perhaps now I can bring myself to speak of Lili and why I had hoped never to have to see her again. She must have been in her early twenties when it happened, when Jack was nearly fifty. He was at the height of his flirtatious career and a trial to me. Whenever we were invited out together I would make some excuse and stay at home reading, so that already people found me distant, cold and unfriendly. In a way that has been a blessing. Having established quite early that I was not a gregarious woman I have been largely left alone. I never could abide drunken conviviality, and when my ennui was compounded by the awareness that I had chosen to marry a foolish and insecure man I vowed never more to go out in society. Jack would say – his body freshly bathed and powdered and his face pink from shaving – 'Come on, darling. Come too. You'll enjoy it. You know you like the so-and-sos.' And I would say, 'No, my dear. You go alone. I am determined to finish *Swann's Way* by the end of the month.' The mention of Proust always alarmed him. He would say, 'Well, if you're sure . . . ' and off he would go, tremulous and excited as a child. (He was very like Syl. My poor Syl . . .)

But I was speaking of Lili: my mind wanders. It must have been a few days after the picnic in the garden. Monica and Derek had just returned from Egypt and Monica was giving a cocktail party as a farewell gesture to Lili and Robert who were about to go back again, and I had pleaded a headache. 'Too much sun,' I think I said: I would have an early night and perhaps come round in the morning to help her clear up and also finish the unpacking. I was about to go to bed when the telephone rang. Monica was in a housewifely state because she couldn't find the crate with the extra glasses. Would I lend her some? She'd send a couple of people round to collect them.

I said she wasn't to bother. If she sent Derek he would feel obliged to insist that I return with him to the party. It wouldn't be seemly to borrow my wine glasses and then leave me in peace. It wouldn't be correct. I said I would put some in a cardboard box and bring them round.

I set off along the path by the golf course, walking very carefully because the glasses were loosely assembled and the bottom of the box was likely to drop open. When I reached the summerhouse I rested the box on the narrow window-ledge in order to readjust my grip. Then, unthinkingly, I looked through the window. My body darkening the window must have given them warning of my presence, for Jack was already staring out at me, his face stiff with dismay, a parody: 'We are discovered.

All is undone . . . ' Lili didn't look at me. I think she was too busy smoothing down her dress. I went on to the house, cold with rage. Not because Jack had been unfaithful to me again, but because Lili knew I knew, and would be harbouring feelings that I should find unacceptable: possibly guilt, but I already knew her well enough to doubt that: pity for me – perhaps compunction – since she was not really a heartless girl. I thought she would not be feeling triumphant, for she was too clever to misunderstand my attitude to Jack.

I had banged down the glasses in the kitchen and realized that what was so infuriating was that she probably knew exactly what I was thinking: knew I didn't love him, knew I didn't care what he did, knew I cared a good deal that I was married to a fool, knew that I knew she knew what she did know. She might even know that somewhere in me was pity for Jack: the coiled contemptuous pity for somebody who, thinking that he is exhibiting his manhood, has merely been caught with his trousers down. I suffered an insupportable, vicarious sense of degradation. When my mother had run away with another man and left me and my father, I had felt bitter hurt but not this extended humiliation. A woman can never seem as ridiculous as a man, since whatever pride she may have is more broadly based and therefore less vulnerable. Her transgressions may arouse great passion, even scorn, but seldom that profound, half-hysterical contempt. Lili had lost no dignity since she had never laid claim to it.

Someone said, 'You must have a drink now you're here.' But as I had come in the guise of a messenger, a porter, and not really as a guest, his words were not pressing and I was allowed to leave.

Soon after, Lili left the country and I thought never to see her again. My sudden appearance had caused Jack such fright and shock that he became what he considered to be a model husband – that is, he hardly went anywhere at all unless I could be prevailed upon to go with him and he frequently stayed in of an evening. He said he didn't know what had come over him and it would never happen again. I could think of nothing to say, but I used to wish that I could get my hands on Lili. I forgot about her, but I never forgave her.

Shortly afterwards Jack died. Sometimes I wished that he could have died before his pride was lost, and sometimes I didn't care. I haven't really cared about anything since – except Syl.

In one way I was relieved that Syl had not married until now. My family had been Catholic since Adam was a lad. They had lived in a remote corner of the North and the upheavals of the 'reformation' had not troubled them. None of us had been called to martyrdom and we all took the Faith for granted, like air and bread. When my mother left my father all those years ago, the gentry and the yeomanry for miles around had been delightfully scandalized, for adultery and divorce were social sins and rare in those parts. But my uncles and aunts, her kin, without talking, or even thinking, about it, feared for her immortal soul. They were ashamed in the social sense and angry with her for so shaming them, but those emotions are bearable. It is the knowledge that somebody you love – one of you – might, by sin, separate herself from you for eternity that is a source of anguish. Embarrassment and wrath kept my family away from the neighbours for a time, but it was not those feelings which would make one of my uncles fall silent, another give a sudden exclamation and bite his lip. It was not because my mother had put her sisters into the awkward position of having to hold their heads high before the curious regard of the neighbours, when what they wanted was to clap their hands over their ears, close their eyes and pretend they were insensate that made one of my aunts weep silently in church and another take to saying Decades of the Rosary at peculiar moments. It was the fear that one of them was lost.

Perhaps it was the fear that marriage presented a choice between temporal misery or eternal hell that kept me single for so long. I had plenty of offers and fell in love a few times, but I felt no inclination to tie myself up. When I really did fall in love I expected and asked too much. I should have known better. I had seen enough of my friends making similar mistakes and given them excellent advice on strategy, on anodyne devices and curative measures. I remembered none of them. When the only man I ever loved finally left me, I married Jack. I had forgotten my dread of marriage when I found a man I couldn't bear to lose, and when I lost him I found I had lost everything – even that lifelong dread. I was nearly forty by then and so had less life to throw away. I liked Jack, and he loved me. He was a little younger than I was but I didn't exploit this. I had learned not to appear too dominating and I left all the major decisions to him. He didn't do badly, and I was fairly content. It wasn't the life I would have chosen but it was comfortable and it had its compensations. We spent most of the time abroad even after Syl was born until we moved here.

Where was I? I was saying that, in the main, I was quite glad that Syl hadn't married until now. He would have, as I had had, less time to rue the day. I wished now that I had brought him up differently and not left him so much in the care of the nannies and schools. He had too fixed a view of what constituted masculinity. He was afraid of showing weakness, and felt called upon to flirt with every female who crossed his path, regardless of whether or not she appreciated his attention. Whether or not he was consciously emulating his father, it was a great pity. I could see that some people found it hard to take him seriously. Jack had always strenuously maintained that there were some things men did and some things for women to do. I was perfectly competent in practical matters, but Jack – who was less competent than I – took all such things upon himself and my skills atrophied. I don't know now that I would remember how to put a washer on a tap. Not that it matters any more. It just seems unfortunate that the sexes should limit each other in this rigid fashion. I had always found satisfaction in being self-sufficient. The idea that two separate beings should restrict themselves to certain roles in order to form one whole seemed to me to be structurally unsound. There was a makeshift ring to it. When the string breaks, as it so frequently does, the wear and tear of the operation will have damaged even further the two parts of the unnatural whole. I had discussed this question with priests I had known, and various religious, and been soundly reprimanded for my thoughts, which they considered, to say the least, unorthodox. I had been bred to respect the priesthood and so never said precisely what I felt – that it was all very fine and large for them, speaking from their superior position of celibacy: it was we, poor foot-soldiers, who had to slog through the mire of matrimony. Despite our staunch adherence to the Faith our family had not been much blessed with vocations. I was not a good Catholic, but I could not have married somebody who wasn't one at all, and I would have been greatly perturbed if Syl had done so. Margaret, in that respect, came as a relief to me.

Margaret? No, I couldn't really understand her. I have said she was like me and, having said it, cannot remember the reason. Undemanding, unobtrusive: I am that now but I wasn't when I was Margaret's age. Those of us with any health in us at all change as we grow and I wondered how Margaret would change, or whether she would stay as she was and simply, in the course of time, wither. Either way, as I considered it, it did not augur well for Syl's peace of mind or his contentment. Then I told myself I was guilty of that male fault of over-analysis, of pointless prognostication, and turned, as it were, to look on the bright side again. The old are too prone to misgivings. It was true that Syl was over-protective towards her, over-indulgent, and sometimes over-attentive – although not always. Once he took her away for the weekend to stay with a man he'd been at school with. The man had an adopted son, who was about Margaret's age and very full of himself. I told Syl I did not think this weekend a good idea and he stared at me in wonder and asked why. I said feebly that if past form was anything to go by he and his friend would spend the time together engaged in manly pursuits and Margaret would be bored. What I really feared was that youth, as they say, would call to youth, and Margaret would come to her senses in the presence of the lad who was, as I remembered, a lively, attractive boy despite his conceit. 'She'll have the kid to talk to,' Syl had said. 'He's going through an anti-blood-sports phase, and sits around indoors all day.' I couldn't think of anything to say. How do you explain to a man that you fear a younger man will cut him out by being lazy and gentle in what could be construed as a feminine fashion, while he himself is ploughing across the countryside proving his masculinity? There is no meeting-ground here. I have never met a man who could see that wit and a kind of reticence – which could almost be called cowardice – make up a combination which, in some men, and perhaps in some women too, is virtually irresistible. Physical prowess has in it an element of boastfulness – 'Watch me' – which inevitably, albeit unjustly, gives its owner a certain appearance of boneheadedness. The sly smile of the aesthete has got more people into bed than the triumphant grin of the long-distance runner. I know. I wondered hopelessly why, after all this time, men didn't know that as well. I see that I have said I feared that Margaret might 'come to her senses', and have exposed my reservations. Another girl of her age might not have been too unsuitable for Syl, but she was.

I put these unpleasant thoughts aside, as is the way of human kind. Increasing age does not increase one's acceptance of anything, not even death.

'Did you have a good time?' I had asked Syl when I saw him at breakfast on the Monday morning.

'Splendid,' said Syl. 'I put a brace of pheasants in the larder.'

'Did Margaret enjoy herself?' I asked.

Syl was eating a boiled egg and looked for a second as though he'd forgotten who she was. 'Oh yes,' he said, through a mouthful of toast, 'she had a splendid time.'

I sipped lukewarm tea while I waited for him to go to work. He'd promised to pluck the pheasants so I hung them even further out of the reach of the dog who had sneaked into the larder and was looking up at them like a poet at the stars. How ridiculous that I should remember that so well.

Lili had left a cigarette packet on the window-seat. I found it in the morning as I sat drinking tea and watching the birds. There were two cigarettes in it and on a whim I went and got a match from the kitchen, came back, sat down and lit one.

It was years since I'd given up smoking. I had stopped when I was expecting my first child – not for reasons of health or morality, but because it made me sick. The child, a girl, had died in infancy and when they told me she was dead I had said, 'Give me a cigarette.'

Infancy: the word is like a little diaphanous shroud to cover up the unbearable. She had been five days old. They came to me and they said, 'Mrs Carter ...' (I had assumed the name. This was before I had married Jack. The child was illegitimate.) They said: 'The child was too small to live. She never really had a chance ...' I drew on my cigarette and said: 'Surely she was a little young to die.' The doctor held my shoulder briefly, and then left without saying anything. The nurse fussed about for a while doing what nurses do, not saying anything either. I think she was humming a little tune under her breath. They were both afraid of me, but they need not have been. I lay and looked at the ceiling and smoked and promised myself that nothing should ever hurt like this again. I didn't cry or rant or do anything much except arrange for the baby to be properly buried in her own baby grave. There were just the priest and me there on a watery spring morning, and all I can remember feeling was disbelief and a desperate yearning for it to end, so that I could smoke. It was soon over. I sat on a gravestone and smoked and smoked, my hand shielding the cigarette until it was possible no longer with the rain pouring down my face.

Then when I was pregnant with Syl I had stopped smoking again. I dreaded the birth of this child. I had not before felt such grief, such pity for the as yet unborn. It was like the grief one feels for the dead. It was worse, for even if there is no God and no abode to share with him, at least the dead are past all pain, while those who are yet to be born must learn to live with us: with our frailty and our cruelty. They must learn in time, in order to survive, to be like us. When Syl was very young I was afraid – more of, than for, him – terrified of the beloved's capacity for pain; and as he grew older I indulged him, trying to protect him from his human heritage. A mistake.

Memories are like possessions: furniture, ornaments. Some are always in the room of your mind, some decayed, some lost; and some are there on the walls – of no further profit or use and never to be shared or revealed. Only you yourself are aware that the small hidden image gleaming barely perceptibly through the dust represents the hinge and focus of your life. You tell yourself it doesn't matter and God alone knows what you think you mean.

I don't know why I said all that. I have never spoken of it to anyone. It was the taste of cigarette smoke that brought it back – more potent than any little biscuit, than any egg sandwich. I never did finish the whole of Proust. There wasn't any point after Jack died. Once I was alone I had no need of feints and ruses and avenues of escape since I could be solitary in truth and fact, not just in metaphor. Poor Jack. He was, while a stupider, also a better person than me, in the sense that he was more truly human. I had a capacity for, and knowledge of, evil, while Jack's misdemeanours seemed somehow on a par with the failings of the dog. Having said that, I do not think I could construct a worse insult if I tried from now until the end of time, and I am glad that Jack is dead and beyond harm for I might once have been angry enough to tell him so. Presumably the offensiveness lies in the nature of evil, and now I am confused. It does not seem to me that I think less clearly than I did, but I get tired more easily and I lose the thread. I was thinking of humanity as a combination of beast and angel. It is the beasts who are sinless and it was the brightest angel in Heaven who turned his face from the light. It is the angel in us who is capable of sin; the poor beast merely seeks gratification. I feel I should apologize to Jack, and then I feel – what the hell, this is nothing but the truth. Except, of course, that it isn't and humanity is yet another order of being, more complex than we can ever know.

I finished the cigarette just as Mrs Raffald arrived. She looked at me with exaggerated surprise, and I stubbed it out in a saucer.

'You look as if you'd been doing that all your life,' she said.

'It isn't difficult,' I told her.

'*You're* not a smoker,' she said, unbuttoning her coat and taking her hat off.

'I used to be,' I said. 'I used to smoke as much as Lili.'

Mrs Raffald paused on her way to the broom-cupboard. '*She* smokes too much,' she remarked. 'You can smell her coming a mile off.'

Mrs Raffald and I enjoyed a cordial, even close, relationship. We understood each other.

'My aunts all smoked until they died in old age,' I said, remembering them. Elegant in age, smoke furling in the lamplight, they had talked and talked in the swift, clipped tones of their generation that would seem artificial now. It was strange to think of those days and their difference. There had been more noise, more bustle: even, it seemed, more light. But that was because there had been fewer lights – no electricity in the farm, gas-lighting in the streets – and so the light had had more significance, had shone more brightly. The street lamps in the road now cast a bland glow half prudish, half prurient. They said, 'Nothing unseemly can go on under our regard, and if it does we will be watching.' I remembered a time when I had walked home to the farm from the village because I had somehow missed the uncle sent to collect me. I had been to a music lesson and I hummed 'Farewell Manchester' until I reached the edge of the houses. It was pitch black beyond. I felt my way along the hedgerow, knowing that I must not stop and turn, for if I did I should have no idea which direction I was headed in. When I came to the moor I half walked, half crawled until I saw the lights of the farmhouse. It was both frightening and not frightening. There had been no marauders or footpads in the district since the previous century, but as I edged through that utter darkness I felt I would welcome the company of any other living thing – a wild animal, a murderer. Only when I saw the lights of home did normal apprehension return and the hairs on my neck rise as I heard a rustle in the marsh grass, breathing behind a low stone wall. When home is within reach, sheep become tigers and the swooping owl the assassin. I think it is hope which makes us cowards.

'Well, don't take it up again,' advised Mrs Raffald, returning equipped with broom and dustpan and brush. 'Not at your age.'

'No,' I said absently, for I was wondering why in total darkness there is nothing to fear but darkness. Then I thought about what she had said. 'If you think about it,' I observed, 'this is the only sensible age to do anything dangerous.'

'Oh you,' said Mrs Raffald. 'Philosopher, you are. You should see what's going on down at The Oaks. Three-ring circus down there. Telephone calls, and wedding dresses, and Lili leaving her stuff all over the place.'

I found it interesting but not surprising that Mrs Raffald should refer to Lili by her Christian name. She would not in a million years have done the same by Monica. 'Weddings are always a nuisance,' I said.

'I prefer a funeral,' said Mrs Raffald. 'Unless it's somebody close,' she added. 'The food's generally better.'

'I suppose that's true,' I said, 'and they don't hand you fizzy drinks. Champagne gives me indigestion these days, and I hate those little nibbles that fill you up but don't stop you feeling hungry.'

'Yes,' said Mrs Raffald with the brevity of the connoisseur. Her own family and friends were always getting married, being christened or dying, and she was also frequently called upon to help when my neighbours found themselves in the midst of these traumatic events.

'Is the dress finished yet?' I asked. Monica had been extremely boring about the dress.

'Dunno,' said Mrs Raffald, sweeping the ashes from the grate. 'Margaret moons about all day like a dying duck in a thunderstorm. S'pose she must be in love.'

She said this with such an airy lack of conviction that I was taken aback. I had somehow assumed that Margaret must be in love with Syl, and thought no more about it. Plenty of women had been. Why not Margaret? But now I remembered other things I had once taken for granted: the illness of one of my uncles which had killed him before we could, any of us, accept even that he was ailing. Nothing could have saved him, but we should have been better prepared.

'Have you seen her in it?' I asked.

'In what?' said Mrs Raffald, dusting the iron bars.

'The dress,' I said patiently, perhaps thinking that if I could hear how she wore her wedding dress I would know how she felt about her wedding.

'No,' said Mrs Raffald. 'Her mum just goes on about it all the time. Dress this, dress that. Too long, too short. Don't know why she doesn't just chuck it out and get a new one.'

'She wore it at her own wedding,' I reminded Mrs Raffald. 'Didn't she tell you?'

'Oh yes,' said Mrs Raffald. 'She told me all right. You'd think she'd want to forget about it, being divorced all this time – not make the poor kid wear it.'

I reflected that Monica would die on the spot if she could hear us: the mother of the groom discussing the bride's family with the charwoman.

'Monica doesn't think a great deal,' I said, out of an obscure sense of vengefulness. I had too often been bored or irritated by her.

'Oh, she's all right really,' said Mrs Raffald generously. 'She just got a bit spoilt having all those servants out East. There's quite a few like that round here.'

It was true. There were, and Monica was far from the worst amongst them. Mrs Trevelyan from The Cedars, for instance, was a poisonous bitch with an entirely tenuous grasp of current reality. No, Monica was not too bad.

'The Colonial experience,' I said aloud, 'had a bad effect on the English underbred.'

Mrs Raffald agreed. She said she didn't know how the poor natives had taken it, but when people like Mrs Trevelyan came back and tried it on with her she soon let them know where they got off.

When she'd finished sweeping the drawing-room I made us both a cup of coffee and I thought about the woman who had worked in my uncles' dairy and had smoked a pipe. She was called Marge, and she called all of us, even the eldest uncle, by our Christian names. I had had maids since then, and native servants when Jack did a stint in Egypt, and they had all made me uneasy. Northern blood does not adapt easily to an atmosphere of voluptuousness, of servility and craft – and all these things are present, in no matter how small a degree, in the type of master–servant relationship which Mrs Raffald and I were presently engaged in denigrating.

'Lili's all right,' said Mrs Raffald as she drank her coffee. 'She shows off a bit, but not so's anyone would mind.'

I couldn't dispute this. I was no longer angry with Lili. Jack was dead.

I sometimes found it strange to realize how little effect the vast cataclysms of existence have on those of us who are not too directly inconvenienced by them. The war for instance. Jack had been too old for active service and was given a job in one of the Ministries, which kept him employed and out of the way and allowed him the additional excitement of fire-watching from the roof when the bombing was at its height; while Syl was unfit. It transpired at his medical examination that his heart was weakened, probably by an undiagnosed attack of rheumatic fever when he was a child. That was possibly the worst fright I had throughout the war. Extraordinarily enough, I knew no one who had lost either a husband or a son and what I remember chiefly about those years is discomfort rather than fear or horror. We had the air-raid shelter dug in the garden, but when I was alone I never bothered to use it. Jack was away most nights – possibly fire-watching, probably not – and when the siren went I would settle in the blacked-out dining-room on a temporary divan bed with a book and a bottle and a supply of candles in case the electricity failed. I had an irrational feeling that I would prefer to sleep downstairs and let the house fall in on me than sleep in the bedroom and come down with the house. Syl was away most of the time working out ciphers and codes, I believe, at some secret place in the country. He never spoke about it. He was out of the front line and I hardly worried. I joined the WVS and I knitted socks for sailors, and I conceived the same hatred as the rest of my countrymen for the sign of the somersaulting child, the swastika. I dealt not at all with the black market, and very little 'under the counter', and I never breached the black-out rules or wasted a single crust of bread. When the war was over we filled in the air raid shelter and built the rockery over it, and as the years went by the only time I thought about the war was when I realized that butter and cream were unrationed and I could swim in them if I liked. I am ashamed of this remoteness: not because, like some idiotic folk I have met, I feel guilty because I did not suffer, but because it seems that only suffering can impress events on our minds and consciousness and this makes us seem paltry.

Lili showed very little bitterness when she spoke of how her family's wealth had been taken away, and I admired her for this. I didn't lose this feeling of admiration even when I understood that, by various shifts and devices, much of her family had contrived to retain much of its riches. Things were not and never would be the same. She had an insouciance which I do not think I should have been capable of in her circumstances. There had been bred in my bones a respect, almost a love, for property which would have made it impossible for me to accept with so little complaint the appropriation of land which belonged to me. By property I mean only land. Other possessions left me cold. If, when I was a girl, the farmhouse had been forcibly taken from us I would have fought and killed to keep it. Now it no longer mattered. The course of life had separated me from my land and it was no longer mine. In truth it never had been. I had never held the deeds to it, after all, but it had belonged to me because I belonged to it. I had felt, like a peasant, that I needed it for sustenance and for identity; but I had drifted away, and now I was nobody but old Mrs Monro, living nowhere but in a meaningless house surrounded by spotted laurels. I told myself that it was probably intensely good for my soul: as was the reluctant esteem which I felt for Lili's seemingly spontaneous renunciation of what had been hers.

*

I still liked to do my own shopping. Most of the tradesmen called at the house, but sometimes I would find an excuse to go to the shops. I needed some exercise and I detested walking in Croydon unless I had an aim in view. I walked slowly, masochistically reminding myself of the times when I had run over the moors and down the lanes. *So long ago.* All I knew of history seemed fresher and more immediate than my own youth. Ann Bullen, poor girl, and Mary Queen of Scots, and Margaret of York who was pressed to death under slabstones for refusing to renege on her faith – I could visualize them, soft-skinned and damp with fear as death faced them – but my own youthful self had disappeared into the past, not come with me to my present state. It was as though, at some point, I had been reinvented – an old woman to take the place of the young one. Did I envy those dead girls? Or had Margaret of York come into my head to remind me of *my* Margaret, and why did I think of her as mine when I did not, to be frank, really much care for her? And why was I walking to the butcher when my hips ached? Silly old woman.

I wished I had brought dog for company. But dog, after a very short while, would have had to be carried, and there were difficulties implicit in carrying both dog and a parcel of meat. I was very sad that day. No gleam showed through the fabric that separates us from eternity, and I felt mortal, carnal and disposed to decay. Perhaps it was merely because I was going to the butcher. He was brisk as ever behind his counter, wielding his cleaver, smiting through the bones and joints of dead animals and addressing his customers with his usual *bonhomie*. Butchers are more aggressively cheerful than any other tradesmen, and I wondered why. I had come across melancholy bakers, grim-faced and truculent grocers, and all female shop assistants seemed reluctant to be in that position, aggrieved and resentful at the necessity of having to serve the public, but butchers always appeared pleased with life, positive and willing in their attitude. I wished I knew some undertakers to see if proximity to death had the same effect on them – not, of course, when they were actively engaged in their trade, but when they were at home with their families or out with the boys.

I was relieved to meet Mrs Raffald outside the newsagents as I walked home with a pound of stewing steak and a sheep's heart for dog.

'What are you doing here?' she asked, with a kind of fond disapproval.

'Shopping,' I said humbly, pleased to have my thoughts interrupted.

'You should've asked *me*,' she said. 'If you'd wanted something I'd've got it for you.'

'I felt like a walk,' I said. 'I get stiff sitting at home all day.'

'You just missed Lili,' she said. 'The butcher says "Who's that tart staying up with them at The Oaks?"' She smiled.

'She does give that impression – ' I began and stopped, for surely nothing demanded that I should dissemble to Mrs Raffald: not female nor class solidarity.

'She *is* a tart,' I agreed and ended lazily, 'but she's got a heart of gold.' Mrs Raffald would not scorn my clichés. She understood Lili, I was sure, as well as I did and no refinement of expression, no careful character analysis were needed from me in order to shelter Lili's worth in the eyes of my charwoman.

Mrs Raffald justified my assessment. 'I like her too,' she said.

She walked with me to the end of the street and I felt better. I forgot about undertakers, which was fortunate, for at my age it does not raise the spirits to dwell too closely on their *raison d'être*.

One Saturday I went for another walk. Not to the shops this time. I went along the path by the bottom of the gardens, taking dog as a treat. He waddled among the dead leaves looking, I suppose, for dead things to devour. I was thinking about something I had once said to a man who loved me, that we had grown too close and must be sundered, and wondering why I had said it. In truth I was again thinking about Margaret, for I sensed in her a revulsion from intimacy. I felt tired and I walked slowly.

As I came to the garden of The Oaks I caught a glimpse of Syl and Margaret standing very close together and I thought that I must have been mistaken about her. She must have loved Syl to permit him to stand so close to her. I walked on, feeling, not reassured, but confused.

As I turned to walk home again I saw Syl in front of me. Dog put on a spurt to catch up with him, wheezing awfully, his little legs seeming inadequate to his ambitions.

'Dog,' I called, 'wait for me.'

Syl stopped and looked round. He smiled when he saw me and I took his arm.

'Where's Margaret?' I asked.

'She went in,' said Syl. 'She was cold.'

He sounded perfectly relaxed and confident but I thought it odd: strange that a girl in love, with nothing to do that day, should go in because she was cold.

'Why didn't she get a coat?' I asked.

Syl laughed. 'Because there was no point. I couldn't stay. I've got a game this afternoon.'

Dog had disappeared. 'Where's dog?' I said. 'Dog, dog . . . ' I raised my voice. He emerged suddenly from a shallow ditch, a dead leaf over one ear. 'Come here you little beast.' I picked him up, all muddy and wet as he was and carried him home.

I had made scones that morning. The smell of them still hung in the air and it broke my heart. It went with the smell of home, and this wasn't home. I had no home, Syl had no home, dog had no home. We just all lived together. I rubbed dog dry with no affection and no enthusiasm. Dead leaf over one ear or not, I no longer found him endearing. He was just an old dog somebody had given me once. Syl was somebody I had given birth to once and I could only feel sorrow for him. I poured myself a sherry and after a while I felt better.

'What are you doing?' asked Syl sharply as he looked in at the sitting-room before going off for his game.

'Drinking,' I said.

He stood looking at me for rather a long time without saying anything.

I took no notice. I knew I grew easily fuddled with drink these days. I could hear myself repeating myself. Myself, myself, I thought, sick of myself and my old bones. In the evenings after a few drinks I was no fit company for anyone.

'I don't care,' I said aloud, and Syl made no reply but went off to play his game.

Lili now began to call on me quite often. She would come in through the back door, calling 'Cuck-oo', stripping off her coat and dropping it at the foot of the stairs. And, do you know, I didn't mind. I began to half wait, half hope that she would come, smelling of scent and cigarettes and talking of things that other people didn't talk about. She never mentioned Jack, but after a while I found myself saying his name as I talked of the past. It would have been unnatural not to do so, like describing a recipe and leaving out a mundane but essential ingredient. Of course she had not forgotten the occasion when she had seduced my husband, but she didn't speak of it, although I would not have been entirely surprised if she had done so. As it was, whenever I said his name she would look straight into my eyes with a smiling, limpid regard and offer me a cigarette. As often as not I would accept it. I did not feel old when Lili was with me because she did not treat me with the strained respect which most people considered appropriate to the elderly. Men who habitually told *risqué* stories would moderate their language in my presence, rendering themselves even more tiresome, since constraint causes such unease. I used to toy with the idea of uttering some unspeakable word, but such words come as ill from withered lips as from the lips of babies. I don't know why this should be so. It is probably that the old have undergone more experiences which require such words to describe them than have the young. Perhaps we are meant to have forgotten them all, and, if I am to be honest, perhaps we have. I could not remember the passions that had once filled me – only the broken splinters of phrases that I had used to express them: '... don't leave me. I'll kill you/myself, I can't bear it.' Of the happier moments I could recall almost nothing, not even the words. This was really a mercy, for people who are in love are like people who are out of their minds, and it is best to forget what they say. Passion dies. Even lost poetry has a faded scent to those who entomb dead desire, and everyday words by everyday people attempting to convey their emotions are possibly the most banal in the language. Lili, I was sure, was not at the moment in love. She was far too lively and interesting, discussing everything under the sun, not half-hypnotized by obsession or limp with wondering what the beloved was up to. She said one day – à propos of nothing much – I don't know what I had said to lead her on:

'It's no use anyone asking me about relationships. When I was a little child I was sometimes spoiled, and sometimes locked in my room, and as a result I find it difficult to form relationships.'

'Who told you that?' I asked.

'I did,' said Lili. 'At one point I was being very bad about relationships and Robert said I should be psychoanalysed. That is very expensive and we were short of money, so I simply asked myself what this psychoanalyst would say. He would say "Lili," he would say to me, "as a child, Lili, it has become evident from what you have told me that you were sometimes spoiled and sometimes locked in your room. This has made it difficult for you to form relationships." Then he would say, "That will be ten guineas. You must come back tomorrow, and the next day, and the next, and the next until you can make perfect relationships" – like perfect omelettes – and we would have been penniless and that would have been worse than the bad relationships. Don't you agree?'

'What bad relationships?' I asked. 'You've been married for donkey's years.'

'I don't really have a relationship with Robert,' explained Lili, 'so it can't be bad. But with other people – I tend to squeeze them like lemons until I have squeezed out all the juice, and then I fling them aside.'

'I see,' I said.

'Not women,' said Lili. 'I have good relationships with women. Only men.'

I said I saw very little value in paying out good money in order to have more mutually satisfactory affairs, and Lili said that of course I was right: that was what she had thought herself. She said she also thought that Robert was unlike a lemon, and more like a potato, in that he was not susceptible to squeezing.

Most people seek to be reassuring when health, whether bodily or mental, is under discussion, so I said that that was fortunate, that Robert's potato-like quality must represent strength, solidarity and endurance. Lili said nothing as I spoke and, since she did not deny what I was saying, after a while I fell to thinking – as I had sometimes thought before – that words could be used as the stuff of illusion: that, marshalled in a certain order so that they made at least grammatical sense, they could be used to silence the dissident, awe the credulous, inflame the mob to violence and almost always dazzle the unintelligent; that words were not like bones, a basic and necessary structure, but more like the inessential finery which people flaunt to gain a better conceit of themselves and impress their fellows.

I said, 'I talk too much. I suppose it's because I'm so often alone.'

'You don't talk too much,' said Lili.

'I sometimes talk a lot of nonsense,' I said, 'but then so do we all.'

'I rather like it,' said Lili, 'when very dim people start giving me advice.'

I wondered, with some amusement, whether she meant me. But she went on.

'Monica does it,' she said. 'Monica's always passing round advice like cucumber sandwiches. Awful, homespun advice. I find it entertaining. Birdbrained old Monica holding forth on world affairs! It's as though the canary had started spouting Carlyle. Very boring stuff, but the circumstance is remarkable. I suppose very stupid people are too stupid to know they're stupid.'

I wanted to tell her that humankind should think more of the skeleton and less of the drapery, but I thought she probably knew that already, even if she hadn't put the knowledge into words. Anyway, I couldn't be bothered. I worried sometimes that there was something I should have done or said before I took it to the grave, beyond reach, but I was no prophet and had no real desire to be one. I must have said something about death, for Lili said, 'People used to die so easily. People in novels. Women especially. Their dear one would leave them, or they'd renounce him for some high-minded reason, and before you could say blood tonic they'd dropped dead. For a while they would grow pale and they would flutter about for a bit and then die.'

'They probably had TB,' I said. 'And they were almost certainly undernourished. Invalids used to be given food we should consider most unsuitable.'

'And people bled them,' said Lili. 'And in my opinion they were already severely anaemic.'

'I wonder if Margaret's anaemic,' I said.

'My mother used to give me iron tonic whenever it got really hot,' said Lili. 'My father's sisters used to laugh at her, but they had very strange medicines of their own – they used to have a kind of competition to see who could stuff me full of the most medicine. I was a crafty little girl. I used to spit it out when they turned round for a lump of *loukoum* to take the taste away. Otherwise I imagine they'd have poisoned me before I was twelve. Pills, potions, suppositories, ointments – they were always experimenting. They'd get the doctor to give them a bottle of something. Then they'd add to it – minced up Spanish Fly was one of their favourite things, but luckily I think they only put it in ointment. They were always boiling oil and mutton fat and messing about with attar-of-roses. I suppose they were bored stiff.'

'Your mother was the English one?' I asked.

'Mmm,' said Lili. 'How funny you should say that. They called her that. The English one. And they used to laugh at her, only she was English enough not to notice. And anyway I don't think she was quite all there. Whether she started out a bit wanting, or living with my aunts drove her mad, I don't know. She certainly made more sense when we moved to a place of our own, only then I think my father felt cheated. He was used to dozens of women fussing round him.'

'It sounds as though you had an interesting childhood,' I remarked conventionally, looking back to my brief visit to Egypt and trying to remember whether I'd met Lili's parents. We had met a great many people in a short space of time and I found it difficult to differentiate between them.

'It's interesting now,' said Lili, 'interesting to look back on, but I'm not sure it was much fun at the time. I remember being too hot. I don't really feel the heat so much now, but I remember trying to sleep on the roof under a mosquito net and still being too hot . . . '

'Do you remember the flowers?' I asked. It was the flowers of childhood that I remembered – wild on the heath and along the lanes, cultivated in my aunts' garden, and I never knew which I preferred. There was always a thrill in finding a growing flower: the thrill of coming across contraband with the harebells and heather, primroses, ragged robin, honeysuckle and the wild rose: the calmer but no less satisfying thrill of seeing purpose fulfilled in the tended borders of the garden – the lupins, the monkshood, the Solomon's seal, the marigolds, sweet pea, and the roses.

I said, 'I do love roses.'

Lili said, 'I remember roses – and little bright snakes. Ugh.'

I remembered suddenly that I had been given brimstone-and-treacle as a child, and I wondered why and by whom. My aunts had never thought of giving me medicine. They had left all that sort of thing to the doctor. It must have been one of the servants. I wondered just how many people *had* died at the hand of poisoners before the long arm and prying fingers of the law had brought forensic science to even the outlying farms and, presumably, to the shaded alleys of the souks and the darkened rooms of Nilotic villas.

'I was brought up by a lot of aunts,' I said to Lili. 'Just like you.' We had been silent for some time while I thought of brimstone-and-treacle and Lili, perhaps, thought of roses and snakes. She was chain-smoking.

'I think my aunts were crazy,' said Lili. 'Looking back, I think they managed to give the impression that it was my mother who was mad, because she was the only one, all by herself in a strange land – and of course that might have made her feel a bit deranged. But in actual fact, and not to put too fine a point on it, my father's sisters were all as mad as hatters.'

'Perhaps it was just that they seemed foreign to you,' I offered politely. 'The ways of foreigners frequently appear like a form of insanity to other people.'

'But they didn't,' said Lili. 'They couldn't have seemed foreign to me because I'd never known anything else. I didn't really think they were mad at the time, although ... ' she added, 'I do remember scuttling through the bazaars with the youngest one veiled up to the eyebrows, giggling her head off, and me wondering what was going on. She said she was buying henna and mud to put on her face, but now I wonder if it was some mild, medical form of poison she was looking for to upset another family member. They'd've killed an outsider who tried to harm one of them but they were always playing tricks on each other. I don't suppose they'd've poisoned anyone to death – not on purpose anyhow – but some of them put aperients in the mint tea or I'm very much mistaken.' She looked thoughtful. 'They had ways of getting their own way,' she said. 'Nothing simple like asking for what they wanted or stamping their foot – although they could do that too – but just quietly, and without referring to anyone else, they would go about getting what they wanted.'

'I think a lot of women do that,' I observed.

'My aunts had brought it to a fine art,' said Lili. 'They were all terribly rich, you know. My family. Any one of them could have had almost anything, but they couldn't live alone and grow up, so they all lived together and didn't ask for anything very much except the opportunity to score over each other and get what they wanted by devious means. Sometimes just a certain seat on the terrace in the cool of the evening would be the goal, and they would contrive the most *filigree* manoeuvres to secure it. And then they would change to quoting-games, and recite bits of Racine and Baudelaire, and the others would pretend either that they knew it or that they found it inferior, and they would quote their own bits.'

'That is not unusual,' I said.

'No, I suppose not,' said Lili. 'Monica goes mad if you quote at her.'

We sat in silence again for a while until I repeated, 'I wonder if Margaret's anaemic?' Lili had earlier, in passing, expressed a desire to die. I had not wished to dwell on Lili's problems because I was preoccupied with Margaret, but now I remembered my manners.

'Never mind. Never mind Margaret. Tell me why you want to die,' I asked civilly.

'I don't any more. I've got over it,' she said. 'I just wanted to annoy Robert. He orders me about sometimes when he forgets himself, and I won't have it. The urge to irritate one's husband is not sufficient justification either for death or adultery. There has to be some more compelling motive.'

'How true,' I said pacifically.

'I never wanted children,' said Lili. 'I never really wanted to get married. I only did it because everybody was doing it. It was most unlike me to want to be one of the herd. Having children makes you inevitably one of the herd. I shan't have even one.'

'Does Robert want children?' I asked.

'Mmm,' said Lili. 'He's just realized I'm probably too old to have any now and he's disappointed.'

'Reproachful?' I asked.

'A bit,' said Lili. 'It's terribly boring.'

'Poor Robert,' I said ill-advisedly – and falsely, for I felt no real pity for him.

Lili's discontent turned to rage. 'Am I a chicken to have eggs?' she inquired. 'Am I a cow to calve for my master? Am I a box for him to keep his trinkets in? Eh?'

'No, of course not,' I said.

'I am mine,' announced Lili passionately, giving herself a glancing blow on the chest.

I laughed.

'Besides,' said Lili, 'having babies is painful.'

'You're quite right,' I said, and Lili said she knew she was.

*

One evening we went to a pub in the town and stayed until it closed. I had thought I would be unbearably tired but I wasn't. When we got back Syl was angry.

'Where have you been?' he asked, as though he was my mother.

'Boozing,' said Lili.

Syl opened his mouth to say something and then closed it again.

I slept well that night, not waking up in the small hours as I usually did, coming downstairs to make a cup of tea and disappointing the dog who, on seeing me, would be gripped with untimely expectations of breakfast.

Syl spoke his mind in the morning, hastily swallowing a boiled egg before setting off for work. He more or less told me not to do it again.

'For God's sake,' I said, preparing to tell him that I was a big girl now, but he shook a minatory finger at me and left in a male rage, puzzled as men always are by unexpected behaviour in their womenfolk. I had a sudden sense of pity for Margaret, but I disregarded it. Syl would look after her and she would have to accept that. Dishonesty is something that even the old are not proof against, and I wanted to believe that Margaret would be happy, for if she was not then neither would Syl be. I forced myself to believe, without considering it too closely, that this marriage would work. Selfishly I wanted only to see Syl settled before I died.

It was while Lili was there that I began to have intimations of death that I had not had before. Before, I had hoped for heaven, which I visualized as a reflection of childhood – the better part of childhood, when I had recovered from the loss of my mother in the love of her brethren. I had appreciated that love very greatly because I felt that, in a sense, I had no absolute right to it. It came as a gift, not perhaps undeserved but unexpected. I missed it now that I was even older than my aunts and uncles had ever been.

Now I sometimes felt close to another mode of being, another reality: something which gleamed spasmodically, diamond bright, just beyond comprehension: something ecstatic and infinitely desirable, a swift, shining glimpse of unimaginable joy. I construed these visions – with the optimism which seems ultimately inseparable from the human condition – as promises, as samples of something yet to come, and, with the greed which also seems inseparable from humanity, I yearned for more. I seemed sometimes to move near to realms where the temporal, the finite, began to end, where eagles might clash with angels and the ice-bright light, shattered like gems, would scatter and dissipate until my soul could see it: low down, and far, and waiting. I admitted to myself that it could be imaginary, or possibly pathological, a symptom of age and decay, but this reasonable view failed to convince and therefore destroy my belief. It gave me not so much comfort as delight, unexpected as it was. I linked the experience in a tenuous way with Lili. I could perceive in her very little that gave evidence of spirituality. She never caused me to think of heaven, and I don't imagine she ever had that effect on anyone. It was something else: something about her that reminded me of those shimmering points of light. The nearest I can get to it is to think of seed packets with their garish pictures of flowers. Every now and then, if you feel receptive, they can give something of the pleasure of a sweeping field of poppies. The source of pleasure may be vulgar pastiche, but the pleasure remains. Not all our delight originates in the sublime, and because we are, after all, perhaps quite simple mechanisms we respond similarly to lesser, even to shameful, joys.

I had not understood before that happiness could make one wish for death. To be honest, I had never really thought about it, apart from hoping that the actual business of dying would not be long-drawn-out and disgusting. One of my aunts had thrown herself from her bed in the agonies of cancer.

This was something I had promised myself that I would one day face. I had not had too painful or distressing a life, and I felt there was much I did not understand, too much I was unaware of, or had refused to see. I had meant to think about insupportable pain. I had intended, metaphorically, to go round and round the abattoir and watch the beasts killed, because it seemed unbalanced and faintly unseemly to look only at the flower packets, ignoring the flayed mask of the pig until it turned up speckled with sweet herbs, transformed into brawn for the luncheon table. On the neighbouring farms in my youth they had killed their pigs themselves, but my middle aunt, who fainted at the sight of blood or the sound of squealing, had forbidden the practice and our pigs went to the slaughterhouse. I had hunted hares and shot pigeons, but that was long ago and I had wrapped my memories in forgetfulness. Jack used to hurry me past street accidents, and Syl had a tendency to take the morning paper to work with him when there was a particularly horrific crime running. I had thought I should make some attempt to see clearly and cope with horror before I departed this life, and in view of all I have just said it is ironic that I reacted as I did to what Lili one day told me.

She came in the morning and she looked tired. I remarked on this and she said she'd been up late. She clearly had something on her mind.

'Coffee?' I said.

'I'd rather have something stronger, as they say,' said Lili, 'if you don't mind.'

I took her into the sitting-room and she walked over to the window.

'Winter is getting me down,' she said.

'And you won't be here for the spring.' I opened the cupboard and peered at the bottles.

'I don't like English spring,' said Lili. 'I like a warm spring with almond and orange blossom and goats in the trees nibbling the leaves.'

'Whisky or gin?' I asked. Goats? I had heard her quite clearly but I couldn't picture a tree with goats in it.

'They climb trees in some nice warm parts of the world,' said Lili, gazing at leafless, goatless Croydon.

'I believe goats are well known for their sure-footedness,' I said with teatime, drawing-room politeness.

'They have golden devil's eyes,' said Lili, 'and they look down at you as you go by and they look clever, and you think how astonishing they are to be clever like that *and* be able to climb trees. Then they start chewing again and that makes them look stupid, and you think what on earth are those dumb animals doing up that tree?'

'I find some people like that,' I said. 'Many people. I can never decide whether they're highly intelligent and disguising the fact, or purely boneheaded and trying to disguise it.'

'People. Ugh,' said Lili.

'Gin or whisky?' I asked again, as she made no move away from the window.

'I got stinking on Gin-and-It last night,' said Lili. 'I think I'll have whisky. Gin is a depressant. Did you know?'

'I believe all alcohol is said to be a depressant,' I observed.

'Not like gin,' said Lili. 'I'll never touch it again. Never.' She shuddered, took a sip of whisky and shuddered again. She sat down on the window seat and took out her cigarettes. 'What a hell of a world,' she remarked.

'Shall I make you some toast?' I offered, not really wanting to go out to the kitchen and fiddle with cutting bread.

Lili seemed to pull herself together. 'No,' she said with sudden, assumed briskness. 'I'll feel better in a minute.' She threw the whisky down her throat and held out her glass for more.

'Did you have breakfast?' I asked, sounding to myself officious and typically old. I didn't really care if she had or not, but I didn't want her to get drunk.

'No,' said Lili. 'Everybody got up late this morning, and I sneaked out before anyone was around. Robert's gone off to the gallery, and as far as I know Monica and Margaret are still festering in bed.'

'Well, have a biscuit,' I said, 'or you'll get gastritis with all that Scotch.'

'All right,' said Lili. She took a Garibaldi from the biscuit barrel and gave half to the dog in an absent-minded fashion. He sat very close to her, waiting avidly for more.

'It's not like Monica to stay in bed,' I said.

'She got drunk too,' said Lili. 'Only not as drunk as me. She told me something and so, of course, I had to tell *her* something, and now I can't remember what it was.'

I worried briefly that she might have confided her adventure with my husband, but it was unlikely and I didn't really care. I wasn't really interested in what Monica had told her either, but it seemed to be on her mind and she had said no more about goats.

'What did Monica tell you?' I asked.

'She told me Derek was a paedophile,' said Lili in a noncommittal tone.

I wondered if I had heard her correctly. Of all the things I had thought she might say – and I hadn't really considered it – this was the least expected. To tell the truth, I had faintly imagined that Monica might have expressed some dissatisfaction with Syl. Or, if not that, she might well have let her hair down about her annoyance with Margaret, whose passivity often manifestly infuriated her.

'What did you say?' I asked, knowing quite well. My hearing was still unimpaired.

'Can I have another Scotch?' asked Lili, leaning forward.

I poured her a large one and then put the bottle in front of her on the table.

'Derek, her husband?' I inquired idiotically.

'It's one of those things you'd rather not know,' said Lili. 'You think you want to know everything and then you realize there are some pieces of information you'd be perfectly happy without. I don't really give a damn if Derek's a child molester, only now I know the details and I wish I didn't.' She lit a cigarette and took another slug of whisky.

'Child molester,' I repeated. It never occurred to me to doubt her. Lili was no liar. She didn't need to be. On the whole things went her way in the manner that she wished; the impression she made on people without using any artifice could hardly have been improved. She liked to startle and even to shock, but she needed no recourse to fantasy. Lili was one of those to whom things happen, and one of those in whom others confide.

'She swore me to secrecy,' said Lili. 'Naturally. It's not the sort of thing you want shouted from the housetops.'

My mind, like a rabbit, hopped after a blade of imagery. I heard the muezzin calling between the hot clear sky and the hot dusty earth.

Lili said that Monica had discovered her husband in their daughter's bedroom in a state of some disarray. She spoke in veiled terms of something that had almost never come to my consciousness, and I knew instantly what she meant. My mind tried, and failed, to make a huge leap and get away from it.

I said, 'What?', and Lili moved in the window seat.

'I never knew,' she said. 'It never, never occurred to me. Clever me, who knows everything that's going on. It made me feel small, I can tell you. That's why I got drunk. I thought nothing could shock me. I thought I was the clever one. Poor silly old Monica, I thought, married to that terrible bore. What a shame. And lucky me flying all round the world, having affairs with everyone in positions Monica never even heard about. And all the time . . . ' She drank some more whisky before putting the glass down. 'And all the time ... I have been in some situations, but Monica made me feel innocent. *Me*.'

I knew what she meant, for Lili was not evil, and here it was – corruption, with all its writhen subtleties of meaning. I could see her, dancing in uncertain lights, in the heat and colour of strange places, yet uncorrupt.

'I couldn't think what to say,' she said. 'I sat there with my mouth open like some big fish.'

I couldn't think what to say myself. I knew what Lili meant about preferring not to know. Such knowledge beginning with one act of wickedness leads to abysses previously unfeared because they were non-existent. Something terrible had happened and nothing was, or could be, the same any more.

'In all my life ...' I began.

'I know,' said Lili. 'You've lived a long life and I've lived a rich life and we never ...'

'What ...' I began again, and stopped again.

The conversation went on like this for some time: unfinished questions and reflections – I suppose because we were trying to discuss the unspeakable. Besides Lili was getting drunk again.

I remembered whispered hintings when I was a girl. Table talk, stable talk – it made no difference. The whispers and the hints were the same, and also in the same category as fairy story, dark myth, or, on another level, the outpourings of the gutter press. I couldn't remember any one person murmuring obliquely of murder, bestiality, incest, and I could remember no details. It all happened, if it happened at all, in the remote farms and labourers' cottages. It was as unreal as the death of Robin Hood or the tales of the Brothers Grimm and went with the sound of the tumbling beck, the racing grasses and the darkness of a moonless moorland night. I had an impression of laughter, contempt for the primitives who could not understand that such deeds were prohibited – as much by the absurdity of their nature as by any moral considerations. The implication was that those who laughed had developed, not in virtue, but in intelligence, and those who were laughed at walked with their knuckles grazing the ground. We lived in the certain knowledge that such things happened only under other, distant roofs, and the horror was dispelled, made harmless, by half-shamed laughter, the refusal to dwell on it. Tales of darkness have always been told, but they are better told in the half-dark, not in the greyness of a winter morning or under electric light.

'When ...?' I asked at last.

'Ages ago,' said Lili, and I remembered the night when Monica had come, all dishevelled, without her child, to threaten hysterics in my sitting-room.

'Well ... hell,' I said.

I couldn't sleep at all that night. I sat up in bed with a book on my lap until my back ached. The room was warm, the light soft.

I had never got used to lights hanging from the ceiling, glaring and cold. I had been brought up with oil lamps, and long before it became fashionable I had lit my present rooms with sidelights: lamps on tables, in corners. Jack used to swear and say he couldn't see what he was doing, but as he was usually only pouring a drink or looking at women's legs I couldn't see that it mattered. I sat there getting steadily angrier with Jack: with his unreasonableness, his stupidity, his habit of leaving his clothes on my dressing-table chair – the angular, mute intransigence that men could show, their cruelty.

At two o'clock I got up and went downstairs. I put the kettle on, spoke to dog and clattered the cutlery in the kitchen drawer as I looked for a teaspoon. Jack could never stand me walking about in the night. He had been a light sleeper and when he slept he liked to think that everyone else was sleeping too. Perhaps he was afraid of missing something. He had frequently shouted at me to come back to bed, to stop fooling around. I wasn't sorry he was dead, but sometimes I wished he was here so that I could tell him a few home truths I had not acquainted him with when he was alive. I didn't know Derek well enough to hate him.

I was whistling under my breath when Syl came down.

'What are you doing?' he asked.

'Standing on my head, waving my legs in the air,' I said, as I stirred the tea.

'You'll get your death of cold,' he prophesied.

'Syl, don't *fuss*,' I said. 'You're turning into a real old woman, flapping and fussing all the time.'

He didn't say anything but turned and went upstairs. I considered calling him back to say I was sorry and I didn't mean it – but then I did mean it, being very, very tired of men telling me what to do. It was unfair. Syl was not his father and he wasn't Derek, and I had no cause to be angry with him. Except that he was a man. The person I loved best in the world was a man, and I had no reason in the world to love men at all. I had been used to thinking of Syl as my son, not as a man, but there it was. He undeniably was one. And therefore, I thought hopelessly, standing up and sipping my tea, he was alien. I had learned to understand men quite well, out of a sense of self-preservation as much as of interest, and while I had known some with minds as subtle as any woman's, I had found them on the whole to be predictable. I had heard my aunts say scornfully, 'Men are all alike.' I thought as I stood in the kitchen, drinking my tea, that men were like machines designed to destroy and kill, and that paradoxically only the best of them were able to deny that tragic destiny; that good and gentle men were aberrations, a sport of nature, stopping short of apotheosis. These are the thoughts that come at two o'clock in the morning, but I do not think they would have come to me then if Lili hadn't told me about Derek.

I poured myself another cup of tea and sat down to think about Derek. Dull, ordinary Derek. Faithless, poor Derek with a young second family to maintain. Grey, aggrieved Derek. Derek and Monica. Derek and . . . I had forgotten the name of his second wife. Derek and Margaret. As soon as this conjunction came into my head I moved to ruin it. I put between them a vast hedge of thorns, a cold ocean, walls, rivers. They were no longer father and daughter but strangers, as distant as my tired mind could make them. I became aware of a weary rage as I realized that Margaret was spoiled in my eyes. If he had merely beaten her I would have felt pity, but she had been defiled and I felt some disgust for her. There was nothing I could do about it. When the dog had peed on a blameless cushion I had thrown it away.

Tomorrow morning I would see the priest.

But the following morning I didn't want to see anybody. Syl called in at my bedroom before he went to work and said something disagreeable about how tired I looked and how it served me right.

I had a spurt of temper and shouted after him, '*Men*', the shortest term of disapprobation I know. He could, I suppose, have riposted with as much justice, '*Women*', but he didn't.

I thought about women as I struggled to be fair to my son and all his kind. I had known bad, boring, selfish and destructive women, but they seemed to me to be as much of an aberration as kindly men. I had been born in the last century when it was customary to regard Woman as the Angel in the Home, and while I had always imagined myself to be proof against this strange idea it now seemed that it had seeped irremovably into my consciousness. My grandfather had been distant and authoritarian and I had scarcely ever seen him. His children, imperceptibly rebelling against his coldness, had done nothing outrageous (I except my mother) but had devoted themselves to being happy. My uncles (I know nothing of what they were like with their women) had been uncritical of me, warm and wide and generous, and my aunts had made me laugh and given me their cast-off dresses and handbags. They would have bought me new clothes, but I never saw anything in a shop as elegant as the clothes my aunts wore. If I had never married or fallen in love, if my uncles were all I had ever known of masculinity, I should have had a different, a positive and loving view of men. Or was I idealizing them after all this time? They might have been dreadful in bed or the market-place but they were unfailingly good to me – because, I now understood, they had very largely left me alone. The words 'meddling' and 'interfering' are bad enough without their sexual connotations and my uncles were splendidly free of these traits. All day they did whatever it was they were doing – mostly in the fresh air – and they came home in the evenings, not tired and disgruntled, but elated and ready for a drink. And they'd laugh and they were witty. I don't remember ever seeing one of them in a sulk, even when he'd lost a bet. They bet on anything and everything – raindrops on the window pane, which bird would fly first from the eaves, the colour of the emergent crocuses – and I wonder now whether betting isn't healthful for men, channelling their need to take risks on to less dangerous tracks. It certainly occupies their minds.

I have wasted all this time thinking about men when I intended to think about women. Mrs Raffald came looking for me when she arrived at 9 o'clock.

'You not well?' she asked.

'Bit tired,' I said.

She moved over and closed the window, which I always left open a crack in the night, and then stood for a moment looking down into the garden. She was a good-looking woman with strong, clear features and I'd never noticed it before. Or, if I had, it hadn't seemed of any significance. I had shrunk to being the sort of person who thinks the face of the servant of no consequence.

'You look well,' I said.

She was unsurprised and I thought perhaps her family and friends complimented her all the time and gave her such confidence that she didn't mind cleaning other people's houses.

'Just had my hair done,' she said.

I lay back on the pillows and closed my eyes. After a while I heard her clanking a bucket and mop down in the hallway. She was one sort of woman, competent, sure of herself: not unlike me. Margaret, I had thought, was not unlike me, and sometimes I had thought I detected a similarity, a fellow feeling in Lili. The world seemed suddenly full of women who were nothing like each other but all a little like me. Monica, I assured myself, was nothing like me. Nor was Mrs Trevelyan.

What a ridiculous way to spend a morning. I got out of bed and dressed slowly, thinking deliberately about the evening meal I should soon start preparing. Celery soup, fish pie, apple tart with oven-baked custard. Simple undemanding food. Unexciting compared with the game and the poultry and the haunches and hams and sirloins, the great mounds of vegetables from the kitchen garden . . .

'Oh *shut* up,' I said to myself aloud. I found it increasingly disconcerting that I had forgotten, or chosen not to remember, the greater part of my life in favour of those early days.

Mrs Raffald, whisking a duster down the banisters, looked faintly startled.

'I've taken to talking to myself,' I explained.

'Better company than some round here,' she said. 'You'll get more sense than up the road.'

'How are they?' I asked.

'Flapping away,' said Mrs Raffald, flapping her duster as though by way of illustration. 'You'd think there'd never been a wedding before.'

'I wouldn't care if there never was another one,' I said. I made coffee to see if it would wake me up and make me feel more alert.

'I'll peel the spuds for you,' said Mrs Raffald. 'Why don't you eat something?'

'I'm not hungry,' I said. 'I'll do the pastry for the tart and then I'll start the soup and then I won't have to do anything more until supper time.'

'You do too much,' said Mrs Raffald.

'I do hardly anything,' I said, but I knew what she meant. She meant I was too old to do anything.

'You have to keep going,' she said, 'but you ought to rest. You worry too much too.'

I considered this, wondering what would constitute a suitable, a reasonable, degree of worry. 'I don't really,' I said, knowing that somewhere in her mind was the reflection that if she had a son of Syl's age who proposed to marry a Margaret she would be worried to death.

'It's all right,' I said. 'Everything will be all right in the end.'

'Of course,' said Mrs Raffald.

The front door bell rang, an unusual happening in the mornings: all the tradesmen went round to the back and called out to announce their presence.

'I'll go,' said Mrs Raffald, dropping a half-peeled potato. I picked it up and finished peeling it before she came back. 'It's Robert,' she said.

'Who?' I asked.

'Lili's husband,' she said. 'I've put him in the sitting-room.'

'What can he want at this time?' I dried my hands and went from the companionable kitchen to see what Robert wanted. He had come one evening with the rest of them but we had hardly spoken. He had looked harassed and rather ill and not as I remembered him. I had had a feeling of unease, knowing what I knew about his wife and my husband.

'Good morning, Robert,' I said, like a polite old lady.

'How are you?' he inquired. It was a conventional enough

greeting, but I was growing over-sensitive and discerned in it an unusual anxiety.

'I am exceedingly well,' I told him. 'Do sit down. Would you care for a drink?'

It was by now about ten-thirty but I was inclined to be mildly spiteful. Lili had been quite drunk by noon yesterday and had said, as she left, that she must go and collect Robert and whisk him off to lunch with his gallery owner. It would have been interesting, I thought, to have been a fly on the wall at that lunch.

'How is Lili?' I asked with a sweet-old-lady smile. I felt no animosity now towards either of them but I was sick of people.

Robert was not a subtle man. He said, 'I bumped into Syl this morning and he said you were a bit under the weather.'

I said, 'I merely stayed in bed for a few minutes longer than is customary. I was a little tired after yesterday.'

Robert looked troubled. 'About yesterday,' he said. 'What was Lili saying to you?'

I had not expected such directness. 'Why, nothing,' I said, for I would never, as long as I lived, discuss with anyone the revelation of the previous morning.

'She seemed to think she might have upset you,' said Robert.

'Did she send you here?' I asked, thinking it unlikely.

'No,' he said. 'Only she did say she wished she hadn't told you – whatever it was she did tell you.'

'Didn't she tell you what it was?' I asked.

Robert said, 'She wouldn't. Said it was nothing to do with me. She just said she wished she hadn't told you.'

'It wasn't important,' I said. 'I can't think what she could have meant. Are you sure you heard her correctly – she'd had quite a bit of Scotch, you know.'

'I know,' said Robert.

'I'm sorry,' I said. 'She drank it here.'

I would have said that I had given it to her, but I hadn't

really. She had mostly helped herself. For an unpleasant moment I wondered whether she had confessed her transgression with Jack, or whether she had told Robert years ago and he had known all along. At this thought I wished that I could divorce, in retrospect, my dead husband, and dissociate myself from the indignity of his behaviour.

'Perhaps you would like a cup of coffee,' I said.

'Oh, yes thanks,' said Robert annoyingly.

I warmed up the coffee while Mrs Raffald cleaned the kitchen sink and the dog mumbled a veal bone, lurking behind a table leg.

'OK?' asked Mrs Raffald.

'I can't think what he wants,' I said unguardedly. I wished he'd go away so that I could stay in the kitchen and talk to the charlady. The initial preparations in cooking, I remembered, were soothing and satisfying. It was the last-minute rush to get everything to the table while it was still hot that exhausted the hostess. I said, 'I forgot to put a damp cloth over the pastry.'

'I did it,' said Mrs Raffald. 'I haven't seen a fly yet, but you don't want it going dry.'

'No,' I said.

'Here,' she said, 'I'll carry the coffee through for you.'

Robert stood up as we came in and said good morning to Mrs Raffald.

She responded briskly, put his coffee cup beside him, thrust a biscuit at him and went out. She was invaluable. I daresay I should not have dropped his coffee over him but my hand was a little shaky again. I sat down and waited.

'Syl's looking well,' remarked Robert, swallowing some biscuit.

I was moderately glad to hear that he thought so, but it seemed an inadequate reason for his call. He could have telephoned to say so. I took a cigarette from the silver box on the table. It was stale but it gave me something to do to ward off the mild hysteria which afflicts us in uneasy social situations. If

I had had some real idea of why Robert was there I could have coped, but I didn't know what he might say next, what embarrassment he might uncover. I was determined to feign ignorance if he so much as mentioned Derek. But he said very little more about anything. We conversed briefly over the falling level of the Nile – or was it rising? I can't remember. Then he left.

Syl came home early and I told him about Robert's visit. I said, 'I had a surprise this morning. Robert called – for no reason at all that I could see. He didn't stay long, thank goodness, but I can't think why he came in the first place.' I thought it wiser to let Syl know in case anyone mentioned it. As it turned out, I don't think anyone would have done.

'Did he mention money?' asked Syl.

'No,' I said. 'Why?'

'He tried to borrow a couple of hundred off me,' said Syl. 'So I said I'd lend him half that. He said on pain of death not to tell Lili – they're in some sort of money trouble.'

'*Money?*' I said. That had not occurred to me: the commonest, most prosaic problem of all. 'I think he must have thought that Lili had been trying to borrow money from me,' I said, looking back to the morning.

'Had she?' asked Syl.

'No,' I said. 'Not yet.'

'They're extravagant,' said Syl. 'They should have plenty to live on *and* travel a bit, but I don't know what they do with it.'

After tea Syl went to the tennis club and I addressed myself to the problem I had been putting aside since yesterday: whether or not to tell Syl what Lili had told me; or rather, whether or not to persuade Lili to tell him, for I could not. Without knowing why, I believed that if Syl were told what had happened to Margaret he would not marry her. Pity could easily slip sideways into disgust, and either feeling was inappropriate to marriage.

Almost as much as I wanted to see Syl settled, I wanted to think that Margaret could be safe. The word fell into my mind as I was trying to think of a less showy word than 'happy'. The word 'happiness' had never suited Margaret and now I supposed it never would, but she could at least be protected from further harm. Don't misunderstand me. I was not particularly fond of Margaret. My feelings were not those of a mother.

Sitting wondering what exactly my feelings were, I had a vision of Long Tom, our neighbour's gamekeeper. He shot foxes and crows and weasels so that the gentry might shoot pheasants and hares and grouse. It had always struck me as somewhat arbitrary. Since the first category of beast was already dead, why – my childish mind had asked – didn't people eat them and let the latter category alone, free from at least some anxiety as their ancient enemies were stripped, gutted and prepared for the table? (Long Tom, I should have made clear, was a figure from my youth. Our Croydon neighbours had no call to employ gamekeepers.) Predators on the whole, being largely inedible, made poor game, although there was always, of course, the exception of the unfortunate fox, and even he, I remembered dimly, was eaten at Christmas time in some part of the world – was it Italy? There was tiger-hunting, but that was dying out as the tigers died. Parts of the tiger were supposed to have magical properties and their chopped-up whiskers were used in tea to dispatch the unwanted wives of rajas. I knew a lot of pointless things. None of this information would ever be much good to me. It was Lili who made me think of tigers.

Remembering this reminded me that I had known Lili much better than I had been admitting. Until the contretemps with Jack, I had always found her amusing, although I do not think she ever really liked me in those days. I didn't laugh very much and she needed laughter as some people needed approval. She had come into my house one summer morning in what would have been a rage if she hadn't found the cause of it so funny.

'I'll tell you a story,' she had said. 'And you shall tell me what you think. Once upon a time a man was walking in the forest when he found a baby sabre-toothed tiger all by itself. No mother, no father. So he took it home and loved it and fed it and watered it and cuddled it, and sometimes he teased it and pulled its tail and tweaked its ears, and if he was mad about something he would kick it in the stomach. And it grew up and he went on loving it and feeding it and pulling its tail and its ears and kicking it in the stomach, and all the time the tiger was thinking . . . What do you think the tiger was thinking?'

I said I had no idea, although I had.

'It was thinking, "One of these days he's going to go too far, and then I'm going to bite his head off." And it was watching him all the time through half-closed eyes, wondering when it could be bothered to do it.'

'Yes, it would be like that,' I said, waiting for Lili to explain that she was the sabre-toothed tiger in question and assuming that the unwary rescuer was Robert – although it need not have been. Lili always had numerous men around her, each imagining himself to be foremost in her awareness and affections.

'Men,' she said, but she calmed down and changed the subject, talked until she got bored with me and then went off in her usual swirl of skirts and I thought I could almost see tail-lights glimmering on her heels. It was difficult to picture Lili in the grip of death.

The thought of death was with me most of the time. I think it always had been. Gamekeepers and death and Margaret circled in my mind, with fear – no, horror – on the periphery. Margaret was one of some protected species of bewildered creatures. Protected only to be killed ... I stopped thinking like that. It led nowhere.

Lili and Robert went off at one point to stay with friends

somewhere up North. I had a fantasy that they might pass the farmhouse, but I couldn't bear to think about it. The real farmhouse undoubtedly still existed, solid and four-square, but I did not – could not – relate it to the farmhouse in my mind, since that would be to admit that I could never return and that if I did the people I loved would not be there. You would think that time and experience would teach us not to mind, that inevitability would cease to seem like intransigence, but I have not found it so. It is not so much age as change that I have found cruel and difficult to bear. I would gladly have caught up in age to my aunts if they could have waited for me, but they had gone without me and I had had to grow old alone.

I had forgotten about Robert's exhibition, which is some indication of my state of mind. It had been in its way a memorable occasion; yet it had fallen from my memory like a fledgeling from the nest, too recent and too frail to conserve. With a little effort I can relive it.

We went in Syl's car, Monica and me in the back and Margaret in the place of honour beside Syl. Margaret was as quiet as usual but seemed somehow more alive, less doughily passive. Most of the time I felt that if someone should make a thumbprint on her it would remain forever, but this evening, at least at the beginning, she showed signs of some resilience. I had dressed up for the occasion in a dark green dress and an old black velvet jacket but nobody except Syl had noticed.

He said, 'You look nice, Mum', and I told him that he too looked nice.

Margaret was pale as always, her profile in the light from the street lamps as pure as milk. She was dressed in brown, but somebody, Lili I imagine, had pinned a crimson chrysanthemum to her collar. I could smell its wintry spice from where I sat.

The gallery when we arrived seemed to me uncomfortably full. I was not a great gallery-goer, but the crowd, I felt sure, was unusually large, and everybody appeared to know everybody else, which I also felt was unusual. We were separated almost at once, and seeing an alcove with a cushioned seat I immediately laid claim to it. I was surely the oldest person present – a grimmish reflection which made me smile just a little, and only to myself. From where I sat I could not see the pictures except when a sudden movement shifted the crowd and I could catch a glimpse of those which hung opposite. One looked faintly familiar: a painting of a villa with a broad iron gate. I had not spent long in Egypt and had visited Monica's friend Marie Claire only once, but there was something about the fall of flowers beside the gate that took me back. They had been like tiny posies rather than individual flowers – a circle of white, a circle of cream and an inner circle of pink ... but perhaps all the villas had looked like that, with a flow of blossoms to prove that not all was dust.

Syl brought me a glass of wine and asked if I was all right. I said I was perfectly fine and that he should go and look at the pictures and talk to the people.

Lili was talking. I could hear her voice above the others somewhere to my right, but not what she was saying. There was no sign of Margaret or Monica. I supposed they were caught up in the crush.

After a while I got to my feet and with some difficulty made my way around to give an appearance of appreciating art. The paintings were innocuous, some rather charming, but I would not have chosen to hang any of them on my walls. I gazed at a representation of the Nile and then moved on, and as I came level with Margaret she seemed, not precisely to stagger, but to droop. I reached out my arms to hold her but Robert was before me. She now looked whiter than milk, as white as ice, and her eyes were blank. Her mother pushed her way through to where Robert supported her failing daughter, and she wore a look of exasperation beyond endurance.

'What *is* wrong with you, Margaret?' she said: not 'What's

wrong with you, Margaret?' with the accent in the normal place, very slightly on the 'wrong', but 'What *is* wrong with you?' which has connotations almost diametrically opposed to the expression of concern. Monica was not concerned, but enraged.

I moved to shield Margaret, but this time Lili was before me and Margaret clung to her. Syl had appeared by now and I saw with regret that he too was displeased. I had long ceased to expect much understanding from men but I had thought Syl was different. In the past he had shown great tenderness towards Margaret and had spoken of her with what had sounded to my ears like love. Now he sounded annoyed. I felt a nervous compulsion to demand 'What *is* wrong with you, Syl?' but suppressed it.

He said, 'I'll take her home', as though she was the dog and not to be consulted, or an inanimate bag of shopping.

'How kind of you,' said Lili, and that was the last thing I heard her say that evening.

She disappeared without another word and I was left with Monica and Robert in the slowly emptying gallery. I worried for a while about Margaret and how Syl might be treating her, but these considerations were superseded by simple social embarrassment. It seemed a table had been booked at a restaurant for six of us and the gallery owner. We were now down to three and the gallery owner, and he, for one, was angry about it.

We walked to this restaurant, which fortunately was not far. The waiters, infected by the general air of disaffection and resentment, snatched away the superfluous covers from the table and pushed aside three unnecessary chairs. I decided that regardless of my age I should have to get just sufficiently drunk to cope with all this without screaming. As a result I do not have a very clear recollection of the rest of the meal. I wondered whether Lili had gone home to look after Margaret or whether she had gone with her *louche* friends to some smoky, moderately riotous club. On the whole I thought that was more likely. Monica sat opposite the gallery owner and talked at him, Lord only knows what about. Once or twice she laughed, put her arms on the table and leaned towards him. I took no interest in what she was saying, fuddled as I was with wine and weariness. I remember telling myself it was decent of her to make an effort – and uncharacteristic. With drunken charity I reflected that Monica had some good in her and was proving it by trying to salvage a scrap of conviviality out of what was, after all, Robert's evening. I tried a little as well, saying how much I had liked the water-colours, especially the one with the ruin.

I saw no sign of Syl when I finally got home. His coat was not in the hall. Robert walked with me to the front door while Monica sat slumped in the car, largely silent as she had been all the way back.

'Thank heaven for that,' I said more or less involuntarily as I stepped into my own house. Base camp, even if it is not your heart's home, is infinitely preferable to wandering in uncharted territory looking at pictures.

I was so relieved I said, 'Would you like a drink?', in an access of grateful generosity, which I regretted as Robert said that he would. He said he'd go and see whether Monica wanted to come in too, or whether he should walk to her gate with her.

'Go home, Monica,' I implored under my breath, but she came in, puffy-eyed with tiredness, and her feet clearly causing her some discomfort. It must have been nearly midnight.

'Can I pour you a drink?' said Robert, who had made like a homing pigeon for where the Scotch stood on a table.

'Just Martini for me,' said Monica.

I was getting my second wind. If I had gone to my bed at my normal time my body would now have been preparing itself to wake and put me through the rest of a sleepless night. I thought I might as well make the most of it. 'Whisky,' I said, and I lit a cigarette.

'I do think that was too bad of Lili,' said Monica when she had downed her first Martini. 'She might've made the effort, I *do* think.'

'I think so too,' said Robert. 'But you know Lili.'

'I don't know why you let her get away with it,' said Monica.

I thought that an extremely irritating remark and was reassured to hear Robert respond mildly, since I could not have endured an argument after the tensions of the dinner table.

'You know Lili,' he said again. 'She does as she pleases.'

Monica settled herself lower in her chair, looking as though she had just said 'Huh', which in fact she hadn't. Possibly she wished she hadn't spoken of Lili.

There was something strange in the atmosphere, something unusual. We were an ill-assorted threesome gathered together at an ill-chosen time. The only parallel I could think of was Christmas mornings long, long ago when I had risen before the sun, gone downstairs by lamp and candlelight while my aunts and uncles still slept, looked through my presents bedecked with holly, and joined the cowmen in the down-house, drinking tea and eating bread and butter with a full and glorious day ahead. This occasion felt a little the same in kind but black where the other had been white.

'I had the impression the opening was a great success,' I said, hauling myself out of the realms of introspection and fantasy.

'Yes,' said Robert, 'I believe it was. That should please the owner.'

'I thought he was charming,' said Monica. 'I don't know why you didn't ask him to come over to dinner before this.'

'I can't stand the fellow,' said Robert simply.

I was surprised to hear that Monica had found him charming. He hadn't looked to me the sort of person to appeal to her.

'That's only because you deal with him professionally,' said Monica, making this meaningless statement in a decisive tone. 'I've asked him to the wedding. I shall send him a proper invitation tomorrow.'

By now I was fully awake and had drunk myself sober, a trick which I thought I had lost, and I could see Robert reacting to this. Or rather I could sense his feelings from what he did not say. He was suffering the usual slight shock of those who, imagining their various sets of acquaintances to be separate and distinct, find that they have run together and the emphasis, the structure, of their social life has shifted. In a word, he was not pleased. He did not say, 'Oh what a good idea. What fun we shall all have together. Whoopee.' He didn't say anything. He was probably wondering how to put the kibosh on the whole thing.

I felt sorry for him. 'But the gallery owner isn't family,' I said. 'We hardly know him.' I felt magnanimous uttering that 'we'.

Monica became extraordinarily annoying and began to lecture me. She said that it was unreasonable, and possibly unhealthy, to confine such celebrations as a wedding merely to close family and friends. It would make the occasion more interesting and memorable if we were to entertain those whom we wished to see for no other reason than that we found their company enjoyable. She mentioned in passing 'angels unawares', and, in fact, told me everything that I believed myself and that she, until this moment, would have dismissed as heretical nonsense. I said nothing.

'Well, I guess it's time for bed,' said Robert, getting up from his chair.

Monica by now was also fully awake and charged with energy. 'Come on then,' she said, 'we can go through the gardens and get a breath of fresh air.'

Now I do not fully know why I said what I did then, except that Syl was not home and I didn't know where Lili was. Until that second I had had no suspicion, no hint of a thought, about it, but there came into my mind an image of Monica's blasted summerhouse, and I said, 'You can't go through the garden.

Mine is complete mud and I've just laid down new lawn seeds.'
Thank God Monica's interest in gardening was confined to a
few pot plants or she would have known that this was an odd
time for such an exercise.

'We'll go by the road,' said Robert very firmly, and I
wondered what was in *his* mind. I have no idea to this day
whether my alarm was justified.

I was getting tired again. I made the dog a small dish of
biscuits and milk and felt that I was truly back. Not back where
I belonged, but just back – back where I had to be; and on that
thought I went to bed, leaving the green dress and the black
jacket on a chair for Mrs Raffald to hang up in the morning.

Mrs Raffald came on a Saturday as a matter of course to help
me put all in order for Sunday, and since she was so near
anyway she had agreed to go to Monica for as long as she had
guests, that is until the wedding was over. She came in at
midday and announced that things were going from bad to
worse at The Oaks.

'Could I get into the lounge to clear up?' she inquired rhetorically. 'No, I couldn't. Lili was there with her feet up, and
Robert roaming around like a bear with a sore head.'

'He got to bed late last night,' I explained. 'So did I. We
went to his show opening.'

'I know,' she said. 'He was going on about his late night and
she was going on about her hangover and Margaret's mum was
going on at Margaret and Margaret was sitting there like a
dying duck in a thunderstorm. The honeymoon's off,' she added.

'What?' I said. I hadn't seen Syl all day and had assumed he
had gone to the club, as he did most Saturdays. 'Is Syl round
there?' I asked. It was ridiculous to worry about a man of Syl's
age, but I still liked to know his whereabouts. 'What do you
mean – the honeymoon's off?' I asked as I gathered the full
import of her words.

'Yes, he's round there,' said Mrs Raffald. 'They're all fussing round that poor girl, driving her mad, I should think. Not Syl,' she said as an afterthought, remembering that I was his mother.

'He does fuss a bit,' I said tiredly. 'He means well.' I knew that she would be thinking that this was unmanly of him and was too polite to say so. Even in a relationship as unusually frank as ours there were certain things not to be said. 'The honeymoon,' I reminded her.

'They'll kill me if they knew I've told you,' she said, and I assured her that they wouldn't know.

'Just tell me quickly,' I said, 'so that I know what to expect. Sit down and tell me.'

'Well, let's go in the kitchen,' she said, 'and have a cup of tea in comfort.' I knew what she meant. The kitchen was the place for confidences.

'Margaret nearly fainted last night,' I told her. 'At the opening. It was very hot and stuffy . . . '

'Was that it?' she said. 'They were all going on about her health this and her health that and she was getting paler and paler, and then Lili said it was mad to go to Egypt because there was disease out there . . . '

'Did Lili say that?' I asked.

'Yes,' said Mrs Raffald, 'and then Margaret said she'd rather go to the seaside. I didn't hear it all. I was trying to polish the hall. Fat chance with everyone going backwards and forwards all over the place.'

'Probably just as well,' I said. 'It's a tiring journey to Egypt, never mind the heat when you get there.'

'Did you feed the dog?' she asked. He was trying to scratch something out from under the cupboard, his claws scrabbling and his eyes brimming with anxious desire.

'What's he after?' I wondered aloud. 'Mouse? Beetles?'

'Not in *my* kitchen,' said Mrs Raffald jocularly. She got down beside him on her hands and knees and also scrabbled. 'Bit of biscuit,' she announced after a moment. 'Wasn't there yester-day.'

'Syl bribes him not to yap when he comes in late,' I explained.

'Cufflink here too,' she said, and for some reason I said that Syl had lost it days ago and had been looking everywhere for it.

'Wasn't here yesterday,' she said, and was as satisfied as I to change the subject, for she prided herself on her meticulous housework.

'They're off to Scotland this week,' she said. 'Lili and Robert. Give me a chance to get the place cleaned up properly.'

Syl drove me to Mass the following morning. Monica was not what is known as a regular church-goer, but Margaret was. When Syl had first become interested in her he had suggested that he should take her to Mass each Sunday as he took me, and she had refused. I can see her now, standing in the hallway, saying with completely unexpected determination that she preferred to walk. Syl had been taken aback and made some joke about her being right – one didn't go up Calvary in a Rolls. She hadn't laughed.

We arrived before the previous Mass was finished. Syl went off to the club since he also was not an ardent church-goer, considering it sufficient to make his Easter Duties and turn up at Midnight Mass, and I sat down near the back.

Margaret was kneeling at a pew a few rows in front of me to my left, a black lace chapel veil over her shiny hair, her head bowed. I watched her as the priest said *Ite missa est*. She raised her head to look at the altar and slowly got up, genuflected and walked up the aisle. She didn't see me and I got the impression she didn't see anything. She was half-smiling. She was rapt. It was cold in the church. I tried in my imagination to clothe her in bridal garments, to see her treading that same path down the aisle, misted in white, radiant with flowers, leaning on Syl's arm. I couldn't. Hell, I said in my mind, and didn't even feel it necessary to apologize, for something was wrong. The next Mass passed more or less without me as I strove to imagine Margaret's wedding. Hats and bridesmaids and sponge-bag trousers. Confetti and old shoes. Laughter and tears. Oh God. The awful banality of weddings oppressed me, and I could not people the church where I sat with the appropriate gathering of cheerful guests. Blasphemous reflections had assailed me as the bell rang three times for the Host, for it had just occurred to me that the bride's father would give her away – and Derek was the bride's father. I sat lost in cruel abstraction as the congregation stood for the gospel, knelt for the consecration. Up, down, up, down. My age excused my sitting throughout the service, but I felt I would need absolution to reconcile myself to the Lord after the thoughts I had entertained during his feast.

Syl was waiting for me outside although I had told him, as I always did, that I could easily get the bus, which passed the end of our private road, but he insisted that as long as the winter lasted he would collect me. In the spring he feared it might rain on me. In summer he mistrusted the heat, in autumn he would say there was already a nip in the air. He was a good son.

'Lili and Robert are going away this week,' I told him in the car. 'Why don't you take Margaret and me out for lunch one day.'

'Would you like that?' asked Syl, surprised. I had refused on many occasions to join them on some expedition, wondering whether Syl was alone among the sons of men in wishing to take his mother on trips with his fiancée.

'I think it would be nice,' I lied. My misgivings about this marriage had been increasing daily. Margaret's white, spellbound face as she turned from the altar had made my heart sink. I had felt it give an unnatural beat and fall a little. It was none of my business, but I was going to make it so: at least to the extent of trying to discover what Margaret truly felt about her wedding, and about Syl. I thought I could not bear to see him rejected and hurt again, but no man could live with a woman who wore that terrible look as she turned from the altar. *Noli me tangere.*

'We could go out to a pub in the country. Take dog and let him chase cats in the forecourt.'

'Dog is past chasing anything,' said Syl.

'He dreams about it,' I said. 'He lies on his side, twitching and chasing dream cats up dream trees. We'll give him a refresher course so he can dream new dreams.'

'New dreams,' said Syl, changing gear and smiling broadly.

I pulled my hat down further over my ears and started thinking about lunch.

A few days later we stopped outside The Oaks and Syl went in to fetch Margaret. I sat in the back seat of the car with dog wondering glumly why I had ever had this stupid idea. Syl and I got on well, all things considered. We didn't bore each other when we were alone. When I say 'bore' I mean that active, almost aggressive quality which some people have. They will, it seems, deliberately set out to bore, refusing to be quiet but telling you things you know already, and things you don't agree with, and things you don't want to know. Monica was like this when she was at her worst. The bore never understands that if he would only shut up he would cease to be boring. Nor does he care. Syl and I were content to be silent together until speech became necessary or until something struck us as worth transmitting. Margaret was not boring in this sense but her presence hung in the car like a heavy, unfamiliar odour: not unpleasant exactly, but impossible to ignore. It was distracting and strange and I could think of no way either to dispel or cope with it. She was, I think, so engrossed in her own thoughts, so remote from us that her intensity became almost palpable. She seemed to belong to another order of being. Dog was more one of us, more easy and everyday than the small girl, heavy as lead with her unexpressed concerns.

Syl whistled as he drove, a ploy that was not needed when we were alone together. I wondered how it would be if I was not there, and whether he would still need to whistle through the bleak winter countryside. I wished I had stayed at home and not had to hear his reedy response to the Jericho walls of Margaret's silence.

Suddenly she said very loudly, 'No.'

I nearly jumped out of my skin and dog whined. '*What?*' I said.

The atmosphere thinned as she spoke. She sounded quite normal. 'I am so sorry,' she said like a polite little girl, 'I was just thinking aloud.'

I knew that tone of politeness. I used it myself when I wished to dissemble. Margaret was quite as unhappy with this trip as I was. What a ridiculous waste of time and petrol when at least two of the car's passengers wished they were somewhere – any-where – else.

Then we arrived at the pub and were able to occupy ourselves ordering drinks and staring at the menu. Even dog had had a wasted journey, as he showed no desire to chase cats: no desire to do anything but lie by my foot, as he could have done at home. The menu was dull – Sunday dinners were all that were on offer and I grew more depressed by the minute. We went through to the restaurant and sat at a table by the window. My back was aching from sitting in the car and now my temper was growing short. Syl was relaxed by his pint of bitter and looked around him with every appearance of contentment, but Margaret was silent again. I thought – battling against the urge to shriek 'Say something, you tiresome little lump' – that I had better discuss the weather.

'It's nice here in the summer,' I remarked. We had once

come here often, years ago, and it had been quite nice, but it was so no longer. The old open fires had been replaced by electric logs and there were juke-boxes in the bars.

Looking around I saw that the genuine beams had been replaced by artificial ones, and wondered again what it was in the human psyche that preferred the ersatz to the real. My temper worsened and I vowed never to come here again.

Syl must have become aware of the new constraint in the atmosphere for he grew awkward. An assumed gaucheness was one of his methods of dealing with embarrassment, and he helped himself to the vegetable dish using his fingers.

This evidence of his anxiety briefly breached my self-control. 'For God's sake, Syl,' I snapped, 'use the spoon, can't you. You're not three any more.'

'Sorry, Mummy,' said Syl, smiling maddeningly, yet still looking unhappy.

Margaret seemed completely unaware of these family tensions. She was pushing her food around her plate and thinking of something else.

And then she suddenly said 'No' again.

It was odd and rather frightening. Even Syl was disconcerted. He said 'Yes' and forced another smile. 'What do you think of her, Mum, talking to herself?'

'I think it's the first sign of madness,' I said in as cold a tone as I could muster. I was very angry: angry with Margaret and her passivity and her sudden display of negativeness; angry with Syl and his unease and his fingers greasy from the vegetable dish; angry with dog; angry with the interior designers who had ruined a perfectly good pub; angry with my aching back and my age and myself. The trifle too, when it arrived, was disgusting. I was so angry that my sight dimmed as though with weeping. When it cleared I looked up and saw Margaret glance at Syl.

There is more to be learned from a quick glance than from a long gaze. People settling down for a good look can compose their features into a suitable mould, while with a split-second glance they can utterly give themselves away. Margaret did not only not love my son. She loathed him.

'My,' I said brightly, 'just look at those cows.'

I was no longer angry. Shock douses rage. I sat up as straight as I could, stared out of the window and gabbled, for now silence would be insupportable. I felt a coldness of pity for Margaret and of fear for Syl. I talked about the time I was chased by heifers, out with my love and his cousin, thousands of years ago it had seemed. I had forgotten, forgotten it because it had once given me such pain to remember. The cousin had come to stay with my love on his father's farm. She was a little older than him, a little older than me. She had red hair and thick ankles, but she was undeniably attractive despite her feet. The heifers of the father of my love had run naughtily away out of their field up on to the moors and the three of us went to chase them back; but my love and his cousin hid from me, and I was chased by the cows. I had been brought up with cows and held them in contempt, but I was frightened then, astonished at my love's betrayal and dreadfully wounded. We were very young. The cousin went away again and my love turned back to me – it was to be many years before he finally betrayed me – but I never reconciled myself to the cows.

I chatted away about heifers and their tendency to violence, but as my story was really about passion and infidelity and I left all that out it was pointless and tedious.

The marriage could not go ahead. Perhaps I should argue that since Syl and Margaret were related, no matter how distantly, it would be an error; plead the Table of Affinities. As much as I didn't want to see my son married to a woman who disliked him, it was Margaret I was worried about. I had never been back to my daughter's grave. My thoughts were inchoate and disjointed. I felt powerless and aged and useless and sad. I felt the way dog looked, and no wiser.

*

When Lili returned from Scotland she came round, bringing a box of biscuits with a picture of white heather on it.

'We're going to go and see Cynthia and Derek and the little ones,' she said. 'We're going to go and check on their frocks, and look in their mouths, and count their teeth.'

I found that the name 'Derek' had the same effect on me as many much worse words – words not to be spoken in family houses. It seemed to me that Derek should have been thrown into outer darkness and the signs of his exit papered over: that he should never have lived at all, and, having done so to do what he did, should be expunged from human memory. I said, 'I don't think I'll be able to look at him.'

'He'll just look exactly the same as everyone else,' said Lili. 'A bit ugly, like most people.'

'I don't see how he can show his face,' I said.

'He's forgotten,' said Lili. 'He's justified his actions to himself. He feels guiltless.'

'And I don't see how Monica can bear to look at him.'

'She's forgotten,' said Lili. 'She's blocked it from her memory. She pretends it never happened.'

'And Margaret . . . '

'She's forgotten,' said Lili. 'She feels guilty. She's blocked it from her memory.'

'I'd like to kill him,' I said.

'He'll be sort of dead already,' said Lili. 'People who've done bad, bad things start to rot away from inside. I wouldn't be in his shoes, I must say.'

'The Bible's quite comforting,' I said. ' . . . better for him that a millstone should be tied about his neck and he should be cast into the depths of the sea . . . '

Lili gave a hoot of laughter. 'At the wedding,' she said, 'shall I creep up behind him and whisper those words in his ear?'

'What about his new children?' I said. I hadn't thought of them before.

Lili shrugged and said she didn't know. 'There's nothing you can do,' she said. 'If you climbed on the roof and denounced him for a child-molester Margaret wouldn't admit it and Derek and Monica would deny it with their dying breath. It isn't respectable, you see.'

'We should do something,' I protested.

'Let Cain pass by,' said Lili, 'for he belongs to God. Don't worry.'

But I did worry: not so much about the new children as about how to prevent this travesty of a wedding. I wondered if I should talk to Lili about it, but the moment didn't seem right. It would sound too much as though I didn't want my son to marry flawed goods, and while that was part of it, it certainly wasn't the whole of it, as I hope I have made clear. Perhaps all motives are always and invariably mixed. I felt increasingly useless. That night I lay awake, for I decided that in all conscience, as a Christian, I must worry about Derek's new family.

Or rather not exactly worry about *them*, but about my own incapacity, my disinclination to interfere. That dreadful word. I thought again that there should be another, better word for it and cast around in my mind. All I could come up with was 'meddle', which is worse. There was an old medical phrase about 'minimal interference', which concept I had always applauded. I believe it was invented by some doctor as he sweated among the wounded on the battlefield and observed his colleagues enthusiastically hacking off those limbs which had not already been severed but merely damaged; probing, cauterizing, anointing and bandaging. In many cases, it seemed to him, nature, left to herself, would have made a better job of it all. I had to make many a conscious effort to return to the plight – if plight there was – of Derek's new family. Frequently I would assure myself that Derek's lapse (I clothed the unspeakable in the Sunday clothes of euphemism) was an isolated instance, a moment's madness, and that he was a harmless, rather pathetic human being, either unjustly accused or unfairly punished by the exaggerated loathing in which Lili and I – if no one else – now held him. I would decide to acquit him, and think about other things such as battlefields, and then, feeling craven and inadequate, would try and force myself to face the facts. It was astonishingly difficult. My mind wandered incorrigibly from the point while I made attempt after attempt to see and think clearly. I made myself consider again the question of interference. If you came across a brute beating a donkey or a dog what did you do? You intervened, I thought to myself. That's what you did, and it wasn't called, or regarded as, interference – except by the beater, of course. And then I began imagining this beater of animals, haranguing him and snatching away his whip, soothing the cicatrices of his wounded and abused beasts. I started again. I decided to talk to Lili. She would, I felt instinctively, be of more practical use than the parish priest, who was the only other person I could think of who could be regarded as concerned in the matter. It was, after all, a question of wickedness, and sin was his business, but he was an old man and I didn't want to worry him. Then I remembered that he was certainly younger than me, and went off to make myself a cup of tea.

The wedding was so close. It seemed an inappropriate time to accuse the father of the bride of nameless crimes. I grew even more cowardly and began to consider the quality of bravery. Mrs Raffald was brave. I wished I could tell her about it, but the prospect reminded me of something my love had once done. He had shot a fox (in my part of the country it was usual to shoot foxes) and had brought it to my uncles' farmhouse. I was alone and he had said, 'Come with me while I do this', and we had gone into a corner of the barn and there by lamplight he had skinned the fox and cut off its feet. I had thought it would be pleasure to be with my love in the lamplight, alone with the smell of the hay and the lamp reek, but it had been some time before I wanted to be alone with him again. If, I thought, I should put this corrupt matter between myself and Mrs Raffald, it would change, if it did not spoil, our friendship. It was a matter for professionals, for slaughterers and undertakers, doctors and priests, this little matter of decay and destruction. It was for others to intervene between Derek and his possible victims. But who knew? The problem was impossible. In the end I did nothing: one more cause of shame to add to a lifetime's roll of those things which I ought to have done.

Syl came home one evening earlier than I had expected. I was tired after all the recent gadding about and had promised myself an evening of solitude by the fire. I was beginning to realize how much I now appreciated warmth and to wonder when I had begun to do so. Time had once passed slowly, each year like a drop of blood from a new, as yet unrealized, unfelt wound. Now the years flowed, clustered, congealed, and the wound was clearly mortal.

'You're back early,' I said, too tired to regret the reproach implicit in these words.

Syl looked tired as well.

'I thought you were dining in the city,' I said, maternal feeling compelling me to some show of interest.

'Decided against it,' said Syl. He had brought in a flat parcel and put it down on the sofa. Since he was silent and obviously upset by something, I had to make a further effort.

'What's in the parcel?' I inquired, as if I cared.

'It's my wedding present to the bride,' said Syl in an offhand tone. I expected him to go up to his room since he was in that sort of mood, but he walked over to the fire and stood looking down at it.

'Oh, what is it?' I asked doggedly. Dog lay at my feet.

'I'll show you if you like,' said Syl.

I could see his mood beginning to thaw. His pleasure over the present was dissipating the annoyance some setback had caused him. He undid string, unfolded paper and produced a framed painting, holding it at arm's length. It was one of Robert's paintings that I had seen at the exhibition.

'Oh, she'll love that,' I said.

'It'll go just opposite the bed,' said Syl, looking at it carefully.

'I'm sure she'll be pleased with it,' I said, in as bright a tone as I could contrive. Syl was now quite cheerful and inclined to sit down and talk, but I had nothing to say that evening and went to bed. I sat reading for a while and wondering whether Syl had taken the painting in exchange for the money he had lent Robert. It was none of my business.

'I won't half be glad when this wedding's over,' said Mrs Raffald. 'I can't get on with anything in that house.'

'Is Margaret still going round like a dying duck in a thunderstorm?' I asked.

'There's something not right with that girl,' she announced, stuffing a duster in her apron pocket. 'Sometimes I think she's not all there.'

'I wonder if she's ill,' I mused, remembering countrywomen's talk of green sickness and trying to remember what they'd meant by it.

'She's always thinking of something else,' said Mrs Raffald. 'Miles away.'

I wondered where she went, and then something connected in my mind. There had been a thunderstorm that night when Monica had come round, distraught, with her hair flying, but I had not previously associated it with Mrs Raffald's dying duck. I heard myself saying 'Ah.'

'Eh?' said Mrs Raffald.

It had sounded even to me like an exclamation of pain. I said I had a twinge of rheumatism.

'Then get out of this kitchen and back in the warm,' said Mrs

Raffald. 'Go and sit down in the sitting-room and I'll bring you a cup of tea.' She brought a plate of Lili's biscuits too, and I crumbled one in the saucer while she watched me.

'You don't look after yourself,' she said.

'Does she ever say anything . . .?' I began.

'Not a lot,' said Mrs Raffald. 'Robert was trying to talk to her the other morning when her mum and Lili went off. I heard Lili telling him to take her out to lunch or something but he couldn't get any change out of her. She's happiest with her own company.'

'I know,' I said. I knew that Mrs Raffald undoubtedly had views of her own about the forthcoming wedding. I was certain that she found it as incongruous as I now found it myself – inexplicable and absurd – and I wanted to talk to her about it. She was the only person in my life with whom I had anything in common at all. She was solid and unpretentious and she didn't give a damn what people thought. I forgot that I had felt myself to be like Lili and Margaret. Perhaps I was, but there was no comfort in the reflection and nothing to be gained from it. What was needed here was the middle-aged quality of common sense. As a girl I had been good and I had had some wisdom, but it had been dissipated by time. Realizing that I had grown old only to grow worse, I felt an immense frustration. Impotence and a weary disinclination ever to do anything again flooded my limbs and I put the cup down before I dropped it. All I longed for was peace and an absence of all feeling: dull death with no prospect of immortality and whatever it might hold. I was too tired even to wish for happiness.

'Right,' said Mrs Raffald, 'I think it's back to bed with you.'

I found I was trembling.

'This bloody wedding,' she said. 'You've been overdoing it, gallivanting all over the place, up all night with that Lili. You're no spring chicken, you know. It'll be the death of you, this wedding.' She went on grumbling as I got back into bed.

'Mrs Raffald,' I said, 'this wedding is ridiculous.'

'I know, I know,' she said. 'Don't you worry your head about it. It'll be all right. You'll see.'

I lay against the pillows thinking how undignified the neighbours would consider my conduct and my conversation with the charwoman, and how much I valued her. Without her, I reflected, I would be insupportably lonely. I had always heard that old age was a time of loneliness and it had never perturbed me, since I had imagined that what was meant was a physical separation from one's fellows. Old people who lived alone, cut off by distance, or senility, or simple crabbedness, were lonely – not me. I had kept myself to myself from choice and I had never understood until now that loneliness was not imposed from outside but had bred and spread in me until I had become its host, and little else. I had not realized until now that I was lonely.

'My Mum overdid it,' said Mrs Raffald. 'She was always on the go until I had her to live with me.'

I had been to the funeral of Mrs Raffald's mum, but not to the baked meats afterwards. This was because in those days I had grown too far from the ways and customs of my youth and had forgotten how to appreciate people with no pretence. I had thought I would feel awkward with Mrs Raffald's relations who shouted their wares from barrows, cleaned windows and drove taxi-cabs for a living. I had thought they would feel uneasy with me, but now I remembered all the time I had spent in the kitchen and the dairy with the people who belonged there and how I had belonged there too. Margaret had never known that security. She had been brought up by a shallow, ambitious and pretentious woman in a precarious, silk-lined vacuum and never really felt the earth under her feet at all. Perhaps her mother had done her as much harm as . . . But I didn't want to think about that.

'Perhaps she should go away for a while . . . Margaret . . .' I said.

'She's been away,' said Mrs Raffald, 'and she's come back more limp than she went.'

I don't know whether it was because of what I had been told, and that I saw Margaret in a different light of my own kindling, or whether she really was changing, but whatever the reason something was different. She was drinking a lot for one thing. In those days I believe people drank more than they do now – some people anyway – and I think it was those who had got into the habit in the East. Monica, I am certain, would never have splashed around the alcohol in the way she did if she hadn't grown accustomed to a way of life in which her compatriots drank more or less all the time. I remembered from my brief stay in Egypt that even the innocent-seeming long drinks were habitually spiked with gin.

Margaret, I felt, did not drink to be sociable, nor even to get drunk, but because the drink was there on offer and she had discovered almost by mistake that it made the days seem shorter and more tolerable. If anyone had reproved her I think she would have abandoned it, but even Monica seemed to see no real harm in what she doubtless thought of as convivial drinking. I never saw Margaret stumble or laugh without reason or flushed with drink, but I saw her eyes go slightly out of focus and watched her not listening – away somewhere on her own. Once or twice I wondered where.

'What are you thinking about?' I asked her one evening – out of curiosity, not in order to make conversation.

'Oh nothing,' she said, but the smile she gave me could only be described as *mocking*, and it was very unlike Margaret's usual style. I persevered.

'I have always found it very difficult to think of nothing,' I said. 'And I believe I am not alone. I believe the ability to think of nothing can only be acquired after years of practice – by Yogis and Sufis and people who spend all their time sitting on top of poles . . . ' If she had been completely sober I should not have spoken like that, but I was a little annoyed. Drink is supposed to loosen the tongue, and her smile had indicated that she was certainly thinking of something.

'I mean it wasn't important,' she explained. 'It wasn't interesting.' I found her composure remarkable. She was shy and too often silent, but when she spoke she sounded assured, cool and rather frightening.

There were quite a number of people present in the bar of the golf club – a ladies' night – and God knows why I had allowed myself to be inveigled into joining them. Feeling more than ready for bed I had nevertheless been persuaded by Syl to accompany him to this festive scene. I knew Margaret was enjoying it no more than I was and I wondered if any of the revellers were. It was hard to tell. A few people were happily tight, some talking, but most were mute – either playing bridge or just sitting there.

'On the other hand,' I said, 'I don't think many of our fellow guests are thinking about anything much. Do you?'

She had, in politeness, to respond. 'I think some of them are thinking their frocks are too tight,' she said, her eyes on a fat woman in red.

'And I'm thinking about bed,' I said. 'Monica, is it time to go home?' She was at an adjacent table talking about weddings to another neighbour.

'It's early yet,' she said and Syl brought Margaret another drink.

I wanted to say that she had had enough, but it was none of my business. I felt sorry for her. There was no real proof that she was bored almost to death but I knew that she was, and I wondered if she was contemplating the future with an infinity of these evenings to live through. I didn't feel that I could bear many more myself and in the nature of things I didn't really need to worry. There couldn't be all that many in store for me.

'I'm going home,' I said.

'Wait just a while,' said Syl, 'and we'll come with you.'

'There's no need,' I told him. 'I can easily go by myself.'

But Syl wouldn't hear of it, and I had to endure nearly another hour in the clubhouse, feeling that on the whole I would rather have been set upon by footpads and summarily despatched on the path home.

I woke again soon after I had finally got to bed, perturbed by a stray half-thought, half-dream. It was to do with images, with reflection and projection, and I lay awake, teasing it out. I had never liked the woman whom Jack had seen as his wife, had never liked Jack's *me* – myself in his eyes. I had seen in his eyes the reflection of the woman he loved and I had despised her; and despised him for loving her, for I could not. I wondered what Margaret thought of the girl she saw in Syl's regard.

I stayed in bed the next day and didn't sleep that night.

Nevertheless I felt somewhat restored the following morning and got up early. It was mild for the time of year and I went out into the garden wondering if I would live to see the green shoots of spring flowers, not being a spring chicken myself. If I would live to see the almond blossom, a goat in its lower branches, peering down with devil's eyes ... Oh, God, I'm wandering, I thought. I'd better go and make some coffee.

I was going slowly towards the back door when Lili came flying over the lawn from the path by the golf course. After a moment's doubt I had to admit I was glad to see her. I knew I would be tired out again by lunchtime, but I had to give her her due: she was good company.

'Derek's wife is awful,' she said, 'I think he must beat her. She's all quiet and silly as though she'd had the stuffing knocked out of her. And she can't cook.'

'Poor thing,' I said. The mention of Derek depressed me.

'I knew a woman like that in Egypt,' said Lili. 'I was ever so sorry for her and then her husband died in terrible agonies and it turned out she came from a family of women who were skilled in herbal medicine just like my aunts. Eating Cynthia's lunch I began to wonder if she was thinking along the same lines.'

'Nasty, was it?' I asked.

'Horrid,' said Lili.

'I'll make you some nice wholesome coffee to take the taste away,' I said.

'We went out to dinner that night,' said Lili, 'with the same thing in mind. I ate a lot of garlic.'

She looked at me sideways and I had the impression there was something she wanted to tell me but didn't know whether she should. I waited.

'Well,' she said after a moment, 'I should think, going by the evidence, that Derek's life is a misery and a burden to him, so that's good.'

'Bit hard on Cynthia,' I said.

'We can't be bothered with Cynthia at the moment. We've got Margaret to think about,' said Lili.

'And Syl,' I said, suddenly rebellious, for I didn't want my son plunged into a loveless marriage like Derek. No, not like Derek. Syl was nothing like Derek.

I said loudly, 'Margaret is too young for him. She is not at all mature. She isn't ready to be married.'

'I know,' said Lili, 'but what's to be done about it?'

'Speak to Monica,' I said hopelessly.

'You can't speak to Monica,' said Lili. 'She doesn't listen.

'Then I don't know what to do. Perhaps I should speak to Syl.' I poured coffee and passed the sugar. It didn't occur to me to speak to Margaret.

'I don't think that would help,' said Lili. She had the air of someone who knew what she was talking about. 'I've skirted round it a few times but he's stubborn. *And* he's bought that picture of Robert's for a wedding present.'

I said before I could stop myself, 'I'll make him keep it whatever happens. He won't want his money back.'

'That's all right,' said Lili abstractedly. 'I'm not worrying about that. I was just thinking he does seem to have made his mind up.'

'He's made it up before,' I said, again before I could stop myself and sounding unexpectedly bitter, even to my own ears. I was glad the issue was out in the open. Perhaps relief was making me unguarded.

'It would be a disaster,' said Lili. 'Most marriages are, but this would be an *absolute* disaster.'

'Maybe . . . ' I began.

'No *maybe* about it,' said Lili. 'It would be dreadful.'

'I was going to say,' I said, 'that maybe we should get the priest to talk to Margaret.'

Lili stirred her coffee. 'I don't know why I didn't tell you before,' she said. 'I tell most people most things without a moment's hesitation but I haven't told you this.'

'What?' I asked.

She placed her spoon carefully in her saucer before she spoke, and I remembered she had been an actress – or was it a dancer?

'Margaret wants to be a nun,' she said, putting her elbows on the table and lacing her fingers together. 'I haven't told anyone this either, but when I went to see Marie Claire just before we came away I went to the convent to see Mother Joseph too – I've known her for years – and she said she'd been sorry to see Margaret go, but she'd eat her wimple if she didn't come back. And she's no fool.'

'A nun,' I said. 'Yes, I see.' What I saw was the recollected face of my intended daughter-in-law as she turned from the Blessed Sacrament. 'Yes, I *see*,' I said again.

'There'd been some trouble,' said Lili. 'Mother Joseph said she didn't know what it was all about but, God forgive me, I think she was lying. She knows everything that happens before it happens. Margaret wanted to get away. That silly Marie Claire wouldn't tell me either – but then she wouldn't tell me anything. She thinks I don't know she'd been having an affair with Robert.'

'Good heavens,' I said.

'Silly cow,' said Lili with some force. She offered me a cigarette and I took it. 'As if I couldn't have stopped it if I'd wanted to.'

I thought this talk of sexual misdemeanour might lead us into dangerous territory in view of Lili's liaison with my husband, although it was refreshing to be with someone who did not, for one moment, think it necessary to tone down her conversation to spare my aged sensibilities. Mrs Raffald was bread, while Lili was croissant – insubstantial and not altogether wholesome, but enjoyable. Despite the increased drinking, and the cigarette smoking which she had led me into, I felt more alive than I had before she returned. I brought the conversation back to the convent.

'Has Mother Joseph written to Margaret?' I asked.

'I don't know,' said Lili, 'I don't think so. They don't go out chasing postulants. She'll just wait. Marie Claire's written to Monica. She says they can't come to the wedding because she's too busy, but what she means is she doesn't want to face me. She's frightened of me.' Lili sounded smug.

'It's just as well,' I said. 'If there isn't going to be a wedding.'

'I think there'd better not be,' said Lili.

After she was gone I wondered briefly about her motives in saying that. Most people, for whatever reason, tended to encourage marriages, but then Lili wasn't much like most people.

Supper was ready for Syl when he came home. I wasn't hungry but I sat down with him at the end of the dining-room table.

'I mustn't be long,' he said, cutting up his baked mackerel. 'I'm taking Margaret's present round to her later.'

I was nervous, but after all I was his mother. I said, 'Syl, do you think this marriage is a good idea?' I thought at once I could have phrased that better, or started from a different angle or possibly have kept my mouth shut, but it was too late now.

Ominously, Syl seemed not to be surprised by my question. He drew his eyebrows together but continued eating mackerel, pouring more mustard sauce over it as he spoke.

'I'm not going to let Margaret down,' he said.

This quite flummoxed me. I don't know what I'd expected him to say, but it wasn't that.

'What do you mean?' I asked stupidly.

'I mean she's had a tough time,' said Syl, 'and I'm not going to let her be hurt any more.'

'But she's so young ...' I said.

'That's just it,' said Syl. 'She needs somebody to look after her. Monica doesn't understand her, her father deserted her, she was bundled off to school and then off abroad and she needs some sort of security.'

Not a word of love, I thought, as Syl continued to speak in between mouthfuls. How interesting. 'Have some cheese,' I offered, as he pushed his plate aside. 'Cheddar.'

'I haven't got time,' he said, and he went out, leaving me with my mouth open.

What was so surprising about his reaction, I thought, was its extraordinary arrogance. I found it difficult to be really angry with Syl but I heard myself saying 'Men' again, under my breath. Here was the same thing, the unquestioning assumption that in the attention of men lay the fulfilment of women.

I cleared the table and gave dog a bit of mackerel skin. It was gone, gobbled up, before I could turn.

'Dog,' I said, 'you men are all the same.'

Now I could feel an uneasy rage curdling somewhere behind my breastbone. Not with Syl: with somebody else, somebody I had almost forgotten. With my eyes closed I imagined this man standing to the left of me, and in my mind I swung out with all my strength with my left arm and felled him. Then there were other men and I moved along and I felled them all. There were tears in my eyes, and I knew what I was mourning. It was my lost virginity. This realization brought me to what sense I had remaining to me, for after all it was rather late to worry about that now. Like one of the seal people, the mermaid or the fairy wife, I felt I had sacrificed my birthright to benefit mortal men and I yearned to return to the sea, to the lake, to my element. Three blows from a man were enough to send these mythical creatures back to the halls of their fathers, and I had put up with more than that. I went and sat down in the sitting-room and lit a cigarette. I got up, poured myself a glass of brandy and sat down again feeling dissolute.

Then Syl came back.

'You weren't long,' I said.

'Margaret's tired,' Syl said.

'Did she like the present?'

'Yes, I think so.'

'You don't sound very sure.'

'I'm sure. She liked it.'

I was silent, for Syl was in a bad mood.

I thought of King David. They used to bring him virgins to sleep in his bed and warm his old bones. Old, cold, bones. Once, in the poor farmhouses, some farmers' families would only have one bedroom and they would all have to sleep together. My mind was like a disobedient dog: it would go off without approval or permission and roll in matters that I wished to know nothing of. It went on sniffing and scratching at the oubliette where the subject of incest lay concealed until I thought I should go mad. The dairy women had held the same biblical superstition that the young should never lie beside the old, for their vitality would all be drained away: they would fade and wither, while the old would rise, rosy-cheeked, with renewed vigour and go on living. I could not, at the moment, imagine why they should want to. I could not, at the moment, see any virtue in living whatsoever.

Yet another morning had come round. Life was like some debilitating, hypnotic game composed of endless repetition: some cosmic fruit-machine – mindless, mechanical, like the monsters in the pub by the river. The mere speeding succession of days was enough to unhinge the reason. I longed to be back – at home, where the days had seemed to flow, not fall in, one upon another, with a jangle and a flash, and be gone again.

I thought of telephoning Father O'Flynn, but what could I say? That I wished I was dead? He might reply that, doubtless, I soon would be, adding that my desire was sinful. That I wished I'd never lived? Even I could see that that was pointless. And it was a lie, for I had once taken great joy in life. That I must prevent my son's marriage? He would think I was a jealous, possessive old woman, for he was not the cleverest of men, our good parish priest.

I sat down, for I knew that Lili would soon be round. She could not tolerate the atmosphere in Monica's house and when she couldn't be bothered to go to town she came to me to smoke and drink my whisky. Have I said that before?

She came, sure enough: light-footed with a dancer's step, her hair like filaments of light and her skirts floating.

'I brought my homework,' she said, and sat at the kitchen table making flowers.

'What do you think would happen,' I asked, 'if I told Syl about Margaret?'

'You mean about *Derek*,' corrected Lili, her fingers busy with a curl of scarlet paper. 'I think he'd hate her, and he'd marry her and hate her more and more, and when she wept at his unkindness he would say, "Don't blame me for your unhappiness, my dear. It's your father who has done this to you. You are incurably deformed in spirit, a filthy and unnatural creature, blighted beyond redemption. There is nothing I can do to help you. Lie down and ..."'

'Syl doesn't talk like that,' I said. My voice was harsh.

She put her head on one side. 'Doesn't he?' she said.

I knew that part of what she said was true. The revelation would not stop Syl from marrying Margaret. He would say that the outrage upon her made it more compelling that he should marry her, and look after and protect her. Everything she said was true.

'Margaret would hate him,' I said. 'She would hate him for knowing that about her.'

'But then,' said Lili, 'on the other hand, he might never tell her what he knew. She might never know. She might never know why *he* hated *her*.'

'Are you sure,' I said, ' . . . are you sure she doesn't remember?'

'I'm sure,' said Lili. 'Couple of weeks ago – do *you* remember – we had tea with you and on the way home she wanted to talk. She wanted to confess something. Now you know me. I *cannot* keep my mouth shut. If I keep it shut sober, I open it drunk. So I told her not to tell me. She trusts me, you see, poor little bitch. Now I think I *know* what she wanted to tell me – I gathered a lot from Marie Claire between the lines – and if she was prepared to tell me that, it wouldn't take much to make her tell me anything. No – she doesn't remember.'

'Why wouldn't you listen to her?' I asked.

'Because,' said Lili patiently, 'if it all came out, if somebody – anybody – talked about it, she'd think it was me. And she trusts me. I like being trusted. Besides,' she added with patent honesty, 'as I already knew what it was I wasn't consumed with curiosity.'

'What was it?' I asked.

'Not going to tell you,' said Lili.

'What are you making?' I asked.

'Flowers,' said Lili, 'for the wedding. For decoration. It's a secret. Don't tell.'

Without shame I felt helpless tears rolling down my cheeks. 'Oh Lili,' I said.

She didn't get up, but leaned across and put her hand on mine. Her fingers were stained scarlet.

'There won't be a wedding,' she promised.

For some reason I believed her: possibly because there was nothing else I could do. I was as weak and dispirited as a newborn child exposed on a river bank. I had seen a dead kingfisher once on a riverbank . . .

I couldn't leave it alone. 'But what can you do?' I asked. I found I was thinking of Monica, of all her preparations, the trouble and expense. She spoke of it whenever I saw her.

'It's so late,' I said. 'We've left it too late.'

'Some things,' said Lili, 'only happen at the very last minute. If you think about it everything happens at the last minute. Things don't happen before they happen, do they?'

Although I found this quite senseless her tone was reassuring. Something out of the common was called for here and Lili was unlike most of human kind. She did not feel the normal constraints of accepted behaviour. She might do anything.

I went and got a bottle of whisky to reinforce the wisp of optimism I was experiencing and poured out two glasses full.

'Wow,' said Lili, 'that's more like it.'

It was now about ten in the morning and these days one glass of whisky made me drunk. I half-consciously wanted to rearrange the pattern of life, to ride across the boundaries which separated the done from the not-done thing. I felt it would make it easier for Lili to do something which normally was not done, and getting drunk on Scotch in the middle of the morning was not the accepted thing for old ladies in my environment.

Mrs Raffald, when she arrived, was noncommittal about this scene of mild debauchery. 'Don't overdo it' was all she said.

'I'd better be off,' said Lili, gathering up her bits of paper and wire. 'I'll finish this in the summerhouse.'

Summerhouse. I laughed to myself and shook my head. Lili was incorrigible. Mrs Raffald made me sit, out of the way, in the drawing-room and I went to sleep. I slept a lot over the next few days and I drank a lot of Scotch as well. Perhaps I should have put that in reverse order.

Mrs Raffald came up to my bedroom carrying a tray of breakfast things: China tea, toast, coddled egg.

'I'm not hungry,' I said. I had a headache that seemed to start at the bottom of my neck.

'There's two aspirins here,' she said, picking them out of a saucer and handing them to me. She poured water from the jug at my bedside and I got them down somehow.

'I called in at The Oaks,' she said , 'and I told her I'd come back later when they'd got things sorted out a bit. The place is full of kids now on top of everything else.'

'Kids?' I said.

'Margaret's dad's new two,' she said.

'Oh, them.' I drank some tea.

'And his new wife's brought everything bar the kitchen sink.'

'Sit down and tell me about it,' I said, with a perverse wish to wallow at second hand in the awkwardness and discomfort that I was sure now characterized The Oaks.

'She doesn't seem to have any luggage. She's brought everything in paper bags,' said Mrs Raffald, 'and left them in the hall-way.'

'Perhaps she can't afford luggage,' I said, thinking of Monica's lifestyle on alimony.

'Don't suppose she can,' said Mrs Raffald, who knew everything about the circumstances of Monica's divorce. 'Only it needn't be alligator skin. Anyone can afford a cloth holdall.'

'I hope it won't mean too much work for you,' I said.

'I won't neglect you,' said Mrs Raffald, familiar with the weak selfishness of the aged.

'That's good,' I said. 'Hand me my top teeth and I'll smile at you.'

'Eat your toast,' she said.

Despite the headache I felt happier that day, more relaxed. I had made a conscious decision not to worry myself to death, since it couldn't be long before he came for me anyway. Why waste strength?

'Where's Lili?' I asked.

'I saw her going down the garden before I left,' said Mrs Raffald. 'She'll probably be along any minute.'

'Will you send her up if she comes?' I asked.

'Yeah,' said Mrs Raffald. 'Shall I tell her to bring anything up with her?'

'Cigarettes,' I said, 'and sherry. I'm not going to drink whisky *all* day long. Only when there's a wedding in the offing I do think one needs something.'

'I'll tell her to bring the dog up too. He's pining down there.' Mrs Raffald had a soft spot for dog despite the mess he made. I think she was one of those unusual folk with a genuine tenderness for the old. It's easy for most people to like babies, but the helplessness of the aged does not have the same appeal.

'Cuck-oo,' came the cry from the stairs.

'Come on in,' I said.

Lili put dog on the bed and his claws scraped at the silk counterpane.

'Put the little beast on the floor,' I said, 'and move those clothes off the chair and sit down.'

She was wearing a bright red coat and was clearly going further than my house. Underneath she wore a black jersey dress, more suitable for tea at the Ritz than a drunken morning with an old lady.

'You're going out,' I said, and I knew I sounded doleful and despised myself for it.

'I have to go and sort out finances at the gallery,' she said, 'and then on to lunch with some people, and then off to dinner with some more.'

'Well, have a nice time,' I said.

'I'd stay,' said Lili, looking at her watch, 'but I must get a move on. I *had* to get out of that house. I'll tell you all about it later . . . ' and she was gone.

I drank a couple of glasses of sherry and left the bottle well in sight on the bedside table. If I was going to end up as a tippler I didn't want anyone to imagine that I was trying to hide it. Drinkers I did not mind. Secret drinkers I could not abide.

'That Lili's a bad influence on you,' said Mrs Raffald, folding a towel. 'You've hit the bottle since she turned up *and* you smoke like a chimney.'

'It's not her,' I said, 'it's the wedding.'

'This wedding's getting everybody down,' said Mrs Raffald. 'Be glad when it's all over.'

I said I'd decided to stay in bed that day and asked her if she'd leave something cold in the dining-room for Syl's supper. She brought me up a library book I hadn't yet opened and the latest copy of the *Croydon Advertiser* and I leaned against the pillows and went back to sleep. I slept on and off for most of the day and in consequence was wide awake as darkness fell.

Syl was late. I put on my dressing-gown and went downstairs. Dog had gone down earlier and acknowledged my descent with a snuffle or two. I supposed Mrs Raffald had fed him, but I gave him a mouthful of the ham she had left for Syl.

'All alone, dog,' I said. 'All alone, you and me by the telephone.'

I was waiting for it to ring: for Syl to tell me he'd stayed late at the office, or had gone with a colleague to a restaurant. I told myself it was ludicrous to worry. If we had been an ordinary family Syl would have left me years ago and be living in his own house with his own family and I would certainly not be staring at the phone, waiting for it to ring, like a lovesick maiden. I resented having been forced into admitting to myself that our situation was not ordinary, and when the telephone did ring I picked up the receiver intending to be very short with Syl.

It wasn't Syl. It was Monica.

Taken by surprise I told the truth and said he wasn't home and I didn't know where he was.

She lied and said Margaret was missing him.

I wanted to implore her to drop the pretence, but I merely said in a conventional voice that I would leave him a message and ask him to return her call.

I knew that there were women whom Syl visited. I had overheard snatches of phone calls. He had recourse to them when he had no regular girl in his life. I was irrationally sure that he had gone to one of them. Fearing the ties of marriage, the end of freedom, the anchor of domesticity, my son had gone to a whore.

'Hell,' I said, startling dog, for I had shouted. It was insane that I, at my age, should be concerned with the private life of Syl, at his age. If you shared a house with someone – no matter who – you become involved in his movements, his comings and goings, his tardiness, his moods.

'God, dog,' I said, 'I'm tired.' The grave presented itself as a most desirable property.

Syl came home as dawn was breaking. I turned my bedside light off and lay down for a while. It was the eve of the wedding. I looked back to my own wedding and found I remembered little about it except that I had felt, on the one hand, bilious and, on the other, determined. Rather, I supposed, as the troops had felt facing the carnage of the trenches. Warfare was one symptom of the insanity of man, and marriage was another. Only a flawed species would indulge in wholesale self-destruction, and only an insecure and uncertain species would have hit on the idea of bonding pairs of its incompatible members together for life as a means of stabilizing society. Musing thus bitterly I got up and dressed. I no longer believed that the wedding would be abandoned. It was too late. I spent the day pottering about, tidying up and making my own tea since Mrs Raffald was engaged at The Oaks, helping to put everything in readiness.

In the evening I put on my green dress, and Syl and I walked along the road to the pre-wedding festivities. The lights were on in every room and the front door stood ajar. Monica was being particularly *grande dame* and welcomed us with more formality, combined with an assumed warmth, than was natural. She kissed my cheek and led me into the drawing-room to meet the other guests.

This fell a little flat, for Cynthia and her children were the only people present whom I hadn't met before. I had brought dog along under my coat, thinking he might ease the awkwardnesses should the children be shy, but they were shyer of dog than anyone. They backed away from him and clung to their mother. She, I concluded, would not permit them to approach any animal for fear of germs, or perhaps rabies.

'Go on, stroke him,' I said to the little girl, but she shook her head and cowered away.

Dog was no more forthcoming. When I sat down he got behind my feet and stayed there. I said good evening to the gallery owner who came and sat beside me, seeming relieved to get the weight off his feet, and talking quite interestingly about the gangs of Soho. Monica, hovering close, gave a little shriek as he spoke of knives and implored him to discuss something pleasanter. The conversation waned. I noticed that Robert kept well away and wondered whether the gallery owner was here to check on his investment.

Margaret was drinking too much. I knew the signs. Lili had commandeered a bottle and went around filling everyone's glass as soon as it emptied. Before we left I had a brief discussion with Cynthia about the uncleanliness of the water in foreign lands and strangled at birth Derek's desultory attempt to reminisce about the old days. I could hardly bring myself to look at him, ordinary and unexceptional as he was. I felt my throat flushing with the drink and a primeval distaste. His presence seemed both purposeless and dangerous, like a cinder from which all visible glow has gone but which is still too hot to touch.

Pleading weariness, I left. Syl walked me home and then went off somewhere. God knows where.

Dog died the next morning. I found him in his basket, stiff and cold as a graven dog, and all the losses and all the deaths came back and washed over me in a flood. I forgot that death brought peace to the dead and wept uncontrollably for the anguish of the living. Syl found me on my knees, unable to rise.

'What on earth is it?' he asked and I thought he probably imagined I was weeping because he was going to marry Margaret that day. As indeed I was: amongst other things.

'Oh dog,' I wept, 'dog, dog.' I liked him now. I wanted him back, snuffling with his bad breath and his hair coming out on my skirt.

I said so, and Syl grew alarmed. He took me up to my room and said he'd send for Mrs Raffald.

I pulled myself together and said I was all right. I said he was to take dog and bury him at once – at the bottom of the garden where the crocuses would grow. He was to do it now before he put on his wedding clothes. Syl left me reluctantly, looking back over his shoulder perhaps to make sure I wouldn't die also on his wedding morning.

I went to the window and watched him walk down the garden, carrying dog and a spade. He began to dig, stopping frequently to straighten his shoulders and look around. He was probably taking deep breaths to remind himself that he still lived. He looked notably free, like a prisoner just released and I felt compunction at my ingratitude. Perhaps he was as constricted as I by our relationship. I wasn't surprised, when he had filled in dog's grave, to see him go out of the garden, along the path to Monica's summerhouse, and thought he must have decided to snatch Mrs Raffald from her duties to come and minister to me. I began to dress for the wedding, not wanting to be too obvious a skeleton at the feast.

Breathless, Mrs Raffald came into my room.

'I'm nearly ready,' I said, trying to give an appearance of sense and decisiveness. 'You needn't have come.'

'You needn't go,' she said. 'The wedding's off.'

I sat on my bed feeling deader than dog, even experiencing the peace of the dead.

'You can take your hat off now,' Mrs Raffald said.

'Have I got it on?' I asked. I raised my hand to my head to make sure, and there it was: the hat I had always worn to weddings. How significant, I thought, that I hadn't bothered to buy a new hat for my son's wedding. It hadn't occurred to me before.

'What happened?' I asked, not caring. 'Where's Syl?'

I realized that I had no idea whether he'd come back from interring dog to get into his wedding clothes. I said, 'I think I'm losing my grip.' I thought, I know now what that means: it means we're all at sea in a storm, clinging to the mizzen mast or the lifeboat's rim or the captain's sleeve, and one by one we tire and we loosen our grip and away we go, down to the depths.

'He went down the pub,' said Mrs Raffald.

That sounded reassuring. People didn't go down the pub to shoot themselves.

This reflection brought me back to life. The cancellation of a wedding at the last, the very last minute, was, if I remembered correctly, not a thing to be taken lightly. I struggled to accommodate myself to this idea, but I didn't want to think about it. I started to speak again but my words were slurred. I could hear them – thick, unsteady and wet round the edges. I said, 'I'm not drunk – I haven't been drinking anything', and then I thought that that was an unseemly remark for a lady to make on the day of her son's wedding.

I began to feel better. Surely all was now well. Few of us had wanted this wedding.

'On the other hand,' I said, and now I was speaking more clearly, 'I could easily be going mad. I feel as though I am.'

'It's shock,' said Mrs Raffald.

I was conscious of myself as though I could see myself in a mirror. I could see an old woman shaking as with the palsy, putting out a tremulous hand for comfort, puzzled and fearful and at a loss.

'Then in that case,' I said, my voice still not quite right, 'we'd better have a drink.'

She went away and came back with the brandy.

I said, 'I prefer a whisky usually, but I'll make do with this. Can I have a cigarette?'

She said, 'That Lili ...'

I said, 'She's a bad influence isn't she?' I was feeling stronger. 'How do you know Syl went to the pub? Did he tell you?'

'I told him,' said Mrs Raffald calmly. She was a calming person. A good influence. 'I told him to go.'

Clearly something momentous must have happened – Mrs Raffald did not habitually give my son orders – but I increasingly did not care what it was. I said, 'Let's have just one more drink', and I wondered briefly what Monica would do with the baked meats – but baked meats were what you had at funerals. This was to have been a wedding. I fell asleep reflecting that while weddings could be definitely cancelled, funerals could only be postponed.

I never really knew exactly what had happened, although I remember Mrs Raffald uttering the word 'summerhouse', and experiencing a swift, hallucinatory image: a sense of *déjà vu* which would have rocked me back on my heels if I had not been sitting down. What she said, or hinted at, was not unexpected. I thought confusedly, 'I know, I know, I saw them.' Past and present were superimposed on each other, everything was repeated, nothing was new. Lili and Jack, Lili and Syl, Lili and all the devils in hell ... Bless her. I never saw her again.

Syl refused to discuss the matter. He said there'd been a scene. They were all mad round there, and Margaret herself had turned out to suffer from religious mania. He said he was going to marry Miss Benson from the office ...

'Mrs Raffald,' I said some time later, 'did Lili ...?' But I didn't really want to know. Details were unimportant and frequently distressing, and Mrs Raffald would not burden me with them. Anyway, perhaps I did know.

She said, 'I'm not saying nothing. All I'm saying is she'll never wear that hat again in public.'

And she laughed and laughed and laughed.

THE FLY IN THE OINTMENT

My coffee had gone cold. It looked, I thought, as though it had died, since it had a grey, inert appearance and only something dead could possibly go cold in such heat. I might have been thinking like this because I was reading the obituary column in an old copy of *The Times* in order to discourage other club members from coming to talk to me, and I was not yet old enough to be cheered by the deaths of strangers. Somebody stood up at a neighbouring table so I read the list of forthcoming marriages with an assumed intense interest, reflecting that strangers who were engaged to each other were even more boring than strangers who had died. Then I saw two names I recognized and immediately I looked up and around to see if there was anyone present who would remember Monica – someone who would appreciate how very peculiar, and indeed amusing, this announcement was. It was quite pointless. Nobody here had met Syl. Nobody here knew the circumstances of our past. Nobody here would be diverted to learn that Syl was going to marry Monica's daughter unless I acquainted them with the facts and I couldn't very well do that. I was already regarded as not *quite*. That was how the women put it: 'Well, darling – Lili is very good company and all that, but she isn't *quite* . . . ' And most of them wouldn't trust their husbands alone with me. Nor could I tell my own husband the details of my last days in England. He was a tolerant man, but there are limits.

I saw him coming towards me across the terrace and stood up waving the newspaper. 'Look,' I said, 'look – Monica's daughter's going to marry Syl.' 'Who?' said Robert. It was an unsatisfactory morning. I poured the dead coffee on to the bank of the Nile and called for a gin.

*

'So,' I said, 'I've decided. I'm coming with you to England.' Clever Robert painted pictures. He was having an exhibition in Soho. I had arranged with God to go regularly to Mass if we could sell a lot of these pictures. Robert said it was too short notice and we couldn't afford it. I said, 'I will sell some jewellery.' Robert said I hadn't got any left. I had. I had some new golden things that my aunt had given me only a short while before. They were an investment. My father, as was the Egyptian custom, had kept all the women of his family, continuing to feel responsible for even the sisters who had married. As a result, whenever my aunts made money – as they frequently did by buying and selling – they thought of it as *family* money and gave me some. They always wanted to invest it for me, to buy a little villa in Portugal, or a share in a little ship, but I would tell them I'd invest it myself in something English and they never felt they could argue with me for my mother had been the *Anglaise* and that made me a little different, not *quite* like them. And then I would spend it, confident that my astute relations would make and give me some more. I seldom had to ask, and never twice. Robert wasn't rich so the extra money was necessary. I said, 'My aunt gave me a parterre ... ' Robert interrupted to remind me, briefly, that he wished I wouldn't take money from my aunts. I said, it wasn't money, it was gold things, but we both knew they were things to sell. Robert could not rid himself of the idea that accepting money from *anybody* was 'sponging'. I could see his point, for I had been a pupil at the English school in Alexandria and there I had learned that many English people felt this way. Monica had felt that way even when she was a little girl. Nevertheless I couldn't really understand it, for was not family *family*? And was not the good of the family the good of all its members? Robert often made me feel alien – oriental and exotic. In the salons of my aunts I became languid and pale like a lily and with Robert I could feel my skin grow darker, my body smaller and my eyes glowing. I went barefoot. I suppose that was why I had married him.

I said, 'It is years since I felt the chill of an English winter, oh my dearest. I want to walk in the fog and kick up the dead leaves.' 'Why?' asked Robert, in a reasonable tone, and I saw that I had approached the matter from the wrong angle. 'Monica is my oldest friend,' I said. 'I have known her all my life and I have known Margaret since she was a tiny little girl. I must go to her wedding. When she was a tiny little child I gave my *word* that I would go to her wedding.' 'You haven't been asked yet,' said Robert.

Oh, the horrible journey and the horrible cold! I had had a little fever before I left home and, as always, had imagined that, by contrast, it would be wonderful to be chilled to the bone. Now I could think of nothing more delightful than sitting in an African garden, baking like a cake. I could feel the fog going up my nose and there was nothing I could do about it. If I complained to Robert I should simply look a fool, for I had brought it all on myself. I was going to have to make the best of it.

We were staying at a dreadful little hotel on the Uxbridge Road. It seemed to me extravagantly, unnecessarily dreadful so I wasted no time in writing to Monica with congratulations on her daughter's engagement. I could have telephoned but letters are safer: more formal, and demanding of a response from the well brought up English gentlewoman. She wrote back immediately inviting us to stay with her, and I danced a bit on the disgusting linoleum of the dreadful hotel bedroom. Robert had gone to the gallery where his pictures were to be shown, so I had some time to decide how to break the news to him. I have found that men often do not like staying in other people's houses. I don't know why. Besides he was bound to assume I had been 'sponging' again.

When I heard his footsteps outside the bedroom door I lit another cigarette. I had already smoked a packet and I had put a lot of shillings into the meter, so the gas-fire had been hissing all afternoon. 'God,' said Robert, 'what a fug!'

'It doesn't matter, my darling,' I said. 'We're not staying.' Robert put his hat on the bed. He was being difficult, but that didn't matter either. I always got my own way. I told him there were cockroaches behind the skirting board, and the lorries roaring down the Uxbridge Road had kept me awake all night. I said the proprietor of this hotel had not changed the sheets since the previous occupant, but had merely ironed them *in situ* on the bed. I said I was convinced the previous occupant had been diseased, for I had found shreds of bloodstained tissue sticking to the sides of the waste-paper basket. I did all the talking while Robert took his coat and his shoes off. I had hoped that he would say we couldn't afford to go anywhere better so that I could announce that we were going to save money by staying with Monica, but he said, 'I suppose you've got hold of Monica,' and I remembered that he knew me well. Sometimes I thought that he didn't like me much. 'It makes perfect sense,' I said. 'Besides Monica leads a most dull life and we will add some interest and glamour to it. This is a kindness we are doing.' It was *true*.

I left the dreadful hotel that afternoon. Robert had gone back into the city in order, I think, to assert his independence. The proprietor of the dreadful hotel took our suitcases down to the cab and stood watching as it drove away. I waved to him and sat back feeling a sense of comfort and gratification since I had done *nothing* to charm him and he was still sorry to see me go. There I was, going to a better place, and there was this unattractive stranger mourning my departure from his dreadful hotel. Clever Lili. I had some tiny misgivings about Robert, but I knew he'd come round in the end. Apart from the fact that he loved me he was much too sensible to turn down the offer of free hospitality. There was a remote chance that he might stay with some other friend, but most of the people we knew in London lived in discomfort in little flats or single rooms or studios, sharing bathrooms and washing their paintbrushes in the lavatory. They thought it was bohemian. Robert was really no fonder of squalor than I was myself. He'd be along in the course of time. Anyway all his clothes and his toothbrush were in a suitcase next to the driver.

Croydon was much as I remembered it. I was not your usual sort of foreigner; not convinced that only Park Lane was fit for human habitation. I liked Croydon, and I found Monica's house very comfortable. It might have been in the country with its big garden and its big rooms. If I could have taken it to Râs-et-Tin I could have lived in it happily for the rest of my life. As it was, I enjoyed its Englishness. Robert didn't like it. He said it was an architectural abortion, but I really didn't care what it looked like from outside. My own little villa – which was all I had left now – didn't look very good from outside. Inside it was different: half oriental, half *rive gauche*. Very *me*. I was a cosmopolitan and happy anywhere if it was warm. I had gypsy blood, for I was an Egyptian. Do you see?

'Oh, Monica,' I said, 'my dearest, how lovely to see you after all this time.' I kissed her on both cheeks, behaving in a foreign way, because it would be more interesting for her and the little Margaret. The little Margaret I didn't recognize for I hadn't seen her for years and years since she was a child. I just assumed it was her because it couldn't really have been anybody else and I said I must congratulate her on her forthcoming nuptials, and Monica said one was meant to congratulate the groom, not the bride, so I said I trusted she was doing the right thing and Monica said one was supposed to wish the bride *happiness*. So I did that and I talked rather a lot because it is always a little awkward meeting again people you have not seen for a long time, and I was remembering the things that Marie Claire had told me that I knew I was not supposed to know, and really it came as a relief when Monica asked where Robert was.

I said vaguely with some large and meaningless gestures that he'd had to go to the gallery. Monica would make allowances for us because I was not wholly English and Robert was an artist. I said he would be along in the course of time and asked if I might go to my room. Margaret took one of the suitcases and I noticed that she did not look healthy. She didn't look as though she would be able to lift a matchbox let alone a suitcase, and also she looked half-witted. When we got to the bedroom she put down the suitcase and stood in the middle of the floor with her shoulders hunched. I thought how satisfying it would be to shake people who stood looking like that. To take them and shake them until their eyelids rolled up in astonishment and they were made to understand that there was life on other planets and other life on this planet. Margaret was locked in some solitary misery and unaware even of *me*. I couldn't have that. I never, never did like to be seen as negligible, not so much out of vanity as because it made *me* doubt my own existence. I was a dancer and I danced because people *have* to look at people dancing. They can't be ignored. No, I wasn't that bad. I felt sorry for Margaret. I really did. I was not going to question her about the events in Egypt when Monica had sent her off to stay with Marie Claire, although I was curious to have her version. Marie Claire – who, I will say immediately, was a terrible pain in the neck – had said that poor little Margaret had fallen madly in love with her son, the silly little Nour. Marie Claire suffered under the delusion that both she and her child were utterly irresistible to persons of the opposite sex, and while it was not impossible that Margaret had indeed fallen prey to the wretched boy, I had laughed dismissively and told Marie Claire not to derange herself about it. That had annoyed her. I told her I had spoken to Margaret's friends, the nuns at the convent where I went to Mass when I stayed with Marie Claire and they had said she was merely homesick. I was lying. Mother Joseph had said she believed that the *petite anglaise* had a true vocation, but I wasn't going to tell Marie Claire that because she would instantly say that broken-hearted girls often took the veil. I hadn't really been very interested in Margaret and her problems for, after all, I hadn't seen her for years, and Marie Claire had grown angry. She said Nour had told her that Margaret had done something *wicked* and I asked what. She wouldn't tell me and, without actually saying so, I had indicated with smiles and flourishes that I knew Nour to be a terrible, *terrible* liar.

I said to Margaret, 'You look as though you haven't been sleeping.' She jumped and muttered something. I lit a cigarette and began to think about the awful boringness of unpacking the suitcases which, after all, I'd only packed an hour or so before in the dreadful hotel. I was not looking my best; not exactly *travel-stained* because what was there to stain you these days? Boats and trains and taxis kept you out of the mud; we had encountered no blood and no one had thrown wine over me. I was unstained, but my clothes were crumpled. I looked at Margaret, wondering whether I could say to her, 'Darling, would you be a little heavenly angel and just press this blouse for me?' But it wouldn't have been any use. You can't really ask people to do things for you if you can't see any signs of life in them. There isn't any point.

'And how is Syl?' I asked when we had sat down to dinner. I asked partly out of politeness, because why should I care how he was after all this time, and partly out of curiosity because I couldn't imagine why she was going to marry him. He was twice her age. 'Is he still handsome?' I said, because it was the politest thing I could think of to say, and Monica said he flew around playing squash and golf and kept himself very fit. Margaret said nothing to add to this unappealing picture and I began to feel rather old, for Syl and I were the same age, were we not, and what was all this talk about keeping in trim? I *was* in trim. I didn't need to play stupid games or jump up and down all over the place. I was fit as a flea. Healthy Lili. Oh, naughty, nasty Margaret to make me feel suddenly old.

Monica said, 'Tell Lili what you thought of Egypt,' as though the girl was a parrot to utter a phrase and be given a nut. 'It-was-very-nice,' said Margaret in her little dull voice as though she feared I would be offended if she said she'd hated it. I don't *own* Egypt – I thought – I'm not *Cleopatra* – I don't care if you hated the sight of the Valley of the Kings and all the accoutre-ments of Tutankhamun. I don't care if you detested the fellahin and feluccas and falafel. Nothing to do with me.

'What did you think of Marie Claire?' I asked her, and I wondered whether perhaps she *had* been in love with the beastly little Nour and was marrying old Syl on the rebound.

'She-was-very-kind,' came the response. I might have known.

'She's very clever,' said Monica.

I wasn't having that. '*Kind* I will allow,' I said, 'Marie Claire is not ungenerous ...' (I thought this magnanimous of me) '... but she hasn't got the sense of a chicken.'

'Oh Lili,' said Monica. 'She was cleverer than all of us in school. She was top of the class, time after time.'

This was *really* annoying. Marie Claire had always cheated. She'd have *aides-mémoire* painted in henna on her arms under her long sleeves and on her legs up to where her socks stopped. I had sometimes cheated too when I could be bothered, but I had never cared about exam results in the way the others did. Monica didn't cheat. She *swotted*. She'd been a stupid girl in many ways. I said, 'What I said *was* – she didn't have any *sense*.' Monica looked at me as though she found me ridiculous. Any minute now I should find myself squabbling as I'd squabbled at school and I lit a cigarette and breathed deeply. I must not allow myself to be drawn into an undignified wrangle. Dinner had been more or less all right, the beds were soft and the rooms warm. I must behave like a grateful and courteous guest, not an undisciplined schoolgirl – no matter how maddening Monica could be, and I was beginning to remember just *how* maddening that was.

'You always did talk frightful nonsense,' she said to me in a tone half-reproving, half-indulgent. I was speechless.

Suddenly Margaret spoke. 'She was *daft*,' she said, and in the twinkling of an eye I saw the child in a different light. Not only did it appear that she held convictions of her own – she held the correct convictions. I reminded myself again how unwise it was to leap to conclusions before a proper period of observation, and I regarded her closely for the first time with these new eyes.

'How you can say that', said Monica to her daughter, 'when Marie Claire was so good to you, I really can't imagine.' She spoke of the ingratitude of guests and I was glad I'd held my tongue earlier. She was really cross. She was cross with me; but just as the good guest cannot roar at her hostess, no more can the good hostess roar at the guest, so she was taking it out on Margaret. Now that I was looking at Margaret properly I saw that she was not as ordinary as I had thought. Not quite. She didn't answer her mother, not – I thought – because she was afraid to, but because she knew it would be a waste of time and energy. She had bones and features and she sat still.

She didn't look to me like a girl who was about to get married. Or maybe she did? It all depended on expectation. There were girls – they were usually the ones who had been good at games – who sort of leapt at marriage with their hair flying and a glint of lasciviousness in their eye. They flew greedily around, buying things to put in their new houses, and hats to put on their heads, and shoes and frocks and knickers and nighties. They were grabbers. They would grab their husband on the wedding night and never willingly relinquish him. They would if they were the *first* to find someone better, but if they were enjoying him and suddenly caught him straying they would cut up his clothes and follow him to his places of assignation where they would stamp and scream curses, and throw things. If they were driving a car they would try and run him over. I had known several such – the kind who made their own marriages. Then there were the kind whose marriages were arranged for them. Many of my friends fell into this category, but they were not usually Christian and most of them had hated games. They went placidly along with the arrangements and let themselves be wed. Sometimes they lived lives of contentment, and if they didn't it was just too bad. Margaret looked like someone being led to the wedding. 'Is everything planned for the day?' I asked. 'Who's coming? Is Derek coming?' Derek was Monica's ex.

'Yes,' said Monica, 'Derek's coming. And his family. Jennifer and Christopher are going to be page and bridesmaid.' She sounded smug and I looked at her closely. Monica was one of the grabbers. She had written to me when Derek married again – not when he left her but when he married again. She had expressed herself in unguarded terms and I daresay when she'd posted the letter she'd wished she hadn't. Something must have happened to reconcile her to the situation. On a moment's reflection it was pretty clear what it was: nothing dramatic like a conversion, a change of heart, a surge of generous forgiveness. No. Looking round at the creamy comfort which characterized Monica's mode of life I realized that she'd grabbed *everything*. Derek was a dreary type of man even by Monica's standards and she'd probably been only too glad to be rid of him, once she'd understood that she could grab and grab and leave him and his new wife to struggle along as best they could, living on alms if need be. She'd kept everything – the knives and forks we were eating with, the tablecloth under the dinner service which could only have been a wedding present, not being the sort of thing you'd buy for yourself. She'd grabbed all the wedding presents and everything that they'd since acquired. I rather admired her. Another thought occurred to me: 'What's she like?' I asked. 'What's the new wife like?'

'A nice little thing,' said Monica.

'Aha,' I said, for these words conveyed much meaning. They meant colourless, dowdy, poor and tedious. I could *see* her, this new wife. She made her own clothes and her wardrobe smelled of moth balls. Her feet smelled of feet for she could not afford much hot water to wash. I would not be one ounce surprised if her feet were flat. Her shoulders would smell of tears and the vomit of children.

'Her name is *Cynthia*,' said Monica. All my suppositions were correct, for what could a *Cynthia* be but tiresome? 'Oh, yuk,' I said, and for a moment Monica and I were in accord.

I got up early. To be truthful I hadn't slept very well. To be absolutely truthful I was a tiny bit worried. I brushed my hair and it went crackle, crackle. I wasn't very pleased with my hair – it wouldn't shine because I had had a fever. It was going a bit grey when I looked at it closely. See how truthful I am being. Truthfully, I had forgotten what colour it really was. My aunts had hennaed it since I was a tiny little baby. It was due for a fresh application. Oh how troublesome everything could be. The curls were natural – oh, all right, I gave them a little help with the curling tongs when it was necessary, but basically they were real. Now the treacherous hair would not behave. I should have to wear a hat.

Where was Robert? Where was Robert? *Where was Robert?*

Of course he would telephone soon. He would telephone or just arrive at the house. He always did. No cause to worry. Nobody ever left Lili. Not for long. Well, almost nobody. I was certainly growing older, for there comes a time in life when you must face the truth. There are two times – once when you are very young and think in terms of absolutes; and then when you have spent your years lying a bit and scheming a little because you must survive, then the time comes again, when you no longer think in terms of absolutes. It had come. I didn't really know why. Perhaps because once you no longer feel invincible the truth is all you have left . . .

I said to the woman – Oh, oh, whatever happened to the girl? Where had that girl gone? – I said to the woman in the looking-glass: 'Pull yourself together, Lili.' I spoke firmly. Peering closely I put lipstick on that woman's lips, mascara on her eyelashes, powder on her nose. And there she was. The girl was back. I dressed her in a very simple frock of black jersey. A very simple Paris frock; and I pulled in my stomach, for the girl had had no stomach at all, and I didn't want to let her down.

'All dressed up and nowhere to go, eh?' said Monica as I came into the kitchen. An irritating remark, you must agree. 'Where's Robert?' she asked, as I ignored this conversational gambit.

'He is terribly taken up with his exhibition, Monica,' I said, in the serious tones I used when speaking of work or money.

'All night?' asked Monica.

'Very possibly,' I said. 'He has to spend much time with the gallery owner. They were quite probably up all night.' Monica knew nothing of the world of art so she couldn't argue. It was maddening for her.

'What do you want for breakfast?' she inquired, sounding rather grudging. I thought I might take the opportunity to have a real English breakfast – bacon and eggs – but I wouldn't have been able to eat it. Not all of it, and Monica would be cross with me.

'I will have just a croissant and some coffee,' I said.

'We don't have croissants in Croydon,' said Monica, and by now she sounded rather grim. 'And until I get round to putting in an order at Selfridges we don't have any coffee beans. Will Nescafé do?'

Oh. I should have to be careful. Monica was under strain. Probably she found Margaret recalcitrant. I must be good. Two difficult females under her roof would be more than she could endure. Stupid people, contrary to popular belief, are not good at endurance like dumb animals. They crack and behave unfairly, blaming the innocent for things they haven't done. I said, like a sweet and grateful innocent, that I would love a cup of Nescafé and a weeny-teeny bit of toast. With perhaps a little marmalade. She was already making toast, so that was all right.

'I'm taking Margaret her breakfast in bed,' she announced, rather, I thought, as a person might remark that she was going to find a leper and give him a smacking kiss. A martyr in search of martyrdom. I would have offered to take up the tray myself, but my coffee would have gone cold, and we all know how much I hate cold coffee. Can't abide it.

'It's easier in the end,' she said, slapping toast on a plate. 'Better than having the kitchen full of people first thing in the morning with the day ahead.'

There were many responses I could have made to this. I could have asked why we did not break our fast in the dining-room. I could have asked why it mattered, having the kitchen full of people. I could have pointed out that every morning the day lay ahead, and there was really no reason to mention it, for I needed no reminder. But would that have been wise? No, it would not. So I ate my toast very carefully and brushed up the crumbs with my finger. The telephone rang and I forgot about the crumbs and flew to answer it. It would be Robert calling, for it had to be Robert. I willed it to be Robert and it was. So that was all right.

'Did I hear the phone?' asked Monica, when she came down. I was in trouble again – answering *her* telephone.

'I answered it,' I said, 'to save you the trouble of flying downstairs and breaking your head on the parquet.'

'Who was it?' she inquired, not really mollified by my care.

'It was Robert,' I said. 'Soon he will be coming.' Oddly enough this seemed to cheer Monica. Perhaps she missed having a man around. There were women, I knew, who felt that life was incomplete without a man around. No reason to cook. No reason, really, to comb your hair. Perhaps, underneath, Monica felt like that. I did myself. Sometimes I did and to be honest sometimes I didn't. It was a matter of mood. Sometimes, when I was little, it was better when my father was away and I was alone with my aunts and my mother. It was easier to laugh and there seemed more to laugh at, but then when he came he brought presents and a certain sense of excitement. He brought me a monkey once. I wonder what happened to it.

Down came Margaret – rather like rain – grey and not cheerful. I said, 'Here comes the bride', and I thought – poor girl. How ridiculous. People who look like that don't get *married*. They sit in corners and people pretend not to notice them. I said out of curiosity: 'When will we be seeing Syl again?' I wasn't all that curious about this, actually. I wanted to see her reaction to his name. She didn't react at all, just said he'd be round in the evening, and nothing more.

She made no effort at all and I began to feel depressed. It was cold outside and I could see things blowing about. I said: 'We can have a party.' Monica would probably quite enjoy a small party, I thought. Then, on the other hand, if she caught me planning parties in her parlour without asking her she'd be mad with me again. 'Maybe we won't have a party,' I said. Quite often I didn't like parties; nasty, noisy occasions. Can't hear yourself think. Too hot. Squashed. When I was Margaret's age I didn't like parties at all unless I was asked to dance. I don't mean May-I-have-the-next-waltz type of thing – I mean me dancing all by myself in a clear space so that everyone could see me. Graceful Lili. Such *talent*.

Monica came in worrying about dinner and looking quite, quite as depressing as the weather. The weather, by contrast, began to look almost inviting. A brisk walk would be good for me. Monica hadn't got enough chops for dinner, poor soul, not if extra people were coming, so I said I'd go and get her some.

'Come on, Margaret,' I said. 'We shall wrap ourselves up warmly and go and buy these chops.' It was nice of me to take Margaret too because she was not easy to converse with. On the other hand she, I imagined, would know the way to the butcher's shop and I didn't want to go wandering all over Croydon in the wind hunting for meat. No fun really. Ach, it was cold out there. I said so. I promised myself that I would buy a new coat. A big, warm English coat for the English winds. English people, I remembered, often went for walks just for the sake of it. Not to go anywhere or do anything – just walk. Silly, I call it. It was very monotonous putting one foot in front of the other.

Margaret, who until then had not opened her mouth, told me that she used to walk in Egypt. Just that. 'I used to walk in Egypt,' she said. How interesting. A lot of people walk in Egypt. *Thousands* of them, up and down the *gisr* and all around the towns.

'How did Syl propose?' I asked. This was something I actually wanted to know – for all sorts of reasons. Well, I was curious for a variety of reasons.

Margaret appeared to give this some thought. I was changing my mind about her again. She was worse than ordinary. Was she, perhaps, mentally retarded? 'He asked me to marry him so I said I would,' she finally told me. Well, what an earth-shattering revelation. Fancy that. How truly amazing. 'Why?' I asked.

'I don't know,' she said, and she looked very sad, so sad that now I began to feel sorry for her. It was no use my pretending that I thought this marriage was a good idea because it wasn't. It was a silly idea. Remember – I knew Syl. I said, 'I wonder if he's queer?' and then thought that perhaps I should not have. It wasn't very tactful, was it? Too late now, anyway. I had sometimes wondered that in the past. 'I mean he's getting on', I said, 'and living with his mother and never got married yet and all that.'

'He's had girlfriends,' said Margaret, as one who states a fact. *I* knew *that*. I wondered if she knew how many. There'd been a time when he changed girls as often as he changed socks. It had looked like a kind of insanity, and sometimes I'd wondered if he wished he'd been a girl, surrounding himself as he did with such heaps of the creatures. Everybody lost count. The minute one affair was over – and often before – he'd be in love again and always with somebody *unlikely*, somebody who, you felt, would have remained forever on the shelf if Syl hadn't reached up and brought her down and dusted her. He seemed to have an ability to see something in the dullest, plainest female; some spark imperceptible to the rest of the world. Having perceived this twinkle he would set about fanning it in his mind to a positive pyre, a great glorious leaping thing of flame and heat. He would describe the new girl in these firelit terms and bring her to meet you, and when he did you'd find the sort of girl you bought your stockings from, or who dealt out your prescription over the chemist's counter. Yes, all right. I *am* a snob. I am particularly a snob in matters of sex. Monica too used to be disgusted. Why did she permit her daughter now to be engaged to him? I thought it was very bad of Monica. I didn't understand her. It was all too peculiar. Maybe I had been away too long and forgotten how the English behaved. What an annoying thought. I am particularly fond of understanding.

The butcher's shop was bright and orderly. It gave a rather comfortable impression which was remarkable considering its purpose. Nice clean bits of animals hung around in neat rows. It was warmer in there out of the wind and I was quite sorry to leave. There were all manner of cuts of meat I hadn't seen for years and the butcher bragged about them. He was as proud of his liver as if it had been his own. I was a bit worried about mine for I drank too much. Oh yes I did. I knew it and I sincerely meant to mend my ways. If Monica intended to stuff us with meat at every meal then I should have to persuade her to give us extra vegetables too. We didn't eat much meat at home. It wasn't really very good. I would have to buy garlic myself since Monica would be bound to consider it vulgar and it was essential for health, cleansing the blood and clearing the skin. I like to look after myself even if I do drink too much. *Because* I drink too much.

Robert was in a rage. He claimed several reasons for this rage – good and sufficient reasons, he said – Croydon, and gallery owners and such things – and me. 'Oh nonsense, Robert,' I said. 'It will all be all right on the night.' Monica had put on some scent. 'Be nice to Monica,' I said in his ear, and I pulled it because I was glad he was there, after all. He gave me what I can only describe as a cold look, which I ignored, but he did set about being nice to Monica. He sat down beside her and conversed – mostly about past events, for that was all they had in common, apart from their humanity, which didn't offer much in the way of social chit-chat. I was, I confess, relieved that Robert was there. He wouldn't have left me for ever, wouldn't have left me for long, but when they're not there you can never be absolutely certain – either as to where they are or whether they truly will be coming back. Not *absolutely* certain; not unless they have huge possessions and a special chair and slippers that they mind about. Our life wasn't like that. Even the house at home was more mine than Robert's. All that held Robert to me was me, and while that should have been sufficient (and indeed was really) sometimes when my hair wouldn't shine and I looked in the looking-glass in the cold grey light – well, sometimes I wondered just a little. Just a *very* little.

I was so glad to see Robert making his effort and being nice to Monica that I'd hardly taken any notice of Syl. He hadn't changed. He was just the same. Same clothes, same face, same Syl. 'How well you look,' I said. I meant well-preserved, for that was the impression he gave. He had put his arm about

Margaret's shoulders and she moved away towards me saying, 'What were you like when you were young?' What a question out of nowhere! Why did she ask it? Did I look a hag? Was I perhaps decaying under her eyes? Monica heard too and seemed to take it personally. 'Do grow up,' she said to her child, which was ironic when you think about it, since she was offended at the suggestion she was no longer young and the more Margaret grew the older *she'd* be. But then Monica was never what you could call logically-minded.

'I take care of myself,' said Syl. 'I like to keep fit.'

This conjured a melancholy picture of Syl jumping up and down, beating his arms around and pouring with sweat.

'Press-ups?' I asked gloomily and felt his biceps. 'Mmm,' I said.

'You look well too,' he remarked without conviction. Syl and I had got off on the wrong foot with all this talk of health and youth. There was an antisocial air of competitiveness, regret and envy floating about. You'd never have thought – well, never mind!

Dinner seemed endless with those ghastly old chops. Monica had graciously permitted me to make the soup and that was all right. I'd used up the spinach she'd been going to serve with the chops and put a lot of garlic in it too. I liked doing a little bit of cooking when I didn't really need to, but Monica had hung around making critical queries – 'Do you have to use *so* much garlic? Why are you taking all the ribs out of the spinach?' – and I decided I wouldn't help in the kitchen any more. We could always eat out quite a lot, Robert and I. It took him ages to cope with his chop and his gravy and potatoes. I felt quite impatient, for it was the sort of food he'd been brought up on. He should have learned how to eat it by now. Margaret drank too much and didn't say anything. Nor did Monica, and I think Syl was sulking, so Robert and I did our world-famous double-act, performed before all the crowned Heads of Europe and the

East. Sometimes I thought that together we might be the reincarnation of Abû Nowwâs. Robert told anecdotes and I added to them. We'd dined out that way more times than I could count. I was beginning to get fed up with it so I was glad when Margaret went to bed. Robert went to bed too and Syl went home and I was left to help Monica clear the table. I didn't offer to help wash up. What if I broke one of her wedding present plates? It is very difficult being a guest. The best thing is to be amusing and keep out of the way.

I offered an added bonus and suggested she leave the washing-up till the morning. 'Come and sit down,' I said, 'and tell me all about *everything*.'

'I'm a bit tired,' said Monica, sitting in an armchair and sagging. 'This wedding . . . '

'You're obviously doing too much,' I said in a solicitous voice. 'Poor darling, it doesn't seem fair.' I don't know what I meant by that, but it went down well.

'Oh Lili, you've no idea,' she said. 'Bringing up a child on your own is no joke.'

'No, it can't be,' I said. Why should it be? No, I didn't say that. I just thought it.

I said rather warily: 'Margaret seems a good girl though.' I wished to compliment Monica's skill in raising this good girl without making light of her achievement in doing it all by herself. 'She's a credit to you,' I added, inspired. 'A really nice girl.' This was praise enough for Monica to allow herself to express some misgivings.

'She's so quiet,' she said. 'She seems to have no go in her at all. I thought when I sent her off to stay with Marie Claire it would do her good – make her see something of the world, make her come out of herself. You know . . . '

'A lot of people would be glad to have a daughter like Margaret,' I said. Oops – wrong thing to say. I was getting tired.

'They wouldn't if they had to live with her,' said Monica

sharply. 'You've no idea what a strain it is. She just moons about like a dying duck and she makes no attempt to do anything for herself. I have to think of everything.'

She sounded overwrought. Any minute now she'd lose her temper or burst into tears. I said: 'You're worried aren't you?' By this time, you see, I felt sorry for her. I really did.

'Oh yes,' she said, wearily. 'I'm worried. I'll be glad when the wedding's over, only . . . '

'What?' I asked.

Monica stirred in her chair. 'I don't know if she's ready. I don't know . . . I've never discussed anything with her. I haven't . . . '

Enlightenment broke upon me. Of course Margaret would have told her mother nothing of the ratty little Nour. 'You don't think she's a virgin, do you?' I cried, wishing simultaneously that I had not, for the events in Egypt, from what little I had gathered, must remain forever shrouded in secrecy or else there would be the most unholy *brouhaha* and I would get the blame for being indiscreet.

Happily Monica's stupidity came to my aid. She gasped like a goldfish. 'Lili, you don't think Syl . . . '

I said in my relief, 'Darling, you can be so stupid sometimes . . . ' there was a sound from the kitchen and we both listened. 'It was nothing,' I said. 'There's nobody there. No, I just meant – is she a virgin? I didn't mean she wasn't. I don't think Syl would sully his bride, do you?'

Monica looked doubtful. 'Oh look here, Monica,' I said, 'we all know what Syl was like, but that was years ago. He must have grown up a bit since then.' I was not being frank. I saw no reason to suppose that Syl had changed at all. Why should he have? I hadn't. If he hadn't slept with Margaret I bet it wasn't his fault. On the other hand it was just possible . . . 'If he is truly in love,' I said with my tongue in cheek, 'he will respect Margaret, will he not?'

'I suppose so,' said Monica, and from her tone I gathered that that was not really what was worrying her. It was something else. 'I sometimes wonder,' said Monica, 'whether she'll *ever* grow up.'

Robert was rather alarmingly quiet. He had been since he arrived. Quiet and polite. I didn't like the signs. He was seldom openly angry with me, for when he was I got angry too and that was dangerous. I don't mean I'd have killed him, but when two people lose their tempers one of them always says more than she intends because one of them – at least – feels she must win at all costs, and I have a reckless streak. It is an important part of my character and I cannot erase it, but I like to keep it under control. Robert called it 'showing off' because he'd been taught in school to despise spontaneity. He was hitting the top of a boiled egg with an egg spoon in a concentrated, silent sort of fashion. It made me nervous.

'The thing about marriage,' I said, too loudly, for being made nervous also made me bad-tempered, 'is that it must be exclusive.' Don't ask me why I said that. I wasn't thinking about the wedding. I wasn't thinking about anything much. It just popped out. Nobody else was saying anything after all, so it was good of me to bring a little cultured conversation to this breakfast table. I'm not being truthful, I said it to please Robert. Robert didn't look pleased. He didn't look anything except like a man eating a boiled egg on a winter's morning, while Monica looked contemptuous. I don't think she meant to look like that for she hadn't got enough brains to *be* contemptuous. It was only her expression but it was irritating. I went on. 'We learn nothing from promiscuity,' I said, 'just that there's very little to choose between one man and another.' I often talk like that when I'm drunk, but seldom first thing in the morning. I was more shaken than I'd realized. Robert had disappeared behind *The Times*. Oh, damn. Might as well be hanged for a sheep as a lamb. I was getting everything wrong. 'In order to understand ourselves,' I said, making one of those honest attempts to clarify matters which led you further into the mud, 'we need to understand each other, and to do that we must live together for a long time. Exclusively.' Even I could see that this didn't mean anything. I knew what I meant but I couldn't seem to express it. I meant it was better to understand one thing properly, using one example (well, all right – one man, one husband) rather than go flying round exploring the possibilities of hundreds of them. I *believed* that. Robert lowered *The Times* and looked at me. Monica spoke: 'What have *you* learned, Lili?' she asked.

Great heavens – she *was* being contemptuous.

I floundered. I felt like a person dancing on a river bank when, lo, the bit she's dancing on breaks away and there she is hopping about like a lunatic on a lump of sinking turf. The way of the entertainer is fraught with danger – with misunderstandings and the risk of failure. And now Robert was looking at me. I began to get really cross. I lost the thread of my argument. Anyway, what did I care? 'Oh, I don't know,' I said. 'Isn't it obvious? All you learn from sleeping around is that men are much the same.'

Robert spoke: 'So are women,' he said.

I was furious. I know it was my own fault for talking philosophically over breakfast; for saying the sort of things that are normally only said in smoke-filled rooms after dark, after dinner, after several bottles of something or other. Nevertheless he had no right to say what he said; to humiliate me before Monica.

'I'm not like other women,' I said. 'I'm different.' Perhaps it was the cold and the greyness that were making me unsubtle – making me vulnerable. Making me sound ordinary and – yes – making me sound like other women.

'Yes,' said Robert, 'you *are* different.' His tone was sardonic. I changed the subject. 'What are you thinking about, Margaret?' I inquired. I might have saved my breath, for she replied that she was thinking about what I'd been saying. 'Don't listen to me,' I said. 'I talk a lot of nonsense.' It was sufficiently irritating to have been forced into making such a statement without what happened next. Monica repeated my words. 'Don't fill her head with nonsense,' she said. 'Only a fool would marry for love. Anyone with any sense uses her head when it comes to marriage – chooses someone with a bit of character; someone with good solid qualities.'

I think she was referring to Syl and this was enough to make me blink, apart from the fact that what she said had absolutely nothing to do with what I'd been saying.

'People don't sleep with people because of their good solid qualities,' I said, also with seeming irrelevance. (Monica doubtless thought of herself as having good solid qualities and no one was sleeping with her.) I was glad to see that this had annoyed her. She said nothing. I thought it was high time I dropped the discussion before I really put my foot in it. 'We're off to town,' I said. 'I'm taking Margaret, too.' At the moment I didn't want to be alone with Robert. He was clearly still displeased with me. Quite unjustifiably, in my view, but there you are. Men take offence at the slightest thing.

'I don't really want to go out,' said Margaret.

'Oh yes you do,' said her mother. 'It'll do you good.' She was leaping at the chance of a day's respite from her daughter. She looked determined.

'What'll you wear?' I asked Margaret hastily before she could argue.

'She can wear her grey tweed,' said Monica, beginning to gather up the breakfast plates.

'I'll go and look in her wardrobe,' I said. 'I like looking in other people's wardrobes.' It was true. I sometimes had a dream that I'd been given a house and I went through all the rooms, along the verandas, looking in other people's wardrobes and chests of drawers. The trouble with this dream was that in the centre of the house lay a vast palm-shaded courtyard and I was never permitted in there. Not ever. It belonged to somebody else. Poor Lili. Oh well.

Margaret's clothes were what you'd expect, but I lent her a jumper of my own and some scent. With a dash of make-up she didn't look too dull. She had a kind of distinction – almost. If she'd concentrated she could have looked rather beautiful, but I was in a hurry and had no time just then to start on artistic endeavours. I could have made her look quite different – but then, what was the point? I'd have got no thanks for it. Besides, why should I create a beauty? I was the beauty here. Who needs two? I was ashamed of this thought. Selfish; unworthy of me. I made Monica lend Margaret her pearls and gave a little lecture on the power of dress.

'Since you're so keen on clothes, Lili,' said Monica, 'you can help me alter her wedding dress.'

'OK,' I said. Real, tangible help from me would do much to reconcile Monica to our presence.

Robert's brother had let us have his car. He was away so he didn't need it. He hadn't wanted us to have it, but he couldn't think of a good reason for refusing. I said, 'I hope we get a good lunch.' I was feeling a bit undernourished.

'Don't expect too much,' said Robert. 'He's in an economical frame of mind.'

'We speak of Robert's gallery owner,' I explained to Margaret. She said, 'Won't he mind if I come too?'

'Who cares?' said Robert. We were both mad with the wretched man who conspicuously failed to appreciate us. He should never have been concerned with art when all he really minded about was money. He hadn't even offered to put us up.

'Is it difficult selling paintings?' asked Margaret.

I felt we must have been careless if she was so aware of the undertones to what we were saying. 'Not at all,' I said. 'Not if they're perfectly superb and they've got me to help sell them. You must watch me at the opening . . .'

Robert kept interrupting me and I had to make an effort to remain cheerful and positive.

I spoke for some minutes on the benefits of being married to a creative person – the added interest and challenge, the absence of boredom. I believe Robert found me unconvincing. He said: 'I told you not to give up dancing.' He spoke too gently for my liking.

I said that I was sick of dancing. I told the truth – the pure, plain truth – which was that I was tired of dancing, and I'd rather spend the time with Robert. Of course it didn't sound like the truth. It sounded as though I was generously pretending that I didn't care about abandoning my own career in order to further Robert's. And it wasn't the whole truth – which was that I was desperately sick of dancing, at that time, lonely and frightened and aching in every limb. You wouldn't believe some of the places I'd danced in. My aunts never knew. Nobody really knew, except perhaps Robert . . . I said, 'I didn't want to go dancing round the world. Do you remember how I was dancing round the world?'

He said, 'Yes. Summer seasons in Fayyum.' He did know really, after all.

'Ha ha, ho ho,' I went, and I was a little afraid again for if he knew me so well then surely he couldn't love me very much. Oh, how I hate feeling humble. Time to fight back. I said: 'I'm glad I didn't marry a successful man. How boring it would have been. As it is, I have had every chance to discover my own potential.'

'You've always been the same, Lili,' said Robert in that gentle voice.

I sat in the car wondering why he'd married me. He must have loved me. I'd make him love me again. Or perhaps he still did? He was faithful to me and that must mean he loved me. But of *course* he loved me. Silly Lili.

*

As soon as we arrived at the gallery I took an intelligent interest in the exhibition. I spoke of framing and hanging and lighting, about all of which I did not know a damn thing and cared less. I was bored by painting and seldom even looked at Robert's pictures. I always said how beautiful they were but I'd never really looked at them. They were something Robert did when he wasn't with me. If he'd been an accountant I wouldn't have had to pay huge attention to his columns of figures, would I? How could I constantly be throwing myself about in transports at the glory of his paintings? I always said all the right things and I helped sell his work. I did. I made people drink a lot and buy it. Now I made several very pertinent and clever remarks and a few suggestions to which nobody listened. The hell with you – I thought – if you won't even listen to me.

We left for the restaurant; Margaret, whom I'd almost forgotten, trailing behind, and me between two silent men, both of whom, for whatever reason, were in something of a rage. I myself began to feel angry. The gallery owner was obviously regretting having agreed to exhibit my husband's paintings and I may as well confess now, for otherwise you will miss some of the complexities of the situation, that, yes, I had had the teeniest fling with this man some years before when he was first wondering whether it was worth taking Robert on. I had helped him make up his mind. A misunderstanding had arisen when he had considered that the fling should be resumed and I could see no good reason why it should. You must see my viewpoint. He had telephoned me at the dreadful hotel and I had been dismissive. Polite, but dismissive. I'm glad that's out in the open. I should not like Robert to know, but I am not, by nature, secretive. Both these men were now unjustly annoyed with me and I was fed up. We plodded on until I said, reflectively, that I loved to see men dancing. A dancing man, if he's doing the right dance, is incomparably sexy. Much more attractive than some sweating fool kicking a ball around. I knew neither of these conventional men would agree with me. They wouldn't understand.

The silence continued until Robert said, 'I was telling Lili she shouldn't have given up dancing.' This was infuriating, for it put him in the position of the superior male chiding his woman for making silly mistakes. All my subtle spite was wasted. I wanted to stop there and then and hit him, but I took a grip of myself and carried on jabbering rubbish in an effort to make things seem normal. They made the odd, uninterested response until I got really cross and said, 'Anyway art is only a snare and a delusion.' Even that didn't get through to Robert. He said: 'If it wasn't for art we wouldn't be about to eat.' I couldn't say what I was thinking, could I? That if it wasn't for me sleeping with Mr Money Bags here we wouldn't be about to eat, and it had fuck all to do with his stupid painting. No, I couldn't say that. The restaurant was of the Middle-Eastern sort, so I went on about Egypt instead. 'What a coincidence,' I cried, or something on those lines.

Money Bags said, 'I chose it specially to make you feel at home.' The liar. He didn't bother to sound as though he was telling the truth. It was cheap, that was all.

Margaret, I need hardly say, was of no help during these exchanges. She was unconscious of the tensions and the unseen currents. I made another effort and introduced the topic of food. Surprisingly she joined in and we had a little chat about the culinary attitudes of different nations. She, I was glad to hear, had no illusions about English food. I don't suppose she could have with her mother's cooking for example, but you can never really tell what people think is edible. Margaret was quite sensible on the subject.

I agreed with her. 'No wonder the English look so awful,' I said. Robert said, 'Margaret doesn't look awful.' What? What have we here? My stern husband complimenting the *petite anglaise*? What was happening? I was half English myself, after all.

I said that *we* had the sense to make some effort to eat properly and maintain our looks. I meant me.

I felt lost. Not really English, not really Egyptian, not really human sometimes. Just a collection of bones and flesh that somebody once had danced in. I'm only a tutu – I thought, and sat speechless while Robert and Money Bags argued, in a disguised sort of way, about the meaning of art. I was boring.

I was more worried about Robert than I cared to admit. I couldn't stop thinking about it. He had wanted children. We never now talked about him wanting children. I couldn't have any. It was too late now, but I never could have had any. I'd been ill ... well, something had gone wrong ... well, I can't talk about it. It wasn't my fault. Not altogether. I'd been unlucky. I didn't like children anyway. They would've spoilt our life together. How can you travel and be free with a lot of screaming children? I had no regrets.

Still, I worried. I had to talk to someone. I couldn't go through all my life with no one to talk to, and I couldn't talk to Robert. Not at the moment. There was something wrong. I talked to Margaret, for it was rather like talking to yourself, and if she did respond I sometimes had the feeling that perhaps she knew what I was talking about. This is a soothing feeling when you are used only to the sort of people you meet at the club who wouldn't understand a word you were saying if you spelt it out in capital letters. She never said much, but I didn't mind. If you're pouring out your soul you don't want other people pouring out theirs. There'd be a flood. Oh, I was full of grief. I don't know why. Perhaps it was the cold of Croydon, although I'd been no happier in the heat of the Nile. I had no reason to feel so sad and I thought and thought about it and finally found that I was lonely. Lonely Lili. What an absurd conception. I had never had to be lonely in all my life. There were people everywhere; people who loved me. Hundreds of people who loved me. I only had to walk to the corner of the street and smile in a way I had and I would bring back several people who, in that moment, had learned to love me. It's true.

So why was I so sad? Empty and cold and sad. I thought sometimes that I had been loved too much – not only by all those lovers, and yes, I admit there had been several; well more than that. I don't care to count because the numbers make me seem trivial and undiscerning – oh, all right, promiscuous. But I wasn't really promiscuous. I didn't like most of those men. I despised them. I knew what love was. I thought for a moment that I knew because I had never really known it; that I knew it by default as warm and real and steadfast, and I knew so well what it was like because I was cold. Not frigid, you understand. Just cold. I thought of how unthinkable it would be to betray that love. Oh, hell. I did love Robert. I would never betray him – not really – but to an observer it might seem that I had. It might even seem so to Robert. I hadn't meant to, not ever, only sometimes he made me so cross and then the only way I could think of to punish him was to go and be nice to somebody else. I said to myself, while Margaret listened, that we could only love once. If we loved more than once then *none* of it counted. It was all meaningless and valueless and we might as well stand under a street lamp and sell ourselves like sugar-cane to whoever cared to buy. When I shut up I saw how Margaret was looking at me, and, lo, I had done it again. The little Margaret loved me. I had made no effort at all and she loved me. There. Do you see? I told you so.

I was slightly cheered. I felt suddenly sufficiently fond of her to wish that she wasn't going to marry old Syl. I could have told her then and there not to be such an ass, but Monica would have killed me, so I said in a roundabout fashion that the conventional marriage could be a rotten way to spend a lifetime. All those wedding presents getting tarnished and discoloured and curling up at the edges; a constant reminder of the death of things. But Margaret had just mentioned Mother Joseph and I grew wary. I must not let her talk of Marie Claire and Nour and her months in Egypt.

'... And did you know Sister Bridget too?' she asked. 'And the other nuns?'

'A long time ago,' I said, and, naturally, Monica chose that moment to appear. However, her invariable habit of taking a discussion off course could sometimes prove useful. She gave us her views on the selfish nature of the religious life, which were of no interest to anybody but at least got us off the subject of love and marriage and away from any *faux pas* I might have made in relation to little Nour.

I am not as stupid as I sometimes sound. Really I'm not. I'm clever and quick and intelligent and you'd see at once what I mean if you knew me properly. I am very good with clothes. I *know* clothes. You may think this unimportant compared with the rigours of life, but clothes are not insignificant. Take Monica's wedding dress. It was bloody awful when she wore it and when she plunged her unfortunate daughter in it – well. For some reason I never could make out she was determined that the poor girl should go to her martyrdom in this appalling garment. Margaret stood on her dressing-table stool draped in the thing and I didn't know whether to laugh or to cry.

'It's lovely,' said Monica decisively. 'It just doesn't fit properly, that's all.' That wasn't all at all. It was out of date, it had never looked any good anyway, and it had dropped out of whatever shape it had ever had. Margaret looked like a badly wrapped joint.

I said I wasn't sure I could do anything with it. I tucked it and turned it and nipped it in here and there, while occasionally suggesting that we should abandon the whole thing as a bad job. This didn't go down well, so I carried on pinning and changed the subject – well, almost. I was remembering my own wedding in the church of St Catherine in Alexandria, an exotic occasion with much of the English community present and also my own relations on my father's side. All the English ladies wore silk and muslin and chiffon, and so did my aunts, but some of them had insisted on wearing their furs too. I had got the giggles as we left home with my mad aunts hung about in fox and sable with the sun glaring down. I was dressed in crimson wild silk with a wreath of crimson rosebuds on my head. Monica had expressed her opinion that people with red hair shouldn't wear crimson, especially not when they were getting married, but she was wrong as usual. I looked *wonderful*. Mind you, I shouldn't have said so while I was fiddling with that frock on poor Margaret. Monica wasn't pleased. She thought I was showing off and making odious comparisons. I was.

She went to bed early that night and I thought if Margaret went too I could spend the evening just with Robert and a bottle of Monica's Scotch. I could make him laugh and get him a bit drunk and then ... but, no. He said he was going to walk to the pub because he fancied a pint of English ale. I was disappointed. I said, 'Since you'll be passing Syl's house why don't you pop in and ask him out for a drink?' Robert never could stand Syl. I'm sure he had no idea that – well, never mind. He simply couldn't stand the sight of him.

'If you ask him very prettily,' I said, 'perhaps he'll play you a tune on his flute.' I had put Robert in a difficult position. He could hardly say, in front of Margaret, that he'd rather go to sea than have a drink with her fiancé. Then I looked at Margaret and felt a little guilty. She was blushing with embarrassment for, as I've already said, she wasn't stupid. She knew how Syl stood in the eyes of his contemporaries, and I was sure that her own generation would find him ridiculous. Robert had noticed too and gave me a highly critical look as he left. Oh damn, damn, damn.

Margaret suddenly said: 'Oh Lili.' And I felt sorry for her. Truly. She looked desperate. But I had bigger worries on my mind. Every time I opened my mouth it seemed I offended Robert. I was only teasing him. He should have taken *me* to the pub. I hoped he had called in at Syl's. I hoped Syl would spend the evening clinging to him like a leech. I was furious.

Then I looked at Margaret properly. Her face was so sad. She looked as sad as me – sadder. I said: 'Margaret, sometimes there are things you think you have to do but often those very things are things you must not do. Sometimes you must grow up and when people tell you you *must* do things – that's when you absolutely must *not*.' *I* could talk. I was beginning to think I'd never grow up myself.

'What shall I do?' said Margaret. 'I'm stupid.'

'No, you're not,' I said. 'You've got no faith in yourself, so you've lost hope. And all I know is, if you hang on long enough hope comes back.' I hoped I was right. My own hope was shaky tonight.

'But I've *got* to go through with it now,' said Margaret. The poor little animal had admitted, without even realizing, that her marriage approached as might her doom. Oh well. How could she have been so idiotic as to let matters go this far?

I lost patience with her. I went to bed.

The next day Syl came round, all dressed up as lamb. 'Why Syl,' I said, 'how young you look. How very young and carefree.' He believed me. He smiled. He was stupid to believe me and I was angry, for it made me feel wicked: wicked and spiteful and rather old and too clever by half. Grown-up people should understand the rules of the game; should know when one is telling tiny lies and being a tiny bit cruel. They should respond in kind. Syl should have said: 'And you, Lili, you too are as fresh and lovely as once you were.' Or something like that. Something polished and untrue and sociable, and then the game could have continued as a pleasant little contest between equals. As it was, all my barbs were wasted and I thought I must sound gushing and ordinary. I thought I might as well go on like that since there was no fun to be had. I turned to Monica and struck up a conventional conversation about her house. At least I *meant* it to be conventional but she grew pompous about it and the devil got back into me. 'Why don't you sell it?' I said after she'd given a sort of lecture on the place. 'It's far too big for you and you'd probably get a lot of money for it.' Monica had that effect on me. She made me want to say vulgar things and I knew she thought there was nothing more vulgar than talking about money. She did look insulted so I added that she was probably right not to sell – the house might have been made for her. It wasn't really a compliment, but she took it as such. So that was all right.

Syl joined in, saying that now was not the time to sell. Margaret left the room as he spoke and I wondered if they'd noticed. I noticed everything. If you want to survive you have to. I told Monica that my own house badly needed painting and the wind had taken all the shine from the stonework. She gave me some advice on the matter and we were friends again. 'Where's Margaret gone?' asked Syl. It was a bit late but he had noticed.

'I think she went into the garden,' said Monica. 'Run out and find her.' Syl got up in what I suppose he thought was a lithe bound and went off in pursuit of his affianced. I waited for Monica to say something like 'Oh, he's so devoted,' but she didn't. Even Monica couldn't keep up a pretence *all* the time. She said she was going to pick some autumn leaves to brighten the hallway and I asked myself if she was intending to spy on Margaret and see how she behaved to Syl; check that her daughter wasn't ruining her chances by being impolite or remote or cheeky to her old suitor. I had a vision of Monica bobbing up from behind a hedge saying 'Margaret, apologize at once' or 'Take no notice of her, Syl. She's just being silly.' It wasn't impossible. Monica was a terrible worrier and worriers can't help interfering. They think if they meddle they won't have to worry so much. Oh, how mistaken they are. Margaret reappeared in the sitting-room. It was getting rather like French farce without the bedroom scenes. 'Where is everyone?' I asked. 'I thought you were all in the garden?' Margaret didn't answer. She'd torn off a hangnail and there was blood dripping everywhere – all over her frock. I hate to see clothes being spoiled. What a messy girl she was. I took her out to the tap and cleaned her up.

'What's going on?' asked Monica suspiciously, appearing at the door. Did she think I'd attacked her child?

'Nothing, nothing,' I said. 'She bit her thumb.'

'She'll probably get blood-poisoning,' said Monica unhelpfully. She didn't really sound as though she cared. I asked where she kept the bandages but she was too busy arranging her autumn leaves to answer me. There were tears in Margaret's eyes, so I started talking a lot. Don't misunderstand me. I'm not afraid of scenes. I just didn't think that was the time for one. At least one person should be drunk when there's a scene, because then everyone can pretend that it didn't happen, or if it did there was a good excuse and reconciliations are unnecessary. A sober scene in the cold light of day can lead to all manner of unfortunate results. Often the bystander gets the blame. Monica could easily have blamed me – for making too much fuss, for encouraging Margaret to be feeble and self-pitying, for being there at all.

'There's no need to cry,' said Monica who seemed bent on trouble.

'She's not *crying*,' I said. 'It was cold out there in the garden, wasn't it, Margaret? It made her nose red, that's all.' I thought that Margaret must have been distant with Syl and Monica had overheard. 'You should see *me* cry,' I said. 'Then you'd know what crying really was.' 'What have *you* got to cry about?' asked Monica rudely. She was the most insensitive woman I'd ever met and I couldn't think why I'd ever bothered with her at all. OK, Monica – I thought – pin your ears back.

I said: 'Sometimes I sink into a grand black horror of depression, but I don't cry so much then. I stay in bed and pluck at the counterpane and listen to the winds of solitude roaring at the edge of infinity and the wolves of evil baying down the void, and I look into the darkness.' There, Monica – I thought – see what you can do with that one.

'Oh, don't be so morbid, Lili,' she said. 'Try and say something cheerful.'

It was a waste of time getting clever with Monica. 'I can't think of anything cheerful,' I said. 'Can you?'

Monica rallied. 'Well, the wedding of *course*,' she said. God, what a stupid woman. She didn't leave it at that. 'It'll be such fun,' she said. I didn't say anything. I was sick of wasting my breath; so Monica went on to describe the awful old wedding menu. She recited it.

'*And* speeches,' I said. '*And* confetti. *And* warm champagne.' I could imagine the whole thing. There was something uniquely dreadful about English weddings. I'd been to dozens of the horrible occasions. Oh, they weren't all so bad, I suppose. Just most of them. They made me think of death, perhaps because there was no music and no dancing. No *zägharit*.

'What's wrong with confetti?' asked Monica aggressively.

'Nothing,' I said. 'Nothing. I just don't like weddings much.'

'You seemed to enjoy your own,' said Monica. I glanced at Margaret but I don't think she was listening. I didn't want to go into details about my wedding. I had enjoyed it – what I could remember of it. It had been all right. I'd asked Robert and he'd laughed and said I'd been all right. 'I should have had a gypsy wedding,' I said. 'I should have jumped over the flames in the darkness of the night.'

'You might have burnt your red frock,' said Monica.

'Robert would have rescued me,' I said, 'stamped out embers and raced with me into the trees.'

'Robert would have turned the fire extinguisher on you,' said Monica. Oops, Monica had that disconcerting way of the very thick of sometimes saying something accurate. Something that hit the nail on the head. That was just what Robert would have done. He had adored me but he had always been sensible. Change the subject. Get Robert out of it.

'I might have married a gypsy,' I said. 'Spotted scarf. Gold earrings.'

Monica wouldn't let it go. 'I thought Robert was the only man in the world for you,' she said. I thought that rather brutal of her considering how well she knew me – not *me* exactly, but she knew more than I liked about what could be described as my Past.

'He is,' I said sincerely. 'I was only fantasizing.' I thought this was a generous concession and should be left untouched but Monica took advantage of it. Bitch. 'You do too much of that.' she said.

Right – I thought – you want to fight dirty. OK. I said in a sweet voice: 'When is Derek coming?' Monica hated him. I knew how much she hated him because I'd been there when she started to. We'd stayed with them here at the time Derek was beginning to play around, and even before that, when they were in Egypt, she'd begun to notice him edging his way towards girls. He liked them young. A thought struck me ...

'They're arriving the night before the wedding,' Monica informed me coldly.

I was thinking about Syl. He liked them young too. Poor Margaret. Her life was full of old men who liked them young.

'No stag night for Syl?' I asked. 'Of course not,' said Monica. I was tired of trying to be tactful. 'I suppose he is a bit old for that sort of thing,' I said.

Margaret went red and I felt sorry for her again, but Monica didn't say anything. Not to me. She knew she'd met her match in me, so she started bullying Margaret.

I had to get out of the house quite often now. Never mind the cold. I was fond of Monica. I was. I always had been but she was impossible in her present mood. Bossy and martyred and *impossible*. It was because she knew she was in the wrong. It was really *very* wrong of her to make Margaret marry Syl, and that was what she was doing. It was obvious. I was amazed that everyone couldn't see it. She knew it but she told herself she was doing the right thing.

'Robert,' I said, as we drove one morning towards Tottenham Court Road, 'what do you think of Margaret?'

'Abishag the Shunamite?' he said.

'Who?' I said.

'You're an ignorant savage, Lili,' he said, for he was feeling fond of me that day. His evil mood had passed. In view of this I let him explain about the girl who was chosen to keep the ancient David warm. One of those dubious Bible stories that they didn't read to us in school. I knew it anyway. I laughed.

Robert laughed too. I wondered for a moment *why* he was in such an agreeable frame of mind. I could see no particular reason for it. 'What's she doing, marrying Syl?' he asked. It wasn't the sort of thing he was usually interested in – human relationships seldom attracted his attention.

'Monica's making her,' I said.

'Nonsense,' said Robert.

'*Robert*,' I said, hoping he wasn't going to annoy me.

'I can see she's in favour of it,' said Robert, 'but she can hardly force her into it.'

'Can't she?' I said.

'How could she?' said Robert.

I wondered how I could begin to explain to him how people make people do things. I wondered why he needed an explanation. He could make me do things by withdrawing his approval.

Often he made me do things he wouldn't approve of by disapproving of me in the first place. Mostly I liked to please him but I have my pride.

'Abishag the Shunamite hasn't got my pride,' I said.

'Just a hot water bottle,' said Robert.

That wasn't what I meant. Not quite. I meant she did what she was told because she had no proper image of herself.

'She has no self-respect,' I said and for some reason Robert laughed again. Why *was* he so cheerful?

Robert had to go and see his solicitor about something. I asked him why he didn't use Syl as his man of business and he told me not to be funny. I spent the afternoon in the Colony Rooms with the painters and the writers and the riff-raff, and my friend Celestine, who had a flat in Bramerton Street. Robert picked me up there but he wouldn't stay. It may have been because famous painters went there and Robert wasn't famous. Not yet. I kissed Celestine goodbye and she winked at me. I had borrowed her spare key. She was out most days and sometimes it was nice to have somewhere to go where I could just put my feet up and not have to be polite to anyone. It was a bit dusty, but so what.

If I wasn't in Monica's house for too long it was a pleasant contrast to the noise and the dust and the paint of the painters. Nice to go home in the evenings and sit in the chintz. No dust. Monica didn't like dust. I couldn't have lived with all that dust for long either, but nor could I have lived forever with all that chintz. Perhaps that was why I was a wanderer. Dirt and grease one minute, shampoo and bath salts the next. Variety.

Monica was still fussing about the wedding dress. I could have done with a little sleep when we got back but duty called. I managed to sew Margaret into the damn thing. I tacked it to her chemise and she got quite upset when she couldn't get out of it. I once sewed a whole skirt seam to a table cover and it *is* annoying, but Margaret made nearly as much fuss as her mother. I was surprised. She said she needed a drink and Monica snapped at her. I was soothing.

'She's got some way to go before she's an alcoholic,' I said. 'She's not like me.'

'Oh nonsense,' said Monica. God, she was irritating. I couldn't even claim to drink too much without being contradicted.

'Don't you worry about my liver?' I asked pitifully. 'Don't you believe me?'

'I've got better things to worry about,' said Monica. She spoke to Margaret: 'Don't forget you're having tea with Syl's mother tomorrow.'

Syl's mother. Yes. I was going to have to think about Syl's mother. There could be a certain awkwardness ...

'Robert will be getting lonely,' I said. 'Down there all by himself.'

'We'll go down now,' said Monica, folding up the dress. She grumbled fitfully as she did so. All about a poor woman on her own and the responsibility of arranging a wedding; the organization, the cost, the wear and tear on the nerves. She turned on Margaret and started nagging her – where was her ring? What about her trousseau? Had she done this? Had she done that? Margaret didn't say anything but I could feel the tension in her. 'You're a lump,' said her mother. 'You don't seem to enjoy anything.' I did so wish she'd shut up. You can push the meekest little mouse too far, and I needed a peaceful evening. I didn't want Robert bothered with all this bad temper and emotion. He'd only blame me.

'She could've got her clothes in Cairo,' I said trying to change the subject again. It was like trying to haul a mule down an alley when it's got its feet splayed.

'She wouldn't think of *that*,' said Monica, implying that Margaret wouldn't think of anything useful.

'But on the other hand,' I said, 'she didn't know she was going to get married then.' I was beginning to feel hysterical.

Monica ignored me. 'Why aren't you seeing Syl tonight?' she demanded of Margaret.

'He's going out.' said Margaret without interest.

Monica lost her temper. She shouted. Well, not loudly, but it *was* a shout. 'Don't you love Syl?' Oh boy – I thought – here we go. Take cover. Margaret's going to tell the truth. But she didn't. She said, of course she loved Syl.

I was so relieved I let out my breath. 'Love?' I said. 'What's that?' I had to say something but I wished I'd thought of something else, for Monica turned on me now. Yes, I know it was a stupid remark but you haven't experienced the atmosphere Monica could create. It addled your brains.

'I thought *you* were the expert,' she said quick as a whiplash.

Ouch. 'Who me?' I said. 'Not me. I know nothing at all about it.' I wish I could describe the look Monica gave me. I can't. Anyway we went downstairs then and Monica behaved herself because of Robert, and we drank a lot and went to bed. Whew.

Yes. Syl's mother. Hmmm. Here was a tricky one. It was some years now but she had reason to be – well, displeased with me. Yes. All right. If I arrived at her house she had every reason to throw me out. I'd have to see her sooner or later. I thought I might as well go with Margaret and get it over with. If there was going to be a scene it had better not be at the wedding. *Courage, mon brave.* Smart frock. Lots of lipstick. Big smile.

Margaret rang the doorbell and the dog barked. I reflected that I'd sooner be paddling in the crocodile pool. Door opened. '*Hallo,*' I said, full of enthusiasm. No point in seeming apologetic.

I was inside. I was sitting down. She hadn't been pleased to see me but she hadn't pointed an accusing finger and ordered me off her doorstep. I certainly didn't feel at ease, but nor did she, poor old trout. She went back and forth carrying cakes and teapots. I smoked like a mad thing and jabbered to the dog and nobody else said a word until she scolded Margaret for not eating up her tea. She went off again to get more hot water and I whispered to Margaret that she should tell her to boil her head.

Margaret said, 'Sshhh', and I lit another cigarette. I was so nervous. The dog was sitting on my foot and I kicked him off – quite gently, but he yelped.

'What are you doing to the dog?' asked Syl's mother who had to pick that moment to come back.

Do you know what I said? Do you know what the devil put it into my head to say? I said the dog was fucking my foot. That's what I said. I wished I could die then and there – slap, face down in the sandwiches. Why, of everything in the world I could have said, did I have to say that? Of all the subjects in the world I had to choose that one. Oh *God*. The last time she'd seen me I was doing that with her husband in Monica's summerhouse at the bottom of the garden – *flagrante delicto*. I hadn't been going to mention it. Well, *of course* I wasn't going to mention it. Oh *dear* God. I considered getting on the window seat and throwing myself out through the glass, but she didn't seem to mind.

She said, perfectly calmly. 'He's not capable of that', and for a second I wondered dementedly if she was talking of her husband. He hadn't really been . . . *Shut up, Lili*.

I said, 'Well, he was thinking about it', amazed that I could speak at all – never mind sound quite composed.

'You can read the minds of animals?' asked Syl's mother, and I wondered if she'd forgotten. Forgotten what I was doing the last time she saw me. I gabbled like a lunatic. God knows what I said but I went on saying it without thinking until I heard myself saying that the dog had simply been overwhelmed by *lust*. I couldn't seem to leave it alone. I suppose some shrink would say it was guilt. Maybe it was. Whatever it was I have never felt such a fool in my life. Oh how I wished I'd died on the doorstep. Oh Lili, how *could* you?

'He's old,' said Syl's mother.

She was still perfectly calm, and I began to pull myself together. I began to talk very, very carefully about travelling, about Egypt, about Tutankhamun, about anything that had nothing whatsoever to do with sex. I was very boring but at least I never mentioned fucking again. Oh *Lili.*

It was cold outside, thank God. I'd been sweating. I have never been so embarrassed ever. And mixed up with all that was a sort of gratitude to Syl's mother. She had taken it very well. The worst thing was I'd always rather liked her. I'd pretended not to because nobody else liked her and it hadn't seemed worth being contrary at the time. There were plenty of other things to be contrary about. When she'd caught me with her husband in the summerhouse I'd disliked her because I'd wronged her, but as the memory faded I remembered her, when I remembered her at all, as different from and better than all the other silly English ladies. I had absolutely meant to pretend that the little contretemps with what's-his-name – Jack, I think, he was called – had never happened. That was how we all managed. Just pretend it never happened. It usually worked fairly well. I couldn't think what had come over me suddenly to mind so much that I could think of nothing else. Oh dear.

Margaret didn't seem to have noticed anything. She walked along in silence until she asked: 'Do you ever bore yourself?'

Bore myself? No, not often. Not today, anyway. 'Yes,' I said, 'I just did.' If she hadn't noticed anything I wasn't going to tell her.

'You weren't boring,' she said.

'Yes I was,' I said. Much better to be boring than what I had been. Tactless was not quite the word.

'I can never think of anything to say to her,' said Margaret. I was growing cooler now and was so chastened by my own performance that I felt well disposed towards her. At the moment I had a lot of leeway to make up in my relationship with the human race. I was not going to be unkind to anybody for several days. I was in no position to be. I said it was very difficult talking to a person of a different age from your own, a person with different experiences. I said one could only really talk to people who had shared one's experience and that *gossip* was the only useful and valid form of conversation. Why did I say that? I was highly wary of gossip, and as to shared experience – well, it could be said that Syl's mother and I had shared an experience, and look where it had got me.

'I wish I was like you,' said Margaret.

The girl was mad. Still, it was sweet of her. 'You are a bit,' I said kindly.

'I'm not happy like you,' she said.

Oh! I told her there wasn't any point in being unhappy. Not if you could help it. Besides I *was* happy basically; most of the time.

We walked on in silence, me breathing deeply. And then she said, 'Lili?'

'Mmm,' I said.

'Can I tell you something?'

'What?'

'I can't tell anyone else.'

Oh hell. Girlish confidences. 'Don't tell anyone,' I said. She could put me in a hopeless position if she told me things. 'If you've got a secret you can't keep,' I said, 'you must either tell everyone or tell nobody.' I wasn't going to be held responsible for one more indiscretion. 'Tell the priest,' I said.

'Did you have a good time?' asked Monica. She was being sarcastic now.

'Terrific,' I said. I really needed a drink. I felt worn out what with one thing and another.

'What did you think of Mrs Monro?' asked Monica who

seemed bent on tormenting me. I said I thought she was wonderful. What was I supposed to say? I was still so annoyed with myself I couldn't really think properly. Somewhere in my mind I entertained the reflection that although she was an old lady singularly lacking in charm she was twice – no several times – the woman Monica was. I wanted to say so but of course I couldn't. I still wished she was a silly, nasty old woman because once I had behaved badly to her. I thought that behaving badly was worse than anyone knew because it distorted relationships. If you poured boiling soup over an angel it would be years before you could like or fully appreciate that angel because he had conspired in being wronged by you to put you in the wrong. Do you see what I mean?

Monica continued assessing Mrs Monro's good points without being accurate at all. She missed all the *really* good points. She said she was a good cook and would make an excellent mother-in-law. Monica was a past master at saying stupid things; things to which there was no answer. I stopped listening. She didn't offer me a drink so I got one for myself. I *needed* it. And where was Robert? Tell me that.

Oh. He came back. Quite early. I was relieved. I was full of gladness to see him. When Lili was wicked she was lonely. Poor Lili. But when Robert was there it meant he was there because he loved me, and I felt like a flower that had been picked up from the path and put in water. I did. I don't care how ridiculous it sounds.

'Hullo,' I said – very casually, because now he was there I didn't need to expand or be enthusiastic. I could relax. 'How does it look?'

'It's all right,' said Robert. He didn't sound too enthusiastic either. I felt a tiny anxiety. We couldn't afford any reversals in our fortunes.

'Do you think we should ask him to dinner?' I said *before* thinking.

Wham. Monica was on to me in a second. 'Who?' she said in a cold, demanding voice. Then Margaret put her foot in it. 'Robert's gallery owner,' she said. I could have smacked her. I'd been going to say that I meant we should take him out to the Ritz or somewhere and take Monica too. I didn't mean that at all but I was going to say I did. Robert said he wouldn't dream of asking the mean bastard to dinner and Monica – who was perverse – said that in that case perhaps she would offer him a simple meal if it would help.

Robert said there was no need. Money Bags couldn't back out of it now. I felt a little chilled to realize that Robert had seen this as a possibility. 'I wouldn't let him back out,' I said, 'I wouldn't.'

'You could hardly stop him,' said Robert. Oh, yes I could. I'd blackmail him or seduce him or hold him at gun point or sit on his head until he agreed to make Robert rich and famous. I wouldn't let him get away with it. I needed Robert to look after me. Perhaps that's why I would have killed to protect him. Love is a peculiar thing. I don't understand it altogether but I can follow its little breadcrumbs of clues for quite a long way. They go round and round and round. Robert was my mother and my child and without him I was desolate. Without him I would be dead.

He went out. Brute. OK – I thought – so go out without me. See if I care. I've had millions of lovers and I don't need *you*. I talked about them in a disguised sort of way, just to let Monica and Margaret know that I didn't need to depend on any one man. You could say it was bravado. Perhaps it was, but I had to survive. I remembered being in love lots of times, and it was like madness because one day you return to your senses and you think – what was all that about? And you look at your lover who you loved so much and you can't imagine *why*. I must have been mad – you say to yourself, and you shake your head to clear it, and you wish quite passionately that you hadn't let anyone see how much you loved him, and you muddy the waters by pretending to love someone else now, and you laugh lightly at the mention of his name. Oh *him* – you say. I'd forgotten about *him*.

Monica didn't want to talk about lovers because she hadn't got any. Margaret was thinking about something else, so I let my talking slow down and drift away. They went to bed and I sat and waited for my husband to come back.

He hadn't been out long. He'd gone to the pub, silly man. When he came back he didn't talk to me. He went to sleep and after a long while I went to sleep too.

The next day I got bored with Monica wondering whether the fish was fresh and talking about it, and I said I would go for a little walk. I went behind the gardens to see Syl's mother. I don't know *quite* why I did that. I couldn't apologize to her because it had not been generally acknowledged that I'd done anything amiss. Do you know – I think I went simply because I wanted to. Because I *liked* her. Yes, I did still feel very bad about what I'd said and, yes, I did sort of want to make amends – without doing anything so embarrassing as saying I was sorry – but mostly I just wanted to go and see her. She made such a change from Monica and Margaret. Like strong cheese and pickles after pudding – if you see what I mean. She wasn't stupid. It was such a *relief*.

Besides I could talk to her and sometimes I needed to talk. I never really meant to tell her anything important but I could talk to her about real proper things. Naturally I found myself talking about Robert. I talked about the past too. I don't know why I was always talking about the past these days. And death. Why did I talk about death? That wasn't very tactful either when you consider the age of Syl's mother. I was obviously a little run-down. What I said was that you could have enough of life. I was thinking about meals. All those meals one had eaten – mostly just to keep alive. But some of the better ones had been too much. For instance it was hard to eat a whole lobster. A delicious bit of lobster was enough. And lamb. Nobody could eat a whole lamb. I sometimes felt that just a little bit of delicious life would be preferable to platefuls and platefuls of it – stretching away into the future forever. The thought gave me indigestion. And I didn't want to find myself, one day, as old as Syl's mother. Oh no. I would settle for the merest *hors-d'oeuvre* of life rather than chew through to that stage. I didn't tell her so. I almost told her how I couldn't have children, but that was because I was feeling guilty about it. I had never felt guilty about it when I was younger. Only now when I was getting older . . . Not very guilty. It was only one more small thing to worry about sometimes – in the night when Robert was asleep. Later we went into London. I was feeling full of pride – hurt pride if you like. Nobody was going to treat me like that and get away with it. No, never. I told Robert to drop me in Sloane Square and I walked down to Celestine's place. I had a few phone calls to make. Well, one in particular. Celestine was there but she was just going out. She stayed a bit longer when I arrived because she liked my company. I made her laugh. We drank some very strong coffee out of dirty mugs. She'd run them under the tap but the lipstick hadn't come off. She looked at her watch and said she must fly. When she got to the doorway she stopped to utter an afterthought. 'Oh,' she said, 'Lili, if you'd just remember to change the sheets.' Even the dirtiest girl can be fussy about some things. I said I would before I remembered that I hadn't told her that the need would arise. Oh well. Never mind. I didn't have to keep secrets from Celestine because she could keep her mouth shut. Her own life was sufficiently exciting without her having to gab about mine. She was quite unlike Monica.

So the day passed as I had intended, which was satisfactory.

Not the best day of my life admittedly but at least I was in control. My arrangements had worked without a flaw and afterwards I said: 'You must go now or you'll be late getting back to work. I'll ring you when I'm here again, or I'll drop in a note with a cryptic message. Goodbye darling ...' I said, '... give me a kiss.'

I should not have done what I had just done, but it wasn't important. Robert had made me angry. Robert had made me feel unwanted. What I had just done served Robert right. Hadn't done anyone any harm. Just made me feel better. A bit better. A very little bit. Oh, God.

Then I tidied up Celestine's place and went shopping. I went to Fortnum's because I felt at home there. I always had. When we were rich I don't think my aunts knew that there was anywhere else to shop in the whole of London – except for Harrods of course – but it was Fortnums they liked best. I bought some cheese for Monica and made the man behind the counter fall in love with me just to show that I could. I kept meaning to stop doing that sort of thing because it could lead to trouble but it was quite hard to resist. Sometimes I felt I would disappear if I couldn't see the person opposite falling in love with me. I just wouldn't be there. Now, however, I felt tranquil because I was in charge and I had proved that I only had to snap my fingers and – lo ...

I felt pleased with myself all the way to the French pub where I was meeting Robert. I could feel the little lines of tiredness and sorrow had gone from my face, and when the taxi driver fell in love with me too I felt quite complete.

'Hi there, husband,' I said, 'how've you been?' Robert didn't like what he called my Americanisms.

'Oh, there you are darling,' he said and I saw that he too looked rested and fulfilled.

'Oh gee,' I said, 'gimme a drink, and fast', for I was suddenly terribly angry. What had made the bastard look so well and so young, and so pleased with himself? *What?* Answer me that.

'I did such a good deal today,' he said.

'Deal?' I said.

'A *good* deal,' he said. 'My brother began it and I finished it ...'

Oh God. He'd been doing a deal and I'd thought ... oh never mind what I'd thought. Oh *God*. Lili, you are such a silly bitch sometimes.

I threw a drink down my throat and I said, 'Tell me about it.' I lit a cigarette and my hands were trembling. Their grandfather had left them some old pictures and books and things and Robert's brother had taken them to a dealer and been offered a thousand pounds, so Robert had gone and seen his dealer and told him to jump in the lake, and he'd taken away the pictures and books and sold them to two different dealers for five thousand pounds. That was very clever. I was very pleased. I said so. What I didn't say was that if the stupid man had told me that that was what he was doing then I wouldn't have been doing what I'd been doing. Not necessarily, anyway. No, I *wouldn't*. It was all Robert's fault.

'Why didn't you tell me before?' I asked. I knew why. Robert told me what I already knew. 'I didn't want to disappoint you if nothing came of it.'

'I see,' I said. 'Let's have another drink to celebrate.'

'You don't sound very pleased,' said Robert.

'I am pleased,' I said. 'I'm *very* pleased.'

'Well, you don't sound it,' said Robert.

'Well, I am,' I said. You can see what was likely to happen next, can't you? A screaming row in the French pub because my husband had made me feel guilty. I felt a fool too, which was worse. Oh, *bugger*.

'Let's go home,' I said. Home. Where was home? Home was where Robert was. What would I do if I lost him? Oh, be quiet Lili. How could you lose him?

In the car I spoke unnaturally of how clever I thought he'd been.

'You needn't go on, Lili,' he said, as though I was a stranger.

I began to say again: 'But I mean it ...' and stopped. I was silent until we got back and he was silent too. Misunderstanding is the worst thing in the world.

There was plenty of misunderstanding in Monica's house. I could sense it in the air. I was tired now but I had to take the stage again. Dash of lipstick. Big smile. Never mind the aching feet. The best thing I could do, I thought, was to talk about the past. The dead old past tucked away with the dried oleander petals, juiceless and inoffensive now.

'Do you remember ...?' I began.

'I remember ...' said Monica. She remembered different things from me. She remembered in different ways. She was talking about going to the tennis club in the school holidays while I was remembering watching an aunt mash up Spanish Fly to put in a jar of mutton grease – the dark shuttered room, the smell of rancid nard and attar of roses, and me not understanding what she was doing or why. I know *now* what she was doing and why, but I didn't know then. She was making a love potion for external application to somebody's straying husband. I don't know why I was thinking about that. It wasn't as though I needed any ointment for a dying desire. I was tired, that was all.

Margaret too seemed to have a different sort of memory from her mother. For one thing she seemed to have liked the people whereas I don't suppose Monica ever noticed them except as a sort of decoration to go with the camels and the pyramids and the palm trees. But then if Margaret had been in love with Nour she would have a different conception of his land. She would have been in love with his land too. Poor little mouse. Whenever my confidence is at a low ebb I begin to feel sorry for other people. A debilitating sense of pity creeps between my bones, making me imperfect and weak. I wondered what had happened in Egypt to give rise to the fuss that Marie Claire had made. She had flown into hysterics and accused Margaret *in absentia* of all manner of indelicacy and even criminal behaviour. It had been quite impossible to get at the truth – even to discover if there was any significant truth to be got at. There had been rumours all over the village. Rumours of sex and even murder – but you know what villages are like. I'd talked to Mother Joseph about it and she said it was all nonsense. She said they were saying that Margaret and Nour had killed a beggar girl who had appeared from nowhere one day. But – said Mother Joseph – she had herself sent away that same beggar girl from the convent gate where she was trying to sell what she shouldn't be selling days after the time when this reported killing had taken place. I thought it more probable – improbable though it was – that Nour had suggested marrying Margaret. That would have been enough to send his mother into fits. If her precious Nour was going to marry anybody he was going to marry an heiress, restore the family fortunes and keep Marie Claire in her accustomed luxury. Not marry an English mouse with no money. It was not impossible that Nour had fallen a little in love with Margaret. Her cold fairness would have held an appeal for him, I know. What I couldn't quite see was why Mother Joseph held Margaret in such high esteem. She really did. I'd been surprised, for she was not one for enthusiasm. I'd known her since I was a little girl and she was seldom enthusiastic. Not even about me. No. I'm joking. I didn't mind that. I didn't mind her talking about Margaret with such interest and fondness. No. I just found it puzzling. It made it seem that there was more to Margaret than met the eye and I couldn't for the life of me think what it could be. You know how annoying that feeling is – that there's something going on that you don't understand. I couldn't make it out at all. Margaret, in fact, *was* a bit of a mystery. Why, for instance, was she going to marry Syl? I know I keep going on about it, but I really couldn't understand it and it made me cross. Syl I could understand. I knew him quite well after all. I knew he'd always been chasing young girls and I thought perhaps I knew why. His father had been the same. One day I had remembered a conversation I'd had with Syl's mother, years ago, before – well before the contretemps – when I had wondered aloud why Syl was such an indefatigable runner-after of girls. I was really curious about his father, but I couldn't say that, could I? I was no angel, I know, but Syl and his papa left me standing. To be honest, his mother seemed as puzzled as I was. Oddly, she was not averse to talking about it. Perhaps she wanted to talk about it because it worried her and she needed to get it out of her mind. We never did reach any conclusions and I couldn't tell her what I was thinking because it wasn't the sort of thing you can tell a mother. At its simplest it is that promiscuous men are bad lovers. I don't want to go into details but it's true. If you think about it you'll find you agree with me. That is, of course, if you have had the poor sense to experiment with a promiscuous man. Yes, I know, I did, but I had reasons of my own. For one brief moment when I was run-down I had been in love with him. It didn't last but I got to know him rather well – *very* well. But as I was saying – the fact is that too much practice makes for staleness. There is a brisk professionalism about the business. You feel that somewhere he keeps a well-thumbed handbook of technique and goes through the motions by rote. Yes. The skill is the skill of the club professional and lacks spontaneity. Almost it is like something that they do for a living and not for love. It is dispiriting. Also they tend to give instructions – do this, do that – and this is insulting. You come away wondering whether his salary will cover the effort or if you should perhaps leave a tip. May heaven preserve me from being the female of this species. What an awful thought. I am not speaking of prostitution. It is something else. Something more depressing because it is unexpected. Oh Lord. I had not slept with Syl for the right reason. By the time I slept with him I was no longer in love with him. Partly it was competitiveness – anything you can do I can do better – and partly it was my most usual reason – to get even with Robert for being mean to me. *Lousy* reasons. I felt positively ashamed of myself. Yes, I did, and now I'd gone and done it again. Aah, let me think of something else.

Once upon a time I had owned a pair of bright green chiffon pyjamas – evening ones, not the sort English men sleep in. I wore very high-heeled soft leather shoes with them. Bright green and tan shoes. They nearly killed me. I danced with the King and he told me how he'd mended the clock in the *hôtel de ville* with his own hands. It's *true*. But he really liked English ladies – big fat fair ones – so we didn't get on all that well. I didn't mind. I didn't find him attractive but he was quite pleasant to talk to. This had all happened years ago in Alexandria before it was spoilt. Monica was there in a velvet kind of wrap with feathers. I could even remember what we had to eat. French food – cold fish and sauces, and chickens and sauces, and salads. I took my shoes off when I sat down on a little gold chair to eat. I left them off to walk home because they wouldn't go on again. Monica – or maybe it wasn't Monica – maybe it was somebody else since they are much of a muchness, these English ladies – said I couldn't possibly walk home, and certainly not without shoes, but I like to go barefoot in the soft subtle dust of the streets. The dirt that God washed off the people's feet was not the dirt of your English sweaty socks but the dirt of the earth. It drifted up past one's ankles and it was a pleasure to wash it off in a bowl of cool water. Do you see? Monica didn't. Monica couldn't really see anything. She didn't like the dirt and she didn't like the heat and she couldn't eat the food. She was quite complimentary about the bay shining under the moon and she thought my monkey was sweet if he kept at a distance and didn't put date stones in her hair, but she didn't think a lot of the pyramids and she absolutely despised Egyptian driving. I rather enjoyed it. There is something exhilarating about a mass of cars and lorries and mules and camels bearing down on you if you get out of the way in time. I like to live dangerously. Mind you, I had been careful with the men. The city was easygoing then and all the English were flirting with each other all the time, but my Dada was an Oriental and it gets into you – the feeling that unchastity deserves death. I never felt really relaxed doing the flirting in Egypt. Once, you see, there was a Sultana who strayed. She must have been completely mad – or perhaps she was English and had been captured by Barbary pirates as a *cadeau* for the King – for she had her little adventure in the palace garden, up against a cypress tree. The Sultan was looking for her for hours, which was bad luck since he had three more wives and three hundred concubines and probably hadn't given her a thought in weeks. So there he was scouring the rooms and balconies and terraces, bending down to look under the divans and behind the jasmine, and all the soldiers of the guard and the eunuchs, black and white, were scuttling round calling 'Cooee' and they *couldn't* find her. Don't ask me why when she was leaning against that cypress all the time. Then when she was finally discovered the Sultan couldn't see the face of her lover, who had prudently done the marathon down the garden path. *But* he had seen the device which the lover wore emblazoned on the back of his cloak and knew by that to which family he belonged. With the cruel guile of the offended potentate he invited all the men of this family to partake of a glass of mint tea, and when they gathered in a little room he called the executioner and his apprentices, and thirty-five heads rolled in the pool in the middle of the floor where the plashing of the fountain cooled the air and pleased the senses. When I was a little girl I used to think what an awful tea party that must have been. I hated tea parties anyway. When I grew older I asked what had happened to the Sultana. Oh – said my aunts – she was *repudiated*. Such a dreadful word. It sounded dreadful when I didn't know what it meant and just as dreadful when I did. Worse. Pish – said my aunts, waving a hand dismissively – she was repudiated. No one spoke to her, no one looked at her, they threw her the crusts the doves had left until she died. A living ghost until death took her. Think how pleased the other wives would have been. Picture the vengeful mirth of the concubines. The wives had their own apartments and the principal wife had the best one, while the concubines had to muddle along together in an upstairs room behind a latticed screen, trying to spit in the wives' sherbet, as they strolled in the garden below, idly plucking the petals off carnations. A bad man makes women bad. Yes, I'm sure it works the other way too, but women are not usually violent and cruel until some man upsets them – then they're nasty to each other. A lot of women have been nasty to me. I could so easily have been that stupid Sultana.

'Oh, give me, give me a drink,' I said, '*Emfadlek.*'

I changed into my Paris frock to cheer myself up and I poured on some scent I may have kept slightly too long. It was definitely just on the turn as wine goes to vinegar. Underneath was still the sweet smell that it started with, but overall the impression was a bit putrefactive. I couldn't be bothered to bathe and wash it off so I pretended it was meant to be that way.

'What a smell,' said Monica. 'That takes me back.'

'Is it not delightful?' I said. 'Is it not erotic?'

'No,' said Monica, 'but it's terribly powerful.' She turned up her nose. How annoying. I knew I smelled odd without her telling everyone. The devil got into me again. It was all Monica's fault.

'Derek used to like it,' I said. Why on earth did I say that? Yes, I know. To upset Monica. I was in a bad mood. She didn't know what to answer and I didn't really blame her. I'd bowled her a nasty one.

301

'He had no sense of smell,' she said, having cast around for some crushing response and failed to find one. I relented towards her. 'No,' I said, 'he hadn't, had he? He didn't go on like the rest of you moaning about the North African odour.' I was not as polite as I might have been because Monica was a difficult woman to be polite to. To be honest I'd never really known Derek very well. He'd been one of the paler, more anonymous husbands and he'd never made a pass at me. If I had indicated that he should, of course he would have, but there was obviously absolutely nothing to be gained from a fling with Derek. No fun, no envy; nothing but making Monica cross, and if I wanted to do that there were a million less drastic ways.

She said, 'I suppose we'd better ring him and make sure he hasn't forgotten the wedding.'

'He could hardly do that, surely,' I said.

'I woudn't put it past him,' said Monica.

'Cynthia wouldn't let him,' said Margaret.

'What do you mean – Cynthia wouldn't let him?' said Monica in a tone of more positive contempt. 'Cynthia. Huh.'

Margaret did seem to have the knack of saying things designed to enrage her mother. I wondered if she did it deliberately. If so she was more interesting than I'd suspected. She could also be more trouble. I would prefer to be the only one to tease Monica. I didn't want her *too* disgruntled for she might get fed up with us. Couldn't have that. Margaret seemed to have gone off in a trance again so I spoke gently to Monica about the inadvisability of second marriages and how they so seldom worked. I didn't know if that was true or not, but it easily could be. Now I come to think of it, I think it probably is.

The evening dragged on. I remembered that I had bought a bottle of gin. I'd thought of keeping it in my room but it would be more useful to produce it now and make Monica tiddly. She was less disapproving when she was tiddly, and like most people she drank more when she wasn't drinking gin she had paid for herself. For some mysterious reason of her own Monica dragged in the subject of Syl's father. I had little to contribute to it, as you can imagine.

'He died of drink,' said Monica lugubriously. 'Drank himself to death.'

'Syl's late,' she added.

I was looking at Margaret as I spoke and Margaret, I can tell you, did not look like a girl waiting, all dewy-eyed, for her beloved. Not a bit. It made me uneasy. I didn't like sleeping with men nobody else wanted. There was no fun in it. I hope you're not shocked that I had resumed my fling with Syl. Why not? Why shouldn't I? Didn't do anybody any harm. Didn't even give me any pleasure. Even less now. It seemed depressingly pointless. Robert wouldn't be jealous if he knew. He'd only be – well, *disgusted* I think is the word. That was why he must never find out. He might have been jealous if I'd slept with the King of England but he'd be contemptuous if he knew I'd slept with Syl. I felt worse and worse as I realized increasingly that Margaret couldn't stand him either. You see my problem. A thief who gets away with the Crown Jewels is a bad person but a successful thief, while a thief who steals a bag of old sandwiches and apple cores from a person who already doesn't want them is a bad person and a bad thief and looks a perfect idiot in the eyes of everybody. Aargh. Nobody must ever know. They would lose all respect for me. I was in a hopeless position all round, and I was worried that Syl might have told his mother. She would despise me for different reasons – not because I had slept with her dear son who was a bit of a twerp, but because I had slept with her dear son without loving him any more. And I had an awful feeling that she had no proper reasons for despising me for sleeping with her husband – not gratifying reasons like jealousy and possessiveness and injured love. She had felt, I faintly realized, that anyone who fell for her husband's line was a bloody fool. That was probably why she seemed – oh God – *sorry* for me. It was pity that made her pleased to see me when I called. She thought I was so inadequate I must seek reassurance in the beds of old men, of other people's fiancés, of anyone who happened to be passing. It wasn't true. It's just that I have this reckless streak. I didn't want Syl's mother to despise me. I'd have to make a great effort to prove to her that I was strong and brave and attractive. Not lost and weak. I had an idea that by sleeping with all her menfolk I might have been trying to get close to *her* – to gain her strength, to *identify* with her. I don't like thinking like this. It takes me too deep and I haven't got time to go down deep. And I never like what I find down there. Often I had thought that the women in the zenana might have been a comfort to each other – like Mother Joseph and her nuns. Well, not quite like that of course, but the ones who hated the Sultan must have had a lot in common. When they were not mad with jealousy they must have been kind to each other.

I would go and see her again and make her laugh, and she would know that I was careless, and in control, and even if she found me shallow she would think me bright, and not be sorry for me at all. I put aside the thought that she might not care.

Robert and Syl came in together. Oh hell. Where had they been? What had they been saying? Was *anything* worth all this worry? What was wrong with me that I danced around on the edge of trouble when there was no need for it? I think they'd just met on the doorstep. I hoped they'd just met on the doorstep. I was vivacious that evening but my eyes didn't meet Syl's once. Abishag the Shunamite went off to bed. Robert went to bed. Syl went home. That left me and Monica and the rest of the gin. I do have a tendency to selfishness. Most people do, but I admit it – freely. I'd been thinking only of myself for days. I asked Monica how she was feeling and she began to tell me. She did look tired and I gave her a lot of gin. That as usual took us back into the past. After a few more gins she came up with a piece of the past I would really have preferred to stay buried in the mud at the bottom of the pool. I knew she hated Derek but I hadn't understood how much. Talking of the past I talked of him for he had been part of it. Not much of it, but he'd been there. Monica grew drunker and more hating. At her drunkest and hatefullest she told me Derek had molested her daughter when she was a little girl.

That silenced me, I can tell you. I couldn't think of a word to say. To be honest, what I mostly felt at first was – thank God I never slept with Derek. Thank *God* I never slept with a child molester. If I had I cannot imagine what it would have done to my self-respect. I am glad to be able to say truthfully that my next feeling was one of pity. Real pity for Monica and Margaret. I am not a very good woman and I am not fond of children, but I know what every human being knows in the depths of his soul – that to hurt a child is a crime for which there is no forgiveness. I don't know about God but I do know that no human being can forgive an injury done to her child. Why should she? I didn't have a child. I didn't want one, but if I had I wouldn't. I have an unforgiving nature already and if someone had injured a child I had budded – oh, how I would have killed him. I gave Monica the rest of the gin and topped it up with vermouth and I had a lot myself and I don't really remember much of what we said after that. I think I may then have made her a whisky and soda as a night-cap, for I knew it would be better by far if she forgot what she had told me.

I woke up early the next day remembering everything about the night before with complete clarity. My mind does this to me sometimes. I forget things I should remember and vice versa. I still felt drunk but clear-minded. Monica and Margaret slept late. Margaret always did but it was most unusual for Monica. I prayed that amnesia had overtaken her in the night. I was in the state where you can't make decisions – not even whether it's worth the effort of making yourself a piece of toast or putting the kettle on. At times like this I find it's easiest to go out. I went to see Syl's mother. What I really needed was another drink and I didn't want Monica to catch me at the Scotch bottle first thing in the morning. If by some fortunate chance she had forgotten her revelations of the night before it would be folly to jog her memory by letting her see how desperately in need of a drink the evening had left me in the morning after. If you follow me.

Syl's mother offered me coffee and I felt I knew her well enough to turn it down and ask for whisky. There aren't all that many people you can do that to, so it was some indication of her worth.

And then, after a while and without too much preamble, I told her what Monica had told me. Now this time I *really* don't know why I did so. I had had no intention of telling her. None whatsoever. Could I have told her because I wanted her to know that there were worse people than me? Worse people who did much, much worse things than I did. Things that made my peccadilloes seem almost like virtues. I hope it wasn't only that. I think it was more that I was still drunk and the sluice gates were open. How careful one should be, and how careful one is not when alcohol has eaten into the brain. I had another drink and a cigarette.

Syl's mother was naturally shocked. Well, she was more than shocked. I shouldn't have told her. It was indiscreet. It was more than indiscreet – it was unkind. On the other hand Monica shouldn't have told *me*. Why should I have to go round with that secret like a cockroach in my head? I *had* to tell someone and I was determined not to tell Syl. If Monica found out I'd told Syl the fat would, as they say, be in the fire. There would be the most frightful fuss. I might even find myself repudiated. You can see what the drink does to you. It suddenly occurred to me – and it felt like a kick in the stomach – that it was pretty damn silly to tell Syl's mother if I didn't want Syl to know. You'd think I might've thought of that before opening my mouth. But then, I thought, she wouldn't tell him because she was too old and too English and too strong. It may have been wishful thinking but it's what I thought. I trusted her. I thought she was strong enough to share another secret with me. Sometimes you love the people you share secrets with, and sometimes you hate them. A lot depends on the secret. Partners in crime can't be very fond of each other, but the recipient of the knowledge of another's frailty is in a rather good position; while the frail one is able to trust because if she's got any sense she knows that she has bowed her head to a superior person who will not dislike or reject her for doing so. It is similar to the dependency of the child on the mother; is it not? Oh well, maybe not. All I'm saying is I didn't really repent of confiding in Mrs Monro – even if I should have done, and if you think I should, I don't agree with you.

The night of the exhibition came rather too soon. Although it was the reason we were in London it somehow caught me unprepared. Too many other things had happened and my mind was taken up with them. Robert was being a little too polite – not just to me. To everyone. It was unnatural. I was always polite when I'd done something I perhaps should not have done. For a while when I'd been a little careless I behaved very beautifully and made sure that everyone had just the amount of sugar he preferred in his coffee. I tiptoed a bit and smiled a lot and tried hard not to seem overbearing. It was obviously a mistake since it was such a give-away. I couldn't help it. I kept on deferring to Robert and Robert kept on being polite to me. *Why?* Do you know who Lilith was? She was Adam's first wife. And do you know why she left him? It was because she was sick and tired of lying underneath and she couldn't see why she should. She said 'Adam, I'm not going to lie underneath you any more. I'm going to be on top.' Adam argued about it because he had developed a liking for being on top and he wasn't prepared to abandon this position of dominance. They quarrelled and fought about it for a long while between time and eternity, and neither would give way until Lilith got into such a rage that she left him. She grew vast black wings and soared above him and away to go and live in the deserts of the earth and brood about what a jerk he was. And Adam married Eve. I was right. Have *you* ever noticed how, when men marry for a second time, they usually chose a perfect drip? Some dumb, obedient female with the brains of a donkey? So she ruined everything by being such a dope and here we all are. Second wives are still the same. They're a push-over for door-to-door salesmen and when their husbands come home they say, 'Oh, darling, such a charming serpent called today and sold me this apple. *Such* a bargain.' A husband with any sense would have made her ring up the parent company and demand her money back. He would if his first wife had done it, but not his second. No. All his confidence has gone and he doesn't want to upset the little woman in case she too might grow big black wings and leave him with his dinner spoiled in the oven.

Lilith grew very bitter when she saw how things were going. She despised Eve when she was pregnant and fat and she couldn't stand the children when they were small. She is still dangerous to pregnant woman and children. I don't really blame her. I would not, myself, push over a pregnant woman in the street or drop poison dust in the babies' cradles, but I can see her point. Having made her stand it was all to no avail because stupid, wet Eve had come along and ruined it all. 'Yes, Adam. No Adam. Ooh, that's lovely, Adam. Do it again.' I sometimes feel very defeated when I remember that Eve is the mother of us all. What hope have we? What hope when we spring from bossy, old Adam and limp, silly Eve? Syl's mother,

I felt, was cast more in the mould of Lilith. Perhaps that was why I liked her. She was like me.

I have been avoiding the subject of the exhibition because of what happened. What happened was this. We all went along in our best frocks. Monica and Margaret and Syl and his mother and Robert and me. And I was going to behave perfectly with *politesse* and charm and sobriety. Behave as only I can behave when I put my mind to it. It was Margaret who opened my eyes. Limp, silly Margaret. Can you believe it? She was drifting up and down, looking at the pictures, and she suddenly opened her mouth and said: 'That's Marie Claire's gate.' I'd seen that picture before. Of course I had. I'd seen all the damn things dozens of times, but I'd never really *looked* at them. Not properly. She was right. It *was* Marie Claire's gate. Why hadn't I seen that before? Because I didn't want to, I suppose. I suppose I *had* seen it and not admitted it to myself. I suppose that was why I'd been feeling so anxious. For a moment I went blind and deaf and senseless. Oh God. I went into automatic. I said a lot of things off the top of my head. I was practised at that. Luckily Celestine was there so I talked to her. Talked and talked and talked. I began to feel better. I began to say to myself that a painting of a person's gateway meant nothing at all. He could have painted it at any time. He could have painted it from memory. I talked to Syl about something or other and had another drink and a fag and took a few deep breaths and moved down the gallery ...

I think they do it to English sheep. They don't just cut their throats. I think they stun them first and then come in with the *coup de grâce*. That's what happened to me. I was beginning to recover from the shock when I came to a picture of a bedroom scene. Now the mad, the stupid thing about this is that I did remember that picture. I had been in the room when Robert was fiddling with it. I had said, 'What a *sluttish* woman with her clothes all over the floor.' I had assumed that he was painting

309

not from memory, but from imagination. Silly Lili, eh? Would anybody have believed that Lili could be so blind? I began to plan what I should do to Marie Claire. A number of ideas occurred to me. Not all of them feasible. I looked at her back and thought how it would be improved by the addition of a great big hat pin. I thought of something to do to Robert too. He had come up beside me and put his hand on my shoulder. I wanted to take his hand and pull away his jacket from his shoulder and bite him in his upper arm until the blood ran, until my teeth met his bone. 'Oh,' I said, 'look at the crocodile pool. How the people shouted when you went too near it.'

'How do you know?' asked Robert, taking his hand away. 'You weren't there.' Did he know that I knew? Had I said enough to let him know that I knew? Had I been sufficiently *dégagée* yet obviously aware? Had I managed to give the impression that I had *always* known? That I didn't really care?

'They kept finding bodies in it,' said Robert, and Margaret fainted.

·I was quite relieved although I did think to myself – What's *she* got to faint about? If anyone should be lying on the floor of the gallery it should be me. Still, it stopped me having to say anything more. I was faintly worried that I was going to lose my temper and hit my husband until he died, there in the crowded gallery, and then everyone would have known how much I minded that he had been unfaithful to me with Marie Claire. With *Marie Claire*, who was even sillier than Eve. Oh, it was insupportable.

People were fussing around Margaret. She was hanging on to me and Monica was demanding to know what she thought she was doing. Syl said he'd take her home and looked at me over the top of her head. I looked back at him, but all I said was, 'How kind.' I didn't need to say any more.

Robert said, 'Well, the evening seems to be over. We'd better get to the restaurant. Coming Lili?' And I said, 'Robert, I'd rather stick needles in my eyes.'

*

I took a taxi all the way back and I smoked and smoked cigarette after cigarette. When I got to Monica's house I went round into the garden. It was dark but the distant street lights meant I could just see my way. I went straight to the summer-house where Syl was waiting for me.

Syl liked to talk afterwards. He always had and it's surprising how people don't change. It was freezing cold and uncomfortable in that damned summerhouse. Well, you can imagine. But I was still so angry I felt hot. I had taken charge over the last half hour. My aunts had had a book which was always given to the residents of the zenana when the Sultan gave the word. A manual of technique. It was wasted on Syl who seemed to take it all for granted. I had never used these esoteric skills with Robert because I thought I loved him enough not to need to. Maybe I should have done. Oh well. What the hell. And if you are thinking these are prostitutes' skills you are wrong. These are the skills of the concubine. Yes, there is a difference, but I haven't got time to argue about it.

'What were you saying, Syl?' I asked. 'Sorry. I wasn't listening.'

He didn't mind my saying this polite and unloverly thing. I was wrapped in a ghastly old blanket, smoking a cigarette and wondering what I could do next to annoy Robert. I was saving up Marie Claire to think about when I had a lot of time and no distractions.

I stretched out my elbow and knocked over a flower pot. Damn. It had Monica's cactus in it. She kept the nasty thing as a pet. It was a winter-flowering thing and she talked about it a lot. Boasted about it. 'Green fingers', she said. I had to put the light on to pick it up. It was a little bit broken. But I turned it round and it looked all right. I could see Syl now the light was on so I turned it off again.

'I should really have married you, Lili,' said Syl. 'We're the same sort of people.'

If I hadn't been so upset already this would have led me to utter a few words. It was just as well I couldn't think of anything to say. I was no more like Syl than I was like the kitchen sink. How extraordinary men are – I thought. I was beginning to feel tired. Married to Syl? Me? I'd rather be married to the kitchen sink. I was also beginning to feel a little disgusted with myself.

'Get your clothes on, Syl,' I said.

'I'm not cold,' he said.

I didn't give a toot whether he was cold or not. I just wanted him to put his clothes on. I put mine on, stumbling about in the dark and getting things back to front. How interesting it would be if I should go to the house with my dress inside out and cigarette ends in my hair and everyone was there, sitting in the drawing-room, sipping coffee and eating biscuits. 'Good evening, Lili. What *have* you been doing?' 'Me? Oh, I've just been ...'

'What's the time, Syl?' I said.

'It's not late,' he said, sliding his hand down my leg. Oh God, now he was going to be affectionate. What a fool you are sometimes, Lili. It *was* late. It was a bit too late to tell him to keep his hands to himself.

'Tell me about Abishag the . . . tell me about Margaret,' I said.

He took his hand off my leg and put it on the back of my neck. I suppose he thought that was a more respectable place if we were going to discuss his forthcoming marriage. He'd always been peculiar about women. He fell in love the way people, who are run-down, catch colds. Yes, I do it too, but not *all* the time. He was prone to it and he did it all the time. Here a thought struck me. What – since Syl had such appalling taste in women – did he see in me? I reminded myself that I was calling the shots here. I had instigated this meeting. It was quite possible that he saw nothing in me at all. I had never thought I should find comfort in picturing myself as undesirable. You see, the twists that you can take once you get off the beaten track. Syl was much too stupid to see the flame in me. I was inviolate. Oh, Lilith.

'You see, Lili,' he said, 'she has these banked-down fires in her . . . ' I was amazed at my percipience. There I was thinking about fires and there was Syl talking about them. 'She's been kept down by her mother all her life,' he went on. 'She has a warm nature and she's capable of passion, but it's all been diverted into other channels. Into mother love . . . ' I thought if Margaret loved her mother I was the cat's granny, but I didn't say anything. 'In her,' he said, 'it's as if the river was running backwards towards the source. She's got this sense of duty towards her mother because her father abandoned her and that makes it difficult for her to show emotion. But it's *there*,' he said with conviction.

I thought – oh nuts, Syl – but I only said '*What* her?'

'What?' said Syl.

'What *her*?' I asked. 'You speak of too many hers. There's the her who's running backwards, and the her who was abandoned and the her who can't show emotion. *What* her?'

'You know perfectly well,' said Syl. He'd always been given to this sort of thing. He'd tried it on me once. It was a kind of guard against rejection. As yet another female turned him down he'd worry at the matter like a rat in a dry well until he'd rationalized his loss and restored his *amour propre*. I had once said to him 'Oh, do put all that away, Syl' – or something on those lines – and he'd said my reason for saying it was that my mother had neglected me. The reason I'd said it was that I was waiting for somebody else to come and spend the night, and the reason he was coming to spend the night wasn't because my mother had neglected me, I can tell you. Try explaining that to Syl.

I was sick of Syl. I'd had a sudden nasty feeling that perhaps we *were* the same sort of people, or, at least, not totally unalike. What a dreadful thought. I had used him. I hated him. The time had come to pull the plug and run. But I *had* been on top.

*

Next day was bad. Really bad. Monica was wild with Margaret for passing out, Robert was wild with me for not going to dinner with them, I was wild with Robert, and Syl was wild because his honeymoon was cancelled. The charlady was wild too. She was trying to do the cleaning and listen to us talking at the same time. Not as easy as you might think. You can only polish one bit of floor for five minutes or so then you have to move on out of earshot. 'Oh,' I had said, being as spiteful as I knew how and speaking as a *Masri*. 'You *can't* take the little one to Egypt at this time of year if she isn't well. She'd catch all manner of things.' Why should Syl go to Egypt? Darling Egypt was too good for him. I really hated him today. I kept remembering parts of the night before and going 'Ouch' and 'Oh God' and closing my eyes and clutching my hair and wishing I'd died. I had to pretend I had a migraine. How *could* I have ... No, never mind. Let's think about something else.

Margaret said, 'I hope I didn't spoil the evening.'

And Robert said. '*You* didn't spoil the evening.' He looked at me and then away. What was I supposed to do when my husband painted pictures of his mistress and hung them around for everyone to see? Call them all to come and watch? 'Now this is Marie Claire. She's just crawled out of bed and my husband thought that would be a good time to do a nice painting of her.' How I wanted to kill him. I was very calm and controlled and I said the exhibition had been a conspicuous success and wasn't that heartening; and I said I'd been tired and come home and gone to bed early, and I looked straight at Robert and dared him to call me a liar and he just *yawned*.

Monica said they'd been looking for me for hours, and I thought that in a way it was a pity they hadn't looked in the summerhouse.

'Sorry,' I said.

What if they had looked through the window at the moment when ...? No, it wasn't funny. I was going to laugh. I turned it into a hiccup and said, 'Sorry,' again. I *was* sorry. I was sorry I'd degraded my person with Syl, but, yes, in some wicked way it was terribly, terribly funny.

'I want to talk to you Lili,' said Robert. Oh God. We were in our bedroom chastely clad in pyjamas and night-gown. He stood at one side of the bed, poised to get in, and I stood at the other waiting for him to do so. I was carefully behaving like a married lady rather than a houri.

'Yes dear?' I said. That was going too far. I never called him 'dear' just like that. He looked at me without smiling. 'Whatsa matter?' I asked. That was the wrong thing to say too. Why should anything be the matter? I began to work myself into a rage. If anything was the matter it was his infidelity. His unforgivable infidelity. Bastard.

But he wanted to talk about money. Robert worried much more about money than he did about human relationships. In this he was quite different from me. All right, in a way I did expect money to grow on trees. In a way, for me, it did. It was the fault of my aunts. They had the minds of merchants. To the merchant there is always something to buy and sell, and even if you don't make a profit the money goes round and round. I did not have the mentality of a merchant. I had the mentality of a child of merchants. That is, I thought money grew on trees. Robert, needlessly, reminded me of this and he intended his remarks as a reproach. I could not see why an ability to account and save should be considered a moral attribute; and I could see nothing wrong in spending money when you had it. Just as long as you always had something to sell should the need arise. He said we were not too badly off at the moment for, while his pictures did not yet command a great price, the exhibition should prove to be a financial success. He said the money he had made in the deal over his grandpapa's things was a help, but he also said that we had to pay off our debts, and to this end he had borrowed a little money from Syl in order to enable us to travel to Scotland without touching the money in the bank.

What? He'd borrowed money from Syl? When? What did they talk about while he was doing this borrowing? And what was that story – the one about the man who wanted to sleep with the merchant's wife? She said it would cost him, so he borrowed the money from the merchant, had his fun, and when the merchant asked for the money back he said he'd already given it to his wife. Why did I think of that story? It was the other way round wasn't it? My mind was fuddled but I was relieved Robert was only talking about money. As for human relationships I'd decided to call it quits for the time being. I knew that no matter what he'd done, when the chips were down I'd be the one to get the blame. *All* the blame. I would just wait, and one of these days ... I made a vow. And I *always* kept my word.

'Why are we going to Scotland, Robert?' I asked, climbing into bed sideways with my knees together and smelling of toothpaste and talcum.

'You don't have to come,' he said. Maybe I didn't, but I was. I was going to stay very close to Robert for a while. We'd been playing a dangerous game. Time to stick together until the boat stopped rocking. I didn't want either of us straying anywhere; not alone. It appeared there was a gallery in Edinburgh which had expressed interest in his work and he was going to discuss the possibility of another exhibition. I vowed that, in future, I too would take a greater interest in his work. I'd follow him round and hold his brushes.

Scotland was cold.

I had bought whisky and biscuits as presents and a large, warm red coat for Lili. A very expensive, large red coat. It suits me. 'Robert,' I had said, 'I don't care what you say, I'm not going to freeze to death for want of a warm red coat. You can sell an extra picture.'

Margaret was pleased when we came back. She must have missed me. She wanted to talk and I felt sorry for her. It must have been so boring when we went away and she was left on her own with Monica. She had a funny idea of social chit-chat, mind you. She was always talking about age and death. Well, not always, because she didn't talk all that much but when she did she usually talked about age and death. I hope she didn't do it because she thought I was the expert. I also had a tendency to talk about age and death when I felt tired. I do us both an injustice. Margaret knew I wasn't as silly as I seemed to some people.

'You mustn't worry about age,' I said. 'It doesn't matter.' Oh, listen to me. Listen to Lili, whistling in the dark. Would Robert love me when my teeth fell out? What if my hair fell out? Would children have kept us together for ever? No, of course not. It was people without children who stayed together for ever. I told her to keep up appearances. Loads of make-up. Expensive clothes. Avoid the elderly. Stick with the young. Oh Lord, what an awful thought – tottering round on your poor swollen old feet, keeping up with the hopelessly, madly boring *young*.

The young are so moral and principled and full of high ideals. I hate them. I didn't say that. You'd be surprised if you knew how sensible I can sound when I talk. You should ask Margaret. I gave her a lot of good advice. I said a number of wise and sensible things. We had an excellent conversation until Monica butted in and that was the end of that. Monica was not only incapable of conversation – she made everyone else start sounding like mother's little idiot child. It was infuriating. Down went the tone of my elevated conversation.

It went down so far that Robert put in his pennyworth and accused me of talking tripe. That did it. I had been as good as gold in Scotland. I had been as good as gold for several days. I had talked about bloody old art and sat with my ankles crossed and crooked my little finger when drinking tea. *Tea.* I hadn't even made any crumbs. Everyone we'd met had fallen in love with me and I'd been gracious to them. No more. Just gracious. And what thanks did I get? I got told I talked tripe. OK, Robert, that was enough of little goody-two-shoes. I wondered where I should go that night. I'd think of somewhere – and I'd think of someone to be there with me. Nobody important, nobody dangerous – just somebody Robert wouldn't approve of. I'd probably settle for Celestine in the end. We could go dancing. I was knitting together this small and none too sinister plot when Monica made one of her daft remarks.

'I'm sure Cynthia will never get the children's clothes right,' she said. Don't ask me why she said it then. Her mind worked that way. It sort of got in and out of the water like a frog on a lily pad and you never knew what it was going to do next.

'Let us go and see,' I said. 'Let us go to Cynthia's house and have a look.' And in case you're wondering I don't know why I said that. Partly boredom, partly curiosity, I suppose. I rather enjoy observing strange creatures in their natural habitat and it would be interesting to see how Monica carried herself. 'Go and ring her,' I said. 'See what she says.'

Monica was very funny on the phone. Not intentionally of course. No, she was polite and condescending. I was surprised she'd agreed so quickly. Perhaps she was curious about Derek's new home too, and nobody had ever been sufficiently considerate to give her the chance of visiting it. She was probably grateful to me.

'We'll go down on Thursday,' she said, 'and have lunch there.'

Came a point when I had to get out of the house again or murder Monica. She wouldn't stop talking about clothes and weddings. I wouldn't have minded if she'd had *anything* interesting to say, but she hadn't. Not a thing. White satin, smoked salmon – oh Yuk. Besides, getting married meant you had to live together and at the moment I thought living together was a lousy idea. For better for worse – and worse. If it had been accepted that we should live apart then Robert, when we met, would have no idea that I'd been up to anything. He would love pure Lili, the angel. On the other hand, I would have no idea what Robert had been up to. This could be a good thing since it would mean less anxiety for me – in a way. I would, perhaps, always be suspicious, and that is so exhausting. Oh, it was *all* too exhausting. All this running around. It made me think of Syl when I didn't really want to. Syl ran around like a puppy dog; like the worst sort of puppy dog you can't take out without trouble. At the sight of a female he'd dash off, tail wagging. *Any* female would get him running around going 'Bark, bark' and scrabbling with his little paws for attention. You'd call 'To heel' and there he'd be dancing round, twirling his moustaches. What I mean is – if he hadn't been a dog he'd have been a moustache-twirler, a Ladies' Man. Oh God. He'd been doing it at the exhibition until Margaret fell over. I was getting madder with Robert by the minute for forcing me into the arms of Syl. Oh, *damn* and blast. *I* didn't scrabble with my paws for attention.

I went to see Mrs Monro. She was refreshing. I couldn't imagine how she'd managed to be the wife and mother of those two men. Not that it's all that unusual. I have known several rather magnificent women with the *most* hopeless husbands and sons. I suppose they seem even more hopeless beside their magnificent woman. I wondered how people saw me and Robert.

I took a box of biccies someone had given me in Scotland round to Mrs Monro as a present, and she was *pleased to see me.* She was. She was really pleased. I can tell. Oh, it is so warming when someone is really pleased to see you. I could talk to her. Not about Robert any more because every time I thought of Robert being so annoying I thought of vengeance and I couldn't tell her that, so I didn't talk about Robert. I sat down and said Monica and I were going to see Cynthia and Derek to make sure they'd put buttons on the kiddies' frocks.

'Eugh,' said Mrs Monro, 'Derek. I don't think I'll be able to look at him. I can't think how Monica can bear to look at him.'

But I knew that even if they remembered what had happened they wouldn't really remember, neither Monica nor Derek. I knew how bad people lived with themselves. After a while they pretended somebody else had done it – no matter what it was. Even now I was beginning to pretend that some other person had spent the better part of a night in a moth-eaten old summer-house. Not me. Not Lili. No.

Mrs Monro wished Derek was dead. I told her that bad people always started to die before they died, that corruption was a sign of death. Dear Lord. But I wasn't bad, not really stinkingly bad, not so bad the angels would have to hold their noses. Was I? I was so glad Syl's mother didn't know the last bad thing I'd done.

Eve, as well as being a gullible mug, was a dreadful housewife. Cynthia was a dreadful housewife and she clearly couldn't cope with little Cain and Abel – or rather little Jennifer and Christopher. Their beastly, depressing small toys lay around everywhere, broken. There was mud in the garden and the children smelt. Cynthia was skinny and hairy and gummy. Much worse than Monica. Derek had married Eve twice, but Eve II was far worse than Eve I. Monica was dumb in many ways but she was moderately competent in the house, and she washed. Cynthia looked as though a good wash wouldn't do her any harm. It was Monica who said this. She whispered it to me when Cynthia wasn't listening. Mind you, she couldn't have been *sure* Cynthia wasn't listening since she'd only that second gone out of the door. Oh, I had to make such an effort to handle the children's little frocks. Both the little children had necks like the necks of dead chickens – dirty dead chickens. Everything here was thin and dirty. How I began to appreciate Monica and her house. How I hated Cynthia's food. I didn't eat it. I sat there hating it and pushing it around the plate. The plate was greasy with old grease. The house was cold with a scum of greasy dust. It was like hell. Derek had married again and gone to hell. Good. I wondered if he abused his new little children and what progression of hells he would go through until he himself crumbled away into greasy dust. I thought that never, never again would I do an impure thing, for I must be different from Derek and free of all that dirt and dust. Once I had believed that transgression led to freedom but now I looked and I saw where it led. Oh no, the place wasn't *really* as bad as that – not in actuality. It was bad enough but something else gave it its atmosphere. Derek, I suppose. I could never be as bad as Derek if I lived for ever, but I wasn't good enough to be comfortable. Oh damn.

Cynthia had put Peter Pan collars on the children's frocks so I took them off again. I didn't bother much with their clothes for there wasn't any point. They would look like dressed-up dead chickens whatever I did. Cynthia gave them pickled red things for their lunch – cabbage and beetroot with bitter, dripping juices designed to ruin blue velvet. I had to be so careful to keep them apart. I wanted to go out and buy a clean towel to sit on. I wanted to get away.

I said, 'Monica, we must go now, for we have things to do this evening.'

'Yes,' said Monica, who was quite good at this game. 'We don't want to keep everybody waiting.' We had given the impression that away from here, in glorious Croydon full of light, there were fascinating and numerous people looking at their watches and wondering eagerly where we were. Cynthia looked wistful.

'Oh Monica,' I said, as we closed the garden gate on the mud and the broken toys.

'I suppose she does her best,' said Monica in a tone of contentment.

I was so glad to be back in Croydon. I know that must sound strange but it's true. I am a little afraid of poverty in all its forms – actual and spiritual. I wonder sometimes what would become of a person who had lost everything; how she would even begin to think about how to begin again if she had nothing at all to sell and nothing to offer freely. It didn't bear thinking about. Monica, admittedly, did not go in for oriental luxury, but her house was a dream of cleanliness and comfort compared with Cynthia's. It didn't frighten me. I could not have stayed a moment longer in Cynthia's house without bursting into tears of fear and depression. This would have been most unlike me. Perhaps I was catching a cold. Perhaps I was growing old. Well, I wasn't a mess. Cynthia was a mess. Her house was a mess, her children were messes, her husband was worse than any mess. Her clothes were almost worse than anything. I was tired. I had to have a drink. Monica had a drink too, but for the other reason. There are two reasons for drinking as far as I'm concerned – because you're happy or because you're sad. Monica was happy now she knew that Derek lived in the dust.

'I want a drink too,' said Margaret. It was really too early for all this drinking, but – so what. I went to the cloakroom in the hall and nearly fell over the cleaning lady's bucket. She had a most disconcerting way of appearing out of nowhere. She had her hat on, so was on her way home. 'Careful,' she said. And then she said, 'You want to watch that husband of yours.' She was looking towards the drawing-room door as she spoke – looking at Margaret slumped in an armchair. She couldn't have said that, could she? I knew she rather liked me. I had seen her grinning to herself at things I had said while she mopped and dusted, but we had never actually spoken directly to each other.

Why should we? Why should she now say such a thing to me? For my sake or for the sake of Margaret? Was that *really* what she had said? I couldn't ask her. I had already smiled at her and moved back to the drawing-room. When she opened her mouth to speak I had assumed that she would say 'Good-evening-lovely-weather-for-the-time-of-year' and it was to that expected remark that I had responded – not 'You should keep your eye on your husband' or whatever it was she'd said. I couldn't think how I should respond to such a remark from the cleaning lady. Did she mean to imply that Robert had spent the day pursuing Abishag the Shunamite round the house? I really couldn't quite visualize this happening. For one thing it seemed to me that Margaret wouldn't run. She would sit there gazing in incomprehension at any male who showed signs of getting up speed in her direction. So, naturally, he would wind down again and pretend that he had merely been trying to take a moth out of her ear. Maybe that's what had happened. Oh hell, what did I care. I did care. Nobody in the world, as long as I lived and all through eternity should ever know how much I minded about Robert. Certainly not Robert. Certainly not Marie Claire, the cow.

I said 'Did Marie Claire explain why she wouldn't come to the wedding?' Monica had been partly aggrieved at this refusal and partly relieved for she didn't want her house overwhelmed with people. You can't keep a house tidy when it's full of people. I thought – she daren't come in case I know about her and Robert. She's frightened I'll kill her. Quite a lot of killing went on where we lived. Well, not a *lot*, but it tended to be more casual than English killing. People tended to disappear sometimes, or they got ill and died. Sometimes their families minded a great deal and sometimes they didn't. I wouldn't have killed Marie Claire. I wouldn't have given her the satisfaction. Monica said Marie Claire was too busy, and then Margaret suddenly said, 'I don't want to marry Syl.' Of course she didn't.

Nobody ever had – not for long anyway. For a second I felt sorry for Syl. He wasn't all that bad. Not really. There was just something a bit wrong with him. Something a bit weird. He wasn't a eunuch. No. But there was something smooth about him, something incomplete. He wasn't really a proper human being, let alone a proper man. Oh, poor Syl. Then I looked at Margaret. Looked at her properly for the first time for days. Ever. And I thought – poor Margaret, and then I thought – poor me, and after a while I even thought – poor Robert. It must have been the gin. No. It wasn't altogether the gin for I am not incapable of human sympathy. I only wish I was. This wouldn't do. Lili was going soft.

I'd made Syl buy one of Robert's paintings. Syl didn't like parting with money. I'd told him it would make a superb wedding present for the bride, and I wouldn't let him off the hook. 'You buy that picture,' I said, 'and I tell you what I'll do. I'll take you out to dinner in a little French restaurant I know.' Syl couldn't resist that – a free meal *and* with Lili. 'Besides,' I told him, 'that picture is a bargain. You can make such a profit on it one day.' It was getting very close to the time for this assignation and I suddenly rather lost my head. 'Let us,' I said, 'go and have dinner in Soho. It will make a nice change for Margaret.' As I spoke I thought to myself – Lili, you've gone mad. What are you doing? What do you think you're doing? I knew what I was doing. I was dicing with death. The reckless streak had overwhelmed me. Sometimes I had swum in crocodile-infested waters. Once I had overturned a stall in the souk. Oh yes, I had. I had been a good girl for days and when I saw the peasants quietly buying mangoes I had seized a support under the stall and pulled it away. There was nothing anyone could do about it. Not to me. The mangoes had rolled everywhere, and after that I had been good again for weeks.

I changed my mind. I thought I would take them to another

restaurant, but Monica said, 'What about Robert? What will Robert do about dinner?' and I remembered the picture of Marie Claire in her dreadful bedroom, and I thought of how *smug* Monica could be, and I thought – oh, so what the hell. What the flaming hell. And I drove to the restaurant of the assignation with Syl. I sang as I drove.

It all fell flat. We sat there in the little restaurant discussing the menu over one of those nasty candlesticks, dripping with wax, and nothing happened. Syl stuck his head round the door but when he saw three of us he bolted like a rabbit. Men are such cowards. Stupid too, I'd been going to smile at him *so* sweetly, and tell him I'd arranged all this as a little extra celebration. If he'd kept his head he could have carried it off but guilt had lent wings to his heels. I did smile as I thought of him flying down the street clutching Robert's picture, his heart pounding; head in a whirl – all confused. 'What is Lili up to?' he would be asking himself. 'What's her game?' Let him stew. I choked on a mouthful of *moules marinières* as something occurred to me. Speaking literally, Syl would be allowed to keep his head, unlike the male relations of the lover of the silly Sultana.

Monica said, 'I could have sworn that was Syl – he opened the door and looked straight at me and went straight out again.'

'Perhaps it was him,' I said. 'He works somewhere round here, doesn't he?'

'Can't have been,' said Monica. 'Why would he go like that? What are you laughing at?' I caught Margaret looking at me and I had the feeling that she knew what I'd been doing. Knew about the assignation and everything. Didn't care. Somewhere inside me I worried about Margaret. She was not fit to take part in these games. She was not like the rest of us. Don't get the wrong idea. I didn't think she was too *good* for the game – not better than the rest of us – only not *designed* for the game.

And I felt that if I was going to bring her into the game then I should have to wash my hands. Yes – here it came, that annoying feeling that one must not sully innocence. Even the knowledge that one is capable of sullying innocence is annoying. It makes one feel corrupt – and old.

I sang all the way home too – out of spite.

Damn. I did feel corrupt. It was all Margaret's fault. Little milky mouse with sad eyes. She looked at me so mournfully sometimes with those eyes, as though she wanted me to save her. To march in and pick her up and send her back to Mother Joseph and the clear fountain. How could I? How was I to explain to Monica the nature of vocation? I wasn't too sure about it myself – it was nothing I'd ever experienced. If Mother Joseph wanted her, let her come and get her. Nothing to do with me. I wasn't her mother. I rather needed a mother myself. I went to see Syl's one. I ran there.

Mrs Monro was unsentimental and strong-minded. I couldn't think how she'd ever conceived Syl, who was neither. But I couldn't discuss Syl with her. I told her about the trip to Cynthia's house. I told her how awful Cynthia was, and her food. I didn't really want to talk about Cynthia. I wanted to tell her how destructive I could be and ask her why she thought that was. I wanted to confess. I couldn't of course, for that would have brought in Syl – not to mention his father. I approached it from another way. I was beginning to feel rather proud of the depth of my concern for Margaret. I wasn't used to worrying about people other than Robert or myself and I felt if I really worried about Margaret I should not only seem, but *be*, a better person.

I heard myself saying, 'We must think about Margaret.'

'And Syl,' said his mother. Oh bother Syl – I thought, but I didn't say it. She went on: 'Margaret is much too young for him. She's not ready for marriage.'

'I know,' I said. I couldn't for the life of me see what was to be done about it. There was no point in talking to Monica, for the whole thing was her idea. I was sure Margaret would never have let things go this far without her mother pushing and pushing.

'This wedding would be most unfortunate,' I said. 'A disaster.' Syl's mother agreed. She *was* a sensible woman. I didn't want to hurt her maternal feelings by remarking that anyone who married Syl would be letting herself in for disaster, so I explained that Margaret had a vocation and thus was in no position to marry anybody without incurring the wrath of God – the jealous God whom no one in her right mind would care to cross. Vocation, the religious life, wasn't something I really wanted to talk about much. I liked Mother Joseph. I was fond of Mother Joseph, but she always made me feel as though I'd do well to go and have a ritual bath and a good scrub – inside and out. I couldn't imagine living the life of a nun although I had to admit it would be peaceful with no men around. But, oh, so boring. I stopped thinking like that for if God knows all our thoughts he would not be flattered to hear me thinking that a life dedicated to his service would be boring. I really didn't feel I could afford to offend anyone at the moment – let alone God.

Syl's mother was interested in all I could tell her about the convent. She kept wanting to know more and I didn't know much more. I just wished I knew more about what Marie Claire had been up to, and I couldn't think of any way of finding out. I rather wished she was coming over for the wedding. It would have offered opportunities for revenge – my favourite condiment. But no. I had to stop thinking like that. It always led to trouble. Mostly trouble for other people, but quite often it splashed up on me.

I said, 'Marie Claire won't come to the wedding. She's frightened of me.' On the face of it this was a pointless remark. Something drove me to say: 'She doesn't know I know she's been having an affair with Robert.' I had to tell somebody. It was rankling in me. 'Good heavens,' said Syl's mother, not sounding too perturbed.

'But she's not sure I won't find out,' I said. I found it difficult to leave the subject alone, but for the moment Syl's mother was more interested in Margaret than in me. I began to try and think of something else. I looked round and tried to picture Margaret living here. It wasn't possible. It was too *sad*, too depressing. The house needed somebody with a bit of sparkle. Syl's mother needed somebody with a bit of sparkle. Margaret would just fade like the curtains, go limp like the cushions and all the lights would get dimmer and dimmer. Poor Margaret.

'A nun,' said Mrs Monro reflectively, 'a nun. Yes, I see.'

'I believe it,' I said. 'There was some fuss in Egypt – some rubbish Marie Claire was going on about – but I think the nun part is all true.'

'I think so too,' said Mrs Monro. 'I really don't think there ought to be a wedding.'

'I don't think there will be,' I said, and I meant that I would stop it.

I don't know when I made up my mind that I must keep my word. It might have been just then when Mrs Monro looked as though she trusted me, as though she thought I might be capable of anything. Well, I *was* capable of anything. In the end I proved it. Or it might have been when the cleaning lady told me Robert was not to be trusted alone with Margaret. Or it might have been when Margaret had looked at me with big trusting eyes and almost asked me aloud to help her – to please, please help her. I don't know. I have a destructive impulse in me – often I have thought of suicide and sometimes of murder – but I don't know what I then had decided to destroy. Monica's hopes? Or Syl's? Or Robert's? Or just me. Or perhaps I simply couldn't resist the compulsion to go centre stage; what Robert called 'showing off'. Oh, I was angry with Robert. Not only because of Marie Claire, but because often he had made me feel insecure. He had assumed superiority over me and I'd let him get away with it. The time of reckoning – I said to myself – had come. Fasten your seat-belts.

And all the time, of course, I told myself that I could change my mind when it came to the point. I was not committed to anything. I let Monica go on fussing – about the wedding and the wedding guests and the food and the wine and the clothes – and occasionally I felt a little mean for it was all to come to nothing, but mostly I let her go on as though I were in a dream. As though in one of those dreams where impossible things happen together, at the same time. I seemed to leave my body as a jinnee leaves a bottle and floats above all the people, invulnerable, omnipotent and – not to be trusted. Everybody knows that the jânn can't be trusted. They share with man the promise of salvation but they go round at night doing bad things. It wasn't my fault. I hadn't let myself out of the bottle, had I? Robert had uncorked the bottle with his infidelity; or maybe it was Margaret with her hopeless trust; or maybe it was the sprite Peri or Lilith and I had liberated myself on huge wings of rage. Also, to be honest, I foresaw some fun. I knew I should cause the most alarming scene but scenes can be such fun – especially years later when the dust has settled and the blood dried. It would come as a shock to Monica, but by then the exhibition would be all over and it wouldn't matter any more. Besides, Monica's sensibilities wouldn't be so refined if she hadn't been so stuck-up in the old days. I could have taken her to places to see all manner of things that would have done a good deal to broaden her mind. She'd always said she didn't care for that type of thing – said it with her nose in the air. Some of us had been unable to avoid that type of thing. Who did she think she was? A dancer has to dance in some strange places. Then sometimes I remembered her when she hadn't been so annoying.

When she was a girl sometimes she was fun. And sometimes, every now and then, I remembered a tiny little thing in a little sashed frock and that was Margaret, and I would think that such a little one should never, never be invited to step into a dancing house in Cairo. I was not getting sentimental. It merely seemed unsuitable. Syl would not have seemed out of place in such an establishment. Especially not since . . . oh, never mind.

We practised wearing our wedding clothes, and I adjusted Monica's collar under her chin and asked how the winter-flowering cactus was coming along, and I smiled into her eyes.

Oh God. Derek and Cynthia arrived with Cain and Abel and their potty. No, I do not regret not having had any children. I hate the small creatures. They cried and whined in tiny voices like the voices of caterpillars. Oh, the poor little things. No, I won't be sorry for them. I won't. I couldn't afford pity. I hadn't got the time for it.

They arrived with a lot of depressing objects; a lot of their smaller broken toys, and I think they all had a bit of mud on their feet. Nobody could possibly be pleased to see them. Nobody was. They dropped things it was hard to see the purpose of. You couldn't imagine why they'd bothered to pack them. You couldn't imagine why they'd come at all.

Monica was haughty and Cynthia was abstracted and everybody else was embarrassed, so I kissed them all – except for Monica, naturally – and I lit a cigarette to take the taste away. I wished *I* was away. I wished I was lying in the sun, drunk somewhere, with somebody terribly, terribly witty and clever, trickling oil into the small of my back. I don't know why people cling so to life when it is so seldom pleasant. But perhaps I exaggerate. No one would want to live for long in the vicinity of Derek and Cynthia, but there were other forms of life around. I think I had been drinking too much again. If I went on it wouldn't be long before the horrors got me. I should have to get back to the sun. Who should I take with me? No, not Robert. Not yet. I didn't know if I could ever forgive him enough to let him rub oil in my back again. I reflected that I hadn't spent a sober night since I had arrived in England. Not good enough, Lili. There was no real cure for the horrors. You had to go on, trying to drink rather less, until they went away. But what if they never went away? Then you died, I suppose. Died in the dark, screaming at the black wings to go away, screaming for your mother and the monkey your father brought you. Screaming that you hadn't meant it, that you never meant to destroy anything – not even yourself. Oh *God*.

I said to Monica that I found Derek and Cynthia acutely lowering to the spirits, hoping she would also feel sufficiently down to suggest a drink. This was the right thing to say. We went into the drawing-room and after a while I felt better.

Cain and Abel had their supper in the kitchen and Eve put them to bed. She stayed up there with them and Derek also went up early. I didn't think about that. I had drunk enough by now to persuade myself that Monica had been lying about her ex-husband for I didn't want to spoil the whisky by gazing at the devil's feet. Derek made me think of the devil's feet. I was getting drunk again, and where was Robert? Abishag the Shunamite had also gone early to bed. At least I supposed she had. Yes, of course, she had. I wasn't drunk enough to imagine she was rolling round in the garden with my husband who had to have an eye kept on him. Nor in the summerhouse.

Next thing I knew I was in the summerhouse, but there was nobody there. Nobody at all.

And the next thing I did was to steal Cain and Abel's hats. I did it the next morning when I was still not entirely sober. Their hats were lying under the kitchen table where I suppose they had torn them from each other's heads, and I was seized with a bright idea – the sort you get when you're not entirely sober. They were made of scarlet crêpe paper and I imagine they'd been handed out at some pre-Christmas party. I slipped them into my pocket and if anyone asked I should say I'd thought they were rubbish and had neatly thrown them in the bin. You may be wondering what appeal these hats held for me, so I will explain that it was not for their beauty but for their utility that I desired them. I cut them up and turned them into red flowers and I told Monica that her cactus was undoubtedly going to bloom in time for the wedding. It was all part of my plot. I told her that from biblical times there had been a belief that there was no more fortunate portent on a nuptial occasion than the blossoming of a cactus. I said it was held to be so by all the people of the Book, by Muslimin and Farangi alike, and it might have been true for all I knew. Certainly a desert people might find it cheering to discover a flower when a wedding was about to take place. Monica, although she was unimaginative, was superstitious, so she swallowed this whole. I told myself she was grasping at the last straw that broke the camel's back, but that was because I still wasn't entirely sober.

I put on my new coat and went out with my paper hats, down to the summerhouse. Margaret was there already, just sitting and staring out of the window at the leaves and the birds blowing around in the cold. So I couldn't finish my flowers there.

She said, 'You look warm.'

I said I wasn't warm really. The coat helped but I felt chilled all through. I told Margaret her mother's cactus was due for a happy event and then I went to see Syl's mother.

We sat at the kitchen table and drank whisky and I got smoke in my eyes trying to make fiddly little flowers with a cigarette between my teeth. No easy matter, I can tell you. Syl's mother was being gloomy about Margaret. As well she might be. She was wondering if she should tell Syl about Derek's misdemeanour towards his daughter.

'Ach, *no*,' I said, 'he'd never forgive her. He'd hate her, and every time she displeased him he'd tell her she was no good. Hopeless. A deformed, unnatural and filthy thing to be used and abused as the fancy took him . . . ' OK. That wasn't tactful either. Not to speak so to a mother of her son, but I knew it was true. I don't know how I knew, but I knew. Anyway, there wasn't going to be a wedding, so there was no point at all in telling Syl such a thing about a person who soon would be a stranger to him.

Syl's mother was rightly offended. 'Syl isn't like that,' she said. But he was. A lot of men were like that, and Syl certainly was. I *knew*. I did not, however, insist. Syl's mother went on worrying about it.

'Are you sure she doesn't remember?' she said.

I was certain. Margaret had wanted to tell me things – about Nour and love and sorrow – and I hadn't let her. I knew about love and sorrow and the subject of nasty little Nour bored me. If she'd remembered what her father had done she'd have tried to tell me about that. I wouldn't have let her because there really are some things I don't want to know. If she'd remembered she'd have been *determined* to tell me. She trusted me. Oh, oh.

Mrs Monro gave up. 'What are you making?' she asked.

'I am making wedding decorations,' I said. 'Secret ones,' and she began to cry. 'Oh, Lili,' she said.

Now you might not have thought it but I can't bear to see people cry – not children or dogs or men or old ladies. This is partly why I hasten so about the world, because I cannot stay and see people cry. I always feel I should do something about it and this is inconvenient. I particularly didn't like to see Syl's mother cry. She was supposed to be a dry old lady; a brave and funny old lady of the sort I would be myself if I lived that long. I held her hand and I said, 'There *won't* be a wedding.' I promised her. So that was that. Boats burned, bridges crossed.

She opened another bottle of whisky and I had another drink and another cigarette and then I left her and went back to the summerhouse because Monica's cleaning lady had arrived. She was Mrs Monro's cleaning lady too. I sometimes felt a bit haunted by her. Margaret had gone. Back to bed probably.

Monica's house was now uninhabitable with Adam and Eve and the little ones. We had really nothing in common. Eve didn't like me. She couldn't see the point of me and I wasn't going to be bothered to enchant her. Why should I? It would have done neither of us any good and she'd undoubtedly have tried to tell me things I didn't want to know. So I had to go out a lot. I began to wish I was back in Iskenderiyeh. I began to miss the smell of dust and chickens and onions. I was a gypsy after all and I began to wish I was walking along a *gisr*, looking down at the river while the sun set red in a haze of dust. Yes, I knew I'd be restless there too, but I was tired of here. A small villa at Râs-et-Tin under the walls of the Khedive's summer palace would have suited me now; figs and jasmine and a mulberry tree. All gone. All gone. Oh my dear ones, the sadness of life.

I went often to Syl's house. Now I felt at peace with Syl's mother. She cared nothing for my transgressions. She trusted me. I felt safe with her. Oh yes, I was a Nazarene, but I began more and more to feel it would not have been so bad to live in the zenana with the women – just so long as the Sultan was away a lot. Safe and quiet with the old wives and the young ones and the children. The children would have rather spoiled it, now I come to think about it. Nothing was ever perfect. Shadowed rooms with the sun fingering its way between the lattice would not be ideal if they were full of hooting children. Perhaps, after all, Margaret had chosen the best way; the convent way. I wasn't well. Not well to be thinking so. I put on my red coat and went out in the cold to see Syl's mother. The cleaning lady was there, cleaning. She grinned at me. Almost she laughed at me. I didn't mind. She was just another woman of the zenana. There could have been few secrets in the zenana. If she could read my thoughts I didn't care. Why should I? Slaves and eunuchs, Osmanli and Circassians, Frankish women and women of the desert – all had lived together in the harem and known each other's thoughts. There was no privacy there, and those who practised secrecy, if they were found out, suffered things I could not tell you about. You would not sleep well. I thought that secrecy was overrated. Keeping secrets was as foolish as keeping scorpions under your hat. I wished I hadn't got any.

Syl's mother was in bed looking so old and tired. Oh my soul, the sorrows of age. I stayed with her until I had to go. I would have stayed longer but I had to go. I had to go and say goodbye to Celestine and the rest, and I thought I might go to Ely Place to confession at the church there. And then I thought I might as well wait to do that.

I said, 'I must go', and I told her not to worry, and I went.

I met Robert at the French pub. I hadn't known he'd be there but he was. I was so pleased to see him. Every time I saw him my heart eased a little. We had not spoken much over the last few days. Things were not well between us but still just to see him there eased my heart. He was standing by the bar, leaning on an elbow and there were people all around us.

I said, 'Hallo, my darling', and he said, 'I'm leaving you, Lili.' So he was a coward. He couldn't have told me when we were alone. He had to wait until we were surrounded by strangers. Never mind that I knew all these people. They were strangers now. They looked at me without embarrassment. They didn't love me now I'd been repudiated.

'You're a hashshâsh, Lili,' said my husband. He had lived long in my country to learn to be so cruel. 'Go and live with the Old Man of the Mountains,' he said. He was drunk.

*

I went to Celestine's but she was out, so I smoked by myself. I'd always used a little hashish. A lot of my countrymen did. It was not so harmful to the liver as drink. Robert disapproved of it in the same way that he disapproved of me 'sponging' – just because it was foreign. He would borrow money from people he didn't like, and sometimes he drank until he fell over. But that was all right.

Yes, sometimes hashish made me indiscreet and do things I would not otherwise have done, but does not drink also have this effect? Yes, it does. Robert was irrational and I was angry with him. I didn't mind being rebuked if I was really in the wrong, but he didn't know I was. He was being needlessly cruel and it wasn't fair.

I picked up the telephone and before I could speak I found I was sobbing. There were tears in the telephone. I never weep. Not usually. It was the cold of this accursed country that had weakened my resistance. 'Oh, I'm so unhappy,' I said.

There was another side to Syl. A side I haven't told you about. I always knew he had this other side, but I had never had to rely on it. I had *despised* him for it. It was a womanly side; a gentle, loving, worrying side. He would wrinkle his forehead with concern and lean over and take your hand. It was anaphrodisiac, but so comforting. He stayed with me until I stopped crying and then we talked. After a while we finished talking about me. There are limits to what can be said about me. So we talked about Syl. I found I rather liked him, I was quite fond of him. I remembered that once upon a time I had faintly loved him before I became aware of this womanly side. Now I lay against the warmth of that womanly side and felt comforted. The ironies of life. We talked for hours, and we only talked. We might have been in the zenana.

Syl didn't love Margaret. I didn't care what anybody said. *He* said he did, but I knew he didn't. I could tell. That made it easier. Dreaming in the dark, I thought Syl was a *mustahāll*.

When a man divorces you – and all he has to do is say so – he can't marry you again until you've married someone else in the meantime. He's called a *mustahàll* and everybody is happier if he is either so old or so unattractive as to render the consummation merely technical and not much fun. Oh well.

Oh God, life goes on. On and on. The next day was the day before the wedding. Robert had come back. It may have been because he still did love me really, but I think it was because he was English. It would not have been *comme il faut* to disappear from the house of his hostess the day before the wedding. I didn't ask him. I still had my pride. Pooh to you, Robert, with your insults and your Englishness and your cowardice. Whatever else *I* was, I was brave. When nothing else is left bravery is the only virtue that counts. Ask the mujahedin. Even death is nothing to the brave.

Death would have been preferable to the night before the wedding with Monica's houseparty. I drank so much whisky it was like committing temporary suicide. I don't remember much about it in consequence. I have tiny lightning memories of Monica being arch. She had asked Money Bags to come and stay. That was mad if you like. She'd done it to prove to Cynthia that she had an admirer. He didn't admire her at all but Cynthia didn't notice. She didn't notice anything, wrapped up as she was in Cain and Abel. Mrs Monro brought the dog and I think I may have trodden on him. I heard him yelp. I didn't care. I didn't care about anything any more. I sat by Margaret and we killed a bottle of whisky.

When they come to guillotine you they say: 'The time has come to be brave.' When they're about to embark on the jihad they give you hashish. It was the day of the wedding.

I put on my wedding clothes; my crimson redingote and shoes and my little Turkish hat and I went to the summerhouse, and I tied the flowers I had made from the hats of Cain and Abel to the nasty cactus and I made my peace with God. Inshallah ... And I had given my word.

'Oh darling, oh my heart,' I said, dancing in the dining-room. 'It's out.'

'What's out?' asked Monica.

Oh God, she was difficult. The trouble I'd gone to and she asked 'What's out?' I said: 'The cactus is out,' and I thought – your bloody, rotten cactus is out, and the devil Eblis is out and all the devils in hell, and Gehennum is empty. I said, 'Finish your breakfast and you must all come to the summerhouse and see, and we will drink champagne.'

And I went back to the summerhouse and Syl came as I had bidden him, for I had said to him: 'Out of the love I bear you, and for old times' sake, we must meet in the morning before the wedding, and I will give you something whereby you will never forget me', for when I smoke too much I revert to the speech form of my childhood. Oh dear God.

When he came he was carrying a dead dog. He said, 'My mother's dog died.' And I thought I had truly gone mad.

I said, 'You must bury the dog', wondering as I spoke whether the dead dog was an illusion of the jânn and Syl would know I was mad. I think he went away and then he came back and then ...

I danced for him. I danced for them all. I looked up and saw them through the window. My audience. Syl's mother saw me as she had seen me before. I had given her my word. Margaret saw me, and to her too, I had given my word. The cleaning lady saw me and grinned, for she was not surprised. Robert saw me as he had never seen me before and I was avenged.

I had danced thus before in dark places. In the dark places of the world. I had thought never to do so again. I had paid my debts – both of love and hate. I was dead now. I was Lilith high on her black wings in the desert air. It was for the living to continue the dance, if dance they could. Adam and Eve and their ruined little children. And if they could not then it was nothing to me. For I had kept my word.

ALICE THOMAS ELLIS (1932–2005) was one of Britain's most widely admired writers. Her dozen novels include *The 27th Kingdom*, which was nominated for a Booker Prize, and *The Inn at the Edge of the World*, which won the 1991 Writers' Guild Award for Best Fiction. She also published many essays and edited books by Penelope Fitzgerald and Beryl Bainbridge. She was a Fellow of the Royal Society of Literature.